Hunted by a Jaguar

Felicity Heaton

ETERNAL MATES SERIES

Kissed by a Dark Prince
Claimed by a Demon King
Tempted by a Rogue Prince
Hunted by a Jaguar
Craved by an Alpha (Coming January 27th 2015)
Bitten by a Hellcat (Coming February 17th 2015)
Taken by a Dragon (Coming March 10th 2015)

Find out more at: www.felicityheaton.co.uk

CHAPTER 1

The air was thicker than he remembered. Like soup in his lungs. Moist. Hot. Stifling. Kyter tipped his head back and inhaled, dragging it over his teeth. It carried a thousand scents unique to the rainforest, smells he hadn't experienced in centuries.

A blend of sounds teased his ears, a cacophony of insects chirruping, birds singing and primates calling. His jaguar side shifted beneath his skin, a product of his restlessness. He wanted to let the change come over him and take to the trees, prowling along the branches to stalk the monkeys and the parrots. A band of bright blue and yellow macaws broke cover, a stunning flash of colour against the green canopy as they flew to another tree.

Kyter drew in another deep breath, holding this one in his lungs, and calmed himself, shaking off his nerves and trying to see the beauty of this place he had once called home.

The trees loomed above him. The monkey chatter mocked him. Everything closed in and his throat closed with it. A deep need to turn back and escape this place and what awaited him at the end of his journey filled him. He exhaled hard and pushed onwards, taking another step towards his destination. Each step was more difficult than the last. Each stride brought him closer to a place he had vowed he would never set foot in again.

But he had to be here.

He had set out from London a week ago, the same night he had received the news via a call from a satellite phone. That news had knocked his entire world off kilter and left him reeling in the middle of his nightclub, numbed from his skin down to his soul.

He had travelled non-stop since then. Through every plane journey that had carried him halfway across the world, all the boats that had taken him down the mighty Amazon river and its tributaries, and every step he had trod during his trek into the rainforest that had followed, what had brought him back here hadn't sunk in.

He still felt numb.

He scrubbed a cloth around the back of his neck, wiping the sweat away, and shoved it into the back pocket of his black combat trousers as he took another hard step closer to his destination.

The forest closed in again, covering his tracks for him, even though he had made sure to conceal his path so humans couldn't find the village nestled far from civilisation. Protected by nature.

Kyter trekked up a steep incline, the path becoming difficult. He struggled to lift his mud-caked boots over each root that threatened to trip him and clung to each tree he could reach, using them as support as he pushed onwards, battling through the fatigue.

The pack on his back was soaked from the sweat that rolled down his spine beneath his black tank. He had emptied his canteen a day back but hadn't stopped for water. Just as he hadn't stopped to rest nor to sleep since he had left the river behind two days ago. He couldn't stop.

Not until he saw the truth for himself.

He wouldn't believe a thing until then.

He wouldn't feel a thing until then.

Not how his feet throbbed and burned from the non-stop trek across harsh terrain. Not the sting of a hundred insect bites. Not the ache in his bones.

Not the agony ripping his heart to pieces.

He reached a vertical wall of mud and bushes, and grabbed a thick root, using it to haul himself up the final few feet of the hill. He planted one knee up on the bank above him and grunted as he pulled his bodyweight up and set his other knee down on the ridge.

Kyter dragged himself onto his feet and clutched the tree to his left for support.

The scars on his back ached as he stared down the other side of the hill, through the trees and the scrub to the clearing in the valley.

The village of his pride.

He couldn't call them family. They had never been family to him.

They had made sure of that, treating him as the outcast he was, ensuring he felt it every day of his long existence. He breathed hard, fighting the memories of this place as they surfaced, shoving them back down inside where they belonged. They had no place in his life now. He had banished them and his pain years ago, or at least he had tried. His fingers tensed against the tree trunk, his claws emerging and tearing through the thin bark to the wood beneath. It curled beneath his fingers, the fresh scent of it filling the air for a moment.

No. They weren't his family.

If the news was true, then he had no family now.

Kyter pressed a hand to his soaked chest and dug his nails into his pectorals. He ground his teeth and chuffed, the short coughing noise escaping him before he could stop it.

No one would answer that call now.

The backs of his eyes burned and he growled, baring his emerging fangs as he stared down at the village, a flicker of grief piercing the numbness within him and setting fire to his heart.

The smaller wooden single-storey buildings stood on stilts on the earth, without glass in their windows and only shutters to close over them. The thatched roofs hung wide from the sides of each building, providing shelter for the windows and the long porch across the front. They looked so basic to him now, with none of the modern conveniences he enjoyed back in England at his nightclub in London, but one had been his home for most of his life, and he remembered that he had been happy at times.

His golden gaze sought the small residence on the outskirts of the village to his right, near trees that he had climbed as a cub and still bore his claw marks from when he had matured and had raked them to scent them. The house looked so small now. Desolate and lonely. Cold.

As cold as he felt inside.

Kyter straightened and took hold of the straps of his backpack. He sucked down another deep breath into too-tight lungs as his gaze swung back to the main area of the village, to the largest building that stood proudly in the centre of a wide open area. He avoided looking at the left side of the building, where a thick wooden column rose from the earth, and focused on his kin gathered in the square.

They filled the area, encircling a sombre scene that made his numb yet burning heart ache. He had no choice but to believe what he had been told now that it was right before him. Many of the buildings were damaged and, in the middle of the circle of his kin, bodies lay on individual stacks of logs and a cushion of palm leaves, all of them dressed in brightly coloured ceremonial tunics.

The flicker of fire in his chest exploded into an inferno that coursed through his veins and ignited his emotions, bringing them back full force, so powerful that they overwhelmed him. He wanted to throw his head back and roar out his fury and his pain as it ravaged him, but he refused to break with tradition even when he despised it.

Instead of unleashing his rage and grief, he clenched his trembling fists at his sides and vowed that he would hunt down whoever had done this. They would pay. By all that was dark and unholy within him—they would pay.

Kyter took one last deep breath and started down the hill, his step faltering as he approached the village. The hill was more a part of him than the village had ever been. He had spent most of his life up on it, looking down on the village, watching from a distance as ceremonies took place. Especially when they were mating ceremonies.

He never could bear being in the village for those. They only reminded him that he would never have such a thing.

There was no fated mate for him out there.

Now he had to take part in the worst ceremony of all.

He entered the boundaries of the village and kept his gaze fixed straight ahead, on the main building and the people gathered there. The acrid scent of smoke still filled the air, reminding him that only a week had passed since the attack on his kin. A week ago, she had been alive and now she was dead.

Murdered.

Had she been afraid? Had she tried to fight or escape? Had she begged for mercy? For her life?

What had he been doing?

Laughing over a glass of Hellfire in his bar with a pretty little mortal female who had been trying to get his attention all night.

She had been fighting for her life, and he had been laughing while it happened.

Tears burned his eyes and he scrubbed them away, refusing to let them fall. He should have been here. He never should have left.

He reached the edge of the gathered and all eyes turned to him, a hush falling over the village. He ignored them and averted his gaze to the earth, shutting out the pointed looks and the silent accusations that pressed down on his already trembling shoulders.

Kyter glanced at the lead elder of the pride, a tall slender male with short greying hair, and caught the coldness in his golden gaze. More ice than usual.

It had been a long time since Kyter had left this place behind, but he hadn't forgotten the hostility of his pride. He could never forget. They had made sure of that. His back burned, each laceration feeling as if it had only just happened. The lash of the whip rang in his ears. His own pitiful cries followed it.

He closed his eyes against the memories and turned away from the older male.

The gathered parted for him, which was more than he had expected from them, and he swallowed hard, his throat tightening by degrees as he lifted his head and approached the dead.

Males. Females. Children. All laid out in rows. They numbered in their twenties. Almost half of the pride, and all of their strongest males. Their finest warriors.

Kyter looked at one of them and stopped dead as a vision of the male as a boy filled his mind. A violent collision of fear and hope flooded Kyter's heart as he stood before the boy, eye-level with him, and the boy pointed at him. The big elder male beside him signalled to two other adult males. Kyter backed away, shaking his head. They clamped strong hands down on his arms and dragged him across the square in front of everyone.

To the column.

The sound of females sobbing yanked him back to the present and he breathed again, his hands shaking as his heart thundered against his ribs.

Kyter stared blankly at the women off to his right, the village of old disappearing to reveal them to him as they clutched each other, consoled by their shared grief and bonded by it.

He flexed his fingers, filled with a need to tell them that he was sorry for their loss, even when he knew that they wouldn't listen to a word he had to say. They would only look upon him with scorn and disgust.

He hadn't come for them anyway.

He had learned long ago not to give a damn about them, because they didn't give a damn about him.

He had come here for one person.

Kyter's eyes shifted to a small form on a pyre off to the left of the square, her body laid apart from the others and covered only in a piece of pale cloth. Ice and fire speared his chest, freezing and burning his heart at the same time. His throat clogged. Tears stung his eyes.

Not only born of grief.

They were born of fury too. Anger that even in death they were punishing her and holding her away from them, when she had loved them all so dearly. All because she had made a mistake. Duped by a male.

A growl curled up his throat, his anger growing as he realised that they blamed her for what had happened to the pride.

He knew they blamed him. They always blamed him.

The product of her mistake.

He slowly walked towards her, his eyes locked on her, his heart labouring in his chest. His legs shook with each step, his strength leaving him as he drew closer to her, and then gave out when he saw her bruised and lacerated face.

His beautiful mother.

He collapsed to his knees beside her and pulled her cold body into his arms, gently lifting the top half from the palm leaves. Her scent filled his senses and he gathered her against him, buried his face in her throat and cried out the grief ripping him apart inside. Tears spilled in an unstoppable flow as he breathed in her scent with each ragged inhale. He shook to his core and clutched her closer, unable to stop the words from spinning around his mind, damning him.

She had been fighting for her life.

He had been laughing.

Kyter rocked with her, with each hard sob that racked his body, and growled against her mottled skin.

"I should have made you come with me. I shouldn't have left you behind."

He chuffed, the low coughing sound that begged for reassurance and comfort reverberating in his throat, but she didn't answer him.

She would never answer him again.

That knowledge tore him apart inside, ripping him to shreds, leaving him in pieces. He growled again, restless with a need to shift and roar out his agony so the entire rainforest would know his pain and know it had lost one of its most beautiful creatures.

He barely leashed that urge, fighting to maintain his human form and to hold with tradition. He had to endure it all in this form.

He was still a slave to tradition, even though he tried not to be. He had tried to break free of the pride, but he had never been able to remove himself from them and view them as strangers.

He was weak.

He had wanted to be strong.

He had wanted to show her that her son was strong. He had wanted her to be proud of him. He had intended to create a place for her where they could be happy and then come for her. He had done the first part, but had never been strong enough to do the second. He had never been strong enough to come back to this place.

Now she was gone.

And he was here.

He sniffed back his tears, laid her down on the pyre and eyed the tattered piece of cloth that covered her. He had known the bastards wouldn't honour her and send her to her ancestors in a manner fit for her.

He removed his backpack, unzipped it and carefully removed the beautiful embroidered brown and gold tunic she had given him as a parting gift. She had called it a reminder of what he was and where his home truly was.

He had told her that his home was with her. It always would be.

A dark-haired male dressed in the traditional blue and gold tunic of an elder stepped forwards with a clear intention of stopping him from dressing her as she should be for her funeral.

Kyter snarled at him, baring his emerging fangs to warn him away.

The male hesitated, but still looked as if he would intervene.

If he did, Kyter would fight him, and the man would have to be a bloody idiot not to know that. There was too much pain in him. Too much fury. He wouldn't be able to stop himself from unleashing his animal form and taking out all that raw pain and anger on anyone who came near him.

The dark-haired male looked to the greying elder, clearly saw an order to stand down, and backed off.

Kyter kept his narrowed gaze locked on the male until he halted at a distance and then returned to his grim task.

He unbuttoned the tunic, his trembling fingers making it slow work. He blinked away his tears whenever they blurred his vision and focused on his task, trying to use it to give him a moment of respite in which he could shut down the pain burning within him and rekindle his strength. The last gold button came free and he opened the two sides, revealing the quilted black interior, and dressed his mother in silence, slipping her slender arms into it and closing it over her body before removing the rag they had dared place on her.

He breathed hard to hold back his tears as he fastened the buttons that formed a line down her chest. When he was done, he brushed his fingers through her long sandy hair, neatening her appearance, and then sat back.

The tunic was too big for her, and it was meant for a male, but she looked beautiful in it. Tears raced down his cheeks. He scrubbed them away and then took hold of her hand, clutching it tightly in his fingers.

They trembled against her cold skin.

"I'm sorry," he whispered, his voice gravelly with tears and thick with the emotions raging out of control inside him. "I swear… I will find who did this and I'll make them pay."

"That will not change what happened." The familiar deep voice stirred hatred in his heart and Kyter brushed his tears away before turning a glare on the grey-haired elder, meeting his golden eyes.

Kyter pulled down a steadying breath to settle his jaguar side, released his mother's hand and rose to his aching feet.

"I know." He stared hard at the male, his shoulders squared and his feet braced apart, ready for the conflict he felt coming. "But it's what I have to do."

The male's gaze darkened. "It won't atone for your sin."

"My sin?" Kyter barked and took a step towards the male, unable to stop himself from closing the distance between them as his hackles rose. "What about your sins? At least I'm willing to do something. You'll do nothing."

Several other males edged closer to him. Coming to defend their precious elder. Kyter shot them all warning looks and fur rippled over his arms, his fingernails briefly transforming into claws. They ground to a halt, maintaining their distance but still watching him closely. They could attack if they wanted. He would welcome a fight right now and welcome tossing a few more bodies onto their pyres.

"How many have died because of you?" the grey-haired elder said, snapping Kyter's attention back to him. "How many because of her?"

Kyter launched a fist at the male, grabbed the front of his blue and gold tunic, and snarled as he dragged him closer, so they were only centimetres apart. He barely leashed his dark fury, the fierce need to lash out and deal pain to the bastard who had given it to him so many times.

"Back off. Leave her out of this. She had nothing to do with this." Kyter shoved the male away from him.

The elder stumbled back a few steps and held his hands out at his sides, stopping the other males in their tracks as they growled and advanced on Kyter.

Kyter eyed them all again, his heart pumping hard, and part of him wanted to goad them into a fight. He needed the violence and the pain. He looked back at his mother and that desire instantly vanished, a calm settling over him and carrying away his dark urges. She valued tradition. He didn't want her to see him break with it.

Kyter turned his glare back on the greying elder. "Just tell me what the fuck happened here. Which pride attacked us?"

Everyone fell silent.

Everything.

It felt as if the whole rainforest had stopped breathing.

He looked around at the faces of his kin, seeing the wariness in their eyes, tension that filled him with a sense of dread.

"It was not another pride."

Those words leaving the elder's lips made Kyter cold inside.

He didn't want to put it out there, or know the answer because he feared it, but he had to ask.

"Who?" He looked back at the elder, sending a prayer to his gods that he didn't say what he knew he was going to say.

"Demons."

Kyter stared at him in shocked silence, reeling from that blow even though he had expected it. Demons had attacked prides in the past, decimating their numbers, but those attacks had ended centuries ago when the prides had left the mortal cities and had settled back in their traditional habitats.

There hadn't been a demon attack on the prides since he had been born.

Kyter's gaze drifted back to his mother and he swallowed hard.

He knew who had orchestrated the attack on his pride and who was responsible for the death of his mother. He knew who he had to hunt down and make pay for what had happened here. It settled like a lead weight in his gut and an angry growl curled from his lips.

His father.

CHAPTER 2

Kyter stood behind the bar of Underworld, rubbing a shot glass with his white towel, his gaze locked on the glass as it reflected all the different colours of the bottles that lined the back of the bar and the spotlights that rotated above him.

"You keep rubbing that glass, there'll be nothing left," Sherry said as she squeezed past him, snapping him out of his daze.

He looked at the glass, set it down on the black rubber mat laid out on the counter above the wine fridges in front of him and tucked his towel back into his belt. He scrubbed a hand over his tousled sandy hair and then around the back of his neck.

Sherry offered him a smile that reached her blue eyes as she took the glass he had been polishing to death and moved on, a bounce in her step that made her blonde ponytail sway as she approached the optics.

The gazes of several men on the other side of the bar followed her. She was always a draw, and was one of the few humans who worked for him.

She had been working twice as hard over the past week since he had been back, picking up his slack. Everyone had been and he knew they were all worried about him. Hell, even the regulars were beginning to notice he was off his game, his usual banter and smiles nowhere to be seen. He felt as if he was sucking the life out of the joint.

Cavanaugh, a big silver-haired male shifter, looked over the heads of the other bar staff to him, a concerned crinkle to his brow. Kyter waved him away, letting the male know that he was fine.

Sherry had probably snitched on him again.

She was the only human employee who knew what sort of creatures she worked with and every time she had caught him spacing out this week, she had gone straight to the only other cat shifter in his employment and told him about it.

She seemed to think that all cat shifters should stick together.

If she knew how many fights cats got into when they wandered into each other's territory, she would think differently about trying to make him and Cavanaugh grow any closer to each other than they already were. She was lucky that the bigger male wasn't a jaguar. They all were. Being in his prime, Kyter couldn't stand other males of the same species being near his territory, let alone in it. For that very reason, there was a sign on the wall outside the club that warned other jaguars away.

Well. There was a plank of wood with his claw marks raked down it and his scent all over it.

The cat shifter equivalent of a sign.

He leaned his back against the bar and stared at his reflection in the mirror behind the bottles, spacing out again, the loud music and buzz of the nightclub fading into the background once more.

Did he look like his father?

His mother had told him that he was a secret. His father hadn't known she had been pregnant when she had escaped him, fleeing back to her pride expecting sanctuary and finding a different world awaiting her, one filled with cold shoulders and dark looks, and blame for something that hadn't been her fault.

He suspected that his father knew now and that what had happened at the village had been brutal retribution for keeping Kyter's existence from him.

Kyter folded his arms across his chest and clutched the white sleeves of his shirt, tugging it into his fingers as he dug them into his arms, his coiled muscles like steel beneath the soft material.

If his father wanted to meet him, he was cool with that. He wanted to meet him too. He had been working on tracking him down since making it out of the rainforest, knowing it was down to him to make that meeting happen. His mother wouldn't have told his father where Kyter lived, and the pride hadn't known until she had used her dying breath to whisper to the head elder where to find his number.

Part of Kyter's heart knew that she wouldn't have wanted him to do this. She would have wanted him to remain safe and hidden, but he couldn't do that. His father had taken something precious from him, and now he wanted to take something precious from the demon.

He wanted to look him in the eye and then take the bastard's head.

The music changed track, the heavy beat a fitting backdrop to the satisfying images playing out in his head. The demon would pay for killing his mother. He would pay for everything she had suffered because of him. He would pay for everything Kyter had endured.

He felt Cavanaugh's steady gaze on him again and shoved away from the bar, flicking the shifter a glance as he went back to work drying the glasses. It was all he was fit for right now, and he wasn't even doing a very good job of it. They kept running out.

He dried and polished another dozen, setting them back with their matching glasses on the rubber mats dotted along the back of the bar. He hung a few wine glasses by their stems on the racks and paused again when he caught his reflection in the mirror behind them. He looked beyond himself to the other person who had snagged his attention.

Owen Nightingale.

Kyter slowly turned and fixed his gaze on the hunter.

The dark-haired male had his back to Kyter, one arm propped casually on the black bar top and his black shirt blending into the wood. There was nothing casual about him though. He had his pale green eyes locked on Cait where she danced at the fringes of the Saturday night crowd, gyrating in time with the beat, her arms thrown above her head. The position lifted her corset-top up to flash her midriff and her leather trousers caught the lights, changing colour in time with them.

Kyter jammed his towel back into the belt of his black slacks and kept an eye on the hunter. He knew what Cait was and he suspected that Owen did too, being a hunter who specialised in shifters. Hellcats were rare, but extremely powerful. If the hunter thought he could tangle with the little kitty and not get burned, he was heading for trouble, not a trophy.

Cait continued her mesmerising dance, drawing hungry eyes her way. He had seen her a few times in his club. Cat shifters were drawn to Underworld because he regularly visited the fae towns to get a one hundred percent effective witch-brewed version of the sort of calming plug-in diffusers that humans bought for their feline pets. He pumped the pheromones out through the air-conditioning and it stopped them from wanting to fight and shift. It normally kept him pretty mellow too.

Not tonight though.

He studied Cait as she ran her hands up her body and her fingers through her long dark hair, lifting it away from her neck. She was doing her best to act casual, but she was giving off a bad vibe, and he hadn't failed to notice that there was another hellcat in the club.

That one was a big male who only had eyes for Cait. It seemed the little kitty had gotten herself into some sort of trouble already, and was looking to make it worse.

Or maybe drag Owen into things.

He had no love for hunters, but Owen was a regular and he knew better than to hunt on Kyter's turf. Kyter had made sure of that a long time ago, when Owen had first come here with his father. A tenth generation Nightingale on his first foray into the shifter underground. Owen had been nothing but a whelp. Now he was a man, and he was watching Cait a little too intently.

Kyter leaned over the bar and clamped his hands down on Owen's shoulders. The human male stiffened, muscles flexing beneath Kyter's grip.

"I'd reconsider if you were thinking of doing something stupid in my club," Kyter said over the pounding music, making sure Owen heard him loud and clear. "I'm not in the mood to see a fellow cat get her tail pulled. I won't be held responsible for how it will end for you."

He released the man and Owen slowly turned to face him, his pale eyes enormous. "I swear, I'm off duty."

Kyter didn't believe him. Hunters were never off duty.

Cait bounced up to the bar and flashed a smile in his direction. Kyter caught the scowl Owen aimed at him and raised his right eyebrow at the male. What was the hunter's deal? Was he jealous?

He wasn't about to trust Owen near Cait, but she slid the hunter a look filled with dark heat, a corona of blue fire around her dilated pupils, and Kyter backed off and left them alone. Cait was a big girl and she could handle herself. He wouldn't step in unless she needed him.

Besides, Owen didn't look as if he wanted to kill Cait. He looked ready to drool. Kyter shrugged it off. It was his funeral.

He turned away and caught Cavanaugh staring along the length of the bar at Owen and Cait, an odd look of longing in his dark eyes.

It wasn't the first time he had seen the big male watching a couple with that same look in his eyes. He had tried to get closer to Cavanaugh over the years they had known each other, but the snow leopard preferred to keep to himself and they had ended up stuck on sometimes-awkward surface-level conversation for the most part.

Kyter headed for the silver-haired male, gliding past Sherry as she dealt with a rowdy group of young human men, and drawing the gazes of several women along the way. They all clamoured for his attention but he paid them no heed. He wasn't in the mood tonight. He hadn't been in the mood for entertaining them since he had returned from the rainforest.

If he was feeling honest, he hadn't been in the mood for female attention since the elf prince Loren had been in his club with his mate around a month ago. Seeing the two in the midst of forming their bond had left a sour taste in Kyter's mouth that no amount of Hellfire, a black potent liquor designed to overcome the most powerful of fae constitutions, could douse.

Cavanaugh took an order from a pretty little redhead who smiled and flirted to no avail, even reaching over the bar to run a hand down his white shirtsleeve and lightly squeeze his muscles through it. When the bigger male turned away to get her drink, Kyter fell in beside him.

"She's pretty," Kyter said, and she was throwing off pheromones like there was no tomorrow, leaving him in no doubt she wanted to tangle with the handsome barman.

Cavanaugh shrugged and mixed her cocktail in a martini glass, his back to her the entire time and his eyes on his work.

"I've never seen you take up a single offer from a woman since you started working with me." Kyter had a feeling he should have taken his own advice about not pulling on the tail of a cat when Cavanaugh turned on him, baring fangs on a low growl, the centre of his irises turning silver.

"Keep your nose out of my business." Cavanaugh shoved past him, set the glass down in front of the woman, and stalked towards the other end of the bar where it was darker and quieter.

He probably needed a moment in the playroom out the back. Kyter kept it stocked with plastic barrels, tyres and logs. The sort of things shifters loved to take out their aggression on when they couldn't ignore the urge to transform.

The bigger male stopped at the end of the bar though, his shoulders heaved beneath his white shirt on a sigh, and he turned, propped his hip against the bar and folded his arms across his broad chest.

Stormy grey eyes slid Kyter's way.

No trace of aggression in them. Only an apology.

Kyter rubbed his neck and approached him, leaving Sherry and the others to tend to the customers. When he reached Cavanaugh, he leaned opposite him and adopted the same pose, crossing his arms.

"Sorry," Kyter said and Cavanaugh shrugged it off.

"You made any progress?" The snow leopard shifter relaxed and unfolded his arms, pressing his palms against the edges of the bar behind him. The position caused his shirt to stretch tight across the impressive width of his shoulders and chest.

It was Kyter's turn to shrug. "I have a lead. Nothing big."

It was hard to play it cool when Cavanaugh was looking at him so intently, as if he could taste the lie in the air.

Maybe Kyter's lead was more than nothing. Maybe it was big.

Kyter had spent the whole night wondering whether the answer to the non-stop hunt for information he had begun the moment he had returned from Brazil was finally within his grasp. He felt as if he had done nothing over the past week except search for a clue as to his father's whereabouts and mull over the information he had managed to find.

He sighed and rubbed his tired eyes. He certainly hadn't slept and he had barely eaten. His entire life had become dominated by the one male he had vowed he would never give a damn about.

The bastard was the only thing he cared about now.

Cavanaugh slapped a hand down on his shoulder, jerking him back to the bar. "You should follow it up."

Kyter knew that. It was going to eat away at him forever if he didn't, and hadn't he vowed to his mother that he would make his father pay for what had happened to her? He had a duty to do as Cavanaugh suggested and see if this lead actually led him somewhere.

He looked over his shoulder at Underworld, scanning the heavy crowd as the colourful lights flashed across them in time with the pumping music.

"We have this," Cavanaugh said, as if reading his thoughts. "Nothing will happen to the club if you take a little time off. Family should come first."

Kyter turned a black look on him. "My only family is dead."

He meant that too.

A deep recess of his heart that refused to die whispered that he didn't. He didn't only want to avenge his mother by taking his father's head. He wanted to show the pride that he was one of them. He was a warrior as fine as any of the ones they valued as part of the pride.

He growled under his breath, hating the fact that he still needed their validation. It made him feel like a cub all over again, desperate to be accepted, when he thought he had hardened his heart to them and shoved them out of it forever.

Cavanaugh smiled knowingly. "We can try our best to separate ourselves from our family, but it doesn't change the fact that they are family."

Kyter had the feeling that the snow leopard was speaking from the heart for once, letting him see past the barriers, and that they had more in common than Kyter had ever thought possible.

Broken ties with their bloodlines.

"Go." Cavanaugh shoved his shoulder. "You're no use here if you can't concentrate for shit anyway."

Kyter smiled. "True."

He had served people the wrong drink more times than he could count and had given up serving people two days ago when he had managed to get nine orders in a row wrong. He hadn't wanted to shoot for double figures.

"You got this?" The thought of leaving Underworld in someone else's hands didn't sit well with him, but Cavanaugh had come good on his promise to take care of the joint when Kyter had received the call that had taken him to the rainforest for two whole weeks.

The first time off he'd had in decades and it hadn't exactly been a vacation. He knew that whatever lay ahead of him, it wouldn't be a vacation either. If he did find his father, he would be lucky to come away from a fight against him in one piece, but he had to do it.

He had made a vow and he meant to keep it.

"I've got this," Cavanaugh said with a steady smile that became a smirk. "Besides, you'll be texting me every minute to check the club hasn't burned down, blown up, or been taken over by nymphs and turned into a harem. I'm really looking forward to experiencing that all over again."

Kyter hit the shifter with a solid right hook to his arm that barely made an impact. "I was worried."

"I think we were all glad when you hit the jungle and lost signal." Cavanaugh's face fell and Kyter looked down at his shoes. "Sorry, Man."

Kyter shrugged it off. "Just let me know if shit goes south."

He lifted his chin and forced a smile.

Cavanaugh didn't bother. His expression remained deadly serious, his stormy grey eyes holding Kyter's golden ones. He resonated strength and power, and a lethalness that Kyter had never sensed in him before.

"You let me know if shit goes south for you too, Boss, and I'll be there."

Kyter didn't doubt that Cavanaugh would come good on that promise. He was familiar with the darkness that shone in his eyes, that edge of menace and coldness that only warriors possessed, males who had been tested in battle and had survived.

He nodded his thanks to the larger male as he edged past him and lifted the hinged section of wood at the end of the bar. He lowered it behind him and glanced back at Cavanaugh.

"And enough with the boss thing already. It's Kyter. Calling me boss makes me feel old."

Cavanaugh cracked a smile, drawing a few heated glances from the women lining the bar, sultry looks that the male didn't notice.

Kyter waved him away again and followed the black wall to his right that ran behind the bar, stalking into the shadows and ignoring the few couples who were making out in the quieter recess of the club. He paused at the black metal door halfway along the wall, made sure no one was watching as he punched the code into the silver security panel, and twisted the knob. He shoved the door open, stepped through into the brightly lit expansive back room and let it slam shut behind him. The thick metal muffled the music.

He leaned his back against it and shook his head as he stared across the concrete floor to the far pale wall.

It had been four years since Cavanaugh had come to Underworld, a shifter who had looked far from home and a little lost. Four years. In all that time, Kyter had barely been able to scratch the surface. Cavanaugh had held him at a distance and had shot down all his attempts to form a closer relationship with him.

Now, Kyter had lost everything, but he felt he had gained a friend.

He had found a way of bonding with the big male and he couldn't help but wonder what had happened to Cavanaugh to make him leave his pride.

Kyter pushed away from the door and crossed the large pale room to the metal staircase that lined the left wall and led up to the apartments where he and the other staff lived. He banked right at the top of the stairs and headed down the long corridor, past the communal kitchen and break rooms, to his small apartment at the end.

He opened the dark wooden door and prowled through the living room to his bedroom.

He kicked off his shoes, stripped off his white shirt and tossed it onto the dark covers of his double bed, and followed it with his trousers, leaving him in only his socks. He padded across the wooden floor to his wardrobe at the foot of his bed, opened it and grabbed his black backpack from the bottom, pausing for a heartbeat to look at it, still covered in dirt from his home village, before grabbing a pair of combats and stuffing them into it, together with some tanks and shirts. He threw in a few pairs of socks from his drawers and a hunting knife, and zipped it closed.

He tossed it near the door and grabbed a pair of black combats from his wardrobe. He tugged them on and buttoned them, and paired them with a black t-shirt. As a shifter, he preferred to keep clothing to the bare minimum, forgoing underwear. It made emergency shifts a lot easier. While he could happily fight with his hind paws stuck in a pair of socks, he preferred not to have to fight looking like a jaguar wearing boxer shorts.

He pulled on his black leather, stuffed his feet into his boots, and snatched his keys from the dresser beside the wardrobe.

On his way out of the bedroom, he picked up the backpack and swung it over his shoulder, not breaking his stride. He slammed the apartment door behind him, jogged down the corridor and then the stairs that led down into the main back room of Underworld. He opened the emergency exit door near the bottom, closed it behind him and smiled at the sight that greeted him in the narrow alley.

Kyter strode across the strip of worn tarmac and swung his leg over the motorbike parked near the red brick wall.

It sank lower as it cushioned his weight and he patted the sleek black fuel tank of the classic motorcycle he had owned for almost two decades now. She was a thing of beauty and he doubted he could love anything as much as he loved her, or anything could come close to matching her looks. She was all spit and fire, chrome and black. A wild lady with a fierce growl.

He turned the key and she roared to life.

Kyter slung the backpack on, kicked the stand up, and switched the lights on. He revved the engine and pulled away, heading along the slick alley towards the main street, the bike's growl reverberating around the brick buildings on either side of him.

When he hit the main street, he banked left and accelerated, speeding through the quiet night towards his destination.

A fae town.

It was the closest one to his club and he had been there countless times. How many of those times had he crossed paths with the male he was going to look for tonight? He didn't want to think about that or the fact he could have found out his father's location years ago and his mother would have still been alive.

The journey passed swiftly, a mixture of motorways and narrow country roads. Dawn was coming as he rolled down the gravel driveway of a palatial sandstone mansion and parked his bike beside a huge black Bentley. He turned off the engine and eased his leg over the bike, coming to face the mansion. Light fae lived in the grand estate. He wasn't here to see them.

He walked to the right of the mansion, into the woods there, and found the entrance to the town set into a large mound of rock. He pushed the heavy iron gate open and stepped into the darkness, following the slick steps in a sweeping curve downwards into the gloom.

A golden glow lit the end of the tunnel as it levelled out and the scents of the town rolled over him. Herbs. Spices. Blood. Sex. This fae town dealt in everything. He followed the tunnel until it opened out onto a high ledge at the edge of the enormous cavern. Below him, stone buildings covered the huge base of the cavern, groups of different styles marking the different districts.

To his left, the tightly packed hotchpotch collection of white square flat-roofed structures of different heights left little room for the thousands of fae who passed along the narrow streets between them.

The witches' district.

It was always bustling with activity, no matter the time of day or night. Most of the fae, demons and other species who visited the town headed there, looking for a potion or a spell.

Amidst the single-storey dwellings were some with two or more levels and bright colourful signs painted on their walls. Others had tattered jewel-coloured canopies reaching out from them, almost touching the canopy of the building opposite as their owners fought for space in the cramped town.

The scents wafting up to him grew stronger, rising from the copper stills, thatched baskets, and terracotta or stone jars that were on display outside the stores in the witches' district.

Kyter turned away from the town and walked down the carved stone steps to his left that followed the curve of the cavern wall and led down into the town, ending near the witches' district. Before he reached the bottom, he stopped and scanned the buildings again, seeking the demons' district.

Banners hung on the walls of the largest buildings that lined the edges of the town, built into the rock. Some were covens, but most belonged to other fae species. He knew the mark of a local pride of tiger shifters and always avoided the area at the far end of the town because of it. He still remembered the day when a wolf pack had set up home right next to the tigers. It hadn't gone down well. They had ended up dragging the ogres into the fight and several blocks of the town had been flattened.

If it hadn't been for the quick thinking of the local succubus clan who resided in the glaringly red four-storey building at that end of the town, the damage would have been far worse. They had employed their charms though, easily winning over the shifters and the ogres. Make love, not war. A motto he had lived by once.

Now he was out to make war.

He spotted the demons' district off to his right on his side of the cavern. The single storey buildings differed in appearance from those of the witches and the rest of the town. Smoke curled from the crooked chimneys on the uneven dark tiled roofs of the black beam and white panelled buildings that had an almost medieval look to them, lazily drifting up into the air before disappearing. Everyone in the town worked as a merchant, selling something.

Kyter hoped that demons sold information.

Or methods of summoning their kin.

He took the last few steps down to the cobbled floor of the town and banked right, making his way through the busy streets towards the demons' district, hugging the wall of the cavern below the entrance where the road was wider to avoid the worst of the crowds.

A flash of silver caught his attention and disappeared just as his eyes darted to it. He frowned and stood taller as he walked, trying to spot what had caused the brief flare.

A woman.

He stumbled into a small old witch and she jabbed him in the leg with her staff. He muttered something he thought might have been an apology and stared after the female he had spotted.

She was stunning.

He had never seen a female like her.

She moved through the crowd like black smoke, disturbing none of the fae milling around as she slipped between them, nimble and graceful.

On the hunt for something.

He recognised hunting behaviour when he saw it.

She sidestepped, turned so she curved around a woman who had looked back at her friend, not paying attention to where she was going, and slipped back into the crowd, reappearing further ahead of him.

Heading towards the demons' district.

Kyter followed her, bumping into several more people as he pursued her, unable to ignore the compulsion to catch another glimpse of her face. The need was visceral and something he had no command over. He couldn't stop himself from tracking her into the darker part of town and trying to catch her scent. Everything on sale and all the fae and demons packed into the town overpowered his senses, making it impossible for him to pinpoint her scent.

She turned, her long black hair swaying with the sudden action, and ducked down an alley on the left of the thoroughfare, her back pressed to the dark brick building. Her gaze tracked someone in the crowd. Who?

He found himself tiptoeing in an attempt to see.

What the hell was he doing?

He cursed when he looked back at her and found she was gone.

His gaze scanned the crowd and he barged through them, shoving them aside as he hurried towards where she had been. Several of the people shoved back, almost knocking him off his feet, and at least one growled at him.

He almost walked straight into a vampire male, saving himself at the last minute by ducking to one side, down the same alley she had used as a hiding spot.

Kyter dragged the air over his teeth and huffed when he still couldn't pick up her scent.

He looked at the crowd and then at the alley behind him. If she was hunting, maybe she had gone that way, where the flow of traffic was weaker, only a few people coming and going. He chanced it and followed the alleyways that wove through the brick buildings between the witches' and demons' districts, and grinned when he spotted her ahead of him down a narrow path between a set of white panelled buildings of the demons' district.

The smile fell off his face when he finally got a good look at her.

Stunning hadn't been a good enough word to describe her.

She stood at least six-feet tall, her dangerous curves clad in black combat trousers, boots made for kicking arse, and a tight black camisole. Black leather cuffs encased her forearms, elaborate silver swirls of metal covering them. Silver. The flash of that colour that had caught his eye. They were beautiful, but would offer her little protection from a blade.

She lingered near the end of the alley, watching the people passing, her back to him so he couldn't see her face.

What he could see gave him pause.

Strapped to her back was a vicious long black and silver blade.

A merc?

Or was the sword meant purely as a visible warning to the men of the town?

She turned her face to her right and Kyter's heart kicked in his chest.

Beautiful wasn't a good enough word either.

She was otherworldly.

Long black lashes framed luminous green eyes and below the fine slope of her nose, rosy lips curved with just enough pout to set a man's heart racing.

A goddess.

He took it back. There was something in this world far more beautiful than his beloved motorbike.

He took a step towards her and she melted into the crowd.

Kyter bit out a curse.

He had to stop letting her give him the slip. He strode to the end of the alley and halted there, scouring the throng for her. How the hell did she keep evading him? With his senses and her height, it should have been easy to keep track of her. Hell, he should have been able to just follow the wake of slavering men she no doubt left behind her.

He eyed all of the men in the crowd, on the verge of growling at them to warn them to keep their eyes off the female.

Kyter froze. What the hell was he doing?

He hadn't come here to chase a woman as if she was a bitch in heat. He had to find the demon and discover whether he finally had a lead he could follow to find his father. Just thinking about the bastard had his heart turning cold in his chest and his rage welling back to the surface, fuelled by the grief that he felt sure would never leave him, not even when he'd had his vengeance.

He shoved into the crowd and scanned the buildings on either side of the wider street, reading the signs that hung above their painted doors. The demons' district. He had taught himself to read the fae and common demon tongues a long time ago, unwilling to be caught off guard in any way during his visits to the fae towns. Jaguars didn't like having wool pulled over their eyes and the towns often drew unsavoury characters who preyed on anyone who looked out of place.

He studied the wooden signpost in the middle of the street. He was close.

Another flash of silver caught his attention again and his eyes darted to it, quicker this time so she couldn't evade him. She knocked on a door and it opened, allowing her to duck inside. The green door closed behind her.

Kyter pushed through the crowd to the small building and growled as he saw the painted sign hanging from a black iron pole jutting out of the white wall.

His mark.

What did she want with the demon he had come to find?

He pressed his back to the white wall close to the door, shut his eyes and focused hard, using his training to filter out all the sounds that covered the ones belonging to his prey. It was hard when people jostled him as they passed, shattering his focus. He clenched his jaw and drew in a deep breath, shifting the whole of his focus back to the building behind him. He sifted through the ruckus in the street until he found the soft melody of a female voice.

He only caught the end of what she said.

"Must find the key to Barafnir. My client desires it."

Kyter's claws shot out and dug into the plaster at his back.

He snarled as anger poured like acid through his veins, burning him up inside.

Barafnir.

His father.

She was after the same object as he was, but he wouldn't let her have it. He needed it more than she did.

It was only a prize to her.

It was everything to him.

CHAPTER 3

Iolanthe despised fae towns. They were always crowded with disgusting creatures and smelled of vile things. She curled her lip at a male approaching her. He was hideous, the rolls of his stomach spilling out from beneath a brown leather vest three sizes too small for him. The repugnant bald-headed thing should have been lurking in the shadows of a damp cave rather than parading himself in public. Huge pustules dotted his meaty and hairy bare shoulders.

She grimaced as she quickly pinned her back against a wall to avoid brushing him. The last thing she needed was one of those blisters of pus bursting all over her. She would vomit and her mood would turn blacker than it already was.

The thing passed her without any contact and she moved on, using a series of side alleys to swiftly cover half of the town. She came out at the edge of the witches' district and checked her crudely drawn map. The demon had done it in a hurry, and with only one hand.

The one she had left him.

The corner of the parchment was smeared with his black blood and it spotted the map in places. She hoped those splotches didn't conceal anything vital. She would hate to have to go back and ask him to draw another one. She had a feeling he wouldn't be happy to see her either.

She moved swiftly through the crowd, gracefully arching around a woman who wasn't looking where she was going, and then diving down a shadowy alley when she spotted a dangerous male ahead of her. Her heart rushed against her chest and she edged towards the end of the wall, her back pressed against it.

She peeked around the corner and ducked back when she saw she had been right about the dark-haired male's identity.

Lord Van der Garde of the Preux Chevaliers.

She slunk back into the shadows, hoping he wouldn't spot her. She didn't need a mercenary seeing her. Especially one as ruthless as this vampire. They had crossed paths, and swords, before over a mission and she had barely come away with her life. She had no doubts that he would want to know why she was in the fae town.

Just as she wanted to know what had brought him out of Hell.

Normally, he had an entourage of vampires with him. The male never travelled without companions who could do any menial work for him, such as dispatching a foe that the vampire felt was beneath him. Not today though. He was alone.

She risked another glance.

And he was as wary as she was.

He moved through the crowd, eyeing everyone, allowing none to go unscrutinised. Was he looking for someone? Or did he feel someone was looking for him? Either way, he was angry about something judging by his crimson irises and how thin the elliptical pupils were in their centres. Most vampires kept low profiles when travelling to fae towns. The witches despised them. Was he looking to stir trouble?

Iolanthe wasn't in the mood to have him stirring trouble with her. She turned away from the main street, intending to use the alleys to reach her destination, and collided with a solid wall of muscle.

The male caught her arms before she could stumble backwards, righting her. "Sorry."

"It is my fault for not looking where I am going." Iolanthe lifted her gaze to his face.

His dark grey eyes held hers and spots of cerulean and gold broke through. She jerked her arms free of his grip and distanced herself. An incubus. She had hoped not to run into one of his kind.

He flashed her a winsome smile.

She tilted her chin up and swept her hand down in an arc between them. "I am not interested in whatever you are attempting to peddle my way."

His smile faded and his eyes turned stormy, his handsome face becoming as cold and hard as ice. "I was being nice. I wasn't trying to peddle you shit."

He shoved his fingers through his short sandy hair, pushing the soft spikes back, and she caught sight of his fae markings that tracked up the underside of his arm to disappear beyond the rolled up sleeves of his dark striped shirt. They shimmered in hues of crimson and ash black, betraying his feelings to her. She had angered the male.

He advanced on her and she stood her ground, refusing to indulge her sudden desire to back off a step. He didn't stop until he was so close she could feel his strength radiating from him, a dark power that warned her that he was a dangerous male and one she didn't want as an enemy.

A hint of magic clung to his earthy scent. Had he come from the witches' district? The smell seemed to run deeper than one he had picked up by passing through the area, almost as if it was branded on his skin, together with something that surprised her and definitely ran as deep as his blood.

The scent of a vampire.

She lifted her eyes to meet his grey ones, filled with a need to know why he smelled of both vampire and incubus.

He waved his left hand in her face and she couldn't miss the brushed platinum band around his ring finger.

"I have a mate," he snapped.

She hadn't realised that incubi could mate or that they would want to devote themselves to a single female when they fed off sex. It wasn't often she learned something new. She wanted to ask about it but she didn't think he would give her the information she desired to assuage her curiosity. She appeared to have deeply offended him.

He pushed past her, muttering to himself. "Do all elves have bad attitudes?"

Iolanthe stared after him, unable to get her apology out before he disappeared into the crowd. She slowly raised her hands to her ears. They weren't pointed, but he had recognised her as an elf. How? And what did he mean—did all elves have bad attitudes? How many had the male met?

There weren't many elves in this world. Only ones who passed through. Had the incubus been to Hell?

She shook herself and pushed him and the vampire to the back of her mind. She was wasting time. A shiver went down her spine and she looked back over her shoulder, sure she had felt someone watching her. She shook that off too. People hadn't stopped looking at her since she had entered the town. It was another of the reasons she hated these places. She preferred mountains and forests, and deserts. Places without people.

She preferred to be alone.

She checked her map and walked down the alleys, following them towards the demons' district. When she reached the street marked on the map, she paused and studied the crowd, the medieval-looking buildings with their black oak beams intersecting white plaster panels, and all the other alleyways that branched off from the wider thoroughfare.

Her senses warned of several strong creatures in the vicinity but she ignored them. It was to be expected after all. Many of the fae towns harboured powerful demons. Unfortunately, none she had visited had been home to the one related to the artefact she needed to locate.

Apparently, he preferred to remain in the Devil's domain in Hell, in service to his dark master.

Barafnir.

He had a nasty reputation. Most of the demons she had asked about him had refused to tell her anything and had kicked her out. They feared him. That had set Iolanthe more on edge than she had already been.

What did her client want with Barafnir?

She refused to believe the tale that Fernandez had spun when she had met him. He had sat behind an enormous obsidian desk in his opulent yet grim office of his mansion in Hell, surrounded by mirrored walls intersected with black marble columns, a marked sign of his vanity together with his expensive tailored black suit.

And the two females who had sat on a black chaise longue in the corner, scantily dressed in sheer red baby-dolls and eyeing him as an addict would eye their next fix, occasionally breaking their silence to beg for his attention.

Fernandez had slid them a smug smile whenever they had, one that had promised he would allow them to pleasure him later, and then returned his focus to Iolanthe.

When she had questioned why he wanted the key, he had pinned her with cold blue eyes that had held a flicker of red around his pupils, his hands resting on the arms of his throne-like chair, and had told her that he wanted the artefact used to summon the demon for his mantelpiece.

That black stone mantelpiece had stood off to her left, a huge fire burning in the grate beneath, throwing heat across her side and providing the only light in the room. Several rare artefacts had already been on display across it, but there had been a space in the centre that had appeared as if it had been waiting for the one he desired her to find.

Iolanthe still didn't believe he merely wanted the key for his collection.

She was no fool.

He wanted dominion over Barafnir.

Normally, Iolanthe would have refused such a quest, but Fernandez had been very persuasive, making her an offer she couldn't turn down.

Satisfied that the coast was clear, she slipped from the alleyway and followed the flow of people down the road to her right, towards a small white-panelled building with a haphazard crooked dark tiled roof. She exited the crowd outside the green painted door framed by black oak beams and rapped her knuckles against the wood.

It swung open.

Iolanthe ducked into the dark room, having to remain hunched over to avoid banging her head on the low ceiling. Her eyes swiftly adjusted to the muted light to reveal a cramped space with a fireplace and two small threadbare green armchairs to her left, and a rickety wooden staircase that led up into the roof on her right. Her gaze sought the demon she had come here to speak with and widened when he stepped around her.

He was nothing like she had expected.

All of the demons she had met in her lifetime had been strong males, taller than she was and broadly built, wearing an almost human appearance with the exception of their horns and the occasional pair of cloven feet.

This one was barely half her height and blue all over. Black horns flared forwards from above his pointed ears, reminding her of a bull, and eerie yellow eyes ran over her from her boots upwards. She raised an eyebrow when his gaze lingered on her breasts.

He glanced up at her face and then down at his shoes, and shuffled off towards the armchairs. His height explained why he lived in a building with such a low ceiling and why the chairs were far smaller than the ones demons normally had in their places of business. They were smaller than the ones mortals used in their homes. She wasn't sure how anyone other than a child or the demon could fit on them.

She would say one thing about the tiny demon though. He dressed far more impeccably than the other demons she had met, wearing a fine pair of black tailored trousers with his waistcoat and shirt.

"Your reputation precedes you." He pulled himself up onto one of the armchairs and eyed the other one.

Iolanthe was certain she wouldn't fit in it but she did her best, unwilling to appear rude to her kind host. She mentally commanded the sword on her back to disappear, using her teleportation abilities to send it back to her bolthole. She didn't like being without the comforting weight of it, but she would be safe now that she was off the streets.

She squatted on the seat and had to tense her thighs to stop herself from sinking into it completely. They flexed hard beneath her black trousers, pulling the material tight. If the chair had possessed springs once, it didn't have them anymore.

The demon's yellow gaze darkened and narrowed. "I am certain that my friend would have been kind enough to tell you my location without you resorting to ambushing him and chopping his hand off."

She wasn't so certain.

"I do not trust demons in the Devil's service. It was easier to convince him to talk rather than ask him nicely and wait to see whether he would help or would attempt to cut my heart out of my chest and feast on it."

The latter had happened too many times to count. She had learned to maim first, ask questions later with demons. They had a strange thing about eating hearts.

"You do not like demons in the Devil's service, and yet you are looking for an artefact belonging to one?"

She nodded. "It is not for me. I am just the middle-woman. There is a party interested in the artefact and I agreed to find it for them."

"And who would your client be?" The small blue demon leaned back in his armchair and eyed her with a shrewd gaze, one that she didn't like.

He could attempt to wheedle information out of her all he liked. He wasn't going to get any. She didn't talk about her business with anyone and she definitely wasn't going to discuss it this time.

Iolanthe smiled sweetly. "I am afraid I cannot discuss such things. Now, if you would not mind. I require the location of an artefact and was told you could help me. Can you help me or not?"

"And what artefact might that be?" He smiled right back at her and she had the feeling it would fall right off his face when he discovered who the artefact belonged to and would refuse to help her, just as all the other demons had.

"I must find the key to Barafnir. My client desires it."

His smile faded. "Barafnir?"

She nodded. He shifted on his seat and eyed the door. He was going to kick her out. At least it wouldn't be as humiliating as all the other times it had happened. She didn't think he was strong enough to pick her up and physically throw her out of his door.

The demon shook his head.

Her heart sank.

"I only have information about it," he said and she blinked. He was going to help her? He shuffled to the edge of his seat and leaned towards her, and she mirrored him, getting as close to him as she could bear considering the foul odour of his breath. "I should warn you to let this particular job go. Barafnir doesn't like people meddling in his affairs and has taken great pains to ensure the method of summoning him remains hidden."

She had come to understand that after she had asked the first forty demons for information and had been told to get out, had been thrown out, or had been told to give up her quest.

"I cannot," she whispered and searched his yellow eyes, seeking a sliver of compassion in them. "You must tell me what you know. I must have that artefact. I have promised delivery of it in eleven days."

His expression turned grave and he had the audacity to touch her knee. Iolanthe barely stopped herself from curling her lip. He patted her, as one would a child, and she regretted desiring compassion from a demon. It felt more like patronisation.

"You must make haste then." He thankfully took his hand back just as she began to consider chopping it off, sparing her bloodying her blade.

"To where?"

He stared deep into her eyes and if she had thought they were past all the riddles and games demons loved so dearly, she had been mistaken.

"Look for knowledge in the shadow of a volcano."

Iolanthe smiled, much to the demon's obvious irritation as he huffed.

That was an easy one for her.

She stood, narrowly avoiding banging her head on the low wooden ceiling by quickly stooping, and teleported her blade back to her. She also transported a small pouch of gold coins and held it out to the demon.

"Thank you." Iolanthe bowed.

The demon nodded and took the coins.

She let herself out, shutting the painted wooden door behind her, and hesitated as a shiver went down her spine again and the sensation that she was being watched returned. She looked around her at the street. No one was looking her way. She frowned, sure she hadn't been mistaken this time. Someone was stalking her and it wasn't her usual escort.

She scanned the crowd one last time before she slipped into the flow.

Knowledge in the shadow of a volcano.

Green-purple light flashed over her body and she disappeared.

Teleporting to a familiar location in what was now known as Italy.

CHAPTER 4

Kyter strolled through the quiet city of Ercolano, heading down the sloping modern streets from the train station towards the ancient ruins. His backpack shifted with each step, his black t-shirt already soaked through from his not-so-pleasant journey. The trains that ran along the line were old, hot, and dangerous.

Well, dangerous if you were human.

He had lost count of the number of shady characters he had spotted during his journey from Naples, which was another hotbed of depravity and crime. He had made fast work of getting from the airport to the train station and had managed to board a train within a few minutes of arriving there, but in that time he had been left with an unpleasant sensation of being stalked.

He preferred not to harm mortals, and normally just a look in their direction was enough to make them think twice about bothering him, but the scum that loitered in the station and rode the trains were a special breed of stupid. It had taken a brief flash of fangs to dissuade many of them and warn them he wasn't in the mood to play.

His rage had only grown more potent since discovering that a female mercenary was after the same thing as he was, part of it now directed at her. He would find the artefact before she could locate it. He had left for Naples as soon as he had figured out the answer to the demon's riddle, catching the first available flight out of London Gatwick. He felt sure that he would beat her to this place and that he would find what he was looking for here.

The key to avenging his mother.

And his pride.

He clenched his fists and growled beneath his breath, unable to tamp down the need. His heart ached in his chest whenever he thought about his mother. During the funeral, he had been so numb that it had felt like a fantasy, a terrible nightmare. He had watched her body burn, her spirit rising to his ancestors on the smoke that twined through the trees up to the starlit sky. It hadn't felt real then. It felt real now. It had sunk in that his mother was gone and he would never see her again or hear her voice on the end of a crackly satellite telephone line.

The sun sank into the sea ahead of him, bathing the sky in gold, and he slowed his pace to take in the beauty of it, letting it wash over him and soothe his weary soul.

He followed the street signs to an impressive stone and brick arch set back in a small area of garden. In the middle of the arch, a locked wrought iron gate allowed him to see beyond the wall to what it contained. It looked like he had found the right spot.

The ancient city of Herculaneum.

He veered right and eyed the three metre high wall that butted up against the arch on either side. Easy. He had expected more security than just a wall, but he wasn't going to complain. He pressed down on the balls of his feet and kicked off, springing over the wall without even touching it. He landed silently on the other side in a crouch and scanned the area, both with his sharp vision and his senses.

When he felt certain that there were no security guards in the area, he rose to his feet and followed the broad path towards a slope.

A green metal fence lined both sides of the slope beneath towering cypress trees, running at hip height to him.

Beyond that fence spread the ruins of a great civilisation.

Kyter slowed to a halt as his gaze scanned over the large archaeological site. He leaned against the top bar of the fence for a moment, marvelling at the arid ruins.

He hadn't expected it to look so well preserved, with so many structures still standing. Some even had roofs over them that weren't modern additions to protect the interiors. Paved roads intersected the stone buildings, complete with high pavements. Incredible.

There was a steep incline down to the site on all sides and only one way of entering via a walkway over at the far side, in the left corner diagonally across from him. There was bound to be security there.

He clambered over the top horizontal pole of the fence in front of him and kicked off, easily clearing the steep grassy bank and landing hard on a broad flat balcony in front of one of the sets of buildings. His legs ached from the impact and he grunted and grimaced as he rose onto his feet. He was out of practice. Was a time he could've made a jump twice that distance and a fall three times further without even wincing on landing.

Kyter stretched, taking pleasure from it as he raised his arms above his head, his hands locked together, and took in his surroundings. He wasn't sure where to begin. He had picked this site over its more famous neighbour, Pompeii, purely because it was closer to Naples. He took his backpack off one shoulder, let it swing beneath his arm, and unzipped the front pocket. He pulled out the guidebook he had purchased in the airport, opened it on the map he had bookmarked, and studied it.

For ten minutes.

Nope. He didn't have a damn clue where he was on it and where he was going. He hopped another smaller fence around the balcony, walked along the top of a section of wall, and then jumped down onto a main street in the ruins.

He tried to follow the map, but the place was a maze of sites, all marked in Italian on the crumbling walls next to iron gates that stopped people from entering them. He stopped at each sign, trying to match it up to the one he was looking for, working his way along the rows of buildings as the light began to fade.

Around the corner of one row, he found a building that had lost half of its walls and his eyebrows shot up. There was a bench and jars set into the ground. A store? Maybe a bar. He liked the idea of ancient Romans all hanging out at a bar and living it up. It probably hadn't been all that fun when the volcano had erupted though.

Vesuvius loomed in the distance, awash with gold as the sun cast dying rays over it.

The poor bastards probably hadn't stood a chance.

All the crazy mortals who lived in its shadow probably wouldn't stand a chance when it went off again either.

He turned away from the possible bar and frowned as a shadowy figure crossed the street far ahead of him, disappearing beyond another building. A security guard?

Kyter tipped his head back and sniffed, catching their scent on the hot still air.

His eyes widened.

The woman from the fae town.

He had managed to catch her scent when he had gone into the building she had exited to meet with the same demon. She smelled like the flowers in the rainforest. Exotic and alluring, and beautiful.

He took a step in her direction before he caught himself. He curled his fingers into fists and clenched them. He wasn't here to hunt her. He was here to hunt his father and he couldn't forget that. He pressed one hand to his chest, over a heart that burned with cold hatred for the demon who had dared to take his mother from him and kill so many of his pride.

The woman from the fae town wasn't a female to pursue.

She was an enemy, and the quicker his body and his mind got that message, the better. It didn't matter that she was breathtaking, or that she stirred his jaguar side and brought it to the fore, awakening a deep instinct to stalk her as if she were prey, something that had never happened to him before.

She was after the same thing as he was and he couldn't let her have it.

He tracked her from a distance, following her scent as he moved through the ruins. He needed to know if she was looking in the location he had been searching for. If she was, he would drive her away.

Her scent grew stronger, a sign that she had been to the area more than once in the past few hours. He slowed his approach when his sensitive ears caught the sound of her breaths and softened his steps, moving silently towards her location.

She was inside the next building, a pale stone affair with several columns made of brick lining the street outside it.

Kyter stalked towards the entrance, his breathing stilled to conceal his presence. He wasn't sure what species she was, but too many had heightened hearing for him to risk breathing.

He peered into the building, his eyes rapidly adjusting to the darkness. She stood at the far end, hefting a pick above her head and bringing it down with force. Sparks flew as it struck the stone floor. She hadn't had the tool a moment ago. Had it been in the room? How long had she been here?

The size of the hole she had already dug said that it had been a while. She must have snuck in before the site had closed for the day and started work as soon as the last visitor had left.

She paused and set her pick down, resting it against her leg.

Kyter stared, mesmerised as she twirled her long black hair up into a knot and stabbed an elegant silver pin through it. He didn't doubt that she could use that as a weapon in a pinch. She seemed irritatingly resourceful. How the hell had she beaten him to the site? Mercs often had money. Maybe she had a private jet.

She huffed and lifted her hand, and wiped her forearm across her brow. Sweat trickled down her back between her shoulders, turning her perfectly pale skin shiny and soaking into her flimsy black camisole. It seemed he wasn't the only one who didn't take well to high temperatures. He cocked his head to one side and raked his gaze down her spine. Was she from cooler climes? She was too pale to come from a hot country like this one.

He ducked behind the wall when she turned towards him. His heart hammered against his chest, his gaze locked on the column opposite him. He had moved fast, but not swiftly enough that he hadn't caught sight of the beads of sweat rolling down her chest and slipping into the valley between her breasts.

Kyter swallowed hard.

The jaguar side of him growled low and the rumble of appreciation almost made it past his lips.

He dug his claws into the palms of his hands, using the pain to tamp down his desire, and listened hard to his prey. The pick struck the stone again. He shifted a few steps to his left, away from the door, and eyed the sign on the wall. It wasn't the building he was looking for. She had a reprieve. There was no point in confronting her and letting her know he was there until it was absolutely necessary.

He brazenly walked past the door, looking in at her, unable to stop himself from taking in her luscious curves as she worked before he moved on. He checked his map again, found the building she was working in, and followed the paved roads up the hill towards the back of the site.

Kyter grinned when he finally found the building he had been searching for. He walked into the larger building, immediately breathing a sigh of sweet relief as cooler air greeted him. It was dark inside with the fading light, but the modern roof over the series of rooms was raised around a foot off the structure, creating an opening through which a modest amount of light could enter. He used his heightened vision to navigate the rooms, seeking the one he had read about.

He found it in the largest room. Half of it was divided into three square rooms by two thick walls. The section to the right had been walled in again, but the parts in the middle and to the left were open. The central part was the reason he had come to this place.

Two columns covered in white and red plaster stood at the end of the walls that enclosed what appeared to be a sort of ancient chapel. The floor in the area there was raised up two steps and the three walls had been painted. Directly ahead of him, in the back wall, there was an arch, and blue and white panels decorated the plaster. There was a small stone plinth in the centre of the arch, as if something sacred or important had once been placed there.

It was the wall to his left that held his attention. The plaster had been decorated with white and grey columns and arches painted on a red background. In the central area of the wall, someone had painted a picture on a white square surrounded by mottled blue and red.

Ancient goddesses and a god.

The answer to the clue the demon had given to him.

The hairs on the back of Kyter's neck prickled and he turned swiftly to face the person behind him.

The female from the fae town stood in the middle of the dusty empty room, a short black blade balanced on her left shoulder and her green eyes filled with a spark of curiosity as she studied him from head to toe.

Slowly.

He shifted his feet into a more solid stance and debated whether he could reach for his backpack and retrieve his knife before she could attack him.

She canted her head towards her blade. "What are you doing here? The site is closed."

Kyter slowly shrugged out of his backpack and let it fall at his heels.

She dropped her eyes to it and then lifted them back to his face, her green gaze piercing his. "I know you understand English. I heard you muttering to yourself outside where I was working."

She had better hearing than he had anticipated, and he clearly had less control over his mouth than he had believed. He hadn't even realised he had muttered to himself after catching a glimpse of the sweat rolling down between her breasts.

His gaze betrayed him and dropped to her chest. A darker V had formed on the black camisole there, luring his eyes to that spot. He forced them to drop lower, taking in the rest of her, allowing his gaze to do a slow leisurely dance over her dangerous curves.

"You don't look like an archaeologist." He dragged his eyes back up to her face, pretending not to notice that the temperature in the room had just risen by around fifty degrees. Or maybe it was just his blood. "So... same question back at you. What are you doing here when the site is closed?"

She smiled and raked her gaze over him again, setting his blood on fire. She had to stop doing that. Whenever her eyes did a slow once over of his body, his instincts roared to the fore and he wanted to stalk towards her, grab the back of her neck and drag her against him to show her just how hard the body she was eyeing was beneath all his clothes.

"I asked first." She lowered the blade to her side.

Kyter stepped back, over his pack, pretending he was doing it to keep his distance from her weapon. He hadn't zipped the front pocket completely closed when he had taken the guidebook out. His knife was in there. He probably had a fifty percent chance of reaching it before she reached him. He had a better chance if he shifted. It might catch her off guard, giving him extra seconds in which to complete his transformation and take her down.

But he couldn't shift yet.

Tradition said he had to wait a period of a month before he could shift and give in to his need to grieve in his jaguar form.

"What are you doing here?" Her tone gained a sharp edge, one that matched her blade. It seemed the mysterious female didn't have much in the way of patience.

He raised his hand and waggled the guidebook he held in it. "I was admiring the fresco."

She looked beyond him and then back at him. "It was more beautiful before."

"Before?" He frowned and edged his feet further apart, shuffling back half a step at the same time so he could come down straight on top of the pack when he went for his knife.

"Before Vesuvius erupted," she said flatly. "It was more beautiful. The whole town was."

Kyter was unsure whether to believe she was saying what he thought she was.

She had been here, before the volcano had erupted.

He wanted to laugh at that. He had to have heard her wrong, or misinterpreted what she had said. Maybe something had happened to the fresco since they had uncovered it years ago or she was talking theoretically. Yeah. That was it. She was being theoretical. Of course the whole town had been more beautiful before it had been covered in ash and buried for centuries.

He couldn't quite convince himself to believe that and his instincts said not to let this chance to get some information out of her slip through his hands. He had a golden opportunity to find out whether she was implying that she was a few millennia old. It would certainly narrow down her potential species to a number he could probably count on his hands and toes.

"I'm no scholar, but didn't Vesuvius erupt like a couple of thousand years ago?"

She smiled and it hit him hard in the chest. "It did. In seventy-nine AD in fact. Thankfully, I was not here at the time. It was a shame what happened. It was a truly beautiful place."

Kyter stared at her. Gawped if he was feeling honest about it. She was over two thousand years old. What the hell was she? She didn't look a day over thirty.

Sorceress? He couldn't scent any magic on her, but maybe she had cast a spell on him the moment he had set eyes on her. He certainly felt as if she had.

Siren? She didn't strike him as one of that kind, although she did seem to have a hold over him, a magnetic pull that he found difficult to resist, one he felt might spell his doom.

Angel? She was beautiful enough to be something as ethereal as one of that kind.

Her green eyes narrowed as her black eyebrows dipped low above them.

All of the light left her expression, leaving it as cold as stone. "I will not ask you again. Why are you really here? I sensed you in the fae town."

Busted. He had thought he had been subtle when tracking her. The only explanation he could come up with was one based on what she had said. Sensed. She had sensed, not seen him. He had been staring at her a lot that night, his focus locked with intent on her. He had stared at her in the same way when she had appeared before him tonight. She must have put two and two together. Clever little kitty.

Kyter adopted a crooked smile, one that normally worked like a charm on the ladies. "You got me. I'm looking for something."

Her fine eyebrows rose. "That is strange. So am I."

She swiftly pointed her blade at him, her eyes narrowed again and her rosy lips compressed into a dangerously thin line.

"Stay out of my way. I will not allow you to interfere in my business."

Kyter growled low in his throat. "This is more than business to me."

He had been right. She was a goddamned mercenary. A treasure hunter looking for a score.

She didn't waver as he stared her down, no longer hiding his anger, aiming all of it at her.

Her blade remained steady. Not even the point shifted.

The jaguar side of him appreciated her grace and strength, and he wanted to growl at her for a whole different reason as he raked his eyes over her, recalling how she had moved through the crowd in the fae town. An agile and beautiful female.

The tip of her blade dipped.

His gaze darted to hers and he caught the brief flash of colour on her cheeks. It seemed the little kitty wasn't as unflappable as he had thought. He could affect her.

Kyter stepped over his backpack, narrowing the distance between them. She stepped back to keep it steady.

"Give up your quest," she said, her tone steady even though her heartbeat had just picked up in his ears. "I will not tolerate interference in my business. Leave."

He lifted his shoulders and her gaze briefly dipped to them before leaping back to his.

"You don't own the place, or whatever it is you're after, so you can't tell me what to do. How about you stay out of my business? I won't tolerate your interference. This is my territory now."

Her eyes widened a fraction before narrowing on him again. "You will regret your actions."

Kyter looked back over his shoulder at the fresco. He had a feeling he was in the right place and that was why she wanted him away from it. She knew something he didn't though. It was there in her eyes. If she knew the city, then she had the advantage. He needed that advantage.

She wasn't impenetrable. He could affect her.

He had made her blush.

He wasn't above playing on that to get what he wanted from her.

CHAPTER 5

Kyter took a step back, his boots scuffing across the dusty stone floor in the old empty building, stooped and unzipped the main compartment of his backpack. He set down his guidebook, took out his canteen and straightened. The female eyed him, her blade still held at the ready. At least she hadn't attacked when he had feigned dropping his guard.

He unscrewed the cap on his canteen and then put it back on as an idea came to him.

He set the canteen down on his backpack. Stood and stared across the narrow strip of ground to the female, making sure he had the whole of her attention. When he had assured himself that she was still staring at him, he grabbed the hem of his black t-shirt and pulled it up.

Her eyes shot wide.

"Wh-what do you think you are doing?" She edged back a step and her blade dropped a few inches before it came back up.

He smirked and pulled the top off over his head, taking his time about it and giving her a nice, leisurely look at his stomach and chest. He dropped the black tee on his pack and she stared at him. No blush. No problem. He could get one out of her.

He swiped the canteen from beneath his tee, unscrewed the cap and raised it above his head. He tipped half of the contents over the longer tufts of his short sandy hair. Water ran down his face and throat and over his chest, blissfully cool against his hot skin.

She stammered. "What… I… what?"

Kyter shot her his best smile as he scrubbed his hand over his hair, tousling the wet strands and squeezing more water from them. It ran in rivulets down his face and his body.

A blush scalded her cheeks.

Bingo.

"I'm hot," he murmured and rubbed the water into his bare chest. "And a little dusty. I'm remedying that."

Because he hated being dirty.

But he could be dirty for her.

She blinked and her mouth flapped but no words came out. Her gaze betrayed her and fell to his chest as he swept his hand across it. The heat on her cheeks flared hotter. She turned her back on him and every inch of her went rigid.

"Put some clothes on."

He smirked. "I have clothes on. I'm damned if I'm going to boil to death for you. Prude. You don't like what you see, get out of my territory."

She turned on him, her green eyes flashing fire.

"I am not a prude... and this is not your territory." Her left eyebrow slowly rose and she murmured, "Territory. You have said that twice now."

And he wouldn't say it again, because he preferred it when people couldn't tell what he was. His mixed genes normally masked his jaguar scent, making it impossible for all but the most experienced fae and demons to detect his species. At her age, she had probably met several jaguars, and he was surprised she hadn't figured him out yet.

He still didn't have a damn clue what she was.

She lowered the blade to her side and smiled at him, fluttering her eyelashes. Trying to play at his game? She was an awful actress. Too forced. Even the stupidest of males would have seen through her attempt to charm him.

She was going to be a tricky customer though. She wanted the artefact. He could see it in her eyes. He had animal magnetism to his advantage, and a better ability at acting, but something about her had him hungry for a taste of her, and he wasn't sure it was purely her beauty or her gracefulness. If she took the stick out of her arse and really turned on the charm, he didn't think he would be able to resist the fierce desire she stirred in him with only a look. Just thinking about it had him aching for her, growing hard in his combats.

He cursed himself for being too damn easy and turned away from her to look at the fresco, giving himself a moment to get his body back under control. He had to keep building on the foundations he had laid. He couldn't give her a chance to pull herself back together. The quickest way to get in her good graces and get information out of her would be pretending to fall for her charms, giving her the impression she was in control of the situation, and then turning the tables on her.

The trouble was, he probably wouldn't be pretending to fall for her poor attempts at seduction and he would probably forget all about the turning the tables part.

He felt her gaze roaming his back, intent and focused.

The scars on it burned.

Kyter whirled to face her, a growl rumbling through his chest, and she dropped her eyes to her boots.

"You not left yet?" he snapped and she straightened, pinning him with a glare.

"You have to leave."

He shook his head and took a swig from his canteen. "Nope. I like it here."

She pointed her blade at him again. "I have a weapon. You do not."

Kyter slowly smiled. "Oh, I have a weapon. It's around this big."

He spaced his hands ten inches apart.

She blushed beautifully again. "You disgust me."

"I was talking about a knife. I don't know what you thought I was talking about... oh... man... you have a dirty mind." He smirked as she huffed and turned away from him. Giving him her back? She either felt confident she could defend herself if he attacked, or she was beginning to feel he wasn't a threat to her and was starting to trust him. "Name's Kyter."

"I have no interest in your name." She swung her blade up onto her shoulder again and looked over it at him. "I shall call you Disgusting Pig."

Kyter shrugged, luring her eyes back down to his body. "I'm not a pig."

Her gaze jumped back up to his face and narrowed. "What are you?"

He shot her another smile. "I told you. I'm Kyter."

Her huff filled the quiet room. "I should have named you Irritating."

She looked as if she was considering leaving. Oddly, he didn't want that to happen. He was enjoying playing with her. She had the most alluring little crinkle between her brows when he was frustrating her and he liked the way her eyes flashed green fire flecked with gold.

"Irritating is my middle name." Kyter held his free hand out to her. "Most people call me Kyter."

She slowly turned back to face him, looked at his hand, but didn't take it. "Iolanthe."

He bet a thousand men had told her what a pretty name she had. It suited her beauty. He was damned if he was going to be number one thousand and one though.

"So, Io." He flinched when she shot down that attempt at friendliness with an icy glare and tried again. "Lanthe?"

She scowled and the sense of danger she constantly emitted grew stronger. "Do not shorten my name without permission."

Tough customer.

He cleared his throat. If they were back at his bar, he would have offered her a drink to break the ice between them and get her to lower her guard. He cast a glance around the empty room, thinking about the arid ruins beyond it and the fact she wasn't likely to want to leave this place to find a joint where they could share a drink. He didn't want to leave either. He would have to do this the hard way.

Kyter offered her his canteen.

She raised an eyebrow at it. "What do you expect me to do with that?"

The unsteady edge to her eyes and her heartbeat said that she thought he meant her to toss water over herself in some sort of private wet t-shirt competition for his eyes only. While he wouldn't say no to seeing her wet all over, it hadn't been his intention and it was probably a little too soon for trying anything so risqué.

"Drink it." He waggled the round container, feeling the water sloshing around inside it.

She shoved her palm towards it. "No, thank you."

"You have no water. I saw your gear. You have a pick and nothing else." He kept holding the canteen out to her. "You need to drink. You must be thirsty."

She shook her head. "I have survived weeks without water before. I do not need it."

Weeks? Impossible.

"You must need liquid to survive. There isn't a species out there, fae or demon, or otherwise, that doesn't need to replenish their liquid levels. If you survived weeks without water, what did you drink?"

Her green gaze slipped to his throat and quickly darted away.

Kyter's pulse hammered frantically against his neck, his heart slamming against his ribs.

Blood.

All of his rushed south at the thought of this lithe female wrapped around him and sucking on his throat.

He stared at her, mouth hanging open.

Giving her the opportunity she had been waiting for.

She was before him in a flash, one leg around his and her free palm slamming like a freight train against his chest. She had him pinned on his back beneath her before he had even expelled the breath she had knocked from him with her blow.

He stared up at her where she crouched on his chest, her knees splayed and her arms between them, holding her black blade against his throat.

What the hell?

Little kitty had claws and it made the jaguar in him roar to the surface, shifting beneath his skin and itching to emerge and play with her.

"What are you?" she hissed, her green eyes narrowed with deadly intent on his. Dangerous. Beautiful. He breathed hard beneath her, stunned by how little she seemed to weigh as she sat perched on top of him. She growled through her teeth at him. "Why do you insist on going after the same artefact as I am?"

She pressed the blade harder against his throat when he didn't respond, drawing blood when he swallowed.

Her eyes fell to her blade and his throat and widened, her rosy lips parting as she stared at the blood he could feel blooming from the shallow cut.

Beautiful.

She was agile, and dangerous, and intelligent, and fast too. Graceful. Incredible. Otherworldly.

His heart beat wildly. His blood thundered.

A primal urge to roar rushed through him and he was as hard as steel in his black combat trousers, aroused by the scent of her that swirled around him and her majesty as she held him pinned beneath her, a flicker of deadly intent in her eyes.

Gods. She was so damned hot. He wanted to sink his fangs into the nape of her neck and impale her on his cock at the same time, hearing her cry out her climax as he claimed her.

Kyter stilled.

Claimed her?

He reeled, staring up into her eyes through ones slowly growing wider as the answer beat within him like a drum. She tensed and pushed the sharp blade harder against his throat.

"I will not ask again." A flicker of nerves danced in her eyes. Her hand trembled, making the blade shake.

Why? Had she felt it too?

It was undeniable.

But impossible.

He didn't have a fated mate.

She hissed and shoved off him, leaving him lying in the dirt as she disappeared from his senses. Gone.

Kyter stared at the ceiling and the sliver of sky he could see through the gap between the roof and the building. Stars emerged, spotting the inky canvas with diamonds.

Every molecule of blood in his body and every instinct he possessed roared that he had a mate.

And she had just got away.

His blood heated at that. A primal urge to give chase went through him and he was on his feet in an instant, breathing hard as it consumed him. He growled low, letting the sound curl from his lips as he eyed the exit. The scent of the night washed over him, carrying her unique fragrance of rare flowers.

He wanted to hunt.

He wanted to hunt her.

The desire ran deep, driving him to stalk towards the exit and out into the cooling night. He tipped his head back and drew the air over his teeth, catching her scent. He savoured it, putting it to memory, taking his time as he drew her into his body. Just the scent of her had him painfully hard for her, salivating and hungry for more.

He still wasn't sure what she was.

But she was his.

She belonged to him.

She would belong to him.

A slow smile spread across his lips.

She would come back to this place.

The hunt was on.

She could run, but she could never hide from him.

He always caught his prey.

CHAPTER 6

Iolanthe appeared at the edge of the ruins and couldn't stop herself from looking back. She couldn't see the male, but she could feel him, and she knew he would be coming for her. She cursed him for wanting what she was after. He couldn't have it. She needed it. Fernandez wasn't the sort of male who changed his mind once he had set it on something. He wanted the item and she had promised to deliver it, and she meant to keep that promise.

She stepped forwards to leave but hesitated, looking back again.

She wasn't sure what Kyter was, other than irritating and too handsome for his own good. She had tried several times to piece together all the clues he had given to her about his breed, but she had failed to draw a solid conclusion. The evidence was too scattered. She couldn't scent or sense it on him either.

He was against her though, and that made him an enemy.

She turned on her heel to face the ruins. Moonlight bathed it, turning the crumbling buildings cold pale blue.

He wouldn't leave the ruins. She knew that much. He seemed a rather stubborn man.

A rather gorgeous stubborn man.

She couldn't get his image out of her head, how he had looked at her with intense golden eyes that shimmered with banked heat and had held her immobile. Those eyes had spoken to her of desire, setting her blood alight. She had been too entranced by him before he had poured the water over his fair, softly spiked hair, and it had run over his sculpted cheekbones, down the fine slope of his straight nose, and rolled along the sharp strong line of his jaw. It had been impossible to stop herself from tracking those beads of moisture over his honed body, watching them as they darted down the hard square slabs of his pectorals and rippled over the powerful muscles of his abdomen, marking his golden skin.

Just thinking about it heated her blood and had her breathing harder, her heart beating quicker.

Iolanthe shoved him out of her mind and shut down her sudden flush of arousal, mastering herself once more.

She picked out the building where they had talked.

Her control slipped again.

She didn't like how she had felt in that moment when they had been against each other. She rubbed her hands over her bare arms and swallowed her racing heart. It unsettled her. She hadn't felt in control of herself. She had experienced an overwhelming compulsion to drop her lips to his throat and run her tongue over the slender red line that marked it, tasting his strong blood. It had an intoxicating scent. He had an intoxicating scent.

And a seriously powerful physique that had felt better beneath her hands than she had thought possible.

Iolanthe cleared her throat and pushed that thought and the images of him pouring water over his sandy hair from her head. They persisted, replaying again how the drops had trickled down his chest, curling around his left nipple before skating down the ridges of his stomach, luring her gaze downwards to the fine trail of fair hair that led down from the sensual dip of his navel to the waist of his black combats.

A need to follow each rivulet with her tongue and tease his golden skin had flooded her in that moment, driving her to cross the room to him, slam his back against the column closest to him, and obey that urge.

The irritating male had done it on purpose. His golden eyes had flashed with satisfaction when she had blushed. Egotistical and disgusting male. He had been playing her. That knowledge should have been enough to douse any desire she felt for him.

But his reaction to her when she had pinned him to the ground had felt real. As real as her reaction to him.

The feel of his hard body beneath hers, his heart hammering against her palm where it pressed into his chest, and his golden eyes locked with hers, flooded and dark with desire, had triggered an alarming response within her.

More than just a desire to taste his blood.

She had desired to let her feet slide from his broad chest, allowing them to land on either side of him, and settle herself against his body. She had hungered to feel his hands claiming her hips, drawing her down against the apex of his thighs.

She had burned with a need to kiss him.

Iolanthe spat out a black curse in her native tongue.

Perhaps he was a sorcerer.

She felt as if he had bewitched her and hijacked her body, bending it to his will and enslaving her.

She took a step back and then another. She would give him his victory tonight, but she would return tomorrow and hope that he had moved on. She didn't want to meet him again, but she had no choice but to risk it and return. She had to investigate the area where he had been.

Whether he knew it or not, he had chosen one of two spots that matched the riddle her demon contact had given her.

The fresco he had been admiring was of Minerva, Juno and Hercules. Minerva. The ancient Roman goddess of wisdom. She looked off to her right, towards the darkness that concealed Vesuvius.

Knowledge in the shadow of a volcano.

Perhaps she should have chosen to look in the most obvious spot first, but the one she had chosen to explore had been one she had recalled from her visits to this place before the city had been decimated. The room she had been digging in had another room beneath it. That chamber had once held a statue of Minerva on a small marble plinth.

She wanted to go back and finish digging, but just the thought of running into the male again had her backing away from the site. He was sinfully handsome and strong. She flushed as she recalled the feel of his hard muscles beneath her fingers and the way he had smiled at her, his sensual lips lopsided and a wicked twinkle in his eyes.

Iolanthe burned inside, aching to press her hands to his golden skin again and feel his heart pounding against them, speaking of his harnessed power.

She took another step back instead and shook her head. It had been too long since she had been with a man, but she wasn't about to sleep with the enemy.

She would return tomorrow night, when the ruins closed, and in the meantime she would build up her defences against the male and she would send a prayer to her gods.

A prayer that the male had moved on.

CHAPTER 7

Kyter smiled to himself, feeling a little smug as he snuck up on the female under the veil of darkness. He had made swift work of crossing the moonlit ruins of Herculaneum, not needing to follow her scent to know where he would find her.

He could hear her digging in the room she had been in before, her pick working overtime with strokes that sounded frantic and rushed when compared with the measured ones she had used yesterday. Why was she in a hurry? Because of him?

He stalked silently towards the open door.

When the sun had risen, he had concealed himself in an underground room in the ruins on the opposite side of Herculaneum, as far from her dig site as possible. He had passed the day there, allowing his scent to clear from the area so she would think he was gone. It hadn't been difficult to remain in one spot all day. He had limitless patience when stalking his prey. He had once waited three days straight to ambush an enemy.

The female had fallen for his ruse and he had caught her scent just five minutes ago as it had drifted down into his makeshift den. She was already hard at work. Either she could conceal her scent, could move extremely quickly, or she had other methods of travelling at her disposal, because he had been on high alert since sunset. He should have picked up her scent the moment she had arrived back at the ruins.

She came into view as his eyes adjusted to the darkness inside the room. She stood with her back to him, her pick coming down hard. Her black combats clung to her backside as she worked, cupping pure perfection and making him a little jealous. He wanted that job. Hell, he wanted to step up behind her, slide his hands around her waist, and play at being her bra by cupping her breasts through her silver-grey camisole.

It was hard, but he managed to resist that urge, knowing it would probably end with him intimately acquainted with the pick she wielded.

Instead of manhandling her, he opted to lean his right shoulder against the doorframe, cross his boots at his ankles and fold his arms across his bare chest, admiring her as she worked.

She had made swift progress with her hole. It was twice as deep as it had been last night and she stood knee-deep in it, her long black hair hanging down her back in tangled ribbons. She muttered to herself in an odd language, one that had a lyrical quality to it. He wasn't familiar with it, but then that hardly surprised him. Besides fae, the common demon tongue of the seven realms and English, he spoke only broken Portuguese.

There were countless languages in this realm and in Hell that he didn't know. Hers could be any one of them. He wished he knew what she was speaking though, because it might give him a clue as to her species. Guessing what she was had kept him awake most of the day and had become his favourite way of passing the time since sunset.

Well, guessing her species and replaying how she had sat crouched on his chest, one slender hand pressed against it, branding his skin with her touch as her beauty seared itself on his heart.

Kyter ran a steady gaze down her, slowly taking in her curves. If she turned to face him, would she be as beautiful as he remembered? Would she be as beautiful as she had been in the dreams he'd had whenever he had succumbed to sleep?

Just recalling the lustful visions of making love to her in the room where they had met last night, pinning her against the plastered column as she clung to him, kissing him fiercely as he took her hard and fast, a primal and violent mating, had him filling with need again. He palmed his length as it twitched to life, fighting to tamp down his rising hunger.

He silently drew her scent over his teeth and wanted to growl at her smell and what it did to him. He was instantly rock hard in his combats, straining against the button fly. He crushed the need to growl, unwilling to reveal what he was. He liked keeping her guessing, and almost couldn't wait for her to notice him and ask him again what he was.

His mixed blood would keep throwing her off his scent.

He had a feeling that despite her age she hadn't met a jaguar before.

"What do you expect to find in that hole?" he said.

She gasped and whirled to face him, sending her long black hair flaring outwards from her shoulders, her eyes enormous and dark in the low light creeping in from outside the room. The smudge of dirt on her left cheek would have made her look adorable if it weren't for his gut-deep feeling she was dangerous.

Her green eyes narrowed. "What do you want?"

She went back to her work, as if he wasn't a threat to her. Nothing for her to worry about. Her acting ability was improving. He knew that he had startled her and he had caught the momentary flicker of self-castigation in her eyes before she had turned her back on him. She was ashamed that he had been able to sneak up on her.

"Go away," she grumbled, hefted her pick and brought it down harder than before. Taking out her frustration on the ground now?

She could take it out on him if she wanted. He had a perfect way of releasing pent up frustration.

"Not going to happen." His gaze drifted down her tall frame again, taking in every inch of her. His mate. He still couldn't quite believe that he had one, or that this female was his. She struck the ground again and spat out something in her strange tongue. He smiled. "There's nothing down there."

She paused and glared over her shoulder at him.

His smile broadened. "I found an entrance in another building last night after you left. I figured that maybe you would have known about it… being so old and all."

Her glare blackened into a scowl and her lips settled into a firm line.

"I know a guy who looks at people that way," Kyter said and scrubbed a hand around the back of his neck. "It's not very becoming of a lady though."

Iolanthe ignored him, nimbly leaped out of the hole, and set her pick down. She leaned forwards and brushed down her black trousers, giving him a wonderful view down her top. Her head snapped up, her accusing glare pointless considering he hadn't stopped looking at her breasts.

She straightened and stalked towards him, a sway to her hips that had his gaze dropping lower and a smile curving his lips again as he imagined claiming those hips and drawing her against him. She lightly pressed two fingers against his left shoulder.

The world whirled past in a blur of sombre night tones and pain exploded across his back as he slammed into something solid.

He dropped hard and crumpled into a heap, dazed and confused for a split-second before his head cleared and his vision stopped swimming. He grunted and frowned at the pavement beneath him. It wasn't possible. She had tossed him across the street with only a touch, sending him crashing into the wall.

What the hell?

He bared his teeth at her and picked himself up, his bones aching from the blow. Bitch. He pressed his hand into his back and arched forwards, cracking his spine back into place, and almost growled when he saw she was already halfway along the narrow paved street.

Kyter stalked after her, swiftly closing in on her. He tamped down his fury with each long-legged stride, determined not to let her get to him and goad him into losing control. He had a plan and he meant to stick to it. Losing his shit was definitely not in the plan, no matter how much he wanted to fight her for what she had just done to him.

"Maybe we should work together." He tossed her another smile as he came up beside her and she threw him a look that said she was considering tossing him across the road again.

She was more powerful than he had thought. It should have unsettled him, warning him away from her, but all it did was make him want her even more. The thought of fighting her had his blood burning, on fire with a need to tangle with his little kitty.

Of course, his hunger to fight her was probably due to the fact that every battle with her that ran through his head ended in a heated kiss that led to him getting between her legs and her screaming his name in pleasure.

The feel of her gaze on him intensified, ringing bells that warned a fight wouldn't go the way of his fantasies and it was dangerous to drop his guard around her.

He sidestepped to place some distance between them but didn't surrender his position beside her.

"I do not require a partner." She turned her cheek to him and picked up her pace.

He huffed and doubled his, falling back into step with her.

She curled her lip at him and tipped her nose up.

She could pull all the faces she wanted, she was still beautiful to him. Moonlight stole all colour from her skin, threaded her long black hair with silver, and turned her eyes a strange shade of turquoise. She looked even more ethereal and otherworldly, captivating him and making him itch with a need to draw her into his arms and kiss her.

"Come on, we'd be great together." Because he was her mate and he was sure that once she realised that, she would do as he asked and would hand over the artefact to him.

She was his woman after all.

A niggling voice at the back of his head chastised him for that thought and said that wasn't how he should treat her, but a stronger voice crushed it, telling him that a jaguar's female always obeyed her male.

It was tradition.

"I am not interested in working with you. Go away." She turned cold eyes on him. "Stop playing at being a treasure hunter. This is my job."

Kyter stopped dead, clenched his fists to stop himself from grabbing hold of her, and fixed his gaze on the back of her head. She slowed to a halt.

"Playing?" he barked, his voice echoing off the crumbling stone buildings around him, and she spun on her heel to face him in the middle of the ancient road. "This isn't a goddamned game to me. What I'm after, I need. For me. Not for a fat pay off like you're after."

Her eyes widened and then narrowed on him and she took a single step towards him, her fingers flexing and eyebrows dipping low. "You know nothing about my business and my reasons for doing it."

Kyter stepped up to her, towering over her despite her height, and snarled, "You know fuck all about mine."

He had to admire her for standing her ground, even when he could smell the acrid scent of fear coming off her.

She breathed hard, her pulse beating fast in his ears, and looked torn between punching him and walking away.

And possibly kissing him.

The muscle in his jaw popped as he ground his teeth, holding her gaze and refusing to give an inch. Silence stretched between them, thick with a collision of desire and anger.

The breeze picked up, filling the tense silence with the soft sway of the cypress trees that surrounded the site. It stirred the dust, lifting it into the air, dampening the scents that swirled around him. Including hers. He wanted to breathe deeper to catch a stronger thread of it again and take her into him, making her a part of him.

Her lips parted and his eyes dropped to them, a fierce hunger to claim them sweeping through him, threatening to obliterate his anger and leave only desire behind. He clenched his jaw again, refusing to let that happen. She had overstepped the mark and he was damned well going to let her know it.

She lowered her head, stepped back, and whispered, "This is not a game to either of us."

She turned away and he reached for her, coming close to catching her arm before his hand fell to his side and he let her walk away. It wasn't a game to her either. What the hell was that supposed to mean?

She made it to the end of the street ten metres ahead of him before he could no longer resist the need to pursue her. He had to give chase. The more she walked away from him, the more fired up he became, driven by a need to hunt her. He couldn't deny that primal instinct.

He stalked her through the dark moonlit streets, his thoughts caught on the words she had whispered. *Whispered.* She hadn't spoken them with her usual confidence. Had the cause of the fear he had detected in her been because of something other than him?

Did she fear her client?

She had refused to speak of her client to the demon she had met. Kyter hadn't thought anything of it at the time, but he did now.

He hurried after her and caught up with her as she reached an open area that had gone to patchy grass, lined by broken white columns.

"You need my help," he said and she did something unexpected.

She laughed, mocking him with the rich sound. "You think you can waltz in and do what... exactly?"

Kyter snarled and lunged for her before she could take another step away from him. He was through playing. She was going to stop and listen to him and she was going to do what he said.

The second his hand wrapped around her bare arm, a thousand volts blazed through his palm and his bones, burning him with the feel of her soft skin giving beneath his fingers.

He spun her to face him and she glared at his hand on her and then up at him.

"Release me." She wriggled and he tightened his grip on her.

"No," he snapped and dragged her closer to him, until they were almost touching and she had to tilt her head back to hold his gaze. Her lips parted. He did his best to ignore the urge to kiss her that tore through him. "You will let me have the artefact and I will let you have it when I'm done with it."

She shoved the flat of her palm against his bare chest and he flew across the courtyard, landed on his back and flipped heels over head to end up face down in the dirt. He grunted, pressed his hands into the patchy grass, and sprang to his feet.

"I will do no such thing." She held her hand out, her palm facing him, and he hesitated, reconsidering launching himself at her and taking her down. She was stronger than he had thought, and had powers he hadn't anticipated. She had tossed him twice now with a touch that should have only knocked him back a step at most. "I have no reason to let you take it from me, and you *will* have to take it. I have no reason to trust you."

Kyter couldn't stop the feral snarl that peeled from his lips as he stalked towards her, his heart pumping hard, fuelled by a dangerous combination of desire, anger and grief. The first emotion was the only one he felt for her, but the other two mingled in with it, his emotions out of control as his primal instincts roared at him to fight her.

To make her submit to him.

Gods, he had been hungry for a fight ever since he had set foot in the rainforest and had seen with his own eyes what had happened there.

That hunger had been steadily growing and he had been bottling it up, storing it for the fight against his father, but he hadn't anticipated this turn of events. His mate stood before him.

Unwilling to trust him.

Treating him as if he was nothing but a stranger to her.

He growled, baring emerging fangs, and she took a step back, her hand shaking as she held it towards him.

"You have every goddamned reason to trust me," he snarled and sprang forwards, ignoring the small voice as it whispered through him again, telling him to halt and consider what he was about to do, because it wasn't like him.

The stronger voice roared above it, drowning it out and commanding him to make her submit. That was the way of pride jaguars. A strong male's female submitted to him.

That was tradition.

The very essence of mates as taught to him by his pride.

He had her wrist locked in his fist before she could withdraw her hand and escape him. He tugged her arm up above his head and dragged her against him, so the full length of her body pressed against his. She wriggled and smashed her other fist against his chest.

Each blow only made his blood burn hotter and his voice was little more than a fierce growl when he said, "You belong to me."

She froze.

Her heart skipped a beat.

Her wide eyes stared unblinkingly into his.

"Excuse me?" she whispered, her voice so weak he almost didn't hear her.

He lowered his other hand to her hip and then slid it around to the small of her back, pinning her against him as his golden gaze devoured the vivid luscious green of hers. She smelled like the rainforest and had eyes as verdant as nature.

His mate.

"You felt it too," he murmured and rubbed her back, slowly lifting the hem of her silver top. He caressed the patch of bare skin he exposed and she trembled in his arms, the reaction drawing a rumbling growl of appreciation from him. His female was perfect. She reacted so sweetly to him. He dipped his head towards her. "I know you did. You're my mate. My fated female. We belong together."

In his dream, she had fallen into his arms like this, and he had awoken shortly after he had taken her home to his pride.

"Say I am your mate," she softly murmured, her voice teasing his ears and delighting them. "You believe that makes me belong to you?"

He nodded. Now she was getting it. She was his mate. She belonged to him. He dropped his head to kiss her.

Her left hook came out of nowhere, smashing into his jaw and snapping his head back. He lost his grip on her arm and she slammed a hard right uppercut into his gut, lifting him off the ground. He dropped to all fours and breathed hard, fighting for air as his side burned and he clutched at the grass.

Dammit.

Kyter coughed and wheezed as he pushed himself up. He lifted his head, catching sight of her boot a split-second before it crashed into the underside of his jaw, flipped him and sent him slamming onto his back.

Bitch.

The coppery tang of blood flooded his mouth and his vision swam. A couple more hits like that and she was going to have him down for the count.

He pushed onto his elbows, struggling to focus on her. She wobbled as she advanced.

A blade appeared in her hand.

Literally appeared.

What the fuck?

Either she had kicked him harder than he had thought or she could use magic.

She advanced on him, a dark vision of beauty as her eyes narrowed on him and her irises began to change colour.

Turning violet.

Kyter had the sinking feeling that he was about to get his arse handed to him.

Now he knew why she hadn't required bulky armour to protect her in the fae town.

Black scales rippled over her body, concealing her breasts just as her top disappeared, giving him a tantalising flash of creamy swells. Those scales swept downwards, covering her torso and arms and spreading over her legs. Her trousers and boots disappeared, revealing the armour to him. The scales crawled over her delicate hands, turning her fingers into vicious serrated claws. She flexed them around the hilt of her blade and stood over him in her skin-tight armour, her black hair whipping around her shoulders, parting to reveal the pointed tips of her ears.

Elf.

"I bow to no male," she snarled in a voice filled with venom and darkness. "I need no male. No master."

She swept her blade through the air between them and her eyes brightened, blazing amethyst that entranced him.

She was beautiful and terrifying.

His.

"Will you persist with this nonsense?"

He didn't move, but she clearly read the answer to her question in his eyes. He would. She was his mate. He had only one in this world. He wouldn't give up until she belonged to him.

"Very well."

She raised her blade to her side, gripped it in both hands above her left shoulder and pointed it at him.

"I will kill you then."

CHAPTER 8

Kyter sprang onto his feet and kicked forwards, narrowly avoiding the black blade as it arced through the air where he had been. Iolanthe hissed and turned on a pinhead, sweeping her sword out in another deadly arc in his direction.

She was serious.

She meant to kill him.

He rolled beneath her blade and onto his feet. He hit the ground running, using speed to his advantage as he darted between the white columns and came around behind her. His claws extended and he launched himself at her.

Green-purple light flashed across his vision and he passed straight through where she should have been, landing hard on his face. His senses blared a warning and he rolled to his left just as her blade punched deep into the dirt beside his head.

"Iolanthe," he said and she didn't even spare him a glance.

She twisted her blade and brought it hard to her right, aiming for his head again.

Kyter growled, pressed his right hand into the dirt behind his shoulder, and shoved hard. He arched in the air, landed on his feet and swept his left leg around in a high kick. It caught her in the back and she stumbled forwards, rolled and turned halfway through it. She sprang at him, her violet eyes flashing as she hissed, revealing her fangs.

He stood his ground.

She thrust the blade ahead of her and he ducked to one side, caught her arm between his side and his arm, and grabbed hold of her shoulder. She snarled and brought her leg over her back in a scorpion kick.

Kyter released her shoulder, swiftly blocked her ankle with his forearm, and twisted his hand. He grabbed her leg, released her arm, and threw her, sending her slamming into the hard ground beside him.

"Iolanthe," he warned and prepared himself again. He refused to fight her all out. He didn't want to hurt her, but she wasn't pulling her punches.

His mate wanted to kill him.

She hissed and teleported. He waited, his senses scanning. Above. He kicked off and hurled himself forwards into a slide that had him skidding across the dusty earth, the sharper stones biting into his right leg. He twisted and pressed one hand into the dirt, righting himself and rising to his full height as he stopped skidding, coming to face her. She frowned, twirled her blade and launched herself at him. It hadn't worked the first time she had tried it and it wasn't going to work the second time.

The moment she was within reach, he sprang into the air, flipped heels over head above her, and came down hard on her back. He kicked, sending her slamming into the ground. She grunted and the scent of her blood filled the air, tugging at his gut.

Dammit. He hadn't meant to hurt her.

He landed and turned to check on her.

Big mistake.

She appeared behind him and kicked him in the head, the front of her booted foot connecting hard with his temple and taking him down onto the thick flagstones of the path. His vision swam and when it came back, she had him pinned to the ground again, her black hair hanging forwards and caressing his bare chest as she loomed over him.

He was beginning to hate it when she did that.

He didn't give her a chance to get her blade against his throat this time.

He shoved his palm into her wrist, hard enough that she loosed a muffled cry and lost her grip on her sword. It tumbled through the air and clattered across the road behind her. Kyter grabbed her around the back of her neck, used his other forearm to pin her arms against her chest, and rolled.

He ended up wedged between her thighs, one hand against her throat and the other clutching both of her wrists.

She hissed at him, baring her fangs, and her pointed ears flared back against the sides of her head, visible through her hair as it fanned out across the flagstones beneath her.

She was one angry little kitty.

Her violet eyes shot wide and she sharply looked to her left. Kyter refused to fall for her feint. She would attack him if he did.

A boot connected hard with his ribs, lifting him off her and sending him violently spinning through the air. What the hell? He twisted and turned, and landed on his feet, skidding backwards across the dirt.

Kyter lifted his head and growled at the male standing between him and Iolanthe.

Demon.

Not the sort in the Devil's service. This one had all the hallmarks of a demon from one of the seven kingdoms and the small blue-grey horns that stuck out of his black hair, curling from behind his ears down to the tip of their lobes, and his matching eyes said that he was from the Seventh Realm. He was head to toe in black, his leather trousers encasing legs that resembled tree trunks, and his long-sleeved t-shirt stretched tight over powerful immense muscles.

The question of the day was whether he was here to hunt for the artefact?

Kyter slid his gaze down to Iolanthe where she was picking herself up off the floor behind the large demon male.

Or was he here because of her?

Either way, the demon was going down.

The second the demon shifted his blue-grey eyes to his left, towards Iolanthe, Kyter sprang forwards and barrelled into him. He wrapped his arms around the demon's meaty waist and sprinted, taking the male with him and slamming him into a thick stone wall. The male grunted, brought his right fist down hard on Kyter's back, knocking the wind from him, and shoved him away, sending him crashing into the wall.

He landed sprawled out on the dirt.

Claws like talons grew from the male's fingertips and Kyter huffed as he used the wall to pull himself back onto his feet.

He really hated demons.

But they weren't the only species to come equipped with built in weapons.

He growled and flexed his fingers as his claws extended. They were shorter than the demon's ones but just as deadly when you knew how to use them. The bigger male smirked and advanced on him.

"No." Iolanthe wobbled on her feet and threw her hand out to one side. Her blade shot into it. "Leave him."

Kyter wasn't sure whether she was talking to him or the demon, but she was shit out of luck either way. Neither of them listened to her. The demon kicked off. Kyter kicked off too, slammed into him in mid-air and landed the first blow, carving his claws down the demon's left cheek. The male growled and bared his huge fangs, and grappled with him. They hit the ground, rolled together and Kyter barely dodged the left hook the demon threw at him. The male's fist hit the dirt, leaving an impact crater in it.

Kyter decided to avoid the demon's punches at all costs. He liked his face the way it was and the way she looked at him at times told him that his mate did too.

He rolled with the demon and slashed across the male's side, ripping through his t-shirt and his skin beneath it, leaving deep gashes in the wake of his claws. The male repaid him in kind, clawing upwards from Kyter's right hip, cleaving diagonal lines across his stomach.

He growled through the pain and grabbed the male's arm as he brought his legs up. He wrapped them around the demon's neck and twisted with him, clamping his thighs at the same time and pulling on his arm. The demon's eyes bulged out of his head, his face turning red as Kyter squeezed harder, blocking his air supply.

Kyter grinned. He was one mean son-of-a-bitch kitty. Even demons couldn't mess with him.

The demon smirked.

Kyter's smile disappeared at the same time as the male did, sucking him down into a black hole with him. Shit. He grabbed the demon as darkness enveloped them and the male tried to shove him away. No damn way he was going to get tossed out of the demon's portal in a random place in Hell. He dug his claws in and clung to the bastard, doing his best impression of a cat being dragged somewhere it didn't want to go.

The demon grunted and wrestled with him, but Kyter refused to give. Whenever the male got one of Kyter's hands off him and tried to work on the other, he gripped hold of him again.

Light engulfed them, driving back the darkness of the teleport. Pain ricocheted through Kyter and he snarled as the demon landed on top of him, rushing to figure out where they had ended up.

Iolanthe's battle cry was the sweetest thing he had ever heard.

He tipped his head back, watching her upside down as she blazed towards him and threw her left hand forwards. The demon flew off him and roared as he slammed into a column. The stone exploded, showering the area in fragments and white dust.

She appeared above Kyter and frowned down at him.

"Get up," she snapped and kicked him in the side.

It was a gentle kick, but it still pissed him off. He was fighting to protect her and she was kicking him for it.

He pressed both hands into the dirt above his shoulders and flipped onto his feet, landing just in time to see Iolanthe flying sideways across the courtyard. She smashed into a wall and collapsed in a heap.

Kyter turned a deadly glare on the demon where he stood with his arm still outstretched from the backhand he had delivered.

"You die for that," Kyter growled through his fangs and darkness swirled through him, twisting along his bones and twining with his muscles.

His jaguar shifted inside him and his claws grew longer, turning black as they emerged, ripping through his skin. He snarled as his canines extended and the darkness swirled stronger, flooding through his veins now. He fought the seductive lure of it, the temptation of all that power at his fingertips, refusing to give in to that demonic part of himself. He would never use it.

Iolanthe moaned.

His control shattered.

His vision sharpened and burned crimson.

The demon stared at him as if he was looking at a monster.

Kyter supposed that he was.

And it was the last thing he would see.

He kicked off and was behind the demon before he could blink, his clawed hands braced against the sides of the male's head beneath his horns. He squeezed hard and gave it a vicious jerk, growling in satisfaction as bones cracked and the male managed to loose the start of a grunt before falling silent.

The darkness within Kyter said to keep twisting until the demon's head popped clean off.

Bathe his hands in blood.

Kyter dropped the body and staggered backwards, breathing hard as he shunned that urge, unwilling to take things that far. The male was dead. Iolanthe was safe. That was enough for him.

His claws shrank back and his vision dimmed, the colour returning to the world. He looked towards Iolanthe, praying to his ancestors that she hadn't witnessed that dark part of himself that he despised.

Born of blood he didn't want.

She finished pulling herself onto her feet and looked across at him. Her violet eyes went impossibly wide and she blinked slowly as she stared at the fallen male.

"No!" She shook her head, light traced over her body, and she suddenly appeared in front of Kyter and the dead demon.

She looked between them, her mouth opening and closing, a maelstrom of emotions swirling like a storm in her eyes and through her scent.

Her gaze finally stopped on Kyter.

She slapped him hard, snapping his head to his left. He closed his eyes, his cheek stinging, and clenched his jaw as he growled. Not quite the thank you he had expected.

"What the hell is your problem?" He flicked his eyes open and growled again when he saw she was walking away from him.

Not a chance.

He stormed after her, grabbed her wrist and twisted her into his arms, pinning her arms between them. The black serrated claws of her armour pressed into his bare chest. A silent warning. He didn't heed it.

Kyter's breathing slowed as he took in the feel of her against him, in his arms. He couldn't deny the pressing urge to touch her. He uncurled one arm and skated his palm down her spine. She felt naked in her black armour, all of her supple curves on show, every dip and swell of her body right there for his eyes and his fingers to explore.

Her breathing quickened and she swallowed hard.

She stared up into his eyes, her violet ones dark, her pupils devouring her irises as they dilated in response to the desire he could smell on her.

He knew what she was feeling. He knew how her blood thundered and her body shook with need, an uncontrollable hunger born of the fight and the fear, and the incredible surge of endorphins when the battle was done and you were the one still standing.

He was hot as hell too.

There was nothing like having your life on the line to get your blood pumping.

Kyter's gaze dropped to her lips.

And make you a little reckless.

He dipped his head and claimed the prize for his victory.

CHAPTER 9

The voice in Iolanthe's head screamed at her to push Kyter away but her hands had a different idea as his lips descended on hers. Her armour peeled away from them as they snaked up to his neck and clutched it, her short nails digging into his bare skin and his scalp as the hard demanding press of his lips sent a violent hot shiver through her blood. She barely stifled the moan that rose in her throat and clung to him as he kissed her, his tongue demanding entrance, stroking the seam of her lips.

She granted it, her lips parting to welcome his invasion. The coppery dark tang of his blood filled her senses, tearing a moan from her before she could contain it. His answering groan was a deep rumble against her breasts.

His hands pressed into her spine, pulling her hard against him, so she had to bend backwards to keep their mouths fused. She ached in response to the feel of his powerful honed body against hers, the ridges of his muscles pressing into her armour and awakening a deep throbbing between her thighs.

Gods help her.

She wasn't strong enough to stop him, even when she dimly recognised that she should. Her hands left his neck to skim over his bare muscular shoulders, her body quivering at the feel of them. Tensed. Strong. Seductive.

His tongue tangled with hers, his head slanting as he brought them into firmer contact, and she felt as if he would devour her. She wanted him to devour her. She wasn't sure whether she was coming or going anymore, or what she was doing, but something about this felt right.

She kissed him harder, stirring his passion as she stroked her tongue along his and flicked the tip of it down the back of one of his fangs.

He had fangs.

He growled like a beast too, a powerful predator. He was agile, fast, and strong.

Strong.

Iolanthe clung to his shoulders, feeling that strength in his sinewy muscles and in his hands as they claimed her waist, his thumbs pressing into her stomach and his fingers into her back, holding her in a tight grip that warned he wouldn't let her go now.

She didn't want him to release her. She needed this moment of madness. She needed it more than she could bear because everything was falling apart and he felt so strong beneath her fingers.

Solid.

His claws pressed into her armour, unable to penetrate the black metal scales.

Claws.

He had raked them over the demon. The demon he had killed.

No. What had he done?

The implications of it loomed over her, a towering wall of darkness and despair that stole her breath, and then came crashing down on her with the force of a tidal wave, dousing her desire and ripping her focus away from Kyter. She couldn't hide in his arms as she wished, as a weaker female would, believing that nothing bad would happen to her if she just shut it out of her mind and pretended it didn't exist.

Kyter had killed one of Fernandez's men.

A chill blasted through her, freezing her blood and numbing her heart.

Fernandez would ensure she knew the full extent of his wrath.

There would be no escaping it.

No appeal she could make would stop him from exacting his punishment for what she had allowed to happen.

She found the strength to shove Kyter away from her as her chest constricted, squeezing the air from her lungs, and cursed him in the elf tongue.

He didn't let her escape him as she had wanted to. He had her back in his arms before she could stop him, wrapping them around her like steel bands and pinning hers between them again, leaving her vulnerable to him.

"You do not understand what you have done!" She wriggled but stopped when it only rubbed his body against hers, reawakening her passion and threatening to cloud her mind with lust once more.

Kyter's sandy eyebrows dropped low above stunning golden eyes. "Was he your partner or something? You said you didn't have partners."

She shook her head and dropped her eyes to his throat. It still bore the mark from her blade. The rich taste of his blood still filled her senses. She stared at his neck, the world and all of her fears fading away again, leaving only Kyter behind. His heart beat steady and strong against her palms, that strength curling around her together with his scent, stealing away the panic that had filled her just seconds ago and leaving her feeling a little dazed.

Her fangs itched to taste his blood.

Blood.

The scent of it was strong, far stronger than it should have been from something as small as a damaged tooth or split lip.

Her eyes widened as she recalled that the demon had injured him, slashing across his stomach and chest. She tried to push out of his arms, filled with a sudden fear that he was hurting himself by holding her so tightly against his wounds. He refused to let her go, his arms tightening around her, pressing her closer.

"Who was he?" Kyter growled and she had the feeling that he had mistaken her attempt to break free of him for an act of anger.

She only wanted to stop him from hurting himself.

She relaxed against him, hoping he would loosen his grip if she did and he felt she wasn't going to attempt to escape his arms.

"He worked for my client. I knew he was there, spying on me and reporting to him." She lifted her eyes back to his. They were softer now but eerily yellow in the moonlight. What was he? A shifter of some sort? He felt too strong to be one of that breed. She had met plenty of shifters from many different breeds, and none of them had been as strong as he was. "When he fails to report on my progress, my client will send more of his men."

The thought of them tracking her down sent a chill through her and revived the anger that had faded again, stoking it until it burned like an inferno within her. Fear joined it, panic that she was wasting time in Kyter's arms when she should have been taking action. She needed to hide the body. She had to teleport it away from this place to somewhere Fernandez would never find it.

A foolish idea, one that the rational part of her knew wouldn't make a difference even as the panicked part of her screamed at her to carry it out.

Whether she hid it or not, Fernandez would discover what had happened.

He would send men after her.

But they wouldn't only come after her this time.

She looked up at Kyter. He had fought well against the demon, but he wouldn't stand a chance if Fernandez sent his best men.

His finest assassins.

"I was trying to protect you."

Those words didn't ease her anger or her fear. She shook her head again and clenched her fists.

"All you have done is make things worse for me. I will be punished for what happened." She hated the pain that filled his eyes as she said that because it was proof of something she didn't want to believe.

His grip on her slackened and he stepped back, letting his hands fall to his sides as he lowered his head and stared at his boots. "I didn't mean to make things worse. I wanted to protect you."

Iolanthe cursed and looked beyond him, unable to see him when her emotions were tearing her in too many directions, leaving her muddled and on the verge of doing something dangerous, like offering him comfort.

She strode past him and grimaced at the sight of the dead demon. She felt Kyter's gaze on her, boring a hole into the back of her aching head, commanding her to look at him. She resisted and glared at the demon, trying to regain control of her colliding emotions so she could think clearly for a second and decide what to do.

It wouldn't stop Fernandez from finding out what had happened to his man, but she had to dispose of the body. She couldn't leave it here, in a public place, where humans would come across it.

"Do not move," she snapped at Kyter, stalked across the dusty stone pavement to the demon, and crouched beside him. She grabbed his arm and looked back at Kyter. "I will return."

He growled, flashing fangs, his golden eyes going wild as he launched at her, reaching for her even though she had sworn to return.

He didn't trust her.

He thought she meant to leave him.

She huffed as she teleported, darkness engulfing her for a second before she appeared at the top of a black cliff in Hell, above a wide snaking river of lava. The Devil's domain. No better place to dispose of a dead demon. Hot wind buffeted her as she hauled the demon to the edge. She stared down at the river several hundred feet below her and kicked the demon off the cliff. He plummeted, spinning in the air, growing smaller and smaller until he hit the lava and burst into flames.

Iolanthe breathed out a sigh and rubbed her hands on her armour, a small voice at the back of her head telling her to remain in Hell, away from Kyter. She couldn't do it. She had promised to return and she preferred to keep her promises.

She told herself that was the sole reason she was returning to him.

It had nothing to do with the ridiculous need to comfort him and ease his guilt that was steadily building inside her.

She focused on Kyter and closed her eyes as she teleported.

His earthy masculine scent hit her as soon as she reappeared in Herculaneum and she flicked her eyes open, pinning them straight on him.

He stood a short distance away, his bare chest straining with each hard breath he drew and his golden eyes flooded with something akin to relief, as if he was glad to see her, as if her return had been vital to him in some way.

Iolanthe pretended not to notice how much that pleased her, sending a warm shiver through her that heated her heart and melted the ice around it a little.

"What did you do with him?" he said, his deep voice gravelly and husky, teasing her ears and stirring her desire for him.

She crushed it and kept a tight hold on it, refusing to let her emotions run rampant when he had placed her, and himself, in terrible danger.

"I dropped him into one of the primary lava rivers in the Devil's domain. It does not change what has happened. My client will know what occurred here and I will be punished." She cursed him when he lowered his gaze to the dusty ground between them and frowned at it, as if her words had cut him.

Kyter lifted his head and his bright golden eyes pierced hers. "He hurt you. What else was I supposed to do?"

He curled his fingers into trembling fists at his sides, his bare arms tensing with the action, and turned his face away from her, closing his eyes at the same time. She cursed him again, in her head this time, hating him for pulling on her heartstrings. Such a powerful male shouldn't be able to look so vulnerable.

He inhaled hard, causing his broad chest to expand, luring her gaze down to it. She had been right. Deep claw marks raked over his golden skin, slashing diagonally from his right hip across his stomach. Rivulets of drying blood tracked downwards from the slashes, some of them reaching the waist of his dark combat trousers where they hung low on his lean hips.

She wanted to mention that he needed to tend to his wounds, but she feared he would suggest with another seductive glint in his eyes that she tend to them for him and she wouldn't be strong enough to say no.

Iolanthe dragged her eyes away from his body and back up to his face, expecting to find him watching her now. He wasn't. He had remained with his head turned away from her, his eyes closed and his sandy eyebrows drawn down in a hard frown.

She tried to steel herself against the urge that welled up inside her, fought it with everything she had, but in the end, it wasn't enough. She couldn't stop herself from taking a step closer to him and reaching for his hand. Her fingers flexed as she hesitated in placing her hand over his fist, showing him that she couldn't blame him for what had happened.

It wasn't his fault.

If she were his mate, then he was driven by a powerful need to protect her from other males and from harm. His instinct to do such a thing would have easily overwhelmed him when he had seen the demon strike her.

Iolanthe lowered her hand back to her side before she could touch him and studied his noble profile.

Perhaps he was her fated male, because hadn't she felt that same powerful need to protect him the whole time she had been with him? Hadn't she tried to drive him away in order to keep him safe from harm?

He slipped his left arm around her waist and tugged her towards him, and she didn't fight him this time. She was too lost in the possibility that the male standing before her was her fated male.

"You're shaking," he husked, his voice deep and smooth as an ocean, lulling her and making her want to shift closer to him.

She tensed instead, mastering her body and stopping the trembling he had mentioned. "I am not."

He turned his head towards her and his gaze met hers as he smiled. She cursed the way her belly fluttered in response to that stupid lopsided grin of his. It was a real smile this time though. Not one designed to entice and seduce. He had seen through her lie and it amused him that she refused to admit that she was afraid.

He lifted his hand and went to brush his knuckles across her cheek. She leaned back, evading his caress, and he paused with his hand mere millimetres from her face. His eyes searched hers in the low light.

"Are you afraid of me... or this client of yours?" he murmured and shifted his hand forwards, bringing them into contact. The softness of his caress startled her, sending a shiver tumbling down her spine and reigniting her desire. He tilted his head to one side and the corners of his mouth curled slightly. "Which is it?"

Both.

"Neither," she said.

His sensual lips quirked in another lopsided smile.

"I messed up," he whispered and ran his fingers down her throat, and she had to fight to resist looking at his. Her fangs itched. "I'll fix my mess."

"How?" She wriggled one arm free and swatted his hand away. "Stop that."

He didn't. His smile gained an unapologetic edge and he traced his fingers over her shoulder, heading back towards her throat. Her skin heated beneath her armour wherever he touched. She scowled at him.

"Why don't you flip your armour a little mental command and make it go away?" He toyed with the scales that flowed around her throat, his deep voice husky and low, speaking of the desire that darkened his eyes.

She caught his hand this time, immobilising it and stopping it from wreaking havoc on her self-control. Much more of his stroking and she would probably end up doing as he wanted and would forget what she wanted.

Which was him answering her question.

"How?" She put a little more force behind it this time.

He sighed. "You won't like my plan."

"Does it involve me handing you the artefact and believing you will actually give it back to me?"

His expression soured. "You still don't trust me?"

He hadn't given her a reason to yet. He hadn't earned the trust he wanted her to give so freely to him.

He huffed and rubbed her spine with his free hand. Persistent irritating male. She refused to let him see how the light stroke of his fingers over her armour affected her, sending tingles tripping across her skin and causing heat to flare in her belly.

"Answer my question." She scowled at him for good measure.

It seemed to work, because he sighed again and stopped driving her mad with gentle caresses across her back, and said, "We can work together to find the artefact. Two heads are better than one. It'll work out if we stick together."

She wasn't sure which head he was talking about in regards to himself, but she was definitely certain that the part about it working out wasn't related to the artefact. He was thinking about them working out.

As mates.

Warning bells jangled in her head but he was leaning towards her again, stealing all of her focus to his sensual lips as they dipped towards hers.

She cursed him for distracting her with the first brush of his mouth across hers and praised him for the second as everything that had been on her mind evaporated again, leaving only him behind. The feel of his hands as they claimed her waist. The possessive press of his fingers into her flesh. The seductive sweep of his tongue over her lips. She parted for him and moaned as he claimed her again, losing herself in the hard demanding kiss that left no part of her untouched.

Her body. Her heart. Her soul.

He reached every part of her, claiming dominion over her entirely and awakening all of her senses to him. He smelled earthy and masculine, a powerful scent that made her think of nature and thundering waterfalls. He tasted like the rich tang of his blood, stirring her hunger to dizzying heights, until her fangs emerged against her will. He felt like rock and steel sheathed in warm velvet beneath her hands as they clutched his shoulders and she held on to him to stop herself from being swept away. Each soft puff of his breath matched hers together with the primal beat of his heart in her ears.

She wanted to open her eyes and drink in the sight of him, to see the passion she stirred in such a powerful male, but she didn't want to end this kiss. She needed it to go on forever.

It was drugging. Delicious.

Dangerous.

She didn't care. Nothing mattered but this moment.

Iolanthe wrapped her arms around his neck and pushed her fingers through the shorter hair at the back of his head. He groaned into her mouth and pulled her closer, the tightness of his grip thrilling her. She moaned and kissed him harder, overwhelmed by her need of him. It wasn't enough. She needed more.

He moved with her, backing her across the courtyard. She didn't fight him. Not when he pressed her back into a column. Not when his hands skimmed down to her backside and he lifted her. Not when he wrapped her legs around his waist.

Definitely not when he ground against her, rubbing the steel length in his combats against the apex of her thighs. She shuddered and moaned, the wanton sound startling her. He chuckled against her lips, a throaty sound of pure male satisfaction. She wanted to hit him for it. He took a little too much pride in eliciting reactions from her.

He wasn't the only one who could make the other tremble with need.

Iolanthe pulled herself higher, seizing control of the kiss at the same time as she tightened her legs around his waist and flexed her hips, rubbing him through his trousers. He grunted and then moaned when she stroked his short fangs with her tongue, teasing them. They grew longer and she flinched when she felt a swift stab of pain under her tongue.

He had lower fangs too.

What was he?

It was on the tip of her tongue to break the kiss and ask but he mastered her again, using her momentary distraction against her. His tongue plundered her mouth, teasing her fangs, and his fingers pressed into her backside as he ground against her again, the whole of his body gliding across hers. His chest rubbed her breasts through her armour and she bit back a moan, unwilling to give him the satisfaction of hearing it.

He had to work harder if he wanted to elicit any more noises from her.

Kyter seemed to get the message.

His lips left hers to trail across her cheek and he swept them down her neck. She tried to stop herself but the persuasive dance of his mouth over her throat had her tipping her head back, raising her face to the starlit sky, and moaning. He growled against her skin, the feral sound thrilling her and sending a hot jolt down from her throat to her belly. It struck like lightning along the way, making her breasts tingle and her body arch against his. He grunted again and held her harder, his short claws digging into her armour.

"Iolanthe," he murmured between wet kisses and nipped her throat.

Her eyes shot wide and she slammed her hands against his shoulders, hitting him with a light blast of telekinesis to drive him away from her. He staggered backwards across the courtyard as she dropped to her feet and slapped her hand over her throat, her heart racing at a million beats per minute.

She brought her hand away from her throat and stared down at it.

No blood.

But he had been on the verge of biting her.

He stopped and scowled at her, his eyes dark but not with passion. Anger laced his scent, an undertone of frustration and dissatisfaction joining it as he advanced on her.

She held her left hand out in front of her and he halted, warily eyeing it. She would hit him with a stronger blast if he dared to come near her.

He had intended to bite her.

If he were her fated mate, it would have triggered a bonding process between them, weakening her until she completed it by biting him and sharing blood.

His earlier words came back to her, taunting her as they ran around her head on repeat.

The irritating male believed that he could own her.

He believed that she was a possession and belonged to him, purely because nature had made it possible for them to achieve the deepest bond imaginable between a couple—the bond of mates.

She didn't want a mate.

She had witnessed what a mate meant for females. It meant giving up everything.

There was no way she was going to give up doing the things that she loved—a career that had been her salvation and had given her purpose. She loved treasure hunting and she loved flying solo on her adventures.

She didn't need anyone tagging along and she certainly didn't intend to give up her life's passion for any male. They weren't worth it.

From the things he had said, she knew he expected her to do just that. He thought that she was his mate and he thought she would throw herself into his arms, and wasn't that exactly what she was doing?

She was letting him own her.

She narrowed her gaze on him, her anger rising as he glared across the narrow strip of courtyard at her, the look in his eyes demanding she back down and allow him near her again.

Even if he were her mate, there was no way in this realm or in her own one that she was going to let him take control of her life. She refused to throw away everything she had worked so hard for. She wouldn't bind herself to a male who acted as if she was a done deal when he didn't even know her and didn't ask for permission.

She didn't want a male who took what he wanted, as if he was entitled to it and she had no right to deny him.

"I cannot do this. I *will* not do this." Iolanthe bared her emerging fangs at him and the pointed tips of her ears flared back against the sides of her head, a sign of aggression rather than desire and one she had no control over when her emotions were running hot, like fire in her veins.

Kyter tensed and then growled at her, the sound strange and like nothing she had heard before.

"What are you?" she said, unable to hold that question in.

He began pacing even though he looked as if he wanted to close the distance between them and grab her. His fists shook at his sides and his motions were stiff, each stride clipped. He breathed hard, his gaze locked on her as he strode back and forth across the courtyard in front of her.

A caged animal.

His eyes brightened to molten gold.

"Your mate," he spat the words at her.

She didn't like that look in his eyes as he turned and paced back the other way, narrowing them on her, a calculating edge to them. She had seen too many males look at females that way. As if they were a possession.

She stiffened and echoed his earlier words. "I belong to you."

He nodded.

She shook her head and his expression shifted, losing its certainty and gaining a dark edge.

"I do not recognise you as my mate. You are wrong." She took a step back when he reached for her, a wild look entering his eyes. "And even if you were right... I do not want a mate."

Iolanthe curled her fingers into tight fists and focused on her bolthole, her heart hammering against her chest at a sickening pace.

Her limbs trembled with the explosive combination of anger and fear flooding her.

"I do not need a collar."

She teleported just as he lunged at her, but in the brief moment between issuing the command and disappearing, she saw the answer to the question she had posed so many times and he had refused to answer.

He transformed mid-leap, beautiful golden fur spotted with black rosettes rippling over his skin as his limbs bent and twisted and his head morphed, becoming sleek and cat-like. A thick long tail tipped with black whipped through the air as he emerged from his trousers and his mouth opened on a roar of fury, flashing enormous canines as he landed where she had been.

An immense and dangerous jaguar.

Iolanthe landed in her small studio apartment, stumbled forwards a few blind steps and collapsed on the wooden floor, her knees striking it hard.

A jaguar she had instantly recognised as her mate.

A shiver went through her, spreading down her back and thighs, and she stared wide-eyed at her dark violet bed in front of her.

He hadn't been lying to her. She looked back over her shoulder, as if she could see him back at the ruins if she did so, and shook her head, her hands trembling against her knees. Her mate. Her male. It tore her in two, sending her head and her heart in circles.

She couldn't let it affect her. She couldn't give in to him and the fierce attraction she felt towards him, desire that had been steadily growing since she had first set eyes on him.

She couldn't because he was playing her.

She was no fool. He had been playing her from the moment they had met.

He was out to take the artefact from her.

He was out to take her life.

CHAPTER 10

Kyter prowled around the moonlit ancient city, his paws silent on the broad stones of the roads that intersected the ruined buildings. He walked with his head down, breathing in all the scents coming off the cooling stones, pinpointing one among the thousands of different smells.

Iolanthe.

He chuffed, paused and raised his head to the starlit canvas above. He dragged the warm dusty air over his large fangs, scenting his female. A growl escaped him when her scent came back weaker than before, fading in time with the night.

He raked his claws over the stones and moved on, anger ruling him and keeping him in his jaguar form, a prisoner of his emotions.

A potent and sharp emotion threaded through those other feelings, riding him hard and making him want to tip his head back and roar. Guilt. It was relentless, lacing everything he felt, a feeling he couldn't escape as he stalked through the shadows in his jaguar form.

He had broken with tradition.

He hadn't been able to stop the change from coming over him though. When she had turned on him, her eyes flashing dangerously, her scent warning him that he had made a terrible mistake with her and he was about to pay the ultimate price for it, fear had swept through him with the force of a tsunami, shattering his control. His primal instincts had demanded that he stop his mate from leaving him and his body had obeyed, responding by forcing him to shift as he moved to capture her.

That shift into his jaguar form had had zero to do with grieving his mother and everything to do with fear and anger, but it didn't change the fact that he had shifted before his month was up.

When Iolanthe had disappeared and he had regained a degree of control over himself, he had realised what he had done and that he was in his jaguar form, and had expected grief to fill him.

He had experienced only despair.

Anguish that his mate was gone and might never return.

Her scent grew stronger and he followed it, a slave to his need to find her even when he knew that she was gone, teleported out of his territory because he had been a fool. Her words taunted him, spoken with a bitter edge and laced with fury, outrage that he had caused.

She didn't want a mate.

Him.

She didn't want a collar.

He lowered his head again, stalking now, taking careful measured steps as his senses mapped everything around him and his ears twitched, listening hard for a sound that might signal danger.

Or her return.

He wanted her to return.

To him.

Kyter found a tree in one of the gardens of the crumbling buildings. He rose onto his hind legs and raked his claws over the trunk, peeling the bark away and leaving deep grooves in the wood. When the trunk bore patches where he had completely scratched away the bark, he settled down onto all fours and rubbed against the tree, not just his cheeks but his back too, arching onto his hind legs to ensure his scent was all over it. His territory now. He dropped to his paws again and sniffed the tree, making sure it smelled of him.

It smelled of other cats too. Small domestic ones. Not a threat.

He chuffed and moved on, following her scent still, aware it was leading him back to the room where she had been digging.

He prowled down the street, heading downhill towards the building, aching with a need to smell her intoxicating fragrance again. He wasn't satisfied with the traces of her that lingered in the warm night air. He needed to smell her.

He needed to smell his female.

His mate.

He found the room she had been digging in and huffed when he saw the pick she had used laying discarded on the stone floor.

He loped over to it and sniffed it, pulling her pleasing scent over his teeth. It was strong on the wooden handle of the tool. He breathed it in, finding comfort in her smell, and then rubbed his cheek against the handle. It wasn't enough. He caught the slim shaft of wood in his front paws, curling them around it, and lifted it so he could rub it harder. He rolled with the tool, holding it to his face, his hind legs sticking in the air as he lost himself in the joy of rubbing her scent across his fur.

She didn't need a collar.

He rolled onto his feet, dropping his toy, and made a low keening noise in his throat, a sound born of sorrow.

She wasn't like the females he had grown up with at the pride.

She viewed having a mate as something equal to wearing a collar. He had acted the same way out of bitterness after he had been told that he had no mate. He had made himself believe that he didn't want one, because the thought that he would never have one had cut him to his soul.

He still couldn't think about that day without wanting to rake his claws and take his fangs to something, tearing into it to unleash his fury.

It had been the day of his rite of passage into adulthood.

The elders had called him into their meeting house, just as they did with all male jaguar shifters when they were due to begin the rite, a period of several weeks in which they would journey from pride to pride with an elder, scenting all the females to see if their mate was among them.

They had stared at him with cold hard eyes and had announced he wouldn't be going through the rite, because there was no mate for him. His mixed blood made it impossible.

He had begun to drift away from his pride after that, distancing himself at first to avoid hearing the way the other males talked about him, speaking of him as if he wasn't a jaguar or a useful member of the pride because he wouldn't have a mate.

Once he had grown immune to the barbs and whispered words, he had started to distance himself to kill the constant ache in his chest, the undeniable yearning for a mate.

He had envied the males of his pride as they had found their mates, bringing them back to the village to live there with them, but he had hidden it from everyone, including his mother. He had taken to the hills during the celebrations of new mates, watching from there, forever at a distance but never able to take that extra step, one down the other side of the hill so he didn't have to witness the joyous occasion.

There had been little point in paining himself by seeing something he could never have, but he had never been able to stop himself from watching.

Now he had a mate, and she was beautiful, everything he desired, but he felt as if he was going to ruin his chance with her.

She didn't want a collar.

She didn't want the change in her life that would happen because of their mating.

The females in his pride had always been honoured to have found their mate and their chance to bear offspring to increase their ravaged numbers.

Kyter had the feeling that if he mentioned getting a child in Iolanthe, he would end up very familiar with her black claws and she would be using his chest as a new sheath for her blade.

He also wasn't sure how the kid would turn out. It was a miracle that he had turned out more jaguar than demon. Normally, demon offspring were born pure demon, the other species obliterated from their blood.

His mother had told him that his jaguar side was strong.

His ancestors were some of the strongest males of their race.

It was that legacy in his veins that had controlled the demon side of his genes and he was thankful for it. If the demon side of him had been stronger, if he had come out demon rather than jaguar, they would have killed him at birth.

Kyter idly rubbed the shaft of the pick again, smelling Iolanthe on it still, using her scent to drive away his dark and sombre thoughts of his past, replacing them with ones of a possible future with her.

Where was she?

Elves could teleport between the mortal realm and their homeland in Hell. Was she down there now, thousands of miles from him, separated by a barrier that was impenetrable to his kind without assistance? The only way he could reach Hell was to hitch a ride with someone who could teleport freely to that realm or hunt down a fae or witch capable of opening one of the permanent portals between the mortal and Hell realm.

He had been a colossal fool.

Would she forgive him if he told her that he had realised his mistake?

Would she forgive him if he said that he was sorry?

He had been so caught up in the fact he had a mate that he had done everything wrong.

He had slipped into some fucked up primal behaviour born of his upbringing at the pride village. It had overwhelmed that small sliver of himself that had remained conscious that he was messing things up with her, behaving nothing like the male he truly was and acting like a complete dick. He should have listened to that whispered voice and not allowed the stronger one belonging to the lessons of his pride and his upbringing to control him.

It was too late now to chastise himself though. It wouldn't change what he had done.

He had approached her all wrong. So damn wrong. She wasn't a female from the villages. She wasn't meek and dependent on males. She was confident and powerful, as old as the damned ancient city around him, and she had a career and an independent streak that was as wide as the one that normally ran in his veins.

One he had apparently forgotten existed in a fit of stupidity.

He picked himself up and loped away from the building, heading back towards the area where they had fought and he had behaved like a royal dick.

He needed to take a different approach with her if he was going to win her. He had been thinking with the wrong head. Hell, he shouldn't have been listening to either head. He needed to listen to that other part of himself. His heart. As much as that made him uncomfortable, he had to do it.

Because what was happening between them was more than a fated bond. He had felt the attraction burning between them before he had realised she was his mate, and she hadn't been lying when she had told him she didn't recognise him as her fated male. But she had desired him anyway, had been all over him before he had stupidly thought about biting her.

He desired her, wanted her because she was a beautiful woman who stole his breath away, but now she thought he only wanted her because she was his mate.

He chuffed and growled, directing the rumble of anger at himself.

He had messed up. Badly.

If he wanted to win her and stop her from walking out of his life forever, he was going to have to fight for her and he was going to have to be the first male of his species to compromise.

He had a feeling she would be worth it though.

He reached the courtyard and his black combats where they lay on the patchy grass. He focused hard and grunted as he began the transformation, his bones snapping back into their human form and his fur receding. He growled as his face returned to normal and panted as he knelt on all fours. Naked.

Kyter waited for the pain to stop ebbing and flowing through his bones and then stood with a wobble and grabbed his combat trousers. He unbuttoned them, tugged them on and fastened them again. A breeze swept across the open area as he finished with the last button, stirring the trees that dotted the ruins around him and picking dust up into the air. It swirled across the stone flags and the grass, and curled around his bare feet.

He reached into the left thigh pocket of his trousers, took out his phone and swiped his thumb across the screen to wake it up.

No messages.

At least Cavanaugh hadn't burned Underworld down yet.

The only big cat burning things was him. He had one huge charred bridge to repair between him and Iolanthe.

He felt as if it was already too late for him and he had driven her away. She had been angry with him tonight because of his behaviour. She had been furious because he had killed that demon who had come after her. She had even been pissed that he had kissed her, for around five seconds, and then she had kissed him back.

That didn't change the fact that she was mad as hell at him because of every single thing he had done since meeting her.

How was he supposed to overcome that?

He hadn't set a foot right in the whole time he had known her.

He sat on a high stone curb and considered firing off a message to Cavanaugh. Saying what? He had found his mate, screwed things up, and now he didn't have a damned clue how to find the item he was looking for or how to win her back?

His right eyebrow rose.

Maybe there was a way to turn everything around and make her see that he wasn't a complete arsehole Neanderthal bent on owning her like a slave. He smiled. No maybe about it. There was a way to make her see that they could both get what they wanted, and this time he wasn't talking about gaining her as his mate.

He was talking about something important to her.

It was important to them both. Common ground. The perfect starting place for building the foundations of a relationship.

The artefact.

He could have his revenge.

She could have her pay off.

And maybe, just maybe, they could have forever.

CHAPTER 11

Kyter's fingers flexed and pressed into Iolanthe's bottom, drawing her against him as his mouth mastered hers. She tunnelled her fingers into his sandy hair, ploughing lines in the shorter hair at the back of his head as she pushed her hands upwards. She curled her fingers as she reached the top of his head and twined them around the longer lengths of his hair, tugging them into her fist. He groaned into her mouth and kissed her harder, each sweep of his tongue and fierce press of his lips heightening her hunger and stirring her need.

She pulled herself up his body, tightening her legs around his waist, and poured that hunger and need into kissing him. He palmed her backside and pinned her against the column, pressing every hard delicious inch of his body into hers. She shuddered and moaned, the steel length of his arousal between her thighs, rubbing against where she needed and ached for him, sending her out of her mind.

"Iolanthe." He murmured and broke away from her lips to feather kisses along her jaw, persuading her to tip her head back.

She loved the way he spoke her name, lacing it with a mixture of reverence and need, speaking it in a way no male had ever spoken it before. There was such hunger in it, such violent need and desperation. It was if he was voicing her feelings, echoing them perfectly.

She clawed at his hair, tugging him closer and pinning him to her throat as his mouth performed a wicked dance over the line of her artery, sending a thousand shivers down her spine. He raised one hand to the back of her neck and palmed it, stroking and teasing, increasing the shivers until she trembled against him, squirming in his arms.

"Kyter," she moaned, the desperate needful sound of her husky voice shocking her.

He groaned and clutched the nape of her neck and brought his mouth back down on hers, kissing the breath from her, giving her a way of unleashing her need and seeking the satisfaction she desired. She kissed him fervently, desperately, clashing with him and not giving him the dominance he wanted. She couldn't. She was a slave to her need now, too lost and wild to tame herself or be tamed by another.

Kyter's grip on her backside and neck increased.

A dog barked in the distance, reminding her that they were in the open, a dangerous place to lose sight of their surroundings as they succumbed to their carnal pleasure.

Before she could stop herself, she focused on her bolthole and darkness engulfed them both. Kyter's startled gasp against her lips ended on a moan as she landed on the bed in her small apartment.

On top of him.

He instantly rolled her, ending up between her thighs, pinning her to the dark violet covers of her double bed.

She tipped her head back into the pillow as he devoured her throat, his lips teasing her and the gentle nip of his teeth awakening a deep need to do the same to him. She wanted to sink her teeth into him and drink her fill of his rich, strong blood.

He moaned and pressed his blunt teeth into her skin, as if he had heard her thoughts and he liked them.

His hands skimmed up her sides and her underarms, and he shoved her arms above her head, wrapped his hands around her wrists and pinned them to the pillows. He pushed himself up, his golden eyes hooded as he looked down at her. She wriggled and he smiled, a lopsided one that had her heart fluttering in response. His grip on her wrists tightened, causing his arms to flex on either side of her, a subtle reminder of his strength.

She wanted to remind him that she was stronger than he was, but she liked him where he was and she was happy being at his mercy.

For now.

He dropped his head towards her and she raised hers, eager for another kiss. He stopped before their lips could touch and drew back. Teasing her. She frowned at him and he lowered his gaze to her black armour.

"Why don't you flip your armour a little mental command and make it go away?"

She felt a passing sensation of irritation as those words sank in, as if she should be angry with him for some reason, but it drifted away, inconsequential when he was between her thighs, his delicious weight holding her immobile, exactly how she wanted things to be.

That lopsided smile grew into a full-blown grin when she did as he wanted, commanding her armour to recede into the twin black and silver bands she wore around her wrists. He released her wrists and pushed off her, coming to kneel between her thighs as the black scales began to obey her command.

His gaze followed the armour as it peeled upwards from her feet, the gold in his irises brightening as he devoured every inch of flesh that was revealed to him. His perusal became almost leisurely as the armour cleared her thighs and swept up her stomach towards her breasts. His smile disappeared and he studied her, the intensity of his gaze eliciting a shiver as she lay before him, naked and exposed.

He ran a hand down his mouth, revealing a hint of fangs.

"Gods... you are incredible."

Iolanthe's eyes widened and she wasn't sure how to respond to that. A blush climbed her cheeks. His smile returned, reaching his eyes. Her reaction had pleased him again. Before she could issue a compliment of her own, he dropped onto all fours and kissed her.

She arched towards him and clutched his shoulders as she kissed him, wanting to feel their bare flesh pressed together. She wanted to know the warmth of his golden skin. He resisted as she tried to pull him down to her, his back tensing as he braced himself above her. She unleashed a noise born of frustration and he chuckled, the rich warm sound increasing the heat inside her, until she was burning with need, on fire with desire that felt as if it would consume her if she didn't find release soon.

Kyter dropped his head to her chest and she melted beneath him, sinking into the soft bed as he kissed around her left breast and teased her other one with his hand. He pinched her nipple and she gasped, the sound filling the heavy silence. He chuckled again and swirled his tongue around her other nipple before pulling it into his mouth. She moaned this time and clutched his shoulders, pressing her fingertips into his corded muscles as she writhed beneath him.

She needed more.

She needed all of him.

He had to know that. He had to be able to sense her need just as she could sense his. Her male hungered. He ached for her. She wanted to satisfy that hunger. She wanted to give him the release he needed.

He rubbed his cheek across her breasts, the action reminding her that he was a shifter. A beautiful, powerful jaguar.

Just as she thought that, fur rippled across his shoulders, as soft as thick velvet beneath her fingers. She followed the intricate pattern of one of his black rosettes, tracing the longer thick dashes that encased a series of dots before it disappeared. Beautiful.

He groaned and shuddered beneath her caress and she didn't stop as his golden skin re-emerged. She stroked his powerful shoulders, feeling his muscles as they flexed and bunched with each of his movements as he kissed down her stomach.

Iolanthe looked down the length of her body to him, drinking in the sight of him as he worshipped her stomach. Her powerful male.

He lifted his gaze to meet hers, looking through his dark lashes, his eyes pure molten gold. They turned hooded and he dropped his lips, kissing her stomach while holding her gaze, keeping her focus locked on him and what he was doing. It heightened her awareness of him and her arousal soared in response, her need for him flaring hotter. She shivered as he watched her, slowly working downwards, a predatory glint to his eyes.

Those eyes promised wild passion and wicked pleasure, everything she needed and craved from him. They promised that he wouldn't stop until they had both found release.

He was going to devour her.

Gods, she wanted him to devour her.

He slipped his hands over her bare thighs, looked down as he spread them, and then locked eyes with her again. She bit back the moan that tried to escape her lips and breathed harder as he slowly lowered his mouth towards her. His hands skimmed upwards and her belly fluttered as his thumbs stroked her plush petals.

"Kyter," she murmured, desperate for him to know that she needed him. She needed her male. She feared he wouldn't keep his sultry promise and would stop and that deep need of him would consume her.

He narrowed his eyes on hers and then lowered them to the neat dark thatch of curls at the apex of her thighs and closed them as he dipped his head.

Iolanthe cried out with the first stroke of his tongue over her aroused nub, her hands darting to clutch his head, mussing his sandy hair even further. She arched off the bed and he groaned against her, the sound reverberating through her most sensitive place, eliciting another moan and shiver of pleasure from her. He grasped her thighs and spread her further, wedging his broad shoulders between them.

She surrendered to him, unable to do anything but feel and moan as he caressed her and swirled his tongue around her clitoris. She burned at a thousand degrees, each teasing flick of his tongue cranking her temperature higher, until she felt certain she would turn to ashes in his hands.

He growled and suckled her nub, the flicker of pain only enhancing her pleasure. She needed more. She rocked against him, her hips moving of their own accord, and he grasped them, forcing her to stop, holding her immobile. A prisoner of his wicked tongue.

It teased and tortured her, swirling and flicking, lapping lower. She raised her hips again, showing him what she needed from him. He groaned and she gasped as his fingers stroked down her and he probed her entrance, teasing her before withdrawing.

"Kyter," she husked, wriggling her hips and rocking against his face.

He teased her again, giving her a brief feel of two fingers before taking them away.

She unleashed a frustrated growl and twisted his hair in her hands, eliciting a deep grunt from him.

And his compliance.

She moaned as he eased two fingers into her sheath, pressing them in deep, and sagged against the bed, her hands relaxing in his hair, as he began to pump her with them. He swirled his tongue around her nub in time with each invasion of his fingers, each deep thrust that sent her spiralling higher towards release. She could almost reach it.

Her hips flexed, an action she had no control over as her arousal reached a crescendo, the point at which she ceased to have the ability to think or do anything other than feel. He grunted and stroked her harder, pumping faster, sending her soaring.

Iolanthe tipped her head back and cried out as the tightness in her belly detonated. Fire seared through her veins and lit her up inside. Fierce hot tingles swept over her stomach and thighs as she quivered, her body flexing around his fingers as they stilled inside her. His hot breath skated across her sensitive flesh and she trembled.

Kyter withdrew his fingers from her and she lay in a daze, drifting on a warm heavenly sea.

She became dimly aware of the bed depressing as he moved and the rustle of material. She felt the flow of his heat and his hunger in her veins, an awareness of him that ran deep, etched in her bones forever. Her mate.

Iolanthe slowly lifted her eyelids, her desire rising again, burning hotter than ever when she took in the magnificent sight of her mate kneeling between her spread thighs, naked and hard, primed for her.

He locked eyes with her and she reached for him, crooking her finger to lure him down to her. Her male needed. He hungered.

She would give him what he needed.

Everything he desired.

He prowled up the length of her, settled his weight on his right elbow, pressing his chest to hers, and clutched his rigid length in his other hand. He ran the crown of it down her slick centre and held it poised at her entrance.

His eyes held hers. Mesmerising. Molten gold.

His sensual lips parted.

His fangs flashed between them as he spoke.

"You will be mine now."

Iolanthe jerked awake, her heart thundering and sweat trickling down her back and between her bare breasts. She threw the violet covers off her with trembling hands and struggled to steady her breathing as she stared around the cluttered small studio apartment, slowly realising that it hadn't been real. A dream. She had dreamed of Kyter.

She growled, baring her fangs.

She wasn't angry about the dream. That had been delicious enough, nothing more than a harmless fantasy. She was angry because Kyter had even managed to ruin that dream. She couldn't even fantasise about him without him trying to claim her as his mate.

She shoved to the edge of the bed and froze, her hands clutching the mattress on either side of her thighs.

She had kissed him at the ruins and she had tasted his blood.

Her heart picked up again, a sickening rapid beat in her veins. She hadn't bitten him though. She pressed her hand to her chest, recalling that she had felt linked to him in her dream, and focused through her fear. Nothing. She had none of the other side effects of an incomplete bond. She wasn't feeling his emotions or pain, and she wasn't weaker than normal.

Iolanthe sucked down a deep breath and expelled it slowly, bringing her racing heart back under control and shutting down her fears.

She hadn't triggered the bonding process when she had kissed him. She was being ridiculous. It required her to bite him and consume a quantity of his blood, not merely taste it in a kiss.

The dream had been just a fantasy then.

She flopped back onto the bed and sighed.

It didn't make her feel any better.

She was having erotic dreams about him. No good would come of that. Her control around him was already shaky enough. With the dream of him pleasuring her rolling around in her head, she would be lucky to survive another encounter with him without succumbing to her attraction to him.

She threw her left arm over her eyes and groaned. What had he done to her?

She had lived for millennia without a male affecting her to one tenth of the degree that Kyter did. The irritating male wreaked havoc on her control with just a stupid smile. She huffed and let her arm fall above her head, and toyed with the damp strands of her blue-black hair, struggling to formulate a plan.

The only one that came to her was avoiding him.

If she could avoid him, then nothing could go wrong. She could find the item Fernandez wanted, deliver it to him within the timeframe, and then she would be free to get on with her life. Everything would return to normal.

The only flaw in her plan was the part about finding the item.

She stared at the ceiling of her apartment.

She had to return to Herculaneum.

CHAPTER 12

Iolanthe's blood churned at a low simmer, refusing to settle no matter what trick she tried. It had been steadily rolling towards a boil since she had made the decision to return to Herculaneum, building as she bathed and dressed, and eventually teleported to her current vantage point above the ruins as the first golden fingers of dawn caressed the fading night sky.

She blew out her breath and stood balanced on the metal railing that surrounded the site, looking down on the streets and buildings of the ancient city.

She told herself again that she hadn't come back to see Kyter. She had come to investigate the fresco before the site opened for the day. That was the only reason she had returned so soon after leaving. It had nothing to do with the irritating jaguar shifter. She was going to avoid him, just as she had planned.

Her heart did a flip in her chest and she pretended it hadn't happened. She couldn't risk running into him. She wasn't strong enough right now, not with the dream still fresh in her mind and still affecting her.

She nurtured her anger, replaying the moments when Kyter had spoken about her and looked at her as if she was a possession, not an equal to him. He wanted to enslave her. She had to remember that. It didn't matter that she desired him. It only mattered that he wanted to own her. She couldn't let herself be swayed by her need, because he would have a collar around her neck before she realised what had happened.

The early glow of dawn lit the sky off to her right, silhouetting Mount Vesuvius where it loomed a short distance away. The wooded slopes were dark, the nature there calling to her, luring her into forgetting her mission and taking a walk amongst the trees, absorbing the calming scent of the forest. It would soothe her ragged nerves and steady her heart, but she didn't have time to waste.

She pulled her focus back to the site and her mission. Not Kyter. She wasn't thinking about him. She had put him out of her head and he was going to stay there for the next thousand years. It didn't matter that he was her fated male. Or that he was handsome, in an irritating sort of way.

Her hands danced down over her clothing before she realised what she was doing, smoothing her dark purple camisole top over the waist of her tight black trousers. She muttered a black curse and shook her hands, stopping them from executing their ridiculous task of fixing her appearance. No one was going to see her. She wasn't here to see anyone either.

She snapped her focus to the low stone building with the fresco and darkness swallowed her, parting to reveal the entrance as she appeared in front of it.

Her pointed ears twitched.

Digging.

Her heart started a slow steady thump against her breast that began to accelerate as her sensitive hearing detected the quiet masculine grunts that came in time with each ring of metal striking stone.

Iolanthe swallowed to wet her dry throat.

She needed a drink. Her sudden parched mouth had nothing to do with the annoying shifter.

Perhaps she could just walk inside and ask to borrow his canteen.

Iolanthe caught herself. What was she doing? She turned her back on the building and folded her arms across her chest. She was not going to enter the building. She would leave and return when it was dark, and hopefully Kyter would be gone.

She bit her lip, catching it with her right canine. She couldn't leave. She didn't want to see the jaguar male, but she didn't have a choice. She had to go into the building and investigate the area where he worked. The one she had chosen had turned up nothing. That left her with only this one. If he found the artefact, he would take it and she would never find it.

Fernandez would take her head.

She drew in another deep breath and exhaled it slowly, fighting for calm as fear flickered through her in response to the thought of failing in her mission. She wouldn't fail. She would get the artefact that Fernandez sought and within the time limit.

Even if she had to seduce it out of Kyter's grasp.

Her hands trembled as she ran them over her sleek blue-black hair and she cursed the sign of weakness. She couldn't go into the room like this, afraid and on edge. Kyter would sense it on her as he had only a few hours ago, detecting her emotions through scent and through sight.

Or touch as the case had been.

She shunned the memories that pushed to the surface, flooding her mind with an instant replay of being in Kyter's arms, his lips claiming hers in a fierce kiss.

Irritating shifter.

It felt as if she couldn't escape him. He was constantly in her thoughts, stealing her focus away from her mission, and had even invaded her dreams. For the first time in millennia, her emotions and physical condition was all over the place. She had spent the last hour pinging from angry to calm, and cold-as-ice to hot-as-fire, her head filled with wicked thoughts about him, and it was all his fault.

Iolanthe fisted her hands and nodded. She could be professional about this. Discovering that he was her fated male hadn't changed anything. He was still a male on a mission to bend her to his will and get her killed in the process. She would walk into the room and see that hadn't changed. He would probably greet her with that stupid lopsided smile of his and spout something ridiculous about knowing she would come back to him and that she was his.

She turned on her heel and stomped through the building to the large empty room where they had first met, ready for the confrontation she felt sure was coming.

And ground to a halt as he came into view, working in the centre of the area where three walls painted with the frescos she had come here to see enclosed a raised platform.

Her mouth dried out again.

The muscles of his bare back worked in a beautiful symphony as he raised her pick above his head and brought it down hard on the floor, sending pieces of stone flying in all directions. Sweat glistened on his back, highlighting every peak and valley. Her eyes followed a single bead as it rolled down his left shoulder, tracking the line of a scar, and joined with another. They melded with more beads, until they became a rivulet that trickled down his spine, luring her gaze down to the waist of his black combat trousers and the twin dips above his buttocks.

The pointed tips of her ears grew longer, a physical response to the arousal rising swiftly within her, stirred by the sight of Kyter.

Gods.

She tried to avert her gaze but he raised the pick again, the powerful muscles of his arms and shoulders bulging a second before he brought it down in another swift arc, striking the stone.

Her mate.

Her fated male.

He was glorious. Stunning. Strong. Beautiful. Dangerous. Deadly.

She didn't want to be swayed by his allure. She couldn't allow her desire to get the better of her, because if she did, it wouldn't end well. Either he would steal the artefact the moment her guard was down, using her desire against her, or her client would use him as a pawn and he would end up hurt.

Or worse.

The thought of Fernandez capturing Kyter made her heart jerk in her chest, pain spreading outwards from it, rapidly becoming fury as it seeped into her veins and flowed through her blood. No. She would never allow such a thing to happen.

Kyter had been right.

This wasn't a game.

He hefted the pick and struck again, and she viewed him with cold eyes, ones devoid of the desire that had been in them just seconds ago.

She couldn't allow herself to fall to Kyter's charms, becoming a victim of her desire. There was too much at risk. His life. Her life. Her freedom.

If she had wanted to shackle herself to a male, she would have stayed in the village where she had grown up and would have done as her parents had wanted—married the male they had chosen for her on her one thousandth birthday.

Kyter paused, lowered the pick in his left hand to his side and ran the back of his right across his brow.

Iolanthe stared at his back, a frown marring her brow as she noticed the number of pale silvery scars that slashed across his golden skin. There were so many of them, concentrated on his shoulders but with some lower down, cutting across his waist and even his hips. Her eyes darted to take them all in. More than she could count. Her stomach turned as she tried to comprehend what terror he had lived through to gain so many scars.

She had a feeling his entire life had been a fight for survival.

That feeling evoked a fierce and commanding response in her, a deep urge to know what terrible things had befallen him, and awakened a sensation that had her lifting her left hand to her chest and pressing it to the spot above her heart as it went out to him.

He was a fighter.

Like her.

She'd had to fight for everything she had now too.

She opened her mouth to say something but her voice fled her, driven away by her tumultuous thoughts. What could she say? If she said anything, he would know she had been standing there, staring at him. If she admitted that they were alike, he would take that as permission granted, a sign that she would be his mate.

He raised the pick and wrapped both hands around it again, returning to his work.

Iolanthe stood in the middle of the full-width section of the room behind him, her gaze locked on him as he worked between the two walls that intersected the rest of it, dividing half of it into three. She watched him in silence, unsure what to do and unable to stop herself from admiring his physique as he dug his hole, standing knee-deep in it.

He had a magnificent body. She had thought it the first night they had met in this very place and he had attempted to seduce her by removing his t-shirt. She hadn't failed to notice that he had chosen not to wear a top since that moment. She had tried to stifle her reaction to the sight of his honed body, but it had been too powerful to contain, and he had seen it.

He was using his body as a weapon, waging war on her defences.

She cursed him for that.

She cursed him for kissing her too.

She should have been stronger. She should have stopped him.

But she had wanted his kiss. She had ached with a need to feel his lips pressed against hers so she could know his taste and his touch. Only for a heartbeat. She had only wanted it for a short time, a moment of madness to wash away her fear and give her back control over her own body.

It hadn't worked.

That kiss had made him the master of her body whether she liked it or not. Whenever she laid her eyes on him, she remembered how good his body had felt against hers, how commanding his mouth had been and how intoxicating his taste was. The sight of him working, his muscles flexing and bunching beneath his golden skin, had heat pooling in her belly and her blood burning with a need to run her hands over him.

He froze with the pick held above his head.

Slowly turned to face her.

Eyes of pure gold held hers.

His black pupils expanded in their centres.

She felt as if she was being hunted as he stared at her.

His prey.

Iolanthe swallowed and took a step back, her boots silent on the dusty stone floor. He lowered the pick and let it fall to the ground as he stepped out of the hole, his chest heaving with each hard breath he drew and his heart a powerful beat in her ears.

A beat that hers matched.

She stood transfixed, unable to move as he stared at her, his mesmerising golden eyes holding her immobile.

He blinked and when his lids lifted, the eerie brightness of his eyes had disappeared and a completely different male stood before her, one far more casual and infinitely less dangerous.

She had been facing the beast within him.

Thick silence stretched taut between them. She hated it. It felt too intimate. She had to break it. She had to say something. Anything.

She cleared her throat and spoke as casually as she could. "What are you doing?"

He folded his arms across his broad bare chest and smiled, and she had another feeling, this one telling her that he knew what he was doing. He had caught her staring and he could probably scent the desire on her. By folding his arms across his chest, he caused the muscles of his arms to tense and could easily clench the ones of his torso, encouraging every ridge on his six-pack to flex. He was showing off his body, luring her back under his spell. She cursed him, and then herself. She was stronger than this.

"Looking for an artefact," he said, his voice a low rumble that rolled over her, stirring unbidden heat in her belly. She doused it with a reminder that he was out to own her and play her too. "What are you doing?"

She looked beyond him, to the hole he had dug with little finesse right in the middle of the raised section of the room. "I am waiting for you to get out of my way so I can look for an artefact."

He didn't take his eyes off her. "I don't think we'll find it here."

We?

She frowned. "Why not?"

He unfurled his big body and pointed to the ground. She couldn't see into the hole from where she stood and he didn't seem inclined to explain. Forcing her to move closer to him? It was a low tactic, one she should have expected from him.

She rounded the rope that cordoned off the area and took the two steps up to the platform. She hovered at the very edge, over a metre from him, but she still couldn't see. She shot him a black look that he answered with a smile and shuffled closer, narrowing the distance between him.

Dangerously close.

When he looked down into the hole, her gaze disobeyed her commands and leaped to his sweat-slicked chest.

The blows the demon had dealt were healing and she found it oddly relieving to see the scratches were already little more than dark pink marks. They would soon fade to scars that would add to the ones that already littered his chest. Those were marks of battle with other shifters. The ones on his back were different. They made her think of lashings, and she wanted to growl at the vision of Kyter on his knees, his arms bound, his back slick with blood from a beating.

His gaze slid towards her and she wasn't quick enough to stop him from catching her looking. She stared down into the hole, her cheek to him, waiting for him to say something teasing.

Part of her hoped he wouldn't, that he would prove her wrong about him and would be a gentleman.

She grimaced when he shattered that hope.

"I thought you came back for the artefact? You sure you didn't come back for another kiss?"

Iolanthe shunned him and moved closer to the hole, edging around it and placing it between them. It was filled with earth and stone, already several feet deep. There was no underground room here.

"I do not understand," she whispered, her violet gaze fixed on the hole to avoid Kyter as he moved a step closer, choosing to stand opposite her.

His scuffed boots appeared in view and she ignored them, refusing to look at them because she knew that if she did, she would end up following those boots up to his black combat trousers and from there she would end up looking at his body again.

She shook her head, causing her black hair to brush her bare shoulders as she tried to make sense of what she was seeing. Panic clawed its way up her throat, tightening it, and she fought it down again. She still had more than a week. She could find the artefact.

But what if it had been below her original location and someone had discovered it and taken it?

What if it was lost?

Would Fernandez believe her?

Her heart skipped several beats and the feel of Kyter's gaze on her intensified.

"Iolanthe?" he murmured, a touch of warmth and concern in his deep voice.

She shook her head again.

"I was told I would find something here." She ground her teeth when her fear coloured her voice, making it tremble a degree, enough that he would no doubt notice it, if he hadn't already sensed her emotions in her scent.

She clenched her fists and pulled herself together. This was a setback. That was all. She would keep looking and she would find the item before her deadline. There was no reason to panic. She had hit dead-ends before and had still found what she was looking for.

Of course, only money and pride had been on the line those times.

Not her life.

She barely resisted leaping down into the hole and taking up the pick. Kyter was right. There was nothing here.

"The demon I met in the fae town told me to look for knowledge in the shadow of a volcano." She lifted her gaze to meet Kyter's, searching his golden eyes in the low light coming in from the gap between the structure and the modern roof above them.

He frowned and rubbed his stubbly jaw, smudging dirt across it. "The demon told me something different."

Iolanthe couldn't contain her knee-jerk response to that as she shifted closer to him or the way her hoped soared, crushing her fear.

Kyter's golden eyes darkened and she silently begged him not to play her, not to make this into a game when he had shouted at her that it wasn't one. She didn't dare hope that he could be a gentleman, a decent man, and do the right thing, not even when she desperately wanted him to prove her wrong about him.

He didn't shatter her hope this time.

"The demon told me to look to the mother of the gods in the shadow of a volcano. I came here first to check this spot out but my next stop is Pompeii."

Her eyes leaped to the fresco behind him, a painting of two women and a man. Minerva, the goddess of wisdom, depicted with her mother, Juno.

The mother of the gods.

She slowly edged her gaze towards Kyter, wondering whether he knew that he had just given her the best lead she'd had since starting out on her mission.

"The Capitolium," she said.

Kyter canted his head and frowned, a quizzical look in his golden eyes as he scrubbed the strong line of his jaw. Gods, he was handsome. She shook off that thought and focused on her mission, unwilling to let him cloud her mind now that she felt as if she was closing in on the item.

"Pompeii. The Capitolium there."

He smiled. "It sounds made up."

Iolanthe closed her eyes and prayed for strength. He was handsome, but he was severely in need of some history lessons. When she opened her eyes again, he had folded his arms across his chest and was glaring at her, his sensual lips flattened into a hard line and his sandy eyebrows meeting low above his fierce golden gaze. She supposed she hadn't exactly been subtle in her response to what he had said. He had no doubt detected her disappointment.

"There is a temple in Pompeii, but it is often listed as Jupiter's temple. It was actually dedicated to the Capitoline Triad." She stooped and caught the handle of her pick, and straightened.

The wooden handle was rough beneath her fingers and she frowned down at it. There were grooves in the shaft. Scratches. She raised an eyebrow at Kyter. He shrugged, no shred of apology in his eyes. He had scent marked *her* pick?

She held his gaze as she teleported it back to her bolthole. As an elf, she possessed the ability to teleport anything she owned to and from any location. It made travelling light a lot easier, and had often been a lifesaver during the more dangerous jobs. She could teleport any bulky equipment back to her bolthole if she had to swim underwater or squeeze through narrow spaces, and then call it back to her when she needed it.

"The Capitoline Triad were three supreme deities. Jupiter, the father of the gods, Juno, the mother of the gods, and Minerva, his daughter and the goddess of wisdom."

Kyter's eyebrows rose. "So... the Jupiter guy is like Zeus?"

She nodded. "I have to go to Pompeii."

She focused on the one location she could remember in the ancient site and Kyter was suddenly before her, his large hand clamping down on her wrist. She twisted her arm in an attempt to break free of his hold but he only tightened his grip.

"Release me." She looked from her arm to his face and he shook his head.

"I can't do that." The steely edge to his eyes warned that he was serious. He meant to stop her from reaching Pompeii first and finding the artefact.

She hissed, her fangs sharpening and ears flaring back against the sides of her head, and prepared to call her armour and her blade.

Kyter's handsome face softened and he caught her off guard by raising his free hand and smoothing his palm across her cheek.

"As much as I love it when you kick my arse, I don't want a rematch. I want to help you." His eyes danced between hers, his sandy eyebrows furrowing above them as he moved closer, his hand settling against her face, softly cupping her cheek.

He brushed his thumb across her skin and her breath hitched. She couldn't believe him. He was casting another spell on her, attempting to lure her into surrendering to him. She shook her head and he smiled, this one laced with sorrow that tugged at her heart and begged her to give him a chance. Why? He only wanted to hurt her by tricking her into finding the artefact and giving it to him. Didn't he?

"Iolanthe," he murmured and her name had never sounded more beautiful than it did issuing from his lips as his eyes held hers, the softness in them enchanting her. "We got off on the wrong foot... and I'm sorry I was a dick. You can trust me. We can work together."

She wanted to accept that honest apology and believe him, but the poisonous dark voice in the back of her mind whispered that she couldn't trust him and another part of her, a warmer and softer part deep in her heart, said that she couldn't take him up on his offer because he would end up dragged into her mess.

Kyter was strong and capable, a powerful warrior, but Fernandez was stronger, and his assassins were legendary.

She lowered her gaze away from Kyter's, unable to bear the thought of hurting him let alone seeing it in his eyes when she spoke.

"You mean to betray me." She swallowed when his hand fell from her face and his other one tensed against her wrist. "You will take the artefact and I need it."

He was silent for too long, unmoving, and she almost crumbled and looked at him.

"I won't take it." Those words leaving his lips made her head snap up and her eyes lock with his. They were steady and still soft, filled with honesty. She couldn't detect any trace of a lie in his scent. "I just need to borrow it."

Her eyebrows dipped low. "Borrow it?"

He nodded. "I don't need the artefact to sell it to someone. I need it to find the location of the demon it summons."

Her heart set off at a pace. Barafnir?

"What do you want with the demon?" She couldn't hold that question back.

Kyter didn't look like the sort of man who wanted to summon a dangerous demon for his own profit or to use it against another, as Fernandez most likely did. At least, she hoped he wasn't that sort of man.

He smiled and there was only sorrow in it again, pain that laced his earthy masculine scent and echoed in his eyes. He released her wrist and turned away from her, as if he didn't want her to see him when he told her of his reason.

His long fingers ploughed through his sandy hair, tousling the longer lengths on top, and then tensed against the back of his head. His broad shoulders heaved on a sigh.

"The demon it summons... it... he... he attacked my pride in the Amazon." Kyter's fingers dug into the nape of his neck as he lowered his head and his voice turned husky and dark, filled with anger and agony, grief that was still so raw that she could feel it in him. "He killed my mother."

His bare shoulders tensed, looked as if they might shake, and then he jerked his head up and let his arm fall to his side, all of the pain she had felt in him evaporating, replaced by cold fury.

"I mean to kill the bastard."

Iolanthe stared at the back of his head, her heart torn in two, ripped between her need of the item and his. His cause was noble. Beautiful. No wonder this wasn't a game to him. He wanted to avenge his pride and his mother. He needed it with a ferocity that she could feel in him. But if she didn't deliver the item in seven days, she was in trouble, and it wasn't the sort that anyone could save her from. Not this time.

She couldn't surrender her quest for the artefact, and she knew he couldn't either. Their paths would keep crossing and eventually Fernandez would send another to check on her and he would discover what Kyter was to her, and she to him. There was only one way of protecting Kyter now, ensuring he didn't become entangled in her problem.

She had to work with him. He was right and they would be quicker to locate the item if they worked together, and she had to admit that sometimes two heads were better than one. He had been given a different clue. Without him, she wouldn't have figured out the location of the item or possibly the next clue.

If they worked together, there was a chance they could find the item or the next clue in this area before someone came to check on her. They could evade Fernandez's new spy by discovering it and moving on before he could arrive. Kyter could summon the demon and then she would take the item to Fernandez. If they could stay one step ahead of the spy, it might work. Fernandez would never know what happened. He would receive the artefact. Kyter would have his vengeance.

She would live to see another day.

Kyter slowly turned to face her, his stunning eyes still laced with pain and anger, and she felt an overwhelming urge to offer him comfort and hope.

"If you are lying to me, I will kill you." She offered her hand to him.

He gave her a lopsided smile and the pain and anger in his eyes eased, just as she had wanted. "So you keep saying... but I'm not dead yet."

He slipped his hand into hers. His skin was warm and a little rough, calloused from working with the pick, but she liked his heat and how gently he held her, his thumb gently gliding along the length of hers, teasing her and sending a shiver dancing up her arm.

"I will teleport us to Pompeii." She regretted offering it the second he released her, grabbed his discarded black tank off the top of his backpack where it leaned against the wall opposite her, and dried himself off with it, taking his time with his chest and stomach, rubbing the fabric over his honed muscles.

Irritating shifter.

The charming edge to the smile he tossed at her said he was doing it on purpose, luring her gaze to his body and knowing it would stir the passion he had unleashed in her when they had kissed, desire that was becoming harder to resist.

It became almost impossible when he stuffed the tank top into his pack, zipped it closed, slung the pack over his shoulder and stalked towards her, his charming smile holding steady. He slid his right arm around her waist and hauled her against him, so there wasn't a point where they weren't touching.

Iolanthe averted her gaze as heat flared white-hot in her veins, awakening a fierce need to kiss the smile off his sensual lips.

It didn't help.

She ended up staring at his bare chest and his throat. Her fangs itched and saliva pooled in her mouth.

Gods, she was hungry.

He smelled so good.

She stared at the pulse ticking on the left side of his throat below the strong straight line of his jaw. It called to her and she pressed closer to him, lost in the need rising within her. Heat rolled off him, his earthy scent filling her senses, evoking memories of how his blood had tasted. Powerful. Potent.

She mustered her strength and closed her eyes, shutting out the temptation before her.

She couldn't bite him.

Because one bite was all it would take.

It would trigger the bonding process between them.

It would change her entire world.

CHAPTER 13

Kyter shifted a pile of twigs and leaf litter with his boot, clearing the corner of the paved area to one side of the ruins of Jupiter's temple in Pompeii. The full moon cast his shadow out long ahead of him, over the high pale stone wall formed by the large rectangular base of the temple, and threw the world into hues of blues and blacks.

He was glad that it was full. The new moon played havoc with his demon genes and he didn't want to have to worry about that side of himself emerging tonight. He wanted to enjoy this moment he had found himself in with Iolanthe.

She worked at the front end of the roofless temple above him, prowling like a shadow between the ruined columns, her footsteps silent on the white stone.

When she had teleported him to Pompeii this morning, they had toured the site, locating the temple. She had asked if he had a place to stay, and he had told him that he would find a quiet spot to hide out rather than heading back to his rented villa and would then play tourist for the day while the site was open, and conceal himself again when it closed. She had pressed him not to do anything without her, a flicker of fear in her striking violet eyes, and he had promised that he wouldn't and hadn't tried to stop her when she had teleported, leaving him alone.

He had used the day to put the site to memory, checking every building in case there was another place where the item might be hidden and learning all about life in Pompeii from the audio guide he had acquired.

He hadn't missed Iolanthe's reaction to what he had said when she had first mentioned the Capitolium.

He was no scholar and had never pretended to be one, but he was damned if he was going to let his lack of knowledge about ancient history tarnish his female's opinion of him. He had covered the entire site while listening to the audio guide, had read a guidebook he had purchased from front cover to back during a break for lunch at the café, and had then gone around the whole site again.

He was a quick study and had already picked up a few handy facts about the buildings and life in Pompeii that he could whip out at any appropriate moment to impress her and change her opinion of him, hopefully erasing how disappointed she had been in him yesterday.

When he had finished stuffing as much knowledge into his head as would stick, he had switched his focus to studying the roofless temple they were here to explore.

The Capitolium.

The front end of the rectangular temple was open, with broken columns lining three sides and a wall running across the middle of the raised platform. That wall formed one side of an enclosed area that filled the rest of the temple's base. He had spent hours staring at the temple and the single gated entrance that led under the base, trying to figure out where the temple hid the secret he needed to find.

They needed to find.

He was beginning to understand that this item was extremely important to her too.

When she had returned at nightfall, he had smelled her scent on the breeze and had made his way back to the temple, finding her already at work. She had greeted him with a shy smile that had made him forget about pressing her for information on why she needed the artefact and had listened intently as she had issued him instructions before she had turned her focus to searching the main area of the temple.

Every time he saw her, she grew even more beautiful.

Tonight, she wore her long dark hair tied in a ponytail and had dressed all in black, from her tight combat trousers tucked into her boots to her camisole that plunged low enough to reveal a modest amount of cleavage. Her ears weren't pointed, a trick elves employed to make themselves blend in with the human world. They could adapt to their surroundings. In her case, her ears transformed to appear human and her eyes changed to a stunning green flecked with gold.

She had kept her eyes violet tonight.

Even the moon couldn't steal their colour. They were bright, vivid despite the cold light. Entrancing.

Kyter forced his focus back to his work, because thinking about how beautiful she was had him itching to leap up to where she worked, pull her into his arms and kiss her before she had a chance to protest.

He didn't doubt that she would respond and return the kiss, but it would harm his progress with her. She was beginning to trust him. She was beginning to relax around him, revealing herself to him. He finally felt as if the bridge he had burned between them was restoring itself, the damage slowly reversing, giving him another shot at things.

He would do everything right this time.

Starting with winning her trust by showing her that they could share the artefact.

He just had to find it first.

Iolanthe had informed him that there would be a chamber beneath the temple, used to store sacrificial items and offerings. That was the gated area. He had agreed when she had said it seem like too obvious a hiding place for something and if the item they were searching for had been down there, it had most likely been found already. They had checked it out and had turned up nothing.

He still wanted to yank the iron gate open and take another look inside. Only his promise that they would investigate the rest of the temple before dawn was stopping him. He hoped that Iolanthe was right and the item was hidden elsewhere, in a secret place, one not obvious to the archaeologists who worked on the ancient site.

In front of the temple steps to his left, the area had been laid with grass and a barrier erected around it, a mixture of brick wall and iron fences. Behind him where he stood to one side of the temple, low square plinths lined the edge of the paved area, a wide gravel path beyond them. Three white columns stood precariously supporting a piece of another structure. Iolanthe had taken a break earlier in the evening to sit at the edge of the temple base above him and point out several things to him, saying what they had once been. He hadn't taken any of it in, and not because he had already read about it in his book.

He had been too transfixed by the sight of her bathed in pure moonlight, her eyes sparkling as she talked about the site, her passion for the city and her work overflowing in them. She talked animatedly about this place, and with an air of authority and a frightening amount of enthusiasm.

When she had hurried away from him, eager to continue her exploration of the temple ruins, Kyter had concluded that his mate was a walking history book, and that he found it endearing in a strange way. It made him smile.

Maybe it was her passion about the subject and her work. He was passionate about his business and could talk the hind legs off a donkey if someone asked him about it, telling them every detail about running Underworld. They probably thought those details were mundane, but they were important to him.

This work was important to her.

He leaped up onto the base of the temple, easily clearing the six-foot-plus height to land quietly on his feet between two broken columns.

"Nothing down there but the chamber." His mission had been to search for possible false walls or stones that could be moved and something could be hidden behind them. He had walked around the entire base of the temple, using his heightened vision and sense of smell to check every stone.

She sighed and paused at her work of scrutinising every inch of the floor and every column in a hunt for a clue.

"If it isn't in the chamber, maybe we'll have to dig for it." He rubbed the back of his neck and slowly approached her, giving her time to adjust to his proximity.

She had turned skittish the only time he had attempted to get close to her tonight. For all her bluster and bite, she was a timid little thing inside, afraid of him. He wasn't out to hurt her or betray her, not as she clearly thought he was, and he wanted to prove that to her.

He didn't want to own her. He didn't want to put a collar on her.

He wanted her to stand at his side, as his equal.

He hadn't exactly given her that impression though, and he knew it was going to take more than a few hours working with her rather than against her to make her see differently.

He diverted his course and went to his black backpack where he had rested it against one of the shorter pieces of column that lined the front of the temple. He crouched, unzipped the main compartment, and took his canteen out. He had filled it at one of the many taps situated around the site and the water was still blissfully cool.

When he rose back to his feet and turned to face Iolanthe, she was watching him.

He brought the canister away from his lips and offered it to her. She shook her head. Her eyes dropped to his throat and then darted off to her right. His heart pumped harder in response to the brief hungry glance. She wanted to bite him.

Whenever she looked as if she might, he lost track of the world. All of it faded away as his focus narrowed to encompass only her, his mind filling with a vision of her wrapped around him as she had been that night in Herculaneum when they had kissed.

Only her kiss this time was the press of her fangs into his throat.

He rubbed a hand over his mouth, the thought of her biting him making him instantly hard in his black combats.

A hint of colour darkened her cheeks and her head dipped lower. She was on to him. She knew that her glance at his throat had triggered a war in him, a battle between desire and duty. Duty had to win, because surrendering to his desire would only set him back with her. He couldn't act on his need for her until she gave him the green light. That was the challenge he had set himself. She had to be the one to come to him, of her own free will, and initiate things again.

"So you've been here too?" he said and she finally looked at him again. The distance between them seemed to shrink as her eyes met his. A flicker of confusion surfaced in hers. He smiled. "I mean when Pompeii was still a thriving city."

The confusion melted away and she smiled.

Gods. She smiled.

He had never seen anything like it. It sucker punched him, sending his head spinning and his heart reeling, and leaving him sure he must have staggered back a step from the blow. But he hadn't moved. Maybe the whole damn Earth had shifted beneath his boots then, because for a moment he hadn't been on solid ground. That smile had lifted him clear off it.

His mate had a smile that could light up the world.

"Yes, I came here a few times back when it was a city. I did a job here." The casual way she put that one out there had his jaw dropping.

"You were working as a treasure hunter two thousand years ago?" He lowered the canteen and stared at her, questions multiplying in his head, and doubling again when she nodded. "How long have you been a treasure hunter?"

She wrinkled her nose up, looking beyond him, and then shifted her eyes back to meet his. "Around twenty-four centuries."

Two thousand four hundred years.

"How old are you?" he blurted and her cheeks darkened again.

He cleared his throat and cursed himself for just tossing that out there with zero finesse. Men weren't meant to ask women how old they were. He hadn't been able to help himself though. He had thought perhaps she was a little over two thousand years old because she had been to Herculaneum when it had been a city, before disaster had struck it. Now he was beginning to suspect she was older.

Much older.

She almost smiled. "I have lived for one thousand years longer than I have worked."

Just the three thousand four hundred years then. Far older than he had ever imagined or could have guessed.

She was close to ten times older than he was.

No wonder she viewed finding a mate as a collar or a form of enslavement. She was used to her freedom and had been a treasure hunter for twenty-four centuries, almost six times longer than he had been alive.

Kyter replaced the cap on his water and dropped the canteen onto his backpack, needing a moment to take everything in and process it.

"I feel like a toy-boy," he muttered. "I guess that makes you a cougar."

A frown pinched her fine black eyebrows. "I am not a cat shifter like you."

He smiled and chuckled. She knew her history, but it seemed she wasn't up to speed on the modern world.

"You're older than I am." He turned to face her again and took a step towards her. "In human circles, that would earn you the title of cougar. Cougars prey on men far younger than they are."

She planted her hands on her hips, pressing her fingers into her tight black trousers, and huffed. "I am not preying on you. If anything, you are preying on me. That makes you the cougar."

He laughed and she looked startled by it. "I can't be the cougar. I'm a guy. Going for a younger woman is the accepted norm for a guy."

Her eyebrow quirked. "Biologically it makes sense for a female to go for a younger male. They are more virile. Stronger. They would produce offspring with a higher chance of survival."

Kyter smirked and ran his gaze over her. "You're so sexy when you talk all scientific and clever... my little scholar."

That earned him another glare and she waved him away.

"You make no sense. Toy-boys. Cougars. I have no interest in your silly way of talking." She turned away and walked a few steps across the temple base before stopping and looking back over her shoulder at him. "I am older than you are?"

He nodded.

"By how much?" She didn't exactly look as if she wanted to know the answer to that question. She looked as if it terrified her. Afraid of being a cougar? Hell, he wasn't exactly thrilled that he was a toy-boy.

He looked up at the stars, drawing out her pain and enjoying teasing her, and raised his eyebrows as he said, "Oh, just the three thousand years."

He dropped his gaze to her in time to catch her eyes widening and the look of horror that crossed her pretty face before she recovered and raked a gaze over him.

"You are only a few centuries old? You are a mere boy."

That stung and he growled at her, stalking towards her and closing the distance between them. She hurried backwards, her eyes going as round as the full moon suspended above her and her hands rising at her sides.

"Cat shifters age differently to elves. I'm a grown man and I have been for the last three centuries." He advanced on her with long-legged strides, backing her towards the end of the temple that was enclosed by walls around his height, perfect for what he had in mind. He needed somewhere private. He dropped his voice to a low husky murmur. "You know I'm not a boy... but if you want... I can prove that I'm more man than you can handle. I can show you just how virile I am."

A fierce blush darkened her cheeks and she blinked rapidly, her heartbeat off the scale in his sensitive ears and her scent of exotic flowers becoming mingled with the heady honeyed smell of her desire.

Enchanting.

Gods, he wanted her when she reacted so sweetly to him, giving away her feelings. She wanted him too. He prowled towards her.

"You are being silly again," she muttered and bolted, moving so swiftly he couldn't track her with his eyes.

He could with his nose though.

He turned to face her where she had stopped near his backpack, her face still flushed and her eyes still dark with her desire.

It thrilled him.

The sight of her so flustered and the rich scent of arousal rolling off her made him want to keep up his pursuit, to drive his prey to surrender to him.

She wanted to know how much of a man he was, even if she refused to admit it.

She stared across the temple at him, the darkness in her eyes luring him in and tempting him into taking a step towards her. He wanted to hunt her. He wanted to stalk towards her and see the desire rising in her eyes, coming to match the ferocity of his need for her. She would run again, but it would only crank his hunger for her up another notch, making the hunt even more intoxicating and the moment when he finally captured her even sweeter.

He wanted to kiss her again.

Kyter dialled back that need, drawing down a deep breath to bring it back under control. She had to come to him. As much as he wanted to stalk and hunt her, he had to bide his time. He was happy with that. His kind were ambush predators. He would wait until his little kitty was within his reach, ready to surrender to him, and then he would make his move.

He backed off a step, towards the enclosed area. "Maybe we should check out this cellar thing you mentioned."

Her rosy lips curved in a small smile. "It is called a *cella*. It is an inner temple. A place where only priests could enter."

"Cella then. Let's check it out anyway because it's the only damned way I'm going to be able to keep my hands off you." He turned his back, catching her startled gasp and smiling to himself as he strode into the inner temple, feeling her gaze drifting down over his body.

She could pretend all she wanted, but she was throwing off pheromones that were driving him crazy, broadcasting her desire for him and her need, and she seemed to have difficulty keeping her eyes off him whenever she thought he wasn't looking.

Of course, the fact he had made sure to pull his tank top off before showing up at the temple tonight probably wasn't helping her self-control.

He liked the feel of her eyes on him though. He loved the slow, unhurried way she would let them drift over him, taking in every inch at her leisure. She could look all she wanted, and touch all she wanted too. He was her male after all. He had been made for her.

She followed him into the enclosed area and began searching at the far end, where the remains of an altar stood. He kept his distance, his focus split between checking out the area around the columns that lined the longer wall at the side of the temple in front of him and checking out her.

She had told him that she had seven days left before she had to deliver the item to her client. She had evaded answering his questions about that client. They were both still quite guarded, unwilling to reveal some things to the other. Thankfully, she had made things easier on him, as she hadn't asked about the demon he sought. She had taken what he had told her as it stood, without probing for more details.

He didn't want her to know that he was the offspring of the demon.

He wasn't sure how she would look at him then.

He had reached the final column and had started on the other side when he realised that she was humming to herself while she worked. He glanced back at her and smiled as he watched her running her hands over the remains of the altar, her gaze fixed on them. She didn't realise she was humming. His smile widened and he went back to checking the area around the columns, losing himself in his work again.

The sudden feeling of being watched made him lift his head and look across at Iolanthe.

She stood only a metre from him, staring at him with a curious edge to her eyes.

"What are you singing?" She canted her head, the curiosity in her eyes only growing.

Singing? He realised he had been singing to himself while he had worked, and smiled as he recalled the song he had been halfway through before he had noticed she had come to stare at him.

He straightened and turned his smile on her. "Bon Jovi."

She crossed her arms over her chest, squashing her breasts together in her black camisole, and he had to fight to stop himself from dropping his eyes to them. A frown marred her brow.

"I am not familiar with this type of music." Her curious gaze turned questioning as it searched his and he felt as if she was seeking an answer from his heart. "It sounded like a serenade."

Kyter shrugged his bare shoulders. "Bon Jovi is a band, not a type of music… but I guess it was a sort of serenade. People tend to call them ballads."

Apparently, he had subconsciously chosen one that turned out to be quite apt for them.

Born to be my baby.

She had been.

The pretty hint of colour on her cheeks and the slight awkward edge to her expression and body language said she had taken it as a sort of serenade, a song about them, sung from his heart to reach hers, and she had liked it.

"Why were you singing it?" She looked around them at the dark moonlit temple. "Do you desire to attract the attention of the security guards?"

Kyter frowned at her. "No… and you were singing first."

Her eyebrows shot up and then she returned his frown. "I was not."

"Was too." He smiled when she huffed. "You were humming. Do you often hum when you're working?"

Her frown lifted and she turned thoughtful, and he realised that he felt at ease around her now, and she felt the same way. They were growing closer, becoming comfortable with each other, and were slowly lowering their guards. He liked it, and liked how he was learning new things about her.

"I am not sure." She tipped her head up and looked him in the eye. "Do you often sing when you are working?"

Kyter blew out his breath, scrubbed a hand through the messy longer lengths of his sandy hair, and shook his head. "It would be difficult since I often can't hear myself think over the music, let alone sing a different tune to the one that's playing."

Her expression shifted, becoming laced with curiosity again, and she moved a step closer. He sat on one of the broken columns and she joined him, balancing on the one next to him. It felt nice. He hadn't expected them to make so much progress so quickly. She had accepted his apology and his help, and they were already growing closer.

"I work at a bar," he said and then figured he might as well be honest, because she might approve of a male who ran his own business, just as she ran her own business. Another thing they had in common. "I own a nightclub."

She didn't look impressed. "And you play this Bon Jovi there?"

"Not anymore." He shook his head, answering her and trying to shake off the way he had deflated inside, his pride taking a knock.

"Why not?" She leaned towards him, resting her elbows on her knees, her violet eyes beginning to shimmer with curiosity again.

He leaned backwards, clasped his hands behind his head and twisted at the same time, shifting his body side on to her so he could rest his shoulders against the wall behind him. She frowned at him and he had the feeling it wasn't because of his pose. It was because he had moved away from her. She had picked up on his subtle change in mood.

For the first time since opening the doors of Underworld, he didn't feel like talking about his business.

"Kyter?" The sound of his name falling from her lips jerked the whole of his focus to her and his golden gaze slid her way, probably relaying his shock to her.

She had never used his name before.

That she did so now made him feel she was letting him know that she was interested in learning about his business and she was sorry she had made him feel otherwise.

He sighed and tipped his head back, staring at the stars, wondering how things were going back in London. Cavanaugh would have texted him if there had been a problem. Kyter had fired off a message to him this afternoon, letting the big shifter know that he had moved location and was closer to finding the item he needed. He hadn't mentioned Iolanthe. Something told him that the snow leopard wouldn't appreciate talk of mates.

Kyter had been like that once.

He looked back down at the female beside him, a beauty who patiently waited, her violet eyes never leaving his face.

"Nightclubs have to move with the times and evolve. They have to play up to date music to draw in the patrons."

"But you prefer the music you were singing?" she said, genuine interest in her eyes. She wanted to know about him.

He lifted his shoulders in an easy shrug. "I like it. A few of the other shifters who work for me like it too."

Her eyebrows slowly rose. "You employ other fae?"

He nodded. "Yeah. Underworld caters to humans, fae and demons, but mainly to our kind. My staff are mostly made up of fae who needed a place… they heard about the club and came to me, and I gave them sanctuary in exchange for a little hard work."

Her violet eyes brightened, finally gaining the impressed edge he had wanted to see in them earlier. She admired him for giving people like him a place they could call home, taking them in and taking care of them.

"I have the song on my phone." He lowered his right hand when she looked confused, dug around in his thigh pocket and pulled it out, flashing the phone at her.

She leaned closer, eyeing it. Hadn't she seen a phone before? He woke up the screen and she darted back, away from it, and then slowly inched forwards again, her face filled with a beautiful look of astonishment.

Kyter smiled, repeating his earlier thought about her. She knew a lot about history, but knew little about the modern world. Elves lived in a realm in Hell. Maybe she didn't come to the mortal realm very often. That and the fact they had both been after the same artefact at the same time left him feeling that fate really had pulled cosmic strings to bring them together. He only wished it hadn't involved the death of his only family. He wasn't sure what his mother would have made of Iolanthe and her independent nature, but he liked to think she would have approved of his fated female.

He found the track he had been singing and played it for her.

Her eyes lit up and she leaned even closer, her face illuminated by the screen. "Fascinating. The male sings better than you do though."

Kyter snatched his phone back, shut it off and shoved it back in his pocket.

She shrank back and flexed her hands against her knees. "I did not mean to offend you. You sing well."

"I do?" He cursed it for coming out as a question. Others had told him that he had a good voice, but he hadn't expected the compliment from Iolanthe. It had caught him off guard.

She looked down at her thighs. "I think you do."

"You hum well," he offered and she flicked a glance at him. He smiled at her.

A blush climbed her cheeks, she muttered something in her strange tongue, and hurried away from him. His little enigma. Had no one ever complimented her?

He grinned at her back and hollered, "You're beautiful too."

She threw a startled look over her shoulder at him. Deer caught in headlights came to mind. He chuckled.

"No one ever tell you how beautiful you are, Iolanthe?" He pushed onto his feet and she swallowed, blinked, but didn't answer his question.

He closed in on her, breaking all his rules, and she didn't run away. She shifted to face him and stood her ground. His smile widened over how defensive she looked, as if she might call her blade to her hand and threaten him to make him shut up. Not this time. A blade to the throat wouldn't stop him. She could carry out her impotent threats to kill him and he would still get the words he had lined up on his tongue out before he drew his last breath.

He slid his right hand along the line of her jaw, feeling the heat of her blush on his palm, and tilted her head up, towards the moon, so he could see her.

"You're more than beautiful... I thought that the first time I saw you... beautiful doesn't do you justice."

"Kyter," she whispered and tried to look away, but he didn't let her. Sure, he was making her uncomfortable. Sure, she wanted to escape him. Sure, he was being a dick again and treading close to overstepping the mark.

But he wanted her to know how he felt about her and know that it had begun long before he had realised she was his mate.

"You bewitched me in that fae town, Iolanthe. You enslaved me and all I could do was follow you, powerless to resist your pull." He swept his thumb across her cheek and she closed her eyes. "No... look at me."

She did as he asked, her long lashes lifting to reveal those stunning violet eyes.

"You're otherworldly... and the more I get to know you, the more beautiful you become."

"I said I did not wish to hear your silly talk," she whispered with little conviction and pulled away. He didn't let her get far. He caught her cheek again and lured her back to him, smiling down into her eyes.

"It isn't silly talk. I'm being serious. I know you think I'm a dick and I acted like one, but you opened my eyes, and that wasn't me... I'm not like that. I don't want to hold you back or take this life away from you." When she tried to break away again, he did as he had vowed he would. He spoke from his heart and laid it all on the line. "I saw my mother treated that way."

She stopped, her gaze coming back to hold his.

He swallowed his fear and pushed onwards. "I saw her pinned by society's conventions and subjected to what others thought she deserved. I would never inflict that sort of life on a female... especially one I care about."

His heart thudded at a sickening pace against his chest. He had faced a hundred male jaguars in battle, had taken on demons and fae more powerful than himself, and he had never experienced the level of fear he was now. The beautiful female before him stripped him of his strength and had him on his knees without lifting a finger. She could crush him without saying a word.

She did break away from him now, her hand coming up to touch the spot on her cheek where his had been, her eyes wild and heart thundering. She stared at him, her colliding emotions colouring her scent, revealing them to him. She was afraid too and confused, and angry. She thought he was playing her again, out to trick her into being his mate by saying what she wanted to hear.

He sighed and backed off a step.

"I wish you could believe me," he said with a small smile, struggling to pull himself together and keep his deepest fear from her—fear that he would lose her because of the things he had done. His one mate. The female born for him. One that he felt sure he had started falling for before realising she was his mate. "I fucked up. I got caught up in everything and turned into something I'm not. I'm not one of the males who lead my pride… hell, I'm not even one of the pride anymore. When I realised how I was treating you… I was horrified. You deserve better than that. I would never expect you to behave according to pride rules."

She still stared at him, her hand still pressing against her cheek.

"You don't have to believe me." He turned his back on her and trudged over to the column where they had sat, returning to his work.

"I do," she whispered.

He didn't look over his shoulder at her as he wanted to, because he knew it had taken a lot of effort for her to allow those two words to slip quietly from her lips. It had taken a lot for her to confess that she believed him after everything he had done.

He took those two words and held them to his heart, using them as a balm to soothe the ache that had started there when he had thought she would reject everything he said and accuse him of lying to her in order to lure her into being his mate.

They worked in silence until the morning came, the sunrise painting the sky in hues of gold and pink. He stretched and pressed his hands into his aching back. Iolanthe stretched too, the action cat-like and alluring as she held her arms above her head, arched forwards, and then wavered side to side.

"We should stick together," he said and she stopped with her hands held high in the air. "I have digs near here. It's just a small rented place in the countryside."

He waited for her to teleport out of his life again without a word.

She smiled, a gentle one that he came to realise was teasing when she spoke. "You must like all the trees and nature, being a cat shifter."

Two could play at her game. "You must like it too, being an elf."

She fell silent and serious. Damn, he needed to figure her out, because whenever he thought he would put a foot right, it went wrong.

"I met your prince once." The second those words left his lips, her eyes grew enormous and she took a step closer. Feeling he was putting feet right for once, he added, "I served him booze and the guy took it hard."

Her expression shifted to one of horror. "You gave my prince alcohol? Are you insane? How dare you defile my prince with such poison?"

He held his hands up at his sides and backed off as she advanced. "The other elf with him didn't see it as poison and he seemed quite good at handling it."

She snapped her mouth shut and then grumbled, "He is probably already tainted by experience with it. No doubt alcohol has little effect on him."

"Hey," Kyter snapped and shot her a deadly glare. "That's my friend you're talking about. No one badmouths my friends."

Her violet eyes shot impossibly wide.

"My apologies." She rushed over to him and grabbed his arm before he could respond, her grip fierce. "We should go, now, before we are spotted."

Kyter frowned at her odd behaviour. Why was she suddenly in a hurry and suddenly so compliant? Was it something he had said or had she sensed someone nearby? Maybe it was another demon sent by her client.

"You're coming with me?" He had to be sure he had understood her intentions, because he was finding it hard to believe that she was coming to his place, without putting up a fight, and he didn't want her to turn on him when he grabbed her arm and started towards the nearby station with her to wait for the first train or pick up a taxi.

She hesitated but then she nodded and did something he hadn't anticipated.

She wrapped her arms around his neck.

"Just tell me the nearest town or landmark you remember and I will teleport us there if I know it."

Suddenly, Kyter was having trouble thinking.

It probably had something to do with the fact that all of his blood had rushed south the moment she had pressed her lithe body against his.

"Well?" she whispered, her mouth tantalisingly close to his, her soft breath fanning across his lips.

Kyter groaned inside, immediately regretting his suggestion that she come back to his place.

His place.

He was going to be alone, in private, all day, with her.

He had the terrible feeling the challenge he had set himself to wait for her to give him the green light was about to become impossible or it was going to kill him.

Gods help him.

CHAPTER 14

Iolanthe stood with her back to the jet of warm water in Kyter's shower, not feeling the spray or aware of her surroundings. She had hurried into the small bathroom in the isolated villa at the base of Mount Vesuvius shortly after they had arrived and it had struck her that she was alone with Kyter.

She had been alone with him all night, but the idea of being alone with him now, in the privacy and safety of his rented single storey house, had her battling a violent bout of nerves that felt uncharacteristic of her. She felt like a different person, no longer strong and confident. He had stripped those two things from her, had steadily worked his magic on her since they had first met, bringing her to this point where she felt vulnerable to him.

Unable to resist the magnetic pull she felt towards him.

She closed her eyes and focused on her breathing, trying to shut out everything that had happened tonight. It didn't help. She moved her focus to the world outside the small villa. Lush nature enclosed the cream stone building, thick vegetation that had called to her when she had been outside with Kyter. The trees were tall, the ground around them dense with scrub. There was a wilderness to this place and a sense of danger in the air, emanating from the looming threat of the active volcano.

The nature around her soothed her but didn't chase away her thoughts of Kyter.

She had detected no lie in the things he had told her tonight. He had spoken to her with his heart in his eyes, all of his emotions on show for her, nothing hidden from her this time. No ulterior motives. No plans to take anything from her. No desire to enslave her with a mate bond.

It had left her feeling that he wouldn't betray her.

His honesty had touched her because she had sensed a sliver of his fear as it had laced his earthy scent. It had taken a lot of strength and courage for him to tell her everything he had, confessing that he found her looks appealing, and that he desired her. It hadn't been a game. Not a ploy. It had come from his heart, and it had spoken to hers.

She pressed a hand between her bare breasts and lowered her head, allowing the water to spray off the back of her head and run through her hair.

He had made it clear that he was attracted to her and had been from before he had even realised there was a bond between them.

She had felt the same way and still did.

She had learned much about him tonight. The time they had spent together in harmony, working with each other and not against each other, made her feel closer to him. He was handsome, had a sense of humour and honour, and was charming in his own way when he wasn't following his instincts.

101

When an elf male found his mate, it affected him deeply, controlling his behaviour and turning him possessive, protective and dangerous. It appeared cat shifters suffered a similar transformation. She wanted to believe Kyter and believe that he had been a victim of the bombardment of emotions triggered by discovering his mate and had lost his head as a result. She wanted to believe that the male she had been with tonight was the real Kyter, back in control of himself, because she had liked that male.

She turned to face the spray of water, tipping her head up towards it and letting it beat over her face. It felt good to shower after exploring the dusty temple.

Kyter moved around in the next room, stealing her focus.

When she had run into the bathroom and locked the door, he had politely knocked and asked whether she was alright. She had read between the lines to what he had wanted to ask, sensing his uneasiness. He had wanted to ask whether she was going to teleport and leave him.

He wanted her to stay with him.

She wanted it too, but she feared it at the same time. She wasn't sure whether she was strong enough to resist him if she stayed with him, but she couldn't bring herself to leave either. Not only because she knew it would hurt him if she disappeared. It would hurt her too in a way. She had the terrible feeling she might miss the irritating jaguar shifter.

She also had the feeling that he would be angry with her and would go out to the temple without her. If he found the artefact during that time, their deal would be void. He might take it out of spite to make her pay for leaving him. She would pay and it would be the ultimate price. She would lose her head.

Iolanthe told herself that the artefact was the only reason she had chosen to stay. It had nothing to do with wanting to be around Kyter.

He moved closer to her and she paused, breathing quietly but unsure why she felt the ridiculous need to attempt to conceal herself. He knew she was in the shower. Her cheeks burned. Was that why he was prowling around the next room?

He could hear the change in how the water fell as she cleaned herself and moved beneath the jet of the shower. He had to know that she was naked in the cramped bathroom, wet all over.

The image of Kyter in her place burst into her mind, a delicious vision of him arching his head back beneath the spray, the warm water bouncing off his shoulders and chest as he ran his hands through his hair. It ran down his chest, trickling over honed muscles that she itched to stroke and caress, to explore at her leisure.

Her belly heated, her hunger swift to rise after spending the night with him at the temple, seeing him half-dressed, his powerful body on display. His confession about how he was having trouble keeping his hands off her didn't help matters, and neither did the things he had said to her, calling her beautiful with an earnest look in his golden eyes.

She muttered a curse directed at him and tried to ignore the ache between her thighs.

He moved away but then stalked closer again, commanding her focus, refusing to let her go. He had done the same thing all night, whether he had realised it or not. He had driven her mad, constantly pulling her focus away from her work and dragging her eyes back to him.

The moon had hid nothing from view as he had worked, his magnificent body shifting with sensual grace. The way he had looked at her at times, his wide dark pupils speaking of hunger and need, passion she had felt in him, had kept firing her up. Did he know what he was doing to her, wreaking havoc on her control?

She was too hot around him.

Whenever she looked at him, she caught a tangled replay of the savage and graceful way he had fought the demon, how handsome he was when he was relaxed around her, and how wicked he had been in her dream. Every replay had ended the same—on the heated kiss they had shared in Herculaneum.

She knew he wanted to kiss her again. It was there in his eyes whenever he looked at her, and in the way he forced himself to pace away when it became too much for him and he was verging on going through with it. She had almost screamed at him tonight, had nearly crumbled and asked him to surrender to that need and kiss her. She needed it too.

Gods help her but she needed it.

She built an image of it in her mind, reconstructing the moment he had held her pressed against the column, his hard body pinning her there and his hands clutching her backside. He had kissed her as if he hadn't been able to get enough of her, igniting the same fierce hunger within her. She had been a slave to her desire too, lost in her need and desperate for more of him.

The water from the shower ran over her breasts and she bit back a moan as it touched their sensitive peaks. She breathed harder, trying to ignore the temptation to imagine Kyter with her, slowly caressing her body, satisfying the need building within her. Her senses tracked him and focusing on him only made it harder to resist. She had raised her hands to her breasts before she had realised what she was doing, cupping the mounds and thumbing her pert nipples.

Heat pooled lower and she tilted her head back and bit her tongue to stop a moan from escaping her as she rolled her nipples, sending tingles sweeping outwards from them, cascading over her breasts. The feel of the water skimming down her stomach to her most private place was too much for her. She writhed, rubbing her thighs together, imagining Kyter on his knees before her.

He would slowly part her thighs and would look up at her as he had in her dream, a hungry edge to his gaze as he sought permission. She moaned and lost herself in her fantasy, dropping her hand and slipping her fingers into her folds. He would part those folds and hold her gaze as he lowered his mouth to her and his tongue darted out to taste her. Her fingers circled where his tongue would, stroking the nub as it eagerly ached for more.

The water would sluice off his beautiful tensed back as he knelt before her, one strong hand grasping her thigh and bringing it over his shoulder so he could delve deeper, devouring all of her as he brought her to a shattering climax.

She dropped her fingers lower, a quiet moan escaping her as she probed her moist sheath.

A growl rumbled through the door.

Iolanthe gasped and whirled to face it, her heart lodged in her throat and a blush blazing across her cheeks. He knew what she was doing.

"Either you finish now, or you damn well let me in."

Those words, snarled in a deep voice husky with desire, had her knees weakening beneath her.

His ultimatum hung in the air as she stared at the wooden door, her pulse racing and her desire flaring hotter, rising higher as she considered which path to choose.

Finish now?

Or let him finish for her?

CHAPTER 15

Kyter stood in the pale yellow bedroom outside the wooden door to the bathroom, his hands braced against the frame. He dug his emerging claws into the wood to keep himself rooted to the spot, carving deep grooves into it. His breath sawed from his lungs, each heavy inhalation dragging more of her scent into him.

Desire.

Arousal.

He could smell it on her and he needed to break down the damn door and put himself out of his misery by seeing her. Naked. Wet. Touching herself. He knew what she was doing. He could hear her breath hitching.

Every little gasp tore at him.

Her breathless moan did him in.

He needed her too, dammit. He had been hungering after a taste of her all night, the memory of their kiss burned on his brain. She couldn't expect him to bear what she was doing without feeling a deep need to join her, to satisfy his female and take care of her needs. It was too much. He couldn't take it.

"Either you finish now, or you damn well let me in."

Those words left his lips on a snarl and he shoved his hands harder against the doorframe, his heart beating frantically against his ribs and his cock aching in the confines of his black combat trousers. He wanted to palm it, to touch himself while she did the same to herself on the other side of the door, in his shower, but more than that, he wanted her to touch him.

He wanted to touch her.

They were attracted to each other. They were both adults. They could do something about their needs together, not separately, shut away from each other. He could make her feel good. She could make him feel as if he had gone to Heaven.

He stared at the panelled door, his breathing coming quicker. She had to let him in. She wasn't going to let him in. She was going to torture him by making him stand here and feel her desire, her need, while unable to do anything about it and satisfy his need to take care of her.

He wanted to be the one to bring her to climax.

He needed to be the one.

He had messed up, but he had apologised, and he had shown her that he wasn't going to force a bond on her. They could be together without ending up fighting each other.

They could do things together now.

He could give her the pleasure she needed and the release.

He hung his head and his hands tensed against the doorframe.

She wasn't going to let him in.

His heart jerked in his chest when the latch on the door slid across and he stared down at the round knob, his mouth going dry. He had to be imagining things. Maybe he had passed out from need and he was dreaming.

Maybe she was going to open the door and tell him she was all done and didn't need him.

He began to growl but the doorknob turning silenced him.

The door swung open and Kyter snapped his head up, his heart accelerating again when he saw her standing before him, wearing nothing but a long white towel wrapped around her slender frame, her long black hair hanging in tangled damp ribbons around her face and down her chest.

He stared at her.

She advanced on him, a spark of something in her violet eyes as she coolly held his gaze.

"If you were a wolf shifter, I might have expected you to huff, puff and blow the door down." She stopped before him and trailed a finger over his cheek, across the two days' worth of stubble on his jaw, and down his neck.

She didn't take her eyes away from his as she swept her fingers across his shoulder and back again.

"You look hot," she flicked his collarbone, "under the collar. Why?"

Kyter unleashed a feral growl, grabbed her around her waist and kissed her hard. She pressed her hand to his chest but didn't push him away. She melted into him and if he had been a wolf shifter, he would have howled out his joy. As it was, he growled it into her mouth and turned with her, pinning her spine to the doorframe and deepening the kiss as she fought him for dominance, rousing his need to be in control and master her.

She moaned against his lips between kisses and shoved her fingers through his hair, tangling them in it and holding him to her. He grasped her hips, the damp towel stoking his need for her as it struck him that she was naked beneath it.

He lifted his left hand to her breast, tugged the towel into his fist and yanked it off her. He swallowed her startled gasp, pressed his right hand into her lower back and pulled her against him. The heat of her bare body scalded his and he moaned, torn between keeping her pinned against him and pushing her back so he could get a look at her.

He held her closer and broke away from her lips, kissing along her jaw.

She stiffened and her hands shot to his shoulders. They trembled against him.

He stilled, breathing hard against her neck, fighting the urge to do exactly what she feared he was going to do. His fangs lengthened, the need to bite her growing stronger by the second, almost overwhelming him. He mastered it, refusing to be that male. He had said he wouldn't treat her as other jaguars would and he had meant it.

He pressed a kiss to her throat and she clutched his shoulders.

"I won't," he murmured against her soft pale skin, feeling her heat and her rapid pulse on his lips. "I swear it. I won't bite you."

She didn't relax.

She didn't hit him with a telekinetic blast either, and he took that as a good sign.

Every primal instinct he possessed wanted him to own her, to master her and dominate her.

The tiny piece of brain still operating warned it wouldn't be a smooth move. His female needed. His objective should have been satisfying that need.

Giving her what she wanted.

He had waited for her to come to him and she had. Now he had to go against all of his instincts and let her take the lead. He needed to let her master him.

It was the only way of satisfying her needs.

He turned with her, so his back was against the doorframe.

"What are you doing?" she whispered, a touch of confusion in her soft voice.

He let her pull back and looked her in the eye. "Going against every instinct I have as a male in my prime. Giving you control."

Her violet eyes darkened, the hunger and need in them, and the desire he could smell on her combining to leave him feeling that he had made the right decision and he wouldn't regret it.

She tiptoed, pressed herself back against him, and kissed him, her lips clashing fiercely with his.

"What if... neither of us... have control?" she murmured breathlessly between kisses. "What if... we just agree... not to bite?"

Gods, he could go along with that.

He shoved his fingers into her wet black hair and kissed her hard, tangling his tongue with hers, driven to devour all of her. His mate was perfect.

He groaned when she ran her palms down his body, her hands racing towards the finish line. She made swift work of unbuttoning his trousers and he stilled and groaned as she slid her palm down the length of him.

She whispered something in her strange tongue. He hoped it was complimentary.

He began to open his eyes to look at her as she moved back, breaking free of his hold, and then screwed them shut again and shoved the back of his head hard into the doorframe as she kneeled on the terracotta tiled floor and swept her tongue over the crown of his cock.

Hell.

He swallowed hard and raised both hands above his head, grasping the frame to stop himself from grabbing hold of her head and keeping her mouth pinned to his length. She was wicked as she caressed him with her tongue, sliding it from base to tip, leaving no part of him untouched.

"Iolanthe," he moaned and she groaned in response and wrapped her lips around the crown, taking him into the wet heat of her mouth. "Gods."

His hips pressed forwards, his body arching away from the doorframe. He dug his claws into it to stop himself from collapsing to his knees. Her tongue stroked around the head, catching every sensitive spot, leaving him quivering and on the verge of ripping the damned doorframe out of the wall. He groaned and breathed harder, his blood thundering as she kissed down his length. She pushed his trousers down his thighs and ran her hands back up them, and he trembled in response, his breathing harsh in the quiet room.

Her torture only grew more divine, threatening to push him over the edge.

She dropped her mouth and licked his sac at the same time as she cupped it in one hand and stroked beneath it. He jerked forwards and grunted, thrusting at air. He couldn't take it. She didn't seem to care. She kept stroking her tongue over him, slowly edging back towards the base of his aching length, her fingers working magic on him. Fuck. He dimly recalled calling her a prude the night they had met.

He couldn't have been more wrong about her.

He grunted as she kissed up the underside of his cock and wrapped her lips around the head again, sucking him into her moist mouth. She took him into her, until the crown touched the back of her throat and he was on the verge of screaming her name, and then rolled back, pressing her tongue in hard to the vein on the underside.

Kyter lost it.

He tipped his head back and roared, his blood burning at a thousand degrees, triggering all of his male instincts. He needed to be inside her now. He needed to pin her to the bed and take her, making her feel every inch of him, until she cried his name and came on him. He needed to possess her.

He barely leashed that need.

He grabbed the back of her neck, dragged her up to him and kissed her hard, pinning his aching length between them, pressing it into the softness of her belly. She didn't give him the moment he needed to cool down. She rubbed her stomach against him and tiptoed, bringing him closer to the apex of her thighs and where he wanted to be.

"Kyter," she murmured, his name a sound of supplication.

She lifted her left leg, wrapped it around his hip, and drew him against her.

Her warm wetness pressed against his balls.

He lost it again.

He grabbed her under her thigh, lifted her and stumbled across the small span of the doorframe, his combats around his ankles hindering him. She moaned as her back slammed into the doorframe on the other side and raised her other leg, wrapping it around his waist. She shoved her left hand between them, colliding with his, and laughed at the same time as he did. It seemed they had both lost it, both becoming slaves to their desire.

He snatched her hand and wrapped it around his steel length, and held it with her as he guided it towards her. She moaned sweetly as he nudged into her slick heat and groaned with him as he pulled their hands away and eased into her, somehow finding the strength to do it slowly and savour their first coupling. She was tight and hot, so wet that he wanted to growl.

She needed him. He would satisfy that need.

Kyter lowered his hands to her backside as she grabbed hold of his shoulders and grunted as he angled her hips so he could go deeper, feeling all of her and making her feel all of him. He wanted to leave no part of her untouched. He wanted her to know that she was his now and he was hers. Mating was just a formality that could wait. They belonged to each other already.

She held on to him and brought her lips down hard on his, stealing his breath in a passionate kiss as he withdrew almost all the way out of her before sliding back in. He couldn't do slow and steady. Not this time. His animal instincts rode him, his need to claim her driving him to take her harder, faster, satisfying both of them. He tried to hold back, thrusting deep with long strokes, fighting for control.

Iolanthe shattered it.

She rocked on him, her feet locked behind his bare backside, and drove him into her, deeper and harder, faster. She wanted it frantic, just as he did. She wanted it wild and untamed, feral and primal.

He growled into her mouth, grabbed her hard and pinned her against the doorframe as he took her, pumping fast and deep, his entire body flexing as he surrendered to his shifter nature and his need to physically claim her body.

She moaned and clawed at him, her fangs nipping at his lips, awakening a deeper need inside him, a desire to have those fangs in his throat. He groaned and clutched her backside, thrusting deeper, until she moaned with each meeting of their bodies. One hand left his shoulders and she held on to the doorframe behind her, her head tipped back and mouth open on a cry as she rode each plunge of his cock into her.

Kyter buried his face in her throat, kissing and licking it, obeying his instincts to lave at her neck as they mated. His balls drew up, tight and heavy, his release rising. He growled and pinned her harder, his heart beating so fast he felt sure it would burst as he pounded her and she took every deep stroke of his length, her blissful cries music to his ears.

He couldn't remember ever being able to be like this with someone. None of them had been strong enough to take him like this, wild and untamed, more beast than man. None of them had awakened this side of him, this primal need to lay claim and possess them.

"Kyter," she whispered, hoarse and beautiful. She dug her nails into his back and said the one thing he hadn't thought he would hear leaving her lips, "More."

More?

She could take more than this?

She wanted more than this?

He snarled and pressed the clawed tips of his fingers into her hips as he drove deeper, harder, faster, obeying her command. She flexed against him and her cry filled his ears, her body quivering around his, drawing him deeper still, scalding him with her climax.

He roared and joined her, thrusting deep as he pushed her down on him and shot hot jets of seed into her, his cock throbbing and entire body shaking as heat spread through him, stealing his strength and leaving him weakened.

He held her on him as she fluttered around him, drawing out his climax and hers, her soft breathy moans teasing his ears as she slowly sagged against him, settling her head on his shoulder.

His knees gave out.

He hit the tiled floor hard, not feeling the pain that ricocheted from his knees up his thighs.

Iolanthe giggled against his neck, the thundering rush of her heart against his chest matching his, and stroked his shoulders. Her wet hair caressed his chest. He breathed hard, struggling to bring himself down, shaking against her. She was shaking too.

Kyter gathered her into his arms, holding her against him, basking in the warmth of her and what they had shared.

She murmured, "I think I need another shower."

Kyter groaned when she pressed a kiss to his shoulder and whispered to him, a seductive quality to her voice that had his hunger rising again and the primal side of him stirring once more.

"I think you need one too."

CHAPTER 16

Iolanthe lay in Kyter's arms in the large bed, her cheek pressed to his bare chest, listening to his soft steady breathing as she stared out of the window across the pale yellow room. He had risen to open it at some point while she had been sleeping and now a cool breeze swept through it, carrying the scent of evening and the noise of insects. Trees swayed and rustled, and nature swirled around her, comforting her together with the feel of his strong arms banded around her.

She couldn't remember the last time she had slept so soundly, even in her bolthole where she was safe and extremely secure thanks to various enchantments and blockers that prevented anyone except her from teleporting into her home.

Something about the feel of Kyter against her, his hard powerful body gently cushioning hers, and the steady beat of his strong heart against her ear had made it easy for her to let down her guard and fall into a deep sleep.

He stroked her left arm, calloused fingers caressing her skin, and she felt his gaze following them, burning her with its intensity.

He had kept his promise today, never once attempting to bite her, and she was grateful for it. She finally believed that the male holding her tucked against his left side was the real Kyter, and the one who had frightened her and had wanted to own her had been nothing but a phantom, a product of the emotions evoked by discovering she was his fated one.

She was glad that she was female and experienced only a sliver of the possessiveness and protectiveness that ruled him.

She still felt those emotions though. She had surrendered to them this morning when making love with Kyter, giving all of herself over to the moment, letting her passion and possessiveness consume her. She had wanted to claim him. She had wanted to ruin him to all other females, so he would never look at another.

He would only ever desire her.

"What are you thinking?" he whispered and ran his fingers back up her arm to her shoulder, brought them to her cheek, and slid them along her jaw. He tipped her head up, angling his body away from hers so he could look at her.

"I do not know... what am I thinking?" She couldn't resist teasing him, because his eyes said that he knew what she was thinking and he just wanted to hear her say it. They were dark again, the gold in them bright against the wide aroused abyss of his pupils.

Hunting her again?

Perhaps he couldn't help himself.

Felicity Heaton

She had quickly learned that the more she evaded him, the more his eyes gained the same look they held now. If she walked away, he felt a powerful need to pursue her. It fascinated her and she wanted to know more about him. She had learned about shifters, and had met many of them from different species, but she had never really cared enough to truly want to know them and how their behaviour and abilities differed from hers.

"You feel as if you're thinking naughty things." He feathered a caress down her throat and around the nape of it, and pressed his fingers there.

Another behaviour that felt cat-like to her. He wanted to control her by holding her neck. If they ever mated, would he need to bite her there?

"I was thinking about shifters," she said and his expression darkened, his sensual lips losing their playful smile as they flattened into a hard line.

"Better not be thinking about males."

"Only one male." She walked her fingers across the delicious expanse of his bare chest. "I am curious about you."

He caught her left wrist and rubbed his thumb over the black and silver band around it. "I'm curious about these."

Evading her? Why? Didn't he want her to know about him and his kind?

"They are my armour." She tried to take her arm back but he tightened his grip, locking his fingers around her.

"Do all elves have it?"

Iolanthe looked away from him, unable to keep her eyes on his as she answered. "No."

His grip on her loosened and he stroked his thumb across the inside of her wrist, sending shivers dancing up her arm. "I get the feeling you weren't given yours."

She shook her head, ashamed to admit that and not wanting to think about how she had come to have the armour that had saved her life countless times.

"Only elves who serve in the army or hold a rank have this armour." Her voice lost its strength and she closed her eyes, afraid that she would find him looking at her differently if she dared to glance at him.

"I'm guessing you neither served nor held rank... and you don't like how you got this armour... but it was necessary." He drew her hand to his lips and pressed a kiss to the inside of her wrist, and then sighed, his breath moist against her skin. "Did you kill someone for it?"

"No." Her eyes shot open, leaping to his, and then dropped to his chest as she said, "Yes... in a manner of speaking."

She closed her eyes again when he released her wrist and his palm cupped her cheek, his tender touch almost too much for her to bear. She didn't deserve it.

"How did you get it?" he whispered and she felt the depth of his desire to know the answer to that question.

He wanted to know her too.

She drew in a deep breath and exhaled it. "I seduced an elf soldier."

112

His hand tensed against her. She had known he wouldn't like the answer to his question, but she hadn't wanted to lie to him, or evade it as he had evaded hers. What had happened had been thousands of years before he had even been born, but he still experienced jealousy, even when he had no reason to feel that emotion. What she had done with that elf had been business, and far from a pleasurable experience. It haunted her.

"I stole the armour from him and every day I have to live with what I did." She slowly opened her eyes and lifted them back to meet his, pain flowing through her, as fresh as it had been back then, all those countless centuries ago. It never eased. "I have to live with my reckless and greedy actions because he came after me, he tracked me down in an attempt to retrieve his armour and restore his honour, and I saw him killed. He would have lived if I had not stolen his armour."

"He would have lived if he had let it go." Kyter stroked her cheek and she shuffled backwards, away from his comforting touch.

"It was a matter of honour. I tarnished that honour when I stole his armour. He would have been punished for it. He had wanted to restore his honour." She shook her head when he opened his mouth to speak, not wanting to hear what he had to say because she knew he would seek to comfort her. "Do not... I would rather forget what I had done, or pretend it was not my fault, but it is a black spot on my life that I must live with."

He nodded and held his left arm out to her, and she returned to his side, nestling against him, her breasts pressed against his ribs and chest.

She moved her right arm so it lay over the top of his one beneath her and settled her palm on his chest, and her chin on the back of her hand. She studied his face as he looked at her, a smile in his golden eyes even though it didn't touch his lips. He was absorbing what she had told him and she hoped he didn't think worse of her because of it.

Iolanthe lowered her gaze to his chest and frowned as she placed her fingers against the start of one set of claw marks, matching a fingertip to each slash. She gently stroked the thin silver scars that darted diagonally towards her, from the right side of his chest to the left of the first set of abdominal muscles on his stomach.

"Earlier... at the temple... you said that your pride is not your pride anymore. What did you mean by that?" She had wanted to ask him at the time, because there had been a wealth of pain and sorrow in his eyes as he had spoken those words.

He sighed and stared up at the ceiling, his profile to her and his gaze distant.

"Was it because of the demon attack and your mother?"

He shook his head and raked the fingers of his right hand through his sandy hair, causing his muscles to flex beneath his golden skin. "It was before that."

She waited for him to elaborate, not wanting to push him because he would push back if she did. He would close up and shut her out.

"Barafnir—" He cut himself off and slid her a wary look. "Don't suppose you'd give me a clue about your stance on mixed species people?"

Iolanthe frowned, unsure why he needed to know. "Barafnir is mixed species? I did not believe that was possible for a demon. All demon offspring are born pure demon or purely the other species involved if that species is genetically stronger."

Kyter closed his eyes and his jaw flexed as he ground out, "Not all offspring."

Her eyes widened and she stared at him for long seconds before she caught herself, realising that she was making him uncomfortable. It wasn't possible. The only species she knew that was powerful enough to overrule the demon genes were elves. Elf offspring born of a union with another species came out purely elf, without any trace of the other species in them.

But Kyter was implying that it was possible for the offspring of a union with a demon to come out as a blend of both species.

And he was implying something else too, something that only made her heart go out to him even more.

"Barafnir is your father," she whispered and he turned his face away from her, confirming her suspicions. She gently caught his cheek with her left hand and drew his gaze back to her. "I have seen you as a jaguar."

"I am a jaguar... but I do have my father's genes too. That problem you had figuring out what I was from scent alone... that's because of my mixed blood." He tried to look away again, a glimmer of pain darkening his striking eyes and fear lacing his scent.

He thought she would reject him because of his mixed blood?

Her eyes went wide again.

He thought it because his pride had done such a thing.

She hissed through her fangs as they dropped and Kyter turned on her and growled, baring his own fangs in a threat. She grabbed his shoulder before he could move, cursing herself for reacting without thinking.

"It was not aimed at you." She held on to him, refusing to let him go until he relaxed again, sinking back into the mattress beneath her. "It was aimed at those who hurt you... they did hurt you, did they not?"

She ran her hand over his right shoulder, to the start of the scars that littered his back, her gaze locked there.

His pain flowed into her through that touch and he trembled beneath her palm.

"That is why they are not your pride." She wanted to find the ones who had wounded him and make them pay for turning on such a beautiful, noble male, rejecting him and leaving him scarred, both inside and out.

He nodded, swallowed hard and forced a smile as he finally looked at her. "Barafnir found my mother when she was hunting one day and tricked her into believing that he was one of the cursed demon species, only able to mate with his fated one. Jaguars value their fated mates. A mate means everything to those in my pride and it fooled her into believing him. He held her captive for months… and she finally escaped him before he could discover that she was pregnant with me."

She still couldn't believe that Kyter had been born jaguar, not fully demon. His will was strong, his blood even stronger. It was the only explanation she had for the fact he had managed to subdue his demon genes. Now, he wanted to kill the male who had given him those genes, an act of vengeance she knew he needed in order to heal his heart.

"When I was born, they thought I was pure jaguar until the new moon. My mother tried to hide the change that came over me, but another female saw it. She told the elders and the elders took me from my mother and showed everyone in the pride what I was. A monster."

Iolanthe bit back her growl and stroked his cheek. "You are not a monster."

"I felt like one."

"They made you feel like one… when they should have accepted you as part of their pride. They are fools for how they treated you. It was not your fault."

Kyter sighed. "They blamed my mother too. She was disgraced by what happened to her to give rise to me. Because of that, she never mated and was always without position within the pride. They made her life hell but she was never strong enough to leave them."

"You were though. You left them."

He nodded. "Eventually. They kept us both at the fringes of the pride and my mother thought that should be enough for us. It wasn't enough for me. I did everything I could to make them accept me as part of the pride and recognise me. I shouldn't have bothered."

She ran her hand over his chest, stroking the scars there again, giving him a moment to gather himself. His pain was growing stronger, flowing from a deeper source, and she regretted pushing him to talk about himself now. She hadn't meant to hurt him.

"When I was young, nothing more than a boy, I began trying to play with the other males my age in the pride. They were wary of me but sometimes they would let me go with them into the forest. I treasured those times… until one day when one of our group ended up injured when trying to leap between the trees. When the elders heard about it, and heard I was part of the group, they punished me for it."

Now she really wanted to find his pride and teach them all a lesson. How dare they punish him for something that evidently hadn't been his fault?

The darkness in his eyes said it hadn't ended there.

"My mother tried to defend me, but they punished her for it too. She never tried again. I avoided the young males of the pride after that, keeping to myself and training in the forest. I wanted to spare my mother the pain of seeing me beaten… but it didn't help." He looked across at her again, the hurt in his eyes too much for her to bear. She wasn't sure how he could bear it or how he had survived what had happened to him, but it was a testament to his incredible strength. "The young males in the village realised that they could escape punishment by simply saying I was there with them whenever they ran into trouble. No one ever asked me if I was there… they just dragged me to the post, tied me and lashed me for it."

She wasn't sure what she could say to him. There weren't adequate words to convey the depth of her anger or her pain, or her desire to comfort him and steal away his pain and suffering and somehow show him that the way his pride had treated him had been wrong and they were the ones who deserved punishment.

"Did no one speak out to defend you?" she whispered, stroking his chest and feeling his heart beating hard. "Someone should have protected you. You were a boy. A child. You should have been protected."

He smiled sorrowfully. "I was a male. Pride males are meant to be strong. We are meant to know our place or fight for a better one."

"That does not excuse what they did to you, Kyter. It does not make it right. They abused you… they hurt you… and they did it on purpose." Her blood boiled at the vision of a young sandy-haired boy chained to a post and lashed, no doubt in front of the entire pride, ridiculed and tortured when he had done nothing wrong.

The ones who should have been punished were those who had lied and placed the blame on Kyter's small shoulders, and those who had carried out the beatings with the knowledge that they were punishing the wrong child.

"I know," he whispered and took hold of her hand, and she realised she had been digging her claws into his chest. He pressed a kiss to each of her fingers. "I put an end to it."

"How?" Her eyes darted between his and the darkness in them this time wasn't born of pain. It was born of violence.

"I had matured and I had grown sick of how the pride treated me. I snapped and refused to take a beating for something I hadn't done. I took the lash from the elder and turned on him with it." He toyed with her fingers, his gaze fixed on them. "I wanted to strike him."

"But you did not." Because he wasn't that sort of male.

He wasn't the kind who would strike someone or fight them without a reason. He had stopped the male from whipping him, and had no doubt frightened the male by turning on him, and that had been enough for Kyter.

He shook his head, released her hand and ran his fingers through his hair again, sighing as he relaxed against the white pillows, his elbow pressing into the wooden headboard of the bed.

"I left the village and took to the rainforest, living among the animals there. Everything the pride had refused to teach me because of my status, I taught myself. I was gone for almost a decade before I returned. Honed. Powerful. Skilful." He closed his eyes and frowned. "Some of the pride males of my age attacked me and tried to drive me away."

"You fought them."

He nodded.

She stroked the deep scars on his chest.

"You won."

He nodded again, slowly opened his eyes and looked across at her, no trace of pride in his eyes. He had bested the males of his age, proving his strength, but it hadn't changed things. The pride had still treated him as an outsider, rejecting him even though he had grown strong and capable. He had become a warrior. She could see it in him, in the shadow of darkness in his eyes at times, and the cold and calculating edge that came over him when he readied himself for a battle. He had transformed himself into the epitome of a powerful male.

A male who was slowly working his way under her skin, slipping past her defences.

"I left them shortly afterwards. I roamed the world and then I settled in London, where I opened Underworld."

His nightclub. He seemed passionate about it and she had upset him earlier when she hadn't shared that passion. She had only been to a few nightclubs in her life, and all of those had been extremely noisy and none had catered towards fae.

"I would like to see your nightclub," she said and his eyes grew larger. "I have only been to ones where mortals go. It would be interesting to see one where different species come together."

"You can visit any time you want, when you're not in the elf kingdom... if you ever come to London that is." He smiled that lopsided smile of his, the one that always claimed a direct hit on her heart. She smiled too, aware that he was choosing his words carefully, not wanting to mention anything about mates and bonds, and being together. She didn't want to spoil the moment either, but she was going to mention it.

"I do not live in the elf kingdom. I left it when I reached my thousandth birthday and had not found my mate."

His smile faded and his sandy eyebrows dipped low above his golden eyes. "Why? Did you come looking for me? Because I hate to say this and bring it up again, but you were around two thousand years too early."

She silently thanked him for lightening the mood and shook her head, apologising at the same time because she was going to dampen it again.

"I left because it is elf tradition that if a female has not found her fated mate by the time she reaches her thousandth birthday she must wed a partner of her parents' choosing."

"What?" Kyter snapped, all the calm fleeing him as he scowled and tensed beneath her. "Your parents tried to set you up with an arranged marriage?"

Iolanthe walked her fingers across his chest, suddenly finding them fascinating, and whispered, "There was no try... I may have run away on my wedding day."

He grabbed her wrist and pulled her closer to him, the swift jerking action tearing a gasp from her and making her look at him. She had never seen such fury in his eyes. They were on fire. Bright gold. Burning.

"*Fuckers*... remind me to let your parents know exactly what I think about their attempt to palm you off onto a guy when I meet them." He growled those words, flashing emerging fangs, and fur rippled over his skin, a brief and tantalising flash of gold and black.

Iolanthe made a mental note to never let Kyter meet her parents. He looked as if his chosen method of letting them know what he thought about the marriage they had arranged for her would be fighting them.

"My mate... tossed callously into the arms of some random male... my beautiful female." He swept the backs of his fingers across her cheek, an earnest look in his eyes that stole her breath. "The thought that you might have married... fuck, that kills me. I never thought I would have a mate, but to think I might have lost you because of a stupid tradition."

She frowned at what he had said but before she could ask him about it, he was kissing her, chasing away her ability to think with each soft sweep of his lips across hers. She tried to resist him but he waged war on her, his tender kiss melting her defences and leaving her heart wide open.

He broke away to press his nose to hers, their foreheads lightly touching. "What happened? Have you never been back?"

She skimmed her hand over his shoulders, savouring the way his hands clutched her hips, trembling against her, and his heart beat against hers. He was angry and it was beautiful, because it reassured her that he hadn't lied and he didn't want to force her into a bond with him.

"My brother hunted me down and he gave me a place to stay until things at home had settled down. I went into the treasure hunting business. My brother lied and told my parents I was looking for my mate."

She smiled at the memory of how sour her brother had looked when she had asked him to do that for her. He loved their parents just as she did, but he hadn't been pleased when he had discovered that they had attempted to marry her off to one of the village males when she had never been given the freedom to roam the kingdom and search for her mate. He had been even more upset with them because they had done it while he had been away with his legion of the army.

"Maybe you were looking for your mate," Kyter said with a wicked smile. "You just took a while to find me."

She supposed it wasn't a lie as she had found her mate. What would her mother and father make of that?

What would her brother make of it?

Iolanthe didn't want to ponder the answer to that question. She had a terrible feeling she would find out one day, and that day would come sooner rather than later.

"What did you mean when you said you did not think you would have a mate?" She wanted to know but she also wanted to direct his attention away from her family, because she feared he would probe into them. She didn't want to talk about them and spoil the calm between her and Kyter.

"The pride elders told me I would never have a mate because of what I am." He said it with a straight face devoid of feelings but she felt the emotions that stirred within him, the hurt that began to surface again.

"Do not speak about yourself as if there is something wrong with you." She pressed her hands to his chest and pleaded him with her eyes. "I see nothing wrong with you."

She traced the scars on his chest. Marks of battle. Worse were the marks on his back. Those marks had left deep scars on his heart. She wanted to kiss every one of them to ease his pain and wanted to keep kissing them until he accepted that there was nothing wrong with him. She didn't see a monster before her. She saw only a man, one hurt by his past but one who was trying to stand tall despite it all and everything that had happened to him.

He was beautiful.

Her male.

And he needed her to lighten the mood again, to chase away the shadows in his eyes and the painful memories.

She had never had to do such a thing and wasn't sure where to begin, but she was determined to try because he needed her to do it. Her male was hurting and needed her to help him escape his past and look towards his future again.

She had teased him before and he had smiled. Perhaps she could tease him again and coax a smile from him.

She stroked his chest. "Do you like having your belly rubbed?"

He cocked an eyebrow. "That's dogs."

She frowned and then smiled, undeterred by his gruff tone. "Then perhaps you like having your ears tickled?"

He grinned, hitting her hard with it. "I know you do."

A blush rose onto her cheeks and some of the storm clouds in his eyes lifted. He liked it when she blushed. She didn't like it. It made her feel weak when she was used to feeling strong. She had never met a male who affected her as Kyter did. There had never been one who made her feel so feminine or that it was alright to let her guard down and just be herself, without fear of him thinking she was weak or taking advantage of her.

She felt safe with him. Secure. Protected.

Loved?

She wasn't sure she would go that far.

Yet.

"If you see a ball rolling or a small fluffy creature running, do you feel a pressing need to chase it?" she said.

"Ha ha… very funny. Any other cat questions?" He mock-scowled at her. "Come on, get them all out now."

She nodded and her eyes turned hooded as she thought about the only other question she wanted to ask him.

His scowl melted away and he stared at her in silence, the intensity of his gaze sending a shiver through her as the gold in his eyes brightened and his pupils expanded. The hunger that shone in them echoed in her and it only grew as she slowly smoothed her palms across his broad chest, stroking his warm golden skin.

She dropped her eyes to his chest, swept her tongue across her lips, feeling his gaze following it and loving the way his entire body quaked beneath her in response, and slowly lifted her eyes back to his.

She gave him a sultry smile and whispered.

"Could I make you purr?"

He growled, the feral sound sending a thrill through her, rolled her onto her back, pinning her beneath him, and uttered two words before his lips descended on hers.

"Gods, yes!"

CHAPTER 17

Iolanthe threaded her fingers into Kyter's sandy hair and held him to her as he kissed her, the soft sweeps of his lips across hers far from what she had expected, but everything she had apparently desired. This quietness between them, a sense of harmony and tenderness, awakened a deep feeling of connection in her. She felt linked to him, not only in body as they kissed, but in soul.

She felt it deep in her heart.

This was what she had needed from him. Not the wild and explosive lovemaking they had shared before. This tender and gentle lovemaking was what she needed right now and she knew he needed it too. He had opened up to her, exposing his heart and leaving himself vulnerable, and he needed her to show him that she would take care of the heart she now held in her hands. She wouldn't crush it as others had. She wouldn't hurt him. She would treasure what he had dared to give to her without even realising he had given it.

Part of her felt sure that she had exchanged hearts with him even though she hadn't intended to do such a thing. She had wanted to open up to him, but what they had shared had gone far deeper than simply revealing who they were and sharing pieces of their past. It had touched her and it had made her fall a little for her mate.

Her powerful male.

He was tender and gentle as he kissed her, his weight held off her as he rested on his elbows, her right thigh between his. His hardness pressed into her hip, hot and heavy, twitching at times, as if eager to take things further.

She stroked down Kyter's neck and he shuddered, a moan escaping him, and then she smiled against his lips as she brought her hands up and teased his ears. She rubbed the spot behind his left one and he groaned, pausing with his lips against hers.

"Stop that," he whispered and she refused, keeping up her rubbing until he was leaning into the touch, stealing his lips away from hers.

His eyebrows furrowed above his closed eyes, the look of sheer bliss on his face making her smile widen. He definitely liked having his ears tickled.

When she took her hand away, his eyes slowly opened, bright gold and mesmerising. His eyebrows dipped into a frown and he scowled at her. Not a real one. He could pretend to be angry all he wanted but she knew his weak spot now.

He moved quicker than she could evade and she gasped as he ran his tongue up the curve of her ear and flicked it over the pointed tip. The tip flared back, her ears growing pointier as he had his revenge, swirling his tongue over her flesh. She moaned and clutched his shoulders, fighting for control of her body as sensation hijacked it, making her writhe against him, seeking an outlet for the desire spiralling within her. She rubbed her hip against his hard length and he groaned, growled and rocked against her.

The feel of him so close to where she needed him drove her mad and she wriggled, trying to get him to shift his focus away from her ear to his own body. She wanted to drive him mad too. She wanted to make him lose control.

He drew back and gave her a wicked smile, one that had her heart fluttering against her chest even as she groaned. He wasn't going to give her what she wanted. He was going to deny her, drawing out the moment, until she was begging him. She felt sure of it.

She hooked her arms around his neck and pulled him back down to her, kissing him but somehow managing to keep it light, teasing his lips with soft sweeps of her tongue. He moaned and clutched her, sliding one arm beneath her back to lift her off the bed and press her against his chest. His other hand curled around her shoulder and he ground against her hip.

He didn't resist her when she rolled with him, pinning him on his back on the soft mattress, and straddled him. His hands jumped to her hips and he threw his head back and moaned as she rocked against his length, rubbing herself on him. Delicious. She stared down at him as she writhed, tracing her hands over his body, caressing every taut peak of his chest and stomach. He grimaced, flashing his short fangs, and pressed the back of his head into the white pillow. The action only made his muscles more pronounced, delighting her eyes.

Iolanthe made them her target.

She leaned over him and explored his body with her mouth, sweeping her lips across his golden skin as he moved her hips and his, rubbing against her sensitive spot. She pressed kisses to his scars, lavishing them with attention and making sure she didn't miss any of them.

The ones from his fight against the demon were still pink. She slowed and took her time over those, earning a husky groan from Kyter as she trailed her lips down each diagonal slash that cut from the left side of his chest down his stomach, having to shift off him to reach the point where they began.

Just above the ridge of muscle that arched over his right hip.

Kyter lifted his hips and rubbed himself between her breasts, the blissful look back on his handsome face. She shook her head at the pleasure he took from the act and kissed across his hip, recalling the pleasure he had taken from having her mouth on him.

He stilled right down to his breathing.

She looked up the length of his honed body to his face and slowly ran her tongue along his steel length, from root to tip. He groaned and fisted the sheets, pulling the white material taut beneath his body. She lowered her mouth and kissed up his cock, tasting herself on him and drinking down each breathless moan of pure male satisfaction she wrung from him. When she reached the crown, she took him in her hand and wrapped her lips around him.

He jerked into her mouth, his breath leaving him in a rush. One hand clamped down onto the back of her head and she moaned as he guided her, forcing her to take him into her mouth. She sucked and licked him as he pumped into her, growing thicker and harder. His hand trembled against her head. His breathing quickened.

He grabbed her, hauled her up his body, and claimed her mouth in a fierce kiss as he rolled with her, ending up between her thighs. He rocked hard against her, his kiss stealing her breath and his hands clutching her tightly, pinning her beneath him. She tried to keep up, her own passion rising as he unleashed his wilder side. She loved him like this. Wild. Untamed. Hungry for her.

She gasped as he broke away from her and his lips descended on her bare breasts, his mouth working black magic as he sucked one nipple into his mouth and rolled it between his teeth. She moaned and arched off the bed, eager for more, unable to stop herself from silently begging him to give it to her. He pinched her other nipple between his finger and thumb, squeezing the bud and sending hot shivers racing through her. They all collided in her belly and pooled there and lower.

Iolanthe writhed again, rubbing herself against his cock, unable to stop herself as her passion seized control.

He groaned and rocked against her, teasing her sensitive nub, taking her higher but not high enough. She needed to soar. She needed to fly again.

He prowled down her body, grasped her hips and shoved her up the bed, so her head hit the pillows. The feel of him using his strength on her thrilled her. No male before him had ever done such a thing with her. None of them could compare with him. Her wild male.

She threw her head back and moaned as he speared her folds with his tongue. His hands wedged her thighs apart and she felt as if she would overload as he swirled his tongue around and lapped at her before flicking the hypersensitive bud and sending fifty thousand volts arcing through her veins.

Her dream of him like this didn't even come close to the reality of the act. He mastered her with his mouth, bringing her close to the edge before backing away and slowing down, waiting for her to begin to relax again before sending her soaring higher towards Heaven.

Iolanthe alternated between clutching the wooden headboard and clutching his sandy hair. He slid his hands beneath her buttocks and raised them off the bed, and she arched upwards as he teased her entrance with his tongue, flicking it around before gently probing.

"Kyter." She rocked against him, her body beyond her control as she sought release.

He slowly eased the tip of his tongue into her sheath and withdrew it the moment she moaned.

Curse him.

She reached down to grab his hair again and her hand fell to her belly when he slid two fingers into her core. Her body eagerly flexed around them, desire pulsing through her. She tried to rock but he held her firm, stopping her. He thrust slowly, groaning low in his throat as he rubbed the pads of his fingers along her sheath.

Maddening.

Iolanthe couldn't take it.

She needed release.

He stroked his tongue over her pert nub and flicked it. She moaned, the desperate sound filling the room, and flexed around his fingers.

Kyter growled.

The room spun past her in a blur as he flipped her onto her front on her knees, knocked them apart and entered her in one swift delicious stroke. She cried out and grasped the pillows as one hand clamped down on the back of her neck and the other pressed hard into her lower back, holding her pinned against the mattress.

She moaned as he pumped her, long deep strokes that had his flesh meeting hers with each thrust. She edged her eyes towards him, her cheek pressed to the pillow, and groaned as she saw him behind her, his golden eyes locked on hers.

He bared emerging fangs and a thrill bolted through her, a powerful need to feel those fangs in her flesh. He was beautiful. Deadly. Hers. And she was his. He claimed every inch of her with every powerful thrust, as lost to his passion as she was to hers, consumed by the need to mate.

The gold in his eyes burned brighter and she knew her eyes looked the same, the violet in them shining. Her fangs dropped, cutting into her lower lip as she bit it, climbing towards her climax as he pumped her hard and deep. Each delicious thrust of his cock took her higher, making her cry out. Each deep plunge had him grunting, his face twisting as his desire peaked.

"Iolanthe," he growled, his lower canines as sharp as his upper ones.

His fingers pressed harder into the back of her neck, his eyes shifting to it as they blazed. She fought the urge to writhe against him, to goad him into losing the last shred of his control, unwilling to surrender to the part of her that wanted him to bite her.

Needed him to lay claim to her.

The fight was right there in his eyes, a battle she wasn't sure whether he was winning or losing. He was resisting his instincts and the needs that burned within him, and she knew he was doing it for her.

"Iolanthe." It came out as a deep guttural moan this time as his hips jerked and his thrusts turned uncoordinated.

She moaned as his cock throbbed and pulsed, his seed pumping into her. His rough hard thrusts sent her plummeting over the edge with him, crying out his name as her entire body convulsed and fiery heat burned through her, sending shivers down her trembling thighs.

Kyter stilled inside her, his cock buried deep, his hand still holding her neck. He breathed hard, his muscular chest heaving with each one, his eyes locked on hers.

The need in them hadn't abated, and it hadn't faded in her either.

He stared down at her for long tense seconds that felt like hours to her as she fought the urge to do something that would coax him into biting her, forcing herself to keep still instead.

He finally closed his eyes, withdrew from her and flopped onto his back beside her. He grabbed her around the waist and she squealed as he dragged her back against his front, and stilled as his hot breath fanned across the back of her neck.

She waited.

Half of her afraid he would bite her.

The other half begging him to do it because she wasn't brave enough to take that leap.

He exhaled hard, his heart settling together with his breathing, and placed a gentle kiss on her neck.

She trembled from it, a rush of tingles racing down her spine, and her fear ebbed away as he did something that made her smile and left her feeling he was content to leave things as they were between them.

For now at least.

A deep rumbling sound echoed through his chest as he rubbed his cheek across her shoulder and settled against her.

He purred.

CHAPTER 18

Kyter rubbed his left hand on his olive-green combat trousers, wiping the dust from it, and then shifted the pick into that hand so he could do the same with his right. They had returned to Pompeii at nightfall to dig in the temple.

Iolanthe had distanced herself after teleporting them back to the site, heading down into the chamber beneath the temple base for another look. He hadn't gone after her. He was coming to learn her patterns now. She would step closer to him, letting her guard down, and then she would ease back. Eventually, she would stop with the easing back, but he had to be patient and wait for that day.

He rested the pick against one of the pale stone blocks that formed the remains of the altar and raked his fingers through his hair, brushing it back as he took a breather. He had been digging around the altar for the past hour, lifting the stones to reveal the mixture of earth and rubble beneath. He hadn't found anything yet.

He crossed the enclosed area of the temple to his backpack where it rested against one of the broken columns that lined the low wall and took his black shirt from on top of it, setting it down on the marble pillar. He unzipped the black pack, swiped his canteen from it, and unscrewed the cap.

It was another stuffy night at the ancient site. Out in the countryside where his villa was, it was cooler and more comfortable. Here it was humid and warm, the stone giving off all the heat it had collected during the day.

Movement out of the corner of his left eye caught his attention and he slowly turned to watch Iolanthe as she approached. His heart beat a little quicker, a reaction to the sight of her that he was coming to think he would always experience. She was trying to kill him though. She had twirled her black hair up, using her long silver pin to hold it in place, lifted away from her neck.

His gums ached as his fangs threatened to emerge.

Hell, he wanted to sink those fangs into her neck.

She realised he was staring at her and dropped her gaze, the shy reaction drawing a smile from him.

"Anything?" he said to break the thick silence and make her more comfortable.

She shook her head and her violet eyes came back up to meet his. "Nothing."

Her hairstyle had another downside. At least for him. It revealed her pointed ears. Before she had emerged from the bathroom tonight with her hair pinned back, exposing her ears, he hadn't realised just how much they added to her otherworldly appearance, drawing him to her, or how they gave away her feelings.

When desire had darkened her eyes on seeing him half-dressed, his upper body exposed, her ears had grown pointier and had flared back a little. He had teased her about it and had earned himself a hiss and a flash of fangs. Her ears had flattened against the sides of her head then.

She fascinated him.

He had half expected her to teleport and leave him at the villa, but she had calmed down and had taken the hand he had offered her, and the kiss he had given her when he had pulled her into his arms.

"Have you found anything?" She peered past him to the stones he had removed and lined up across the front of the altar, ready to replace before they left the site so the humans didn't know they had been digging here.

Kyter swigged his water and then offered the canteen to her. She held her hand up and shook her head.

"Nothing." He echoed her earlier words. "But there is earth and rubble to dig through. We might find something."

She didn't look hopeful.

Another pick appeared in her hand. "I will look with you."

He still wasn't used to her ability to teleport things to her. She had explained how it worked and he had started to wish that his was a species that could do what she could. It would beat having to fly everywhere and it would be nice to just think about something in his apartment and have it pop into his hand no matter where he was in the world.

Kyter walked back to her and grabbed his pick. She began digging at one end and he worked in the opposite corner. His mind kept drifting back to the hours they had spent in his villa, tangled up in bed together, making love and talking, his digging slowing whenever it did.

He dragged his focus back to his work for what must have been the twentieth time, slamming the pointed end of his pick into the dirt and pulling it up to break the ground.

Something glinted in the moonlight.

He crouched and picked up the gold and silver discs, rubbed them to reveal their faces, and studied them. Coins. He went to toss them onto the stones lining the edge of his hole but Iolanthe was there, crouched beside him. She held her hand out and he placed the coins into her palm.

She looked at each one in turn, studying both sides, and discarded every single one of them. "Are there more?"

He went back to the hole, swung his pick and cut into the earth around the place where he had found the coins. Iolanthe joined him, breaking up the dirt and revealing larger coins. These ones looked more like gold medallions.

She rubbed them on her black combats, tilted them towards the moonlight, and studied them. She discarded the first two.

She stopped on the third.

"What is it?" He closed the distance between them and peered down at the one she held, wanting to see it too because her eyes had gone wide again and he was sure that she had paled.

"I know this mountain range," she whispered, her voice distant as she stared at the relief on the medallion.

The mountains were a series of cragged, dangerous-looking peaks that looked impossible to scale. He had never seen mountains like them, not in all his travels.

"I'm not familiar with them. Are they around here?"

She shook her head and swallowed hard, her hand lowering as she lifted her gaze to meet his. "They are in Hell... the borderland with the Devil's domain. My first mission took me there. I almost died."

He didn't like the sound of that, or the burst of fear that laced her scent. She raised the medallion towards him and froze.

Four more scents joined hers.

Kyter growled and shifted in front of her, guiding her behind him as he turned to face the four males who had appeared in the open area of the temple ruins. All of them wore black, just like the demon he had defeated at Herculaneum.

Iolanthe's client had sent more men after her.

These four radiated danger, a lethal air to their scents. They were powerful. More powerful than the demon he had fought.

Two were demons from different realms, almost human in appearance with the exception of the short horns that curled from behind their ears. One smelled human, with an undertone of herbs. A sorcerer.

The fourth male, a tall slender one with pale eyes and short black hair, Kyter wasn't sure about. Whatever he was, Kyter had never met one of his kind before.

Iolanthe shifted out from behind him and her short black blade appeared in her hand as her armour swept over her body, transforming her fingers into vicious claws.

The mystery male slid her a dark look edged with desire.

Kyter couldn't contain the fury that burned through his veins, the need to annihilate the male for daring to look upon his female with lust in his eyes. He launched himself at the male, growling through his fangs.

The male smirked, a cold look in his pale blue eyes, and disappeared.

Kyter screamed as white-hot pain ripped up his right leg and stumbled a step before slamming into the stone floor. Fire radiated through his bones and he snarled over his shoulder at the dark-haired male who now stood behind him, a silver katana tipped with blood in his right hand, his smirk still in place.

Kyter wanted to punch it off his face but he could only clutch at his leg and growl through the agony. His animal side snarled with him, the pain of having his Achilles tendon severed too much for him to handle.

One blow. One goddamned blow.

It was all it had taken for the male to defeat him and the bastard knew it.

He loomed over Kyter, victory in his icy eyes laced with disgust and disappointment.

Whatever the male was, he knew how to disable a shifter of his breed. The pain was too strong, stopping Kyter from transforming into a jaguar, the form in which he was at his most powerful. The male had seen straight through his mixed blood to what he was.

Kyter's gaze shifted to Iolanthe and he caught the fear in her violet eyes and her need to come to him. She was barely holding herself back. The part of him that was disappointed that she hadn't called his name or come to him when he had been bested burned away as the male stepped on his bleeding ankle, crushing it beneath his weight and sending fresh agony tearing through Kyter. He threw his head back and bellowed in agony, the sound so loud it drowned everything out together with the throbbing in his head.

The world dimmed and he fought towards the light, refusing to pass out and leave Iolanthe vulnerable.

He would make the male pay for daring to look at her with desire in his eyes and he would show the bastard that he was stronger than he had thought. He could still fight.

Kyter brought his other leg up, slamming his boot into the male's thigh before he could evade it, knocking him sideways. The moment the male's weight left him, Kyter rolled onto his front and pushed up onto his good leg. He turned on the male with a snarl and the male charged him, raising his blade at the same time.

Iolanthe appeared between them just as the male brought that blade down and blocked it with her own sword, knocking it away from her and Kyter. She hissed and attacked, each swift strike of her black blade driving the male backwards.

The two demons launched into the fray, the first slamming into her back and knocking a cry from her as she staggered forwards.

"We only want to talk," the dark-haired male said and evaded her, sidestepping when she swept her blade in a deadly arc towards him. "I would say it is in your best interest to cooperate."

The male slid a pointed look towards Kyter.

Pain blazed up Kyter's leg again and he crumpled, his knees hitting the stone flags with jarring force.

"Son of a bitch," Kyter snarled and clawed at the stones as his vision wobbled again.

Iolanthe froze, her fine black eyebrows furrowing as she looked back at him, fear and concern filling her beautiful eyes and lacing her scent.

She turned towards him but the males didn't give her a chance to reach him. The two big demons grabbed her arms, one twisting the sword from her grip, and the sorcerer flicked his hand towards her, binding her ankles together.

Kyter tried to stand, making it onto his knees before the sorcerer hit him with a spell that pinned his arms behind his back. All he could do was kneel and watch as the dark-haired male advanced on Iolanthe. She stood perfectly still, her violet eyes turning cold, no trace of fear in them now.

Kyter growled low in his throat as the men closed rank. The demons turned at angles to face her, their bodies pressed against hers. Intimately. He snarled at the way the dark-haired male didn't stop until he was almost pressed against her too, his front to hers. When the man dared to touch her cheek, to cup it and tilt her head up towards him, bringing her lips close to his, Kyter roared and tried to move.

The man looked over his shoulder at Kyter and slid him another cruel smile.

Kyter bellowed again as pain ripped through him. He arched backwards and screamed at the moon until he was hoarse and his voice died, every inch of him tensing as he fought the agony tearing him to pieces.

The pain subsided and he collapsed forwards, his bound arms aching as they pressed against his back with each ragged breath he drew.

What the hell? It felt as if the male had struck him again. It had felt that way earlier too. Both times the man hadn't touched him, but it felt as if he had. Did it have something to do with his sword? Did it give him some sort of control over the wound he inflicted?

Iolanthe looked down at him.

The black-haired man returned his gaze to her, raking it down her body with dark possession in his eyes. Kyter growled again, warning the male in the only way he could, his anger rising and growing stronger, pushing his pain to the back of his mind.

The darkness in him began to curl through his veins. If he tapped into that demonic side of himself, could he overcome the pain of his ankle, the male's control over the wound, and the spell that held him?

The male wetted his lips and Kyter had the gut-turning feeling that shit could go badly south at any moment, and if it did, if the male so much as looked as if he was going to lay his hands on Iolanthe to violate her, Kyter was taking the bastard down one way or another.

She stood with her head high, undaunted, but he knew her now and he could read the feelings she refused to show in her eyes in the subtle, almost imperceptible change in her scent.

She was masking it, but she was rattled beneath her calm exterior. Afraid. It made him burn with a need to reach her and shield her from the males around her, and burn with anger when he realised he couldn't fulfil that need. If he tried to stand, either the sorcerer would take him down, or the male would, and he had caught the look in Iolanthe's eyes when she had glanced at him.

She didn't want him to fight these males.

She feared for him.

"Report. We know the male behind me killed the fourth under my command. Our master is not pleased by this turn of events," the dark-haired male said in the demon tongue.

Master? Iolanthe's client was their master?

"We are close... but I require the jaguar male to assist me."

The male slid Kyter a dark look and curled his lip. "I did not know you had a partner. There was no information regarding one when we selected you for this job."

"He was away for many decades but I required his skills on this job, so I contacted him."

The male didn't look as if he believed her. He stared at Kyter for almost a full minute, something dark and sinister brewing in his pale eyes, before turning back to her.

"Very well. There have been some alterations to the job."

Iolanthe paled. "Changes?"

"Yes. Since you have a partner, you will not require as much time to find the item. Master Fernandez has brought delivery forwards. You have four days, Iolanthe. Either you deliver the item he desires, or it is your head he places on his mantelpiece." The male leaned closer and brushed his lips across her cheek as he spoke. "It is such a pretty head... Master Fernandez has been kind. Before you lose it, I will get one night with you."

Kyter roared and wrestled against his bonds, the muscles of his shoulders and chest burning as they strained to break his arms free from behind him so he could wrap his hands around the bastard's scrawny neck. The spell didn't give. He snarled and kept fighting, determined to break free and tear the male's head off for daring to lay his lips on Iolanthe and talk of bedding her.

"And Iolanthe?" The male stroked her cheek, unbothered by Kyter's outburst, which only made him fight harder to get the son of a bitch's attention. "Since he is your partner... he will share the reward... and the penalty for failure."

Penalty?

That word and Iolanthe's reaction stopped him cold. A sharp burst of fear swept over him, a tangible wave that emanated from her, lasting only a split second before she regained control and it turned to fury, but long enough that he sensed it.

"No," she snapped, her eyes wild. "That was not part of the deal. I will get the item. Leave him out of this."

"It is a nice try, but we have been watching you, Iolanthe. I am always watching you. I know what he is... and I will make him watch while I make you mine... and then I will kill him."

The male smiled coldly.

Kyter opened his mouth to roar at the bastard but ended up screaming as pain ripped up his leg again. He fell onto his side, breathing hard through gritted teeth as he fought the fresh waves of agony burning through him, threatening to render him unconscious. He couldn't leave Iolanthe alone to face these men. He had to protect her. His heart laboured and his head swam as he fought the pain, battling through it, determined to remain with his mate. She needed him.

When it had subsided enough for his senses to come back online, he opened his eyes and sought the men, fearing they would have hurt Iolanthe while he had been fighting for consciousness.

They were gone.

He was free of his bonds too.

He panted hard, struggling to tamp down the throbbing in his ankle and gain control over his emotions. They were too powerful, colliding and fusing together inside him, a mixture of fury and fear. His jaguar side stirred and prowled beneath his skin, caged by his injury, raw with rage. He wouldn't let the dark-haired male or his master anywhere near Iolanthe.

He wouldn't let her fail.

Now he understood why she hadn't wanted to talk about her client. The one they had referred to as Fernandez was the master of powerful and dangerous men, and that meant he was even more powerful and dangerous than they were. Now he understood why this wasn't a game to her either.

If she failed to find the artefact, her life was forfeit, and he had the impression that her death wouldn't be swift. It would be torturous and she would be begging for death by the time the fiends were done with her.

The thought of Iolanthe suffering at the hands of the dark-haired male, the thought of her dying, almost did him in. He had just found her, but his need to protect her was fierce, driving him forwards and giving him the strength he needed to face his enemies.

If they failed to locate the item that could summon Barafnir, Kyter would find a way to protect her from her client and his twisted goons. He wouldn't let anything happen to her.

She stood firm before him, steady and unwavering, her eyes fixed straight ahead.

His brave female.

The colour drained from her face, turning her skin the colour of moonlight, and she collapsed to her knees, pressing one hand into the stone flags.

Kyter instantly shoved onto his feet and limped to her, hesitating only long enough to consider that he was asking for her to lash out at him before deciding that he would take the blows she needed to deal if he could give her just a sliver of comfort and hope. He kneeled, gritting his teeth against the pain, and pulled her into his arms.

She trembled against his bare chest, her breathing ragged and fast, her fear flowing over him. Strong now. He could easily sense it in her. She had bottled it up and concealed it, and she had done her best to face the monsters her client had sent after her, but now it was flowing out of her, and it made him want to growl. He wanted to hold her close and never let her go. He wanted to make everything better somehow.

She nuzzled his chest, her short nails pressing into his bare flesh, her trembling growing worse.

Thunder rolled in the distance and the sky grew dark. The scent of rain filled the air. The temperature dropped.

Iolanthe remained pressed against him.

Kyter stayed where he was, holding her as the rain began to fall, hammering against his bare back and the dusty ground, mixing his blood with the dirt. The wind picked up and the swaying of the trees and the pounding rain covered the sound of her breaths as they grew rougher.

The rain was cold against his shoulders and scalp.

Her tears were hot against his chest.

He clutched her closer to him, a tidal wave of emotions rocking him, threatening to rip him apart inside. Desire to hunt down her client and the male who had dared to lay his hands on her was strong, compelling him to rise to his feet and demand that she tell him where they were so he could take them down. Desire to comfort her kept him where he was though, his instincts commanding him to shelter her in his arms and hold her, to give her what she needed.

He ached as she trembled against him, such a contrast to the steady, strong and fearless woman he had come to know.

He slowly grew aware of their location as the storm closed in and how vulnerable they were out in the open. He needed to get her back to his villa and dried off, and then see to his wound. After that, they could find the item she needed. They knew where to go now. She still had time to find it and get it to her client.

As much as he wanted to avenge his mother and make his father pay, he wouldn't do it at the cost of his mate's life. She was more important to him.

"We should move. You'll get cold," he whispered.

Her shoulders stilled and then she was out of his arms, faster than he could track. She stood at the altar with her back to him. The rain glistened on her black armour and dripped from the end of the silver spike that held her dark hair twirled at the back of her head.

She inhaled deeply and thunder rolled overhead, the lightning striking nearby.

Iolanthe turned cold eyes on him.

"Leave," she said and he frowned at her, sure that he had heard her wrong. "*Leave.*"

Fear was an acrid note in her normally soothing scent and it flickered in the depths of her eyes too.

He shook his head. "I can't do that."

Pain briefly danced in her eyes and echoed in his heart. He knew what she was doing, but he wouldn't let her do it. She snarled and hissed at him, baring her fangs as her black blade reappeared in her hand. She pointed it at him and the tip wavered.

His beautiful female.

She was hurting herself.

"The deal is off." She straightened her arm but it didn't stop her blade from shaking. "If you try to locate the artefact… if you come after me… you will leave me no choice. I will kill you."

Her purple eyes turned wild and she looked more like a feral beast than he ever had. She was cornered and dangerous.

She was hurting.

Afraid.

She feared for her life, and she feared for his too.

Kyter grimaced and grunted as he slowly got onto his feet, keeping his weight off his right leg as much as possible. White-hot fire streaked down the back of it but he ignored it and continued. He rose to his full height and looked her straight in the eye.

"I know… but I still can't do it, Iolanthe."

He knew that she couldn't do it either. She wanted to protect him and now he could see that she had been trying to protect him from the very beginning. She had kept trying to drive him away by threatening him. She had been desperate to keep him away from the group who were watching her, a dangerous band of males, and he had been too stubborn to notice that she was trying to protect him.

Kyter held his hand out to her. "We have four days. We know where to look. We can find the item, Iolanthe."

Tears lined her black lashes as she stared at him, her violet eyes overflowing with pain and fear that he wanted to ease.

He hopped a step towards her.

She shook her head.

"We can do this… together." He stretched for her, desperate for her to take his hand.

She bit out something vicious-sounding in her elf tongue.

"I cannot." She backed off a step and shook her head again, causing tears to spill down her cheeks and mingle with the rain on them. "I… I am sorry, Kyter."

Green-purple light flashed over her body.

Kyter launched himself at her, screaming as his leg gave out and pain burned through him. He pushed through it and reached for her arm, determined to catch it before she teleported.

She disappeared, leaving him flailing at thin air.

He landed face down on the cold wet stones, rolled onto his back and arched off the slabs as he roared, unleashing every drop of his fury and all of his fear in a feral noise that rivalled the thunder.

He couldn't do as she asked.

He couldn't let her go alone.

There was no point in saving himself if it meant losing her.

He collapsed against the wet flagstones, closed his eyes, bared his clenched fangs and pulled down a deep breath, drawing it over his teeth. Her scent lingered among the smells of the earth and the rain. He could track her, but only if he could find out where she had gone.

He hauled himself onto his hands and knees and looked across the inner temple to the scattered coins and medallions. The one she had studied was there, laying on the wet mud with the others.

His next clue.

His only hope of saving her.

He crawled over to it, picked up the medallion and rubbed his thumb across the dirty wet surface, revealing the jagged peaks she had said were near the Devil's domain.

He was going to need a little help from a friend.

He needed someone familiar with Hell.

He had just the guy for the job.

CHAPTER 19

Iolanthe landed in a remote region of Hell, at the border with the Devil's domain, a short distance from her destination. She stood on a plateau across the black valley from the mountains, her heart on fire in her chest, burning with a need to return to Kyter and with the pain of leaving him behind.

She'd had to do it.

She knew she had hurt him by leaving him, but it was the only way of protecting him and she needed to protect him. Her life was already on the line. She refused to put his on the line too.

She could do this alone, and perhaps she could save both of them.

He would be coming for her though. His wound would slow him down. Even if he bound it, he would need at least half a day to a day to heal it enough for him to move from his current location. Once he was on the move, he would need to find a way of entering Hell. It would take him time to find that pathway, and even longer to locate her.

She had time. She could put an end to this before Kyter could reach her. All she had to do was locate the artefact.

It was waiting for her just a brief teleport away.

The black mountains were dangerous, but she had discovered a route into them during her first job as a treasure hunter. Deep within one there was a cavern that had contained countless treasures. She had only taken the item she had been tasked to find. The rest were possibly still there.

She could get the artefact and hand it over to Fernandez, and then his guild of assassins would leave Kyter alone.

But Kyter wouldn't get his revenge.

She looked up at the jagged black peaks that towered ahead of her, a formidable sight against the dark sky beyond them.

Kyter needed his revenge.

It was more than important to him. It was vital.

The hunger to avenge his mother and his kin, and make the demon who had fathered him pay, consumed him and drove him, a relentless urge that he wouldn't be able to extinguish. If he didn't get this chance, he would probably go after the artefact. He would go after the assassins.

Those assassins would kill him.

She gritted her teeth and glared at the mountains.

There had to be a way for everyone to get what they wanted. Kyter had wanted to use the artefact to summon his father before handing it over to the assassins. Could she still do that? She could summon Barafnir and uncover the location of his home in the Devil's domain, and then hand the artefact over to

Fernandez. Afterwards, she could return to Kyter and tell him where to find his father.

Surely all parties would be satisfied then?

Kyter would have to be satisfied with it, and with her accompanying him into the Devil's domain. The demons there were more than powerful. They made the assassins that had come after her tonight look like kittens. There was no way she would allow him to go alone. He would try to stop her but she would fight him on it, because he would need strong people at his side to survive long enough in that realm to find his father.

Iolanthe focused on a point close to six hundred metres below the peak of the tallest mountain, in the middle of the range. Light traced over her body and she disappeared into the dark, reappearing on a broad deep ledge at the mouth of a crack in the black rock. The crack was barely half a metre at its widest point near the base, but she could easily squeeze through it. She couldn't teleport until she was on the other side, able to see whether any changes had taken place to the interior of the mountain. She couldn't risk teleporting to the cavern where the treasure was either. If it had caved in, she would reappear within the rock.

It would kill her.

She crouched and then shifted onto her hands and knees, and crawled through the widest part of the crack. Her eyes adjusted to the darkness but not enough for her to see clearly. The crack narrowed and she turned onto her side and reached ahead of her, grasping the rocks to pull herself through and sliding along the rough ground.

The air grew thick and stale as she left the outside world behind. She grimaced at the stench. Something had crawled into the hole at some point and had evidently failed to make it out. She pushed onwards, not wanting to think about what she would find when she made it past the crack and into the tunnel.

The end finally appeared in sight and she hauled herself towards it. The hole grew wider again, allowing her to move back onto her hands and knees and crawl. The rocks beneath her stabbed into her palms and knees through her armour. It protected her from being cut, but it didn't stop her from being jabbed by things. It just meant she ended up bruised rather than bleeding.

Iolanthe crawled out into the tunnel, sat back on her knees, and teleported a battery-operated lantern to her. She fumbled with it, found the switch, and flinched as it powered up. Light chased the shadows from the wide tunnel that had been cut out of the rock. Deep grooves slashed down the black walls in places, always four of them in line with each other. They were as thick as her wrists, spaced around half a metre apart.

Dragons.

They had long since moved on from this part of Hell, but one had made this place many centuries before she had come here, carving a home out of the black rock.

She had met dragons before.

One had captured her when she had tried to sneak through their village, looking for a dragon egg made of gold. Two had then fought over her, desiring her as their mate. She had used the pandemonium caused by their battle to escape.

With the egg.

Iolanthe had avoided dragons since then. The males were dangerously possessive and fought over everything. The females were dangerous too, but they mostly fought over the males. Dragon society apparently had a tradition of sharing partners and satisfying their urges with whoever caught their eye. They didn't seem to be interested in monogamy until they had found their fated one.

She held the lamp higher, peering towards the far end of the corridor.

When she saw it was clear, she teleported there, landing on her feet. She scoured the path ahead of her again. Clear. She fell into a rhythm of teleporting to the furthest point she could see, checking the next section, and teleporting again. The stench eventually disappeared. Whatever had died in the tunnel was behind her. She shuddered and was thankful that she wouldn't have to see it. Once she had found the artefact, she could teleport directly to the ledge outside in the fresher air.

The tunnel led upwards and then curved and dipped downwards. She didn't recall any details about the path that had taken her down to the cavern. Not because it had been two thousand years since she had been here. She didn't recall any details because she had been running flat out with an ogre on her tail. The great grey beast had become lost in the tunnels and she had run into him near the start. She had surmised he had been there a long time, trapped inside the mountain since the entrance had caved in, because he had started drooling from between his tusks the moment he had looked at her and had given chase shortly afterwards.

Iolanthe hadn't wanted to be eaten, so she had run.

The ogre had tracked her right down to the cavern and had blocked her exit.

She had tried to fight him, but he had been almost four times her height and ten times her width, and some of his muscles had been bigger than her entire body. He had easily defeated her and had dragged her towards the exit of the tunnels where they had crossed paths, holding her by her ankle, talking to himself about the various ways he wanted to prepare her.

Eat her.

Iolanthe had known that she was going to die.

She had passed out and had feared she would never open her eyes again.

When she had finally come around, the ogre's head had been sitting beside his body, surrounded by a thick pool of blood. The gruesome sight had startled her and she had looked around for the beast who had managed to not only defeat an ogre but decapitate it too.

And that was the moment her eyes had fallen on her brother where he had stood beside the dead ogre, his arms folded across his chest and an unimpressed look on his handsome face.

It was also the first time she had been thankful that she had such an overprotective sibling. If he hadn't insisted she tell him where she was going, and if he hadn't insisted she tell him precisely when she would be back, a date and time she had missed by three whole days, she would have been ogre food.

Iolanthe smiled to herself and walked into the enormous cavern. Violet and pure white crystals stuck out of the ceiling, her lamp catching and illuminating them so they shone. Hints of gold and silver streaked their numerous faces, reflected up from the hoard of treasure stretching before her.

It was still here.

She set the lamp on a crystal that rose from the floor of the cavern and began searching through the treasure, looking for something that matched what had been inscribed on the back of the coin.

A language she hadn't recognised.

She checked each piece before setting it down near the entrance, in a pile away from the items she had yet to study. Swords. Lanterns. Belts. Chains. Jewellery. The dragon had been busy, gathering items from all over Hell. There were probably several artefacts that belonged to demons among the ones the shifter had gathered, but there was only one that she wanted.

It had to be here.

Iolanthe had checked half the items, almost five hundred of them, before she took a break and looked around her. On the black walls of the cave, the dragon had carved pictures, crude drawings of dragons in flight and people, and even mountains. She wandered over to a section of the mural and stroked her fingers over the images. The male or female must have used a tool, because there were multiple grooves at an angle, as if the stone had been chipped away.

The drawings were also limited to just above her height, leaving the top of the black wall untouched.

They had done it while in their mortal form.

She traced the shape of a mountain. It resembled the one she was in. In the dale below it, there was a village, and to the far right, where the last mountain dropped into the valley, there was a temple. It looked almost like the ones she had seen in the glory days of the Romans and the Greeks. A set of four columns held a triangular roof over the entrance. That roof butted up against another roof, this one a dome. Below the dome, more columns stretched between the base and the roof, following the circle.

When she had come to the mountains two thousand years ago, she hadn't seen any temple. There had been the remains of some stone huts and perhaps there had been a stone circle. She wasn't sure even the remains or the stone circle were there anymore, but she decided she would investigate the valley once she had finished searching through the treasure and had found the item she needed.

She hoped it wasn't another clue.

Iolanthe pulled the silver pin from her hair, brushed her fingers through the long black lengths, and twisted it into a neat knot at the back of her head. She jabbed the pin back through it to hold it in place and went back to her work, checking each piece and discarding it. The cavern began to heat up, slowly enough that she didn't notice it at first. It was only when her head turned that she realised the air was running out, making the cavern feel stuffy. She forced herself to continue, breathing as shallowly as possible as she discarded another piece, this one a necklace.

She picked up a gold platter and froze, her eyes on the silver dagger it had concealed.

She knew that writing.

She snatched hold of the dagger, her hand curling around the striped black and silver grip. The claws at the end of it held a smooth round ruby, the colour of blood. She turned the short double-edged blade over, her eyes scanning the inscription on it. She couldn't read it, but it was definitely the same language as the writing on the medallion.

She muttered a few choice curses at herself for forgetting to bring it with her. It might have offered her a clue to deciphering what the dagger said. Either the dagger was just another clue, and one she couldn't read, or it was the item she had been looking for.

She had two options now.

She could find a book or someone who could read the language and translate it, or she could try to find the location where Barafnir could be summoned from and attempt to use the dagger.

Her head turned again. Either way, she needed to get out of the cavern and tunnels before the air ran out and she lost consciousness. She focused on the wide ledge outside the tunnel into the mountain and teleported there. The cool air washed over her the second she appeared and she breathed deep of it, filling her lungs and sighing it out as her head cleared.

When she felt better, she flexed her fingers around the dagger and stared at the writing on it.

Was it just another clue?

Or was it the key to saving her life and giving Kyter his vengeance?

Iolanthe lifted her head to look down into the valley.

The air between her and the dark horizon shimmered.

A teleportation trail. Someone was coming.

A familiar sensation went through her.

Her blood turned to ice in her veins and her stomach dropped into her feet. It couldn't be.

CHAPTER 20

Kyter sat with his back against the wall of the inner temple in Pompeii, soaked through from the rain that had finally passed and in agony. His ankle wasn't the only thing on fire. His heart burned too, the need to find Iolanthe and protect her a relentless force within him, driving him to bear the pain of his injury and focus only on her welfare. She was more important than a busted Achilles tendon.

She was more important than everything, including his own life.

He would lay it on the line to save her. He would do whatever it took to ensure she lived to see another day.

He gritted his teeth as his ankle pulsed with a fresh wave of fire and palmed the small leaf-shaped amethyst crystal, his eyes fixed on it and his focus locked there too. Everything depended on this small innocuous trinket. All of his hope. His life. Her life.

He had been keeping it on his keys to Underworld since Bleu, an elf commander, had given it to him a month ago. Since receiving it, he had used it only once to send the elf a message, testing it out while the male had been visiting one of the Archangel facilities with his prince. Prince Loren's mate was an Archangel doctor. Archangel were the leading force in the world of hunters, institutions dedicated to protecting humans from the fae and demons. Most of the humans in this world didn't have a clue they shared it with everything from shifters to vampires, to incubi and succubi, and to things from fairy tales and mythology.

Angels included.

"Come on, Bleu," Kyter muttered to the crystal, his patience wearing thin.

He wasn't sure whether the elf had received his message. He wasn't even sure how the system worked. Bleu had explained that there was magic in the amethyst leaf, a spell that connected it to him. When Kyter had pressed for more information, the elf had simply told him to think of it as a sort of telepathy.

He had to hold it in his palm and focus on Bleu, and then speak the words of his message in his head.

Bleu would pick them up.

Hopefully.

Apparently sometimes it didn't work. If the distance was too great or there was magical interference, Bleu wouldn't hear him.

Kyter prayed to every god available that the elf heard him.

"Iolanthe," he whispered, curling his fingers over the crystal and clutching it tightly. He needed to find her. He needed to reach her before she ran into those men again, or worse, went to see her client.

Kyter feared that the male was out to deceive her. Whether she brought Fernandez the item or not, he was going to hand her over to that wretched dark-haired male who had dared to lay his filthy hands on her, and then he was going to kill her.

The air ahead of him shimmered and Kyter had never been more glad to see the male who appeared before him.

Standing at the same height as Kyter, an impressive six-feet-five, the elf male had the sort of looks that turned a hell of a lot of female heads and even some male ones. His violet eyes were as clear as the amethyst Kyter clutched in his palm, and his blue-black hair was overlong and wild, pushed back from his face tonight.

He towered over Kyter, a formidable sight in his tight black scale-like armour. It hugged his lithe figure, accentuating every honed muscle that hid beneath, broadcasting how powerful this male was.

Kyter wouldn't mess with him.

Bleu always radiated danger, his handsome face often locked in grim lines that only added to the sensation that he was liable to tear your heart out of your chest if you made a wrong move, but tonight he was throwing off stronger waves of it than normal.

His face bore several cuts, including one that darted across his nose, and he reeked of blood. Not only his own. Kyter could scent multiple species on him. Vampires. Shifters. Demons. Even some magic bearers.

"What happened to you?" Kyter tipped his head back and breathed through his pain as he tried to smile.

It ended up as a grimace.

Bleu raised an eyebrow but his violet eyes remained narrowed and hard, and his lips stayed locked in a grim line.

The elf appeared to be in an even worse mood than usual.

"I could ask you the same thing," Bleu said, his deep voice at odds with his athletic figure. "I do not wish to talk about it. I am here because I need to take my mind off something, so out with it. What's your problem?"

Kyter did smile this time. Bleu had always been a forthright bastard.

He grimaced again as he tried to push himself up into a more comfortable position, jarring his ankle in the process. The scent of his blood in the air grew thicker.

Bleu arched an eyebrow again, his violet gaze dropping straight to the source of the scent. The elf crouched before him and produced a black vial that resembled an upside down teardrop and popped the leaf-shaped lid off with his thumb.

"Drink."

Kyter wasn't about to refuse that order. He had seen the effects of elf medicine with his own eyes and had no reason to doubt that Bleu meant to help him.

He took the vial and brought it to his lips, his eyes watering as he caught the vile scent of it. He held his breath and drank down the contents in one swift go, retching as the taste matched the scent. He really didn't want to ask what was in it, but he had the horrible feeling it was made of things as disgusting as the smell and taste indicated.

The liquid was cold in his mouth but burned as it went down his throat. Incredible heat spread through him. It felt pleasant and Kyter relaxed against the wall, enjoying the way the heat chased the chill from his wet skin.

It reached his ankle.

Kyter threw his head back and screamed as white-hot agony ripped up his leg, the sudden intense pain threatening to render him unconscious. Bleu grabbed his shoulders and pinned him to the wall as he struggled, writhing as the fire lashed at him, burning him to ashes from the inside. He fought the elf, his fangs emerging and a feral snarl leaving his lips as the urge to shift came over him. He had to escape. He needed to get out of his own damned body.

His snarl became a roar and Bleu braced him harder, immobilising him.

"Calm down." The elf's deep voice brooked no argument and Kyter wasn't in a position to make one, not when he was all messed up inside, convinced that he was in his jaguar form even as he was vaguely aware he still wore his normal one.

He cried out, the mournful sound echoing from his throat, not born of his agony this time. It was born of a need to find his mate and hear her answer him.

The pain began to ease and Bleu's grip on him loosened. Kyter breathed hard, slowly settling his racing heart and piecing himself back together. Son of a bitch. He sagged against the wall, all of his strength leaving him, and opened his eyes to look at Bleu.

The elf male eased back, still balanced in a crouch on his toes. "Better?"

Kyter bared his fangs at the male. "You could've fucking warned me."

Bleu's violet eyes glimmered with the smile his lips refused to issue. "Why spoil the fun?"

Kyter huffed, pushed himself up into a sitting position and carefully parted the slash in his boot to reveal his ankle. Perfect, healed skin. Elf medicine was a miracle, even if it had felt as if the damned stuff had repaired his wound by tearing pieces off other parts of him.

"Is this why you called?" Bleu said and Kyter shook his head.

The elf male adopted his normal frown-come-glare. Iolanthe had given him that look countless times. It didn't suit her. He preferred it when she smiled.

He wasn't sure Bleu knew how to really smile.

They always seemed to come out sarcastic or strained.

"I have an elf in danger. I need you to teleport me to a location in Hell that is on this medallion." Kyter looked for it and spotted it across the flagstones.

He must have knocked it flying when he had been fighting Bleu. He grabbed hold of the wall and eased himself onto his feet, not daring to place any weight on his ankle in case it crumpled beneath him.

"I am not your personal taxi service." Bleu huffed, rose onto his feet and folded his arms across his chest.

"It's important. I'll owe you." Kyter went to move towards the medallion.

Bleu pressed a hand to his shoulder to stop him and pointed towards the gold disc. "This medallion?"

Kyter nodded and the elf strode over to it. He stooped, swiped it from the stone flags and straightened. He frowned at it and then flipped it over. His lips flattened again, a dark edge entering his violet eyes.

"You know the place?" Kyter didn't dare hope that he did.

"A female elf gave this to you?" Bleu turned his dark eyes on him, the black slashes of his eyebrows meeting hard above them and his nostrils flaring.

Kyter shook his head and grimaced again as he tried to place some weight on his ankle and it throbbed. "We found it together here… it's meant to reveal the location of an artefact."

"Artefact?" Bleu canted his head and looked from Kyter to the medallion and back again. "What artefact?"

"I don't have time to explain," Kyter barked and hobbled towards him. "Some guy named Fernandez sent men after her."

Bleu's face darkened and the sense of danger that swirled around him rose, his anger lacing his scent as he whispered, "Fernandez. The Mercury Assassins Guild master?"

Assassins?

Kyter didn't like the sound of that.

He reached out to grab Bleu's arm and force an explanation out of him, but the elf grabbed him instead and the world descended into darkness.

Kyter's stomach turned and he clutched Bleu's arm, shivering as cold swept over him. He hadn't enjoyed teleporting with the demon, but he definitely didn't like teleporting with Bleu. He hadn't noticed how cold and dark it was in the void when he had been teleporting with Iolanthe, her slender warm body held tucked close to his.

Iolanthe.

The darkness evaporated and she stood before him, as if his mind had conjured her. For a moment, he thought that it had and she was only a fantasy created by his desperate need to see her and see she was safe.

Then he realised that the darkness behind her was black rock.

And his fantasy Iolanthe would definitely have looked more pleased to see him.

She scowled at him.

Kyter hobbled towards her, his blood racing as he realised that Bleu had been able to bring him straight to where she had gone, and straight to her.

Damn, the elf was good. He would thank him later but right now, he wanted her back in his arms. He needed to feel that she was safe.

Bleu's hand clamped down on Kyter's bare shoulder and the black jagged claws of the elf's armour bit into his flesh as he shoved Kyter behind him.

Kyter stumbled and flailed as he came dangerously close to the edge of a ledge, his eyes shooting wide as he saw the thousand-foot drop to the rocky slope of the mountain below. He barely managed to stop himself from falling over the edge and tripped a few steps forwards, placing some distance between himself and certain death, before looking towards Bleu, an angry snarl balanced on his lips.

Had the elf been trying to kill him?

Iolanthe shot him a glare that made him forget about taking things up with Bleu. Why the hell was she angry with him?

"Iolanthe." Bleu's stern tone had her gaze leaping to the elf male and Kyter's blood boiled, a red mist descending as the two elves locked gazes.

Kyter growled, flashing his fangs, and pounced, placing himself between Bleu and Iolanthe. He shoved the male elf in the chest, sending him stumbling back towards the edge of the ledge.

"Back off," Kyter snarled and his nails transformed into claws. "The female is mine."

Bleu's violet eyes lost their dark edge and gained an incredulous one as they briefly flickered to Kyter.

"What the hell did you just say?" Bleu looked beyond Kyter's shoulder to Iolanthe and the darkness returned in force, turning the elf's expression murderous. "Explain this to me, Io."

"Io?" Kyter growled at that one and turned on Iolanthe too. "So it's okay for him to call you a pet name but it's not okay for me? Why the fuck is that the case? Because he's an elf?"

His face fell as something dawned on him and he grabbed her shoulders, pressing his claws into her armour as he searched her violet eyes.

"Is he your lover?"

She paled and her eyes slowly widened.

Son of a bitch. He was.

Kyter turned on Bleu with a dark snarl and fur rippled across his shoulders. He flexed his fingers as his claws grew longer, breaking through his skin as darkness swirled through his veins, awakened by a violent need to remove the elf's head so Iolanthe would only have eyes for him.

He was her male.

Not the elf.

Bleu dared to look beyond him at Iolanthe.

Kyter roared.

"Keep your damned eyes off my fated female." He launched himself at Bleu.

Bleu sidestepped and Kyter almost skidded off the edge of the ledge, back peddling fast to stop himself from plummeting to his death. He spun on his toes and roared as he saw Bleu standing right next to Iolanthe.

He sprang at the male and Bleu didn't dodge him this time. Kyter grinned as he slammed into the elf, his claws raking over the male's shoulders as he grabbed them and shoved him hard, sending him crashing into the black wall of the mountain. Bleu grunted, his eyes brightened and he hissed, flashing long white daggers.

The elf kicked him hard in the back of his right ankle and Kyter bellowed as fire spread up his healing leg. The world whirled past him in a streak of black and his back slammed into the jagged rocks, his breath leaving him in a rush as pain exploded across his ribs and along his spine.

Kyter managed to get his arm free and wrapped his hand around Bleu's neck.

Bleu drew back and cocked his fist.

Iolanthe shrieked.

"Brother!"

Bleu stopped dead. Kyter blinked. Brother? He looked at Iolanthe at the same time as Bleu did and then slowly edged his focus back to the male elf.

"Brother?" Kyter said, unable to get his voice above a weak whisper as it tried to sink in and he fought it, not wanting it to be true.

Bleu smacked Kyter's hand away from his throat and took a step back.

"*Older.*" Bleu folded his arms across his chest and scowled at him. "You want to explain what you have been doing with my little sister?"

Before Kyter could even think of a way of answering that question without the elf removing his heart from his chest, Bleu turned on Iolanthe again.

"And what the hell is this about you being in deep with assassins?"

She swallowed hard and clutched her hands in front of her, twisting her fingers together, her gaze downcast. Kyter could only stare at her as her meek behaviour made it all sink in too fast for him to handle. It wasn't a twisted joke. Bleu was her older brother.

"How could you come back here after what happened last time? I barely got you out alive," Bleu snapped and advanced on Iolanthe, and her head dipped lower.

Where was the fearless beauty Kyter knew her to be now? He didn't like seeing her like this, subservient and afraid. He refused to see her like this.

"Back off," Kyter growled and both Bleu and Iolanthe looked at him.

Bleu's eyes narrowed and Kyter had the feeling that the elf was sizing him up for a coffin and blaming him for Iolanthe's situation.

If he had realised that she was Bleu's sister, he wouldn't have fallen for her.

Kyter stiffened.

Gods.

He had fallen for her and he had fallen hard, and he really didn't think her status as his friend's kid sister would have changed that even if he had known it from the start. She'd had him on a leash since the moment he had set eyes on her in the fae town.

Iolanthe's expression softened and her purple eyes warmed, holding his and entrancing him, revealing a touch of concern and tenderness that left him feeling he wasn't alone. She had fallen for him too.

Bleu snorted, shattering the moment.

"I had to come." Iolanthe's tone held the same sharp and commanding edge he had heard in Bleu's voice so many times. Now he knew where she got it from, and where she got half of her expressions from too, particularly the one designed to make people feel as if they were dirt on her boot and unlikely to survive another second without being wiped out. "I needed to get the artefact."

She held a small silver dagger out to her brother. Bleu snatched it and didn't even look at it. He kept his eyes locked on Iolanthe, a bitter and disappointed edge to them that had her close to lowering her gaze again.

"I do not give a damn about an artefact. I give a damn that you are in trouble with assassins. *Assassins*, Io." Bleu lowered the dagger to his side.

Kyter wanted to ram it into his jugular.

"It isn't as if she has a fucking choice." Kyter pushed away from the wall and came up beside her, and she flicked him a glance that told him that she welcomed his support. He had her back. He always would.

"Kyter is right. I have to give the artefact to Fernandez. If I do not deliver it in four days…" She lowered her gaze again and stared at her brother's boots. "He is going to kill me."

Bleu barked out something that Kyter thought might have been a vile curse, because Iolanthe flinched and backed into Kyter, her left shoulder pressing against his right side. He wanted to sling his arm around her and pull her against him, but Bleu was looking as if he would take any excuse to restart their fight. Manhandling his little sister in front of him would be too much for the elf male right now. Kyter resisted the urge, willing to give Bleu some time to grow accustomed to what was happening between him and Iolanthe.

He would only give the elf time though.

He wouldn't leave her.

She was his female and Bleu would just have to get used to it.

"We should take Iolanthe to Underworld while we figure out what to do," Kyter offered and Bleu shot the suggestion down with a black scowl.

"I am taking my sister to somewhere she will be safe." Bleu held his hand out to Iolanthe. "Come, Sister."

Kyter bristled and stepped in front of her, shielding her with his body, his bare chest heaving as he fought to contain his growing need to protect her. He wanted to give into that powerful urge, even when he knew that fighting Bleu wasn't the answer and it wouldn't gain him any favour with Iolanthe.

It wouldn't exactly make him feel very good about himself either. Bleu had proven himself a friend and they had been growing closer over the past month. He didn't want to wreck that friendship by letting his instinct to keep his mate safe overrule his heart and common sense. Bleu wasn't his enemy. He was a valuable ally.

"I can protect her," Kyter said, adopting a firm tone that he hoped would leave the elf little room to argue. "She will be safe at Underworld... with me."

Bleu snarled, flashing fangs as his pointed ears flared back against the sides of his head, visible through the tangled strands of his black hair.

"You are doing a wonderful job of keeping her safe," the elf bit out and advanced on Kyter, the murderous look back in his darkening eyes. "She has assassins after her!"

Iolanthe stepped out from behind Kyter and planted her hands on her hips, looking as if she was on the verge of pulling the silver pin from her black hair and jabbing one of them with it. "They were after me before I met Kyter."

Bleu paid her no heed. He kept advancing, each slow step closing the gap between him and Kyter, and Kyter refused to move. He wouldn't back down and he wouldn't let Bleu have the upper hand by shifting back a step. It wasn't in his nature. Jaguars faced enemies head on, and right now Bleu was throwing off a scent trail that said he was an enemy, not an ally.

"How do you intend to protect her anyway?" Bleu flicked a pointed look down at Kyter's ankle. "I doubt my sister severed that tendon of yours. You bore no other wounds. They took you down and had you out of the fight with one hit. A male who only needs a single blow to take him out of action is not a male capable of protecting my sister nor one I would trust with the task."

Kyter lowered his head, keeping his eyes on Bleu's, and growled through his exposed fangs. He didn't need the damned reminder that he had messed up. His pride was still dented from his encounter with the dark-haired male and what had happened. He wouldn't let it happen again and he wouldn't stand for Bleu rubbing salt in his wounds. Fur rippled over his shoulders and over his clenched fists.

"Brother," Iolanthe whispered, something akin to shock in her voice. Or perhaps disappointment. Both of them were seeing a new side of Bleu, and it seemed neither of them liked it.

Kyter didn't take his eyes off Bleu.

The elf stood barely a metre from him, anger brimming in the cold depths of his eyes, his armour in place and covering his hands, keeping his fingers as serrated claws. Kyter calculated his chances of surviving a fight against the elf. Slim. He had no weapon and the ledge was only a few metres wide, meaning he was at a severe disadvantage. He couldn't rely on his stronger form. He needed space to fight as a jaguar.

Kyter flexed his fingers and then curled them into fists. "Iolanthe will be safe with me. What happened won't happen again."

"It happened once. Next time, you might get her killed."

Kyter stared hard at the elf male. There was no talking to him. Bleu wasn't going to listen to a word he had to say. He was hell-bent on blaming Kyter for his sister's predicament and Kyter was tired of taking the blame for everything.

"She will be safe with me." He took a step towards Bleu, rising to his full height and squaring his shoulders.

"She is safest with me," Bleu shot back.

Iolanthe made a noise of frustration and grated out, "I can take care of myself."

Bleu turned dark violet eyes on her. "What a fine job you're doing of that. Assassins? You didn't think perhaps you should have mentioned it when I last saw you? Or that you should have sent me word?"

Iolanthe's fingers tensed against her hips, pressing into the black scales of her armour, and Kyter sensed her hurt. Bleu's lack of belief in her ability to handle the situation and get herself out of it, belittling her strength, pained her. He knew it to be true because he had been in her position countless times, wanting the one who stood before him to be proud of him, not punish him for his mistakes, or others' actions.

"Lay off her." Kyter narrowed his golden eyes on Bleu and couldn't stop the dark inky ribbons as they twined around his bones, his demonic genes awakening as he called on every shred of his strength and every ounce of his power, knowing that Bleu would sense it and how dangerous he was.

How serious he was.

Bleu shifted his gaze to Kyter, sliding him a look that promised pain. Kyter didn't flinch. If the elf wanted to fight, he would slug it out with him, and he wouldn't hold back.

He wouldn't stop until Bleu was pissing blood and begging for mercy.

Iolanthe appearing between them sent his blood from a raging boil to a simmer. Her slender hand pressed against his bare chest, warm on his skin, her touch soothing him. She had her other hand against her brother, holding him back.

She swung between them, looking at both of them several times. "I will do what I think is right. I am old enough to make my own decisions."

Kyter's shoulders relaxed and he leaned back on his heels, crushing his need to fight Bleu for Iolanthe's sake when he realised that it was upsetting her. She didn't show it, but he knew her well enough now to see it in her eyes and in how her hand trembled against his chest.

She didn't want a collar.

She didn't want a master.

She didn't want a male who treated her as a possession, something he owned.

Both he and her brother were guilty of doing such a thing, trying to control her and making her do as they wanted.

He sighed and risked his balls by settling his left hand in the small of her back. She looked down at his arm and then up into his eyes, a soft look in hers. The corners of her lips twitched, as if she wanted to smile but couldn't quite manage one. He smiled for her, raised his other hand and placed it over the one she held against his chest. He curled his fingers around her slender hand, pressing their tips into her palm.

"What do you want to do?" he said in a low voice he hoped conveyed that he was sorry he had lost his head again and had tried to make her decisions for her.

It was her life on the line. She was entitled to decide the path she would take to save it, no matter what.

Iolanthe looked between him and Bleu again, her eyes lingering longest on him. She sighed.

"I hate to say this, but Bleu is right. His apartment is within the castle of the elf kingdom, and the assassins cannot enter it. It would be the wisest choice. I would be surprised if any of the assassins could slip into the elf kingdom. Besides, I need access to the library there." She took the dagger from Bleu and held it up for Kyter to see, clutching the twisted black and silver hilt of the short double-edged blade. There was writing on it. Strange symbols. "We need to know what the inscription says if we are going to find your father."

He felt Bleu's gaze shoot to him. "Father?"

Kyter wasn't in the mood to explain. He was too tired and everything was catching up with him, including the fact that Iolanthe was still talking about using the artefact to give him his vengeance.

He took the dagger from her, surprised that she let him and that she trusted him with it when it was the price for her life.

Her life.

He slid the hand on her back around her waist and pulled her against him, filled with a fierce need to hold her and feel her in his arms. He wrapped both of them around her, pinning her against him, and pressed his cheek to hers.

"Don't disappear like that again," he whispered and tightened his hold on her, clutching her and crushing her to his bare chest.

"I will not. I wanted to protect you. I thought—"

"I know what you thought," he interjected and closed his eyes, absorbing the feel of her, his strength fading as it sank in that she was safe and back with him. He wouldn't let anything happen to her. He would do a better job as her male. He would keep her safe. "It hurt... the thought that I might have lost you."

His throat closed and he couldn't voice the rest of what he wanted to say.

She managed to wriggle her arms free beneath his and he sighed as she wrapped them around him, pressing her palms to his bare back, and feathered kisses across his shoulder.

"That would never happen." Her light tone held a teasing note and she settled her cheek against him as he rubbed his against hers, taking pleasure from the feel of her skin on his and her scent. "I do not seem to be able to escape you."

He smiled at that and pressed a light kiss to her cheek. "I will never let you escape me."

Bleu grunted. "We are leaving."

Iolanthe pulled back, looked over her shoulder at her brother and nodded.

"We can discuss everything back at the castle once I gain permission for you to remain there, and I will arrange access to the library for you." Bleu caught hold of her arm and tugged her out of Kyter's embrace, and not-so-subtly inserted himself between her and Kyter, wedging them apart.

Iolanthe sighed.

Kyter wanted to throttle Bleu, but he could also understand where the male was coming from and that it would take a while for him to get used to Iolanthe having another male in her life.

By the sounds of things, Bleu had saved Iolanthe's life more than once. In Bleu's eyes, Kyter was probably another problem to rescue her from, one he would handle in tandem with saving her from the assassins.

The elf was just going to have to deal with the fact that Kyter was going nowhere, at least not until Iolanthe was safe from the assassins forever.

After that?

It was down to Iolanthe.

She was right and it was her decision to make, not his nor Bleu's.

Kyter wanted to be in her life, and he would fight to stay with her and make her see that they belonged together, but in the end, he would abide whatever decision she made.

He only hoped the feeling that had come over him earlier, when she had looked at him, and the deep primal instinct it had awakened in him was right.

She had already made that decision.

She wanted to be his mate.

CHAPTER 21

Kyter gasped beside Iolanthe as they appeared in the enormous verdant courtyard of the castle of the elf kingdom. She glanced past her brother to him and found him staring at the beautiful pale and dark stone castle that loomed before them, made up of tall towers topped with conical tiled roofs set on a series of large square buildings with balconies. The main building had five storeys, and the thick towers that rose above it to spear the darkening sky added another six levels.

Bleu had chased her up one of the towers when she had been nothing but a child, laughing the whole time. She had wanted to see the nest of eagles at the top. She had never seen the rare birds before and had only heard of them, the stories people told of them something like legends in her land.

When they had reached the very top level of the tower, where huge arched windows without glass allowed the breeze to cut straight through the circular room, she had gasped like Kyter had done a moment ago, shocked by what she had seen.

The great tawny birds had been gigantic, the single chick large enough to carry her off. Bleu had caught her shoulder and pulled her close to him, and she had ended up wrapping her arms around his leg, clutching him as excitement had given way to fear.

He had told her that he wouldn't let them hurt her.

He would protect her.

He would always protect her.

She sighed and touched her brother's hand. He looked down at it and the black scales drew back, funnelling into his wristband and leaving his hand exposed. She brushed the back of his hand with hers, an action she had done often over the centuries, a silent signal that she was glad he was with her.

He knocked his knuckles against hers and shot her a smile as he led the way into the imposing castle.

The two males guarding the massive arched entrance lowered their long black spears to block his path, crossing them in front of the door.

"I am taking my sister and her... fated male... to my apartment. Prince Loren has given his blessing."

The males exchanged a glance and withdrew their spears, granting her brother entrance. Her brother was a liar, but she appreciated it. She didn't want to wait in the courtyard while he spoke to their prince, because the guards and high-ranking elves were already looking at her.

Or more specifically her armour.

She squirmed under their scrutiny and wished Bleu had given her a chance to change into something else before teleporting them to the castle.

Kyter took hold of her hand and squeezed lightly, and she lifted her eyes to his face. He smiled at her and started towards the door, leading her into the castle. She could sense the change in him, the wariness that had started the moment they had appeared in the courtyard. He was on edge and on the defensive. It was there in the way he prowled along the pale stone corridor, a dangerous yet sensual edge to his gait.

The unadorned walls glittered in the light coming in from the door. Bleu led them through the corridors towards the back of the castle, and Kyter's pace slowed as they reached the hallway where statues of their former kings and queens lined the walls. His gaze leaped over them and he pointed towards the statue at the far end, beyond the stone staircase.

"I know him," he said, a charming edge to his smile, one that told her that being familiar with one single thing in the castle, and the prince at that, had made him feel more comfortable in this place.

"Yes, apparently you got him drunk," she countered and Bleu chuckled.

It had been a long time since she had heard her brother laugh. So long that it caught her off guard and she could only stare at him, absorbing the rich sound of it as it wrapped around her, echoing off the high ceilings of the castle and transporting her back to better times, when she had been a child and her brother had laughed freely as he had played with her. When it faded, she looked between Kyter and Bleu.

"Was it funny?" She found that difficult to believe.

"He trashed my club... but it was kind of funny when it happened. One minute he's cool as a cucumber and the next he was out of control. Fought a demon too. All because the demon touched Olivia." Kyter grinned but she still didn't think it sounded like a particularly fun time, especially for their prince.

Bleu stopped at the bottom of the staircase and looked back at her. "It was quite funny. Gods, I hope I never find my fated female if I am destined to act like a prick like every male I have met who found theirs."

Iolanthe scowled at him.

Kyter's grin only widened. "True... but it is worth it. Having the one female made for you in your arms is a pretty priceless thing."

Iolanthe blushed and Bleu glared daggers at Kyter, huffed and stomped up the stairs. Kyter went to follow him but Iolanthe remained where she was and he stopped on the bottom step, his hand still holding hers.

"What?" he said.

Her gaze followed her brother and her heart throbbed, aching for him. Kyter couldn't see it, but Bleu was hurting, and she had a terrible feeling she knew the source of his pain.

A female.

She shook her head. "Nothing."

Kyter frowned and she smiled, brushed her thumb over his and then sighed when she realised he wasn't going to let it go at that. She looked beyond him to her brother where he waited at the top of the elegant staircase and then back at him.

"Just… try to keep mention of females and fated ones to a minimum," she whispered, not wanting her brother to hear, because he would be angry if he did.

He had too much pride sometimes, and not enough at others.

"He has to get used to us being fated." Kyter stepped down beside her.

Iolanthe shook her head. "I am not speaking about us. I cannot explain… but… please?"

He searched her eyes and then nodded. "Whatever you want."

She had a feeling he was talking about more than just not speaking about women or fated mates in front of her brother. She had caught the look in his golden eyes when they had been back at the ledge, the one that had clearly told her that he was giving power over their relationship to her. He was letting her be in control—of their future, and of him.

She led Kyter up the stairs towards her brother, ignoring Bleu's curious gaze. When she reached him, he walked on, turning the corner towards the next set of stairs off to her left. The stone on this floor was dark and Bleu had warned her before that the prince had his apartment on this level and that she had to be quiet when moving around on it.

She had only met Prince Loren once, around five centuries ago, and the male had been formidable, issuing orders to several legions of the army that had gathered in the courtyard. Bleu had been seeing her off at the time and had explained that they were going after Prince Vail.

At her last meeting with Bleu, he had told her that Prince Vail was no longer a threat to their species. He hadn't seemed pleased by the news, but she knew without asking that was because he was close to Prince Loren and saw the prince in private, and knew his innermost feelings about his brother and their war. Bleu feared Prince Vail would still be the death of Prince Loren one day.

They followed Bleu up to the next level and he stopped in front of a wooden door, hesitated, and then sighed and pushed it open.

Iolanthe gaped at the mess.

Kyter chuckled. "Bachelor life looks the same no matter the species."

Bleu grumbled something and began teleporting the clothes strewn across the floor of the expansive room, and then all the weaponry, using his powers to send the clothes somewhere, she didn't want to know where, and stack the weapons in the corner to her left near a set of low cupboards.

The pale blue covers on the double bed directly in front of her, opposite the door, were rumpled.

She sighed. Her brother never had been very neat.

The three arched windows above the bed allowed light to flood into the dark stone room. Bleu crossed the room to the tall arched door to their right and opened it, letting air into the room. It smelled like home. The scent of the blue flowers blooming on the carved wooden structure of beams and braces over the balcony carried through the room, teasing her and relaxing her at the same time.

Kyter drifted towards the open door and she smiled. She wanted to see the view too and breathe it all in, but she suspected the need was more pressing for him. Her homeland held countless new scents and sights for him to experience.

She waited until he was out of the room and her brother was walking back to her before moving deeper into it. She eyed the dark wooden wardrobes that lined the deep grey stone wall to her right, next to an arched opening to another room, and then looked back towards the balcony. Her gaze snagged on the low wooden side table beside the bed.

She smiled at the picture in the silver frame. "You kept it?"

Bleu nodded and smiled. "It is a good picture. You look stupid in it."

She mock-frowned at him. "You are supposed to say I look beautiful in it."

"Beautiful... stupid... both." His smile became a smirk and her frown became real. His expression lost all emotion again. "I must go."

He went to pass her and she caught his right wrist, stopping him in his tracks. He looked down at her hand on him and then up into her eyes, and then behind him towards the balcony.

Towards Kyter.

"Was he telling the truth?" Bleu said in the elf tongue.

Iolanthe nodded. "He is my fated male."

Bleu scrubbed his left hand down his face and muttered, "Everyone is getting sucked into this mate thing."

"I am not sure what I will do yet." Iolanthe turned her focus back to Kyter and watched him through the windows as he walked along the balcony, taking everything in.

Bleu looked there too and was silent for long seconds before heaving a sigh. "I have only known Kyter a short time, but he is a good male."

Iolanthe couldn't hide her shock on hearing those words leaving his lips and couldn't stop herself from looking back at him to see whether he was only teasing her with what she had wanted to hear. Her brother smiled at her, this one reaching his violet eyes, and stroked his free hand over her hair.

"You almost sound as if you are giving your blessing to the match," she whispered, studying his face to see whether she had imagined it or whether he really did approve of Kyter.

He leaned towards her and pressed a kiss to her forehead. "Not even close, but I will give you time to speak with him and decide what you want to do. I will return in the morning."

He tried to pull away but she refused to release him. She held him firm, her hand shaking against his wrist and nerves setting her heart off at a pace. She didn't want to hurt him, but she had to ask. She had to know.

"Iolanthe?"

She closed her eyes, steeled herself for his reaction, and then opened her eyes and raised them to meet his. "What happened with the mortal female?"

A brief shadow of hurt danced across his handsome features before it disappeared, replaced by a cold and distant look. "Sometimes things do not work out."

Iolanthe slipped her hand down to his and held it. "She was not your ki'ara though."

"No." The flat, emotionless way he spoke that word told Iolanthe just how much the female had hurt him.

Her brother had never been very good at expressing his emotions, at least not around people other than her, or handling them well. He was passionate though, a male capable of great devotion and tenderness, one who held a wealth of love inside him. He hid that side of himself behind a wall of ice at times, affecting the air of a male who could have dalliances with a female and not feel anything for them, or who could never have his heart broken.

It was all a lie.

Her brother's heart was broken.

"You will meet her one day," she offered, pressing her fingers to his palm and refusing to let him look away from her.

He smiled and touched her cheek, but the sorrow in his eyes lingered. "You are the only female who could love me forever, Io… the rest only love me for now or not at all."

Tears lined her lashes and she clutched his hand tighter, shaking her head as the belief behind those words tore at her heart.

When she had been a child, Bleu had often visited her, taking her on long walks and teaching her things. He had talked to her of finding his mate one day and she had hoped his female would be able to match his passion and devotion to those he loved. He had never stopped talking about finding his ki'ara, not until everything that had been happening between the two princes had grown more intense and dangerous. He had dedicated his life to Prince Loren then, becoming his right hand man, relinquishing his desire to find his mate.

He had devoted himself to his prince and now that prince had found his mate.

And that mate's friend had broken Bleu's heart.

Iolanthe blamed Prince Loren for her brother's pain too. He had taken Bleu with him to the Third Realm, where a demon king reigned. A demon king who was the mortal female's fated male. Bleu had told Iolanthe that he would fight for the female, and part of her had hoped that he would win, even when she had known it wouldn't end well for her brother.

Now Bleu had to see his prince happily mated and see his prince's mate at the castle, and most likely the woman he had been falling for too.

It was cruel.

Too cruel.

Her beautiful brother deserved better than that.

She pulled on his hand, tugging him towards her, and wrapped her arms around his neck. He was still for a moment and then slipped his arms around her back and held her, his head on her shoulder. He didn't have to be strong around her. He didn't have to cover his hurt and pretend it didn't exist. She was his sister. She was always in his corner and on his side and she would never hurt him.

She held him to her and brought her lips to his ear.

"One day you will discover that I am not the only female who could love you forever, Bleu." She kissed his cheek and he sighed. "But I am a female who will mourn on the day your love for me is shared with another."

He held her closer, pressing his hands into her lower back. "I will love you forever, Io, whether I find my mate or not… no one can take my love from you."

She closed her eyes and savoured the feel of him in her arms, her beloved brother. She felt blessed to have him.

"None can take my love from you, either," she whispered.

He pulled back and smiled. "Not even an annoying jaguar shifter?"

Her lips curved. "Not even Kyter."

Bleu lowered his gaze and then lifted it back to hers and nodded before stepping away from her, his hands falling from her waist. "I will go and speak with Prince Loren to inform him of the situation and request permission to use the library, and will return tomorrow. Stay in my apartments until then."

She nodded, tiptoed and pressed a kiss to his cheek. "Thank you for lending your apartments to us."

Bleu grimaced against her lips. "Be silent now… because I do not want to think about my little sister with a male, let alone with a male in my bedroom."

She wanted to laugh at how uncomfortable he looked when she settled back on her feet and released him but held it inside. He grumbled to himself, pale green-purple light traced over the contours of his body, and he disappeared.

Iolanthe was still smiling as she walked towards the balcony, heading towards her male where he waited for her.

Feeling as if she was heading towards her future.

CHAPTER 22

"Is Bleu okay?" Kyter looked back at her as Iolanthe stepped out onto the balcony and lifted her arm, brushing her fingers through the beautiful leafy green canopy and the pale blue flowers. Their fragrance hung in the air, a sweet smell that made her feel she had come home.

"About us?" Iolanthe asked and he ran his golden eyes over her from head to toe and back again. They gained a dark edge that sent a thrill through her, awakening a desire to slide into his arms and steal a kiss.

Kyter leaned his back against the dark stone balustrade of the balcony.

The lush green rolling countryside beyond the castle's high stone walls was a fitting backdrop for him, a beautiful display of nature at her finest, made possible by an ingenious portal thought up by Prince Loren and Prince Vail. It brought light from the mortal world into theirs. They harnessed the power of her species to form portals that allowed water to flow into their lands too. Their two princes had made this verdant and thriving land possible in the darkest reaches of Hell, making her kind the envy of the other realms. She could see those realms in the distance all around her, where the light from the portal above her gave way to darkness.

"No." Kyter raked another appreciative look over her. "Not us. I'm not sure what has upset him. Back in Pompeii, he said that he wanted to take his mind off something. He seems off... I've never seen him like this."

Iolanthe warmed inside, touched that Kyter was concerned about her brother and that he knew Bleu well enough already to detect when something was wrong with him. She hoped that they could become even closer friends. She liked the idea of having Kyter and her brother in her life, all of them together.

"Is it something to do with that huntress from Archangel?"

That question caught her off guard and she couldn't conceal her surprise as she looked into Kyter's eyes. He knew about the mortal female? She recalled that he had mentioned her brother being at his bar with their prince, and the prince's mate. It stood to reason that the female hunter would have been there too. Kyter had witnessed her brother's behaviour around the female, and that female's behaviour towards him. He must have seen what Bleu had feared— that the female didn't share his feelings.

She considered shaking her head, wanting to protect her brother, but then nodded, because Bleu would need support now. Friends. If Kyter knew, he could tread carefully around Bleu and might be able to help him through this troubled time.

Kyter sighed. "I had a bad feeling it might be. Think he'll be okay?"

It was her turn to sigh as she stared out at the beautiful vista, over the orchard below them within the pale stone walls of the courtyard, to the rolling hills and the villages beyond that. Her village was there. The village where she had grown up learning how to fight from Bleu and eagerly awaiting his visits, and listening to him speak of his fated female.

"I believe he will be. It will hurt, but he will overcome it. I can only hope that he can find his ki'ara."

"Ki'ara?" Kyter frowned across his shoulder at her as she leaned against the balcony railing beside him, facing the courtyard and the realm beyond it, her elbows resting on the dark stone.

"It is the elf term for a fated female. The male's eternal mate." She looked away from the beautiful view, settling her eyes on one that felt more beautiful right now.

Her fated mate. Her male.

His golden eyes were bright in the evening light. That warm light hung matching golden threads in his sandy hair. It was still damp, tousled and wild. When he had been injured, she had felt as if her heart would split in two and had been paralyzed by her fear that the male Fernandez had sent, one of his top assassins, would deal the finishing blow.

A blow that would take Kyter from her.

The thought of losing him had driven her to comply with the assassins, to do whatever it took to keep him safe and alive. Even leave him when it had killed her to do such a thing.

It had also made her aware of the depth of her feelings for the jaguar shifter.

She turned towards him and ran her hand down his bare arm, tracing the contours of his powerful muscles. "You would be my ki'aro."

"Ki'aro," he said but she could see from his eyes that he was stuck on how she had phrased things, specifically using him as her reference for the elf term for a fated male rather than speaking in general as she had for females.

She nodded and went to look back at the view, but he shifted to face her and caught her cheek, keeping her eyes on him, his filled with warmth and an intensity she couldn't decipher.

"Iolanthe?" he murmured and shifted closer, until his body brushed hers, sending a warm shiver through her that had her leaning closer to him. "Whatever happens... whether we mate or we never mate... it won't change my feelings for you. I can't lie and say I don't want you as my bonded mate, but I am willing to wait. If I have to wait forever, I will wait forever. Just being with you is enough for me."

She wasn't sure how to respond to that. It touched her deeply and she knew he was speaking from his heart again. He didn't want to pressure her into mating with him and forming a bond between them. That he would do that for her only made her fall harder for him.

He would wait for her. Being with her was enough for him.

She didn't want to wait. This wasn't enough for her.

Speaking with her brother had made her realise that.

Kyter was the male who had been made just for her. Her one shot at a love that would last forever.

And she did love him.

She knew now that he would never force her to do anything, would never seek to control her, or tell her what to do. He wanted to stand at her side and keep her safe, to protect her and take care of her. She wanted to do the same with him.

She wanted forever with him.

There was a vast difference in their natural lifespans though. In order to have forever with him, she needed to bind them through a mating. It would significantly increase his lifespan, allowing him to live for thousands of years as she could.

Iolanthe slipped her hand into his and led him away from the balcony.

"Where are we going?" he husked, the raspy edge to his deep voice speaking to her of his desire, stirring her own.

"Not to the bed." She looked back over her shoulder at him and he frowned at her, disappointment colouring his expression. A smile tugged at her lips and she pulled him towards the arched entrance to the next room, off to her left. "The waters in my realm are very pure and have healing properties. I want to bathe your ankle."

His golden eyes took on a wicked shimmer. "And the rest of me? Because I'm fairly damp and dirty from Pompeii."

She raked a look over him, not showing a single drop of the arousal that bolted through her at the thought of bathing with him. "I would say you are dirty, but perhaps not in the manner you mean it."

He grinned, flashing short fangs, and passed her, tugging her along now. Her eyes slowly lowered down his lean back to the sensual dips above his backside and then traversed his long legs to his ankles. There was a cut in the back of his right boot where the sword had sliced clean through the leather. Her stomach somersaulted at the memory of seeing that blow happen, hobbling him before her eyes, and she tightened her grip on his hand, reassuring herself that he was here and he was well again now.

He entered the bathing chamber ahead of her and stopped dead.

"I never knew Bleu had such a swanky place." Kyter stared at the room, his eyes darting over the elegant stone basins that hung from the wall to her right below large mirrors and the other facilities, and settling back on the bathing pool.

It was raised from the floor, three broad steps leading up to the wide rim, made from the same dark stone as the floor and walls.

"It looks like a bloody swimming pool."

She smiled at Kyter's shock and moved past him, stepping into the light cast through the first of the three arched windows in the left wall. "All of the apartments in the castle have such bathing facilities. The warm water is pumped up from a natural hot spring. Bleu is fortunate to have rooms here in the castle. I have heard the quarters in the barracks for normal soldiers are cramped, with two or more to a room, and they share a single communal bathing pool."

Kyter shuddered. "Good thing for us your brother is the prince's best friend."

Her eyebrows rose. She supposed Bleu was in a way Prince Loren's closest companion. She had never really thought about it before. It pleased her that her brother had such friends, but made her angrier with the prince at the same time. Prince Loren had allowed Bleu's feelings to be hurt by the mortal huntress and insisted on having her around him. A good friend wouldn't put her brother through such cruelty.

"You do not like the thought of sharing a bath?" she said to shake off her anger at the prince and bring her focus back to Kyter.

She pulled the silver pin from her black hair and teleported it away from her. Her long black hair tumbled down her back as she took the stone steps up to the huge rectangular bathing pool, commanding her armour to disappear at the same time. Kyter's gaze burned into her, setting her on fire as the black scales swept over her body, revealing it to him.

"Hell no... not with anyone other than you." He stalked after her and she swayed her hips, teasing him as her armour finally finished obeying her command, leaving her nude with the exception of the twin black and silver bands around her wrists. "The thought of you bathing in a communal pool... gods, I think I would kill every male in the vicinity."

She took the deep step down into the pool that also acted as a seat and looked back at him over her shoulder as she took the second step to the bottom and sank down into the hot water.

Kyter growled.

Iolanthe smiled as she rolled to face him, enjoying the way the water heated her right down to her bones and soothed all her aches away. She ducked her head backwards, wetting her hair, and ran her hands over it, smoothing it back from her face.

"Does the kitty not want to get wet?" she teased and his eyes darkened and then brightened to liquid gold.

He toed off his boots, grimacing as he removed his right one, and made swift work of unbuttoning his olive combat trousers.

She almost purred as he shoved them down, revealing his glorious body to her hungry eyes. He kicked out of his trousers, tugged his socks off, and prowled towards her, a sensual yet lethal predator stalking his prey.

"I'll have you know that jaguars love to swim. We're water babies and we like hunting prey in water."

He ascended the stone stairs and then stepped down into the water.

His pained grimace as his right ankle hit the water spoiled his seductive allure and she got to her feet and waded towards him, concern making her move.

She caught his arm and helped him sit on the deep stone step in the water, trying not to smile at his sour expression or the bitter disappointment that laced his earthy scent. His pride looked a little dented but she was sure he would bounce back.

"Let me take a look." She kneeled in the water before him and he regained his seductive air, splaying his arms out along the side of the pool and looking down at her through hooded eyes. Water glistened on his bare chest, clinging to powerful honed muscles that she wanted to explore with her lips and tongue.

She tamped down that desire and focused on his ankle.

Iolanthe carefully took hold of it and lifted it from the water. He grimaced again and she caught it, issuing an apologetic smile as she lowered his leg back towards the surface of the water, lessening the strain on his Achilles tendon.

The wound was healed but still dark pink. She flinched whenever he did as she probed it gently, feeling her way along the tendon and over the bones of his ankle.

"Bleu gave me elf medicine for it." His deep voice echoed in the chamber, curling around her, teasing her ears and making her mind leap to imagine how he would sound as she pleasured him.

She wanted to hear him growl and roar in this place and have it encompass her, speaking to her of his strength and power.

"I can imagine that hurt." She probed the tendon again. Elf medicine such as the type her brother had given to Kyter accelerated the healing process, but it meant suffering all of the pain he would have endured during that healing process in one short numbing burst.

She looked up at him but he didn't give away whether it had hurt or not. He stared at her, eyes hooded and dark with desire, a predator eyeing his prey again. She surmised it had hurt and he wasn't willing to admit it, in case it damaged her opinion of him as a strong male and his pride suffered another blow.

"Bleu hates it," she said to Kyter's ankle as she finished checking it. "He complains whenever he has to use it. He believes it is akin to torture and will often go without it if he can, coping with his injury until it heals naturally."

She glanced at him and he still didn't give away whether it had hurt him or not. Males. She wouldn't think any less of him if he admitted that he had experienced great pain. He had endured it. That made him strong in her eyes.

He had endured the injury when it had happened too, dealing with it far better than she could have, or most of the males she had met in her life. Most would have passed out from the pain, but he hadn't. Because he had felt the need to remain awake in order to protect her?

Had he suffered with the pain just so he would be there if she needed him?

Her heart said that he had. He hadn't wanted to leave her vulnerable to the four males. It must have taken incredible willpower to remain conscious and incredible strength to move as he had, trying to protect her from the males and then comforting her after they had gone.

It must have been painful for him to see that male touch her as he had and know he could do nothing to stop him.

She lowered Kyter's ankle and her gaze with it, staring into the clear water at the bottom of the pool between his legs.

"I am sorry they hurt you... I am sorry you have been dragged into this. It was not what I wanted."

He leaned forwards, smoothed his palm along her jaw and gently raised her eyes up to his. There was only warmth in his golden gaze, tenderness that flooded her with heat and soothed her.

"I know. You tried to protect me from them. You don't need to, Iolanthe. We're stronger if we do things together. I won't let that guy get the jump on me again. I won't let him near you. Understand?" His eyes searched hers, intense and focused, filled with dark promise that spoke to her heart and made her believe that he would keep that vow and would kill the male if they ever saw him again. She nodded and he half-smiled as he stroked her cheek. "You are mine to protect now, and I'm yours. We'll have each other's backs... as partners should."

Partners.

She smiled at the meaning behind that word. They were more than lovers. More than fated mates. They were partners. They would face everything together.

Not with her held behind him, shielded and unable to act freely.

But side by side, on equal footing.

Iolanthe released his leg, rose out of the water while remaining on her knees, and brought her lips close to his. He dropped his head and claimed them, his kiss sweet and tender, filled with emotion that spread through her, making her feel light and airy inside, as if she was floating. Each barely-there sweep of his lips across hers sent her higher and warmth mixed with light flowed through her body, leaving her craving more of his kiss.

More of the wonderful feeling of being with him, sharing a quiet intimate moment, one that would stay with her forever.

She shifted closer to him, kneeling between his thighs, and he cupped the nape of her neck and deepened the kiss, turning all of the warmth and light inside her into heat and fire.

He moaned into her mouth as his other hand dropped beneath the water to clutch her backside and she joined him as he tugged her closer, shifting to the edge of the stone seat at the same time. His body pressed against hers and she lowered her hands to it, unable to resist her need to touch him again.

She stroked her hands over the broad slabs of his chest, his taut nipples grazing her palms, and drifted them lower, caressing and teasing every ridge of muscle on his stomach. She slowly worked her way downwards as she kissed him and smiled against his lips as her hands reached the water and the head of his hard shaft and he groaned into her mouth.

"Iolanthe." The plea in her name and the gravelly edge of desire in his voice made her give him what he desired.

She wrapped her left hand around his rigid length and stroked downwards, revealing the crown and feeling him pulse against her palm. He kissed her hard, the demanding press of his mouth on hers sending hot shivers through her, and she stroked him, gliding her hand up and down his length, teasing him until he felt like iron and was groaning into her mouth.

She bit back a squeak as he suddenly grabbed her around the waist, hauled her from the water as if she weighed nothing, and settled her astride his thighs. The cooler air chilled her skin and goose bumps broke out across it, her nipples tightening into hard peaks. Water ran from the tangled threads of her long black hair, rolling down her back to the water that lapped at her waist.

Kyter didn't break the kiss. He angled his head and claimed the nape of her neck with his right hand, pressing his fingers in hard as he held her to his mouth. She moaned and slid down his thighs, another hot blast of tingles racing through her as their bodies came into contact, his hard length pressing deliciously between her plush petals.

Iolanthe wrapped her arms around his neck and clung to him as she kissed him, tangling her tongue with his, and rocked against him, rubbing herself along his length beneath the water. Ripples spread outwards from them, gentle waves that rolled towards the sides of the pool, bounced off it and came back again.

Kyter dropped his free hand beneath the water and clutched her backside as he sank lower, bringing his bottom away from the edge of the pool and his body more underneath hers. The position placed him closer to her, so she could feel every inch of his cock as she rubbed against him, and she forgot everything she had intended to do.

They could wash later.

All she wanted to do right now was lose herself in Kyter again.

His hungry mouth devoured hers, mastering and driving her into submission. She ran her hands over his shoulders and down his chest, delighting in the feel of his powerful body. Each sweep of her hands had the fire in her belly growing hotter, stoking her need for him. She moaned as she ground against him, fevered and aching for more.

"Iolanthe," he murmured, husky and beautiful, his need for her lacing her name in a way that she would always love.

He hid nothing from her.

She moaned in response to him and shifted forwards again, so her knees pressed against the side of the pool behind him and they were as close as they could get.

"Kyter," she whispered against his lips and feathered them with kisses, teasing him as she rolled her hips under the water, rubbing herself against his hard shaft.

He groaned and his length kicked against her. Both hands dropped to her backside and he moved her, sliding her up and down, further than she had been shifting. The head of his length rubbed her aroused nub and she moaned and forgot about kissing him as she breathed hard against his face, lost in the feel of him and the sensations lighting her up inside.

"Can't wait." He caught her under her backside with one hand, raised her up his body, and then pushed her down.

Iolanthe tipped her head back and groaned as the head of his hard length nudged into her slick centre and he lowered her onto him, the slow joining driving her wild with need. She wanted to press down onto him, taking him quickly into her, but she also wanted to savour it and feel every inch of him as he entered her.

Slow won and she moaned with him as she slid down onto his cock until she couldn't take any more of him. He angled his hips then, sinking lower still in the water, enough that he could drive deeper, claiming all of her as the head struck her deepest point. She had never felt so full. So wonderful.

He grunted and grasped her hips and moved her on him, slow and steady, raising her almost all the way off him before driving her back down. The waves that flowed outwards from them across the pool grew larger, the sounds of the splashing joining their deep moans and groans as passion and need overtook them, seizing control of both of them.

Iolanthe clutched his shoulders, pressing her nails into his muscles, and tipped her head back, arching forwards as she rode him. She writhed, shifting her hips in an almost circular motion with each thrust, a slave to her desire. Kyter groaned, pressed one hand to her back and pulled her stomach against his. His lips descended on her breasts, his mouth wrapping around her left nipple and tugging on it as he drove into her, deeper and harder, his tempo building in time with her arousal as it soared and consumed her.

She gave herself over to it, riding him harder, driven by Kyter's grunts and growls as he plunged into her on every downwards thrust and suckled her nipples, alternating between them.

Each deep plunge onto him had her pert nub brushing against his hard body, sending thrills chasing through her that only made her move faster as she sought her release.

She lost awareness of the raw and primal sounds of their lovemaking as she raised her head and looked down at Kyter, watching his pleasure as he suckled her breasts, his handsome face etched with a frown.

She lost awareness of their wild and untamed movements as her eyes slowly glided over his damp sandy tousled hair to the strong line of his throat.

She was only aware of one thing as she stared at his pulse hammering beneath his skin.

Kyter was her fated male.

"Iolanthe?" He lifted his head from her breasts, his eyes coming up to meet hers.

Kyter would be her mate.

She struck hard, sinking her fangs into the strong curve of the right side of his throat. His roar deafened her as he threw his head back, echoing around the room, and he jerked against her, his claws slicing into her skin where he clutched her back and bottom.

Iolanthe closed her eyes and moaned as she made her first pull on his vein. His strong hot blood flowed into her, sliding down her throat, and she wanted to scream out her pleasure as that heat spread through her and Kyter thrust into her at the same time. Not only her pleasure.

His too.

It swirled through her, growing in strength as his blood in her body forged a powerful connection between them, the beginning of a bond that she felt sure would last forever.

He pumped into her, hard and fast, grunting into her ear as she drank from his vein, unwilling to surrender it. The intoxicating taste of him was too divine, too addictive, and the connection blossoming between them with each drop more she drank was too beautiful. Their feelings collided in a mind-numbing rush that had her heart thundering in time with his, their bodies and souls becoming as one for a glorious moment.

He growled and then roared again as she took a final pull on his vein, stealing another mouthful of his rich blood.

He turned with her, sending water spilling across the floor, and pressed one knee onto the seat of the pool and her back into the wall as he took her. Each wild deep thrust of his body into hers tore a cry from her as she released his throat and held on to him, unable to do anything other than cling to him as he brought them both to the brink.

He snarled, flashing his upper and lower fangs, his eyes bright gold as he frowned down at her, driving her into submission, every inch of him tensed and straining.

Her eyes dropped to the right side of his throat and the twin trails of blood running down it towards his chest.

He growled, grunted and roared as the fire that had been building within her finally exploded through her veins and she cried out as she quivered from head to toe, her body throbbing around his. He clutched her in place on him and breathed hard as he spilled inside her, his heart beating in time with hers and his feelings flowing through her. Pleasure gave way to shock and his eyes slowly opened and found hers.

A touch of colour rose onto his cheeks as he looked down at her and the position he held her in, pinned against the hard edge of the pool, one leg dangling into the water and the other wrapped around his back.

He didn't need to apologise for the way he had taken her. She had been the one to awaken that primal side of him, the wild part of him that felt a demanding need to mate with her too.

He gently lowered her into the water, turned with her and settled with his back against the wall of the pool and her astride his thighs, their bodies still intimately entwined.

Iolanthe dipped her head and stroked her tongue over the twin trails of blood on his chest, following them up to the puncture wounds on his throat. She laved them, savouring his rich blood and how he trembled and moaned in response to each sweep of her tongue.

"Iolanthe?" he husked and she felt sure her voice would sound just as hoarse if she could find it to answer him.

She had screamed at the top of her lungs when she had climaxed.

A blush stained her cheeks now, awareness of where they were sinking in and making her want to bury her face in Kyter's shoulder. She didn't want to think about how many people in the castle had heard her, or Kyter.

"Mmm?" she murmured, halfway to hiding against his neck.

He caught her arms and peeled her off him. She tried to stifle her blush and managed to lift her eyes to his. There was only one question in them, and it looked to her as if the answer meant the world to him.

She stroked his chest, feeling his heart beating hard against it.

A heart that beat in time with hers and would do until they had completed the bond she had just triggered. It was faster than she was used to, a rapid tempo that would take her some time to grow comfortable with, but one she wouldn't change for anything in the world.

She took hold of his hand and pressed it against her chest, holding it there while she touched his.

His eyes widened, his shock rippling through her. It was a strange sensation, and one she would have to become accustomed to since that part of their bond was permanent. She would always be able to sense his feelings, and he would be able to sense hers. They were linked now, and forever.

"Iolanthe?" he whispered again, his eyes searching hers now, desperate for the answer to his unspoken question.

She smiled to show him that his suspicions were correct and finally found her voice as she leaned in to kiss him.

"Yes, Ki'aro?"

He growled and swooped on her mouth, his kiss tender yet filled with the raw passion she had come to love about him.

Would always love about him.

Nothing would change that or her feelings for him.

She relaxed into him and let him kiss her, chasing away the fear that began to rise at the back of her mind again, unwilling to allow it into her heart to spoil this moment with him. Tonight she would celebrate their love and the beginning of their bond.

Tomorrow she would face her fears again and she would overcome them, because with Kyter at her side she could do anything.

Even outwit a master assassin and kill a legendary demon.

CHAPTER 23

Kyter lay on his front on the enormous bed in the huge stone room, his bare legs tangled in the silky blue covers and his head turned to his right, towards the open arched doors that led to the balcony. It wasn't the pale blue curtains dancing in the warm breeze that had his attention though.

It was the picture on the dark wooden side table.

The silver frame was elegant, fitting of the beauty in the photograph. She wore a sky blue dress made of sheer layers, held in place over her torso by thick swirls of silver metal that he guessed was a sort of corset in this land. Her violet eyes were bright, shimmering with her wide smile as she held aloft a huge blue tear-drop-shaped sapphire attached to a chain.

His heart pounded at the sight of her.

The corners of his lips curved as he sensed Iolanthe's arrival in the room. She had gone back to Pompeii to retrieve his pack. He had insisted on going with her but she had been far more persistent in insisting that he stay in bed, because teleporting him that far would apparently drain her powers. Something about the more powerful the being an elf transported with them, the bigger the drain on their powers. Iolanthe didn't want to risk weakening herself, and he didn't want that either.

"Why are you smiling?" She rounded the bed and set the pack down beside him.

He looked at her out of the corner of his eye and then back at the photograph. "Do you have a sister? Because there's a picture of a very beautiful woman who looks like you... but who couldn't possibly be you because she's wearing feminine clothing and is sporting a big goofy smile."

Iolanthe huffed, snatched the photo from the side table, and looked as if she was considering hitting him with it.

"Bleu took it years ago. I spent centuries on and off trying to find that stone. I took it to show him and my parents. They always make me wear dresses when I am with them." She slid him a hard look. "Do not expect to see me in such attire very often. It is most impractical."

He rolled onto his back, caught her wrist at the same time, and pulled her towards him. She landed at an angle on the bed, her top half draped across his bare chest, the photograph ending up on her lap.

"I don't mind. I prefer you practical. I'll take you surviving something due to wearing practical clothing over you ending up hurt or worse because you were wearing a dress." He ran his left hand down her thigh, over the black scales of her armour, and took the picture from her, bringing it up between them so he could see it again. "However... I think you should smile more. You're even more beautiful when you smile."

She blushed, swiped the picture from him, and tried to escape him. He wrapped his arms around her, twisted with her, and hauled her over the top of him, so she landed on her back on the bed and his chest pressed against hers.

Her armour was cold against his bare flesh.

"Do that mental command thing," he murmured before dropping his head to kiss her.

The photograph flopped onto the bed beside her and she wrapped her arms around him, sighing into his mouth. She kissed him back, each sweep of her lips across his stirring his hunger, and then doused it by pulling away and saying something he really hadn't wanted to hear and he had been trying not to think about all night.

"Bleu will be back soon and I do not think he would like to catch us naked in his bed."

Bleu's bed.

Kyter shuddered.

The thought that he had slept with her, among other things, in her brother's bed, his friend's bed, sent ice through his veins and he released her.

"Spoil sport." He rolled off her, landing with his legs over the edge of the bed, and grabbed his black backpack. He unzipped it, pulled out his black combats, and held them up. They were dirty.

Iolanthe shimmied on her knees to the edge of the bed beside him and looked at them too. "I am sure Bleu has some trousers he could lend you."

Kyter shuddered again. In a toss up between wearing dusty combat trousers or wearing Bleu's trousers, his own dirty clothing won. He had zero doubts that Bleu was like him and preferred to be nude beneath his trousers. For Bleu, it meant one less thing to teleport away from him when he called his armour. For Kyter, it was much easier to shift and escape his clothing.

The thought of his junk being where Bleu's junk had been disturbed him.

"You do not want them?" She canted her head and he shook his.

"These'll do." He slipped them over his feet, tugged them up his legs and then stood and pulled them up the rest of the way. He buttoned them as Iolanthe moved off the bed and padded across the room to the bathroom.

She retrieved his boots for him and the clothing he had removed last night. She set them down on the bed near his pack and then looked at him, her eyes straying to his throat and the marks on the right side of it.

She had triggered the bond between them and it had been mind-blowing. If only triggering the bond had sent him nearly shooting into the stratosphere, he couldn't imagine how good it would feel when they completed it, sharing blood in a mating.

He growled at the thought, his fangs emerging, eager to press into the back of her neck as he claimed her as his mate.

She stared hard at the marks and then her armour began to race up her legs, revealing their shapely forms.

"Iolanthe?" Kyter said, unsure whether she had changed her mind and he was going to get a morning encore after all. She cried out in pain and heat and ice swept in a wave of prickles across his skin. "Iolanthe!"

She staggered backwards, clutched at her chest as her armour disappeared into her wristbands, and lifted her head and cried out again. Her fangs were longer than normal, and her lower canines were growing too, becoming pointed. She stumbled away from him and his heart thundered, nearly breaking out of his chest as she arched forwards and her limbs contorted.

She couldn't be.

He stood dumbstruck by the sight of her and the single thought pounding in his head.

Iolanthe collapsed to the ground and writhed, her pained grunts becoming growls as black fur rippled across her bare flesh. A tail sprouted from the base of her spine and her ribcage changed shape. Her legs snapped and transformed, becoming cat-like.

She was shifting.

"What the fuck?" Kyter rushed to her as she completed her transformation.

She rolled to lay on her stomach on the dark stone floor and hissed at him, her round ears pinned backwards and fangs enormous.

His jaguar heeded the warning and he backed off, giving her space.

She lumbered onto her feet and stumbled a few steps before gaining balance. Her long tail swished back and forth, speaking of the excitement he could feel in her, pumping through his veins as if it was his own.

His own body responded with a need to shift, fur sweeping over his shoulders, but he tamped it down. He wanted to surrender to it and be in his jaguar form, to be like her, but he needed to figure out what the hell was going on. To do that, he needed to be in his human form.

The light streaming in from outside washed over her black fur as she paced around the apartment, her stunning violet eyes taking in everything as she lifted her head, scenting the air. She wasn't completely black. He could see the typical rosettes of a jaguar in her fur, darker than the rest of it.

She turned towards him, a beautiful black beast that lured him into surrendering to his desire to shift and be with her in the same form as she wore.

The door burst open.

Kyter's gaze leaped to Bleu.

He stared at Iolanthe. "What did you do?"

"Nothing!" Kyter rushed out, sure the elf male was about to pin the blame for what had happened to his sister on him, just as he had tried to blame him for the trouble she was in with the assassins. "She was fine a minute ago and then she was in pain and then she bloody shifted. Does she have mixed blood?"

Bleu shook his head and shot him an incredulous look. "Of course not. Elves are a dominant species. All children born of them are born fully elf."

Kyter stared at him. If he and Iolanthe had children, they would be one hundred percent elf. It was a relief in a way. He had often thought about fathering jaguar offspring, but had feared they would carry his demon genes too. He was glad that any children they might have wouldn't carry those genes, even if they wouldn't carry any jaguar ones either.

Bleu looked at his sister, an unimpressed edge to his violet eyes as she padded around the room, investigating everything, seemingly unconcerned by Kyter's panic and her brother's anger.

"This is a different sort of mixing of blood." Bleu closed the door behind him.

Kyter's stomach turned. Had he tainted her with his blood? The thought that he might have made him ill. If he had known he would taint her, he would have stopped her from biting him.

Iolanthe prowled across the room to her brother and rubbed her sleek body across his legs, getting fur on his black trousers and the long rectangular tails of his jacket. Bleu sighed and looked as if he might pet her, but folded his arms across his chest and shook his head instead.

"Elves can temporarily take on the abilities of a blood host if they are fae or demon." The elf male cast a pointed look at the right side of Kyter's throat and the marks on it tingled. "In this case, she has stolen your shifting ability."

It took a moment for that to sink in and chase away all of his fears. "She can control it?"

Iolanthe turned and rubbed across Bleu's legs again.

"Of course." Bleu still didn't pet her. He cast her another unimpressed look.

Kyter stared at her, amazed by what Bleu was saying and the evidence right in front of him. "So she chose to shift?"

Bleu nodded and sighed as he finally gave up and stroked her rounded ears, pushing his fingers through her thick black fur. "She always was adventurous."

Kyter couldn't believe it. His mate was incredible. Not only did she have amazing abilities of her own but she could take on new ones by drinking blood from fae.

She looked across at him, her bright violet eyes vivid against her velvety black fur.

A deep need filled him. One he couldn't deny.

He stared down into her eyes and chuffed, the low coughing sound echoing in his throat.

She blinked slowly and he didn't realise he had been holding his breath until she chuffed back at him.

Heat swept through him, a rush of tingles that pulled all his emotions to the surface and left him feeling raw inside.

He kneeled on the stone floor and chuffed again.

She stalked towards him, lowered her head and answered him, and then rubbed against him, her fur as soft as spun silk against his bare arm and back as she rounded him. She purred.

Kyter closed his eyes, hiding from her brother how much this affected him but knowing that he couldn't hide it from her. She could sense it all in him through their bond and she responded by rubbing him and then licking his cheek, her tongue rough against his skin. She purred the whole time.

She could be like him.

If he wanted to run in the jungle, she could run with him. They could hunt together. They could play in the trees. They could take in the scents and the sounds. They could share that experience.

And if he called to her, she could answer him.

She could give his animal side, the jaguar he was first and foremost, the comfort of knowing he wasn't alone.

That part of himself demanded that he shift and be with her in that form.

Bleu shattered the moment.

"We need to discuss what we are going to do... but I shall give you two a moment to get dressed."

The elf male stepped outside and Kyter stroked Iolanthe between her ears. His mate was truly incredible. He couldn't have wished for a more wonderful female.

She distanced herself and transformed back, grunting and snarling as her body bent back into shape and her fur disappeared. She kneeled on all fours and looked back at the tail that had remained, a wicked edge to her eyes, and then it disappeared too.

"That hurt more than I had expected." She gave him a pained grimace and sat back, revealing her bare body to him.

He rose onto his feet and helped her up onto hers.

"You could've warned me." He frowned down at her and she smiled and sidled closer to him.

It was a struggle to hold on to his anger when she was naked, stalking towards him with a sensual swing to her hips, luring his gaze down to her body. He jerked it back up to her face and managed to keep scowling.

She pressed her hands to his bare chest. "I wanted to surprise you."

"You almost gave me a heart attack." He took hold of her hands and clutched them above his heart.

"Liar." Her smile widened and she twisted her hands free of his and placed her palms back against his chest. "I can feel your feelings and our hearts beat as one. You were not in any danger."

"It's a turn of phrase... a little like I almost had a heart attack when I realised Bleu was your brother." He released her and rifled through his backpack for a top, needing to distract himself and do something to keep his eyes off her body and his mind off the wicked thoughts spinning through it.

He pulled out a black tank and tugged it on.

When he had finished, he found Iolanthe had dressed, pairing tight black combats with a black camisole top that hugged her breasts. She brushed her fingers through her long blue-black hair and plaited it.

"You could have warned me that you were friends with my brother." She tied the plait and released it, and it swung against her back, the tip reaching midway down it.

Kyter pulled on a pair of socks and jammed his feet into his black leather boots. "I didn't know. It wasn't as if either of us mentioned him by name. You could have told me."

"Would it have changed anything if I had?" She stepped closer to him and her eyes gained an edge that he tried to decipher through her feelings.

He failed. It was going to take him some time to become accustomed to feeling her emotions and understanding what the more subtle ones were.

He shook his head, slid his arm around her waist, and pulled her against him. "What about you?"

A smile curved her rosy lips. "When you mentioned Prince Loren visited your nightclub, I had a suspicion that you had met my brother."

His face fell as he recalled her grumbling that alcohol probably had little effect on the other elf because he was already tainted with an experience of it. She had been talking about Bleu.

Kyter frowned at her. "That was a while back when I told you that."

Before they had grown closer and had gotten together. She had kept it from him. Why? Because she had feared it would drive him away?

It also meant something else.

She nodded and swirled her fingers across his chest. "Who my brother is has no impact on my feelings or my decisions."

Kyter brushed his fingers over her cheek, opened his palm and cupped it before sliding his hand around the nape of her neck, beneath her thick braid. "Good... because it sure as hell wouldn't have stopped me from falling in love with you."

She stiffened.

He smiled.

A blush climbed her cheeks.

"Want me to say it again?" he murmured huskily.

She nodded.

"I'm in love with you." He lowered his head towards hers but stopped short of kissing her. Her sweet breath danced across his lips, tempting him into capturing them. "Iolanthe... my beautiful fated female... my eternal mate... I love you."

She beamed up at him, the same warm and heartfelt smile she wore in the photograph he would be taking a copy of to keep with him wherever he went, filled with light and overflowing with happiness.

Kyter waited.

And waited.

He huffed. "Surely you've got something to say?"

Her smile turned wicked and she rose onto her tiptoes, bringing her lips up to his for the sweetest kiss he had ever experienced, one that would stay with him forever.

"I love you, Ki'aro... my fated male... my eternal mate," she whispered the words against his lips and he gathered her closer, pressing the full length of her soft body into his. She clutched his shoulders, her need sweeping through him as if it was his own, and her violet eyes darkened with desire. "Gods... I want to mate with you."

He chuckled and brushed a kiss across her cheek, feeling that pressing need echoing within him, growing in strength as it mingled with hers.

"Later," he murmured, his lips sweeping across her skin. "I don't think Bleu will stand outside that door much longer and we have some things to take care of before we can think about what happens next. I need to know you're safe."

He feathered kisses down her jaw and her throat, his fangs emerging as he thought about mating with her.

"We'll deal with everything standing between us and our forever... and then I know the perfect place... I'll take you there and we'll complete this bond with a mating you'll never forget... one worthy of my beautiful mate. My Iolanthe."

She nodded and wrapped her arms around his neck as he pressed a long kiss to her throat.

"My Kyter."

He liked the sound of that. Hell, he *loved* the sound of that.

Her Kyter.

He had never been anyone's before. No one had ever wanted him, not in the way Iolanthe did. She accepted all of him.

She loved all of him.

He wanted to roar out his joy at that, and he would, when he took her to the rainforest and the hidden waterfall, and they completed their mating.

But first he needed to ensure his female, his Iolanthe, was free of the assassins.

And his father lost his head.

CHAPTER 24

Iolanthe pulled away from Kyter as the door opened and her brother stepped into the room. The rectangular tails of his long black jacket shifted with his purposeful stride as he closed the door behind him and approached her. He always had looked handsome in formal attire, the tight black trousers, polished knee-high boots, and crisp jacket decorated with pale blue embroidery suiting him. The raw pain that had been in his violet eyes yesterday seemed duller today and she was glad that his hurt was already fading, pushed out of his mind by her predicament.

She had never liked pulling him into her problems and relying on him to get her out of trouble, but today she was happy that it was happening, because it was giving him something else to focus on.

The cuts on his face were healing well and she wanted to ask him about the battle he had participated in for the Third King of the demons, but didn't want to mention that male. It would only remind her brother of what that king now held and had taken from Bleu—a female she suspected had been far more precious to him than he would ever admit.

Bleu's scowl deepened as his gaze settled on her and his eyes only darkened further when he looked at Kyter.

More specifically, he looked at Kyter's throat.

Her brother's violet eyes shifted back to her and he huffed, a flicker of relief softening his expression for a heartbeat before it passed, leaving him looking ready to kill something.

"I hope you know what you are doing." He stopped in front of her and she nodded.

He scrubbed a hand over his wild blue-black hair and around the back of his neck. His eyes gained a glimmer of concern that warmed her and she took his hand, wanting to reassure him that she did know what she was doing.

"Leaving the bond incomplete will weaken you, Io," he whispered.

"What?" Kyter barked and caught hold of her arm, tugging her around to face him. His wide golden eyes echoed the shock and fear she could feel sweeping through him. She placed her hand over his on her arm.

"I had expected it to weaken me, but I actually feel stronger. I can only surmise that you are stronger than I am, so being tied to you physically is not weakening me. It is weakening you."

He frowned. "I don't feel weaker."

Perhaps it was because of the demon side of his blood. She had known he was strong, but she hadn't imagined he was as strong as she could tell he was now that they were bound, their bodies linked. He had power within him that surpassed that of any male she had met before him and something told her that

176

he didn't even realise how powerful he really was. He denied his demonic heritage, holding it back and relying solely on the strength of his more dominant jaguar side.

If he tapped into his demon side, how powerful and dangerous would he become?

Would he be strong enough to defeat his father as he desired?

"I have permission to escort you to the library," Bleu said pulling her back to the room.

She nodded, released Kyter and rounded the bed to the side table where she had placed the dagger. They needed to translate it if they were going to discover whether it was another clue or the artefact she had been searching for.

She picked it up by the twisted black and silver hilt, and the light from the arched window in front of her reflected off it, blinding her. She flinched away and tilted the blade before opening her eyes again and staring down at it.

The language engraved on the double-edged blade was familiar.

Her heart beat harder and she slowly tilted the dagger back towards the light. "I can read this."

"What?" Kyter's deep voice swept over her and Bleu's joined it. Both males approached her back and she turned to face them.

Iolanthe held the dagger out between them. The light had been poor at the cave entrance and she had been tired and worried about Kyter, swept up in everything that had happened and feeling as if she was close to drowning.

"It speaks of a temple in Hell." She cursed herself as she realised where the temple was. She had been right on top of it. She had looked for it from the ledge. "We could have been there already if I had tried harder to understand the language on the blade. We could have dealt with your father and the assassins already."

"Father? That's twice Io has called the one related to the dagger your father," Bleu said with a sideways glance at Kyter. "I thought the artefact summoned a demon?"

Kyter slid him a dark look. "Don't ask."

Bleu looked as if he might press Kyter for the information she could feel he didn't want to give to her brother. He feared Bleu would look at him differently if he knew of Kyter's demonic lineage, just as he had feared she would look at him differently.

"Focus," she snapped and both males looked back at her.

Bleu gave her his full attention again. Kyter shot her a relieved look laced with gratitude. She wished he could keep avoiding revealing it to Bleu, but it wasn't possible. Bleu would come with them to the temple and when Barafnir appeared, he would know for certain that Kyter had demon blood in him.

"What does it say?" Kyter peered at the blade of the dagger, moving closer to her at the same time.

His heat curled around her and she lost focus now, finding it hard to concentrate when he was so close to her and the urge to shift her free hand to bridge the few centimetres between them and brush it across his was strong, compelling her to surrender to it.

She swallowed and forced her focus to the dagger, studying the engravings.

"It mentions a temple near the mountain." She turned the weapon over and scanned the other side. "A key and, I think, a gate."

It sounded promising.

"Doesn't seem like a clue to me." Kyter took the dagger from her and flipped it over and over, his gaze locked on it. "You think this is it? This is what we've all been looking for?"

She nodded. "I do. I think we need to go to the temple and investigate it and try to discover what it means by a key and a gate."

"How long do we have before you need to get this to Fernandez?" Kyter looked from the blade to her, his golden eyes intense and focused, sending a shiver through her.

"Three days, but I want it in his hands in two. Do you think that will be enough time?"

He stared deep into her eyes. "It'll have to be. We'll figure this out, Iolanthe, and if we can't, you'll take the dagger to Fernandez. Understood?"

"But Kyter—"

He cut her off with a shake of his head. "You're more important than my need to settle a score with my old man. I won't risk you. I won't let him take someone else I love from me."

Bleu gagged.

Kyter shot him a glare.

Iolanthe smiled at both of them. She could see that life with the two of them was going to be interesting. Never a dull moment.

She took the dagger from Kyter and teleported it, sending it to her bolthole where it would be safe.

"Back to the mountain?" Bleu said and she nodded. Her brother took hold of her arm and grabbed Kyter's too.

"To the valley, where the village was." She wrapped her hand around her brother's arm and slipped her other hand into Kyter's.

He shifted his hand and linked their fingers, pressing his palm against hers, his warm skin and the strength of his grip soothing her nerves and sending heat flowing through her.

Darkness engulfed them and she tightened her grip on Kyter, unwilling to lose him during the teleport. If they were separated, he would end up in a random point in Hell. It could take them years to find each other again.

She didn't think she could wait years to complete her bond with him.

The thought of having to wait a few days was torture enough.

The darkness evaporated, revealing the desolate black valley and the jagged mountains that rose above it into the inky sky. The round buildings that had stood in the village were now in ruins around her, their stone walls crumbled and scattered, leaving only vague ghosts of them behind. Some of the stones had been used as grave markers ahead of her, names crudely carved into the black square slabs of rock.

The fragments of stone that covered the dark ground crunched beneath her boots as she walked towards the edge of the village, Bleu and Kyter beside her, sandwiching her between them.

"The temple is a short distance up the incline, closer to the base of the mountains." She pointed towards the rise where she remembered it being.

Her brother and Kyter picked up pace, their eyes constantly scanning their surroundings, on high alert. She was right there with them, heart steady but muscles tight, ready for anything as she hurried towards the remains of the temple. She couldn't sense anyone in the vicinity, but that didn't mean they weren't being watched. There were countless species in Hell who could mask their signatures and scents, concealing themselves from their prey.

The trek to the temple ruins passed quickly and Bleu and Kyter broke away from her as they stepped up onto the circular base that remained.

The dome and triangular roofs that had been in the dragon's drawing in the cave were gone, broken into pieces and scattered around the landscape, as if some powerful force had detonated in the centre of the temple, shattering the roofs and sending the shards flying. The columns that lined the round base of the temple and the square section that formed the entrance were all broken at different heights.

"Look for any inscriptions on the stones… or anything that might be a key or a gate." She headed towards the altar end of the circle and paused in the centre of the temple, above a set of markings engraved on the obsidian stones that formed the base.

Iolanthe crouched and teleported the dagger to her. The engravings matched the ones on the weapon. They were in the right place. The images were different though, forming a wide circle in the middle of the floor, with a band of symbols around the outside of it and a triangle of smaller markings in the centre.

She ran her fingers over the engravings while Bleu and Kyter searched around the broken columns that followed the circular base, turning over the fragments of them that littered the floor and the ground around it.

The triangle pointed towards the crumbled altar ahead of her, but also pointed towards the village off to her left and the mountains off to her right. Beyond those mountains was the Devil's domain.

This was definitely the place where a demon could be summoned, but it wasn't necessarily linked to Barafnir. It was entirely possible that what she held was the method of summoning a different demon. She hadn't exactly checked every item in the dragon's treasure trove. She might have missed something.

Her gaze scanned the darkness around them again, a sensation that something was out there unsettling her. In the far distance, a gentle glow lit the dark sky. The elf kingdom. The light of her land reached the realms around it, chasing back the gloom of Hell. It barely touched this place, giving only enough light for her to make things out with the aid of her heightened vision.

Bleu huffed and shoved a piece of column with his foot, sending it tumbling off the edge of the temple base and crashing to the black ground below.

"There is nothing on them." He trudged back to her and she looked across her shoulder at Kyter.

Her mate shook his head, silently telling her that it was the same on his side of the temple.

That left only the mark on the floor.

She looked between the dagger and the circular mark, studying both of them and trying to figure out how they were linked. This was the temple. She needed a key and a gate.

Iolanthe focused harder on the symbols but none of them made sense to her. Only the ones on the dagger did and even those were beginning to look more like pictures than symbols with meaning. Was it something about this area that made it impossible for her to read them? She had been able to back in Bleu's apartment, but now she couldn't understand the language at all.

Bleu walked towards the altar ahead of her, Kyter trailing after him. The answer had to be here. She could figure it out.

She clutched the dagger.

"I do hope you were not planning to betray me, Iolanthe."

A shiver went down her spine.

Bleu spun on his heel to face her, his clothing disappearing and his armour sweeping over his body, covering him from neck to toe and transforming his fingers into long serrated claws. A black blade appeared in his grip. He teleported another silver sword to him and tossed it to Kyter.

Kyter caught it and narrowed his golden gaze on the owner of the voice behind her.

She calmly rose onto her feet, turning as she did so, her own armour covering her fingers and changing them into deadly talons. She was out of time. He had come for her personally. She should have known she wouldn't be able to fool him. He was always watching her. She lifted her eyes.

Her heart lodged in her throat.

Fernandez stood at the entrance of the ruined temple, his vivid red eyes locked on her and his two favourite assassins at his back—the sorcerer and the one who possessed god powers. The dark-haired male stood to the left of Fernandez, dressed head to toe in black, his pale blue eyes fixed on her. She shuddered under his cold and hungry scrutiny, every instinct she possessed telling her to move back a step, towards Kyter and her brother.

The red eyes of Fernandez held her immobile though. She had only met him the once, when the dark-haired assassin had captured her and brought her before him so he could demand she locate the way of summoning Barafnir.

She had felt the power in Fernandez then and the evil, but she hadn't realised what he was. He had hidden it from her, but he wasn't hiding it today. He stood before her in his true form, no doubt using it to issue a warning to her, one that cautioned her not to fight him.

Darkness clung to him, writhing like mist over the heavy black armour that moulded to his seven-foot frame, mimicking the muscles concealed beneath. His clawed black gloves gripped the hilt of the huge obsidian sword he held point down in front of him. The horned helm of his armour flared back from above his nose, covering his silver-grey hair.

He looked like a vampire with his elliptical pupils stretched thin in the centre of his crimson irises, but he was infinitely more dangerous. A deadly foe she stood no chance against.

Fernandez advanced a step, his eyes narrowing, and the shadows shifted, rising to sweep over the part of him that had frozen her feet in place and chilled her blood.

Black wings.

Their enormous feathered forms arched from his back to a point two feet above the top of his head and almost brushed the ground at his feet. Only one species in Hell had such wings, and it was one she had hoped she would never cross paths with let alone swords.

A fallen angel.

Only one species in Hell was more powerful than a fallen angel.

Kyter roared and shot past her, heading straight for Fernandez.

A demon of the Devil's domain.

CHAPTER 25

Iolanthe burst into action the second her brother passed her, sweeping his hand down the length of his black blade at the same time, transforming it into a long spear. She teleported the dagger from her palm and replaced it with her short black sword.

Ahead of her, Kyter clashed hard with Fernandez, slamming his right shoulder into the fallen angel's armoured stomach and driving him backwards off the edge of the circular black stone base of the temple. Fernandez's eyes flashed vivid red, glowing like hot embers, and her heart leaped in her chest as he shot his left hand out, wrapped it around Kyter's throat, and hurled him across the temple. Kyter grunted as he crashed into the remains of the altar, shattering the ancient stone, and collapsed onto the floor.

Iolanthe hissed, her pointed ears flaring back against the sides of her head and her violet eyes pinned on Fernandez.

He would pay for hurting her mate.

She ran at him as Bleu took on the sorcerer, nimbly teleporting whenever the fair-haired male launched a spell at him. Her brother was faster than she remembered, impressing her as he evaded every spell the male cast and closed in on him, forcing the sorcerer to fight hand to hand. Bleu's black spear was a blur as he attacked, slashing and thrusting, driving the sorcerer away from his companions.

Fernandez spread his black wings and threw his left hand forwards, towards Kyter.

Iolanthe feared the worst and looked back at her mate, only to realise that nothing had happened. It hadn't been an attack.

It had been an order.

The dark-haired male beside Fernandez pressed one hand to his chest, bowed his head, and then disappeared, moving so swiftly that her eyes couldn't track him.

"Kyter." She skidded as she changed direction, turning away from Fernandez and towards her male.

Kyter shoved onto his feet and reached for his fallen weapon. Not quick enough.

The dark-haired male appeared before him, one hand wrapped around the hilt of the katana sheathed at his side. He drew the weapon. A swift silver arc cut through the darkness, a deadly blur aimed straight at Kyter's neck.

Iolanthe teleported, her heart thundering against her breast, and appeared between Kyter and the male. She leaned back as she brought her arm up, the black scales of her armour rapidly flowing from the twin bands around her wrist to cover it, and flinched as the blade struck her forearm a split second after her armour had reached that point.

The force of the blow sent pain lancing through her arm even though her armour stopped the blade from cutting into her and drove her backwards into Kyter. He grabbed her waist to steady her and growled into her ear, the feral snarl directed at the male pressing forwards with the attack.

Her armour burned where the silver blade pressed into it, searing her skin beneath the black scales. Panic rushed through her and she shoved forwards with her arm, knocking the blade away from her before it could do serious damage. Her armour was only weak against the same metal. Or it should have been. It wasn't possible that his blade could cut through it, but it had felt as if it had been on the verge of doing so.

She growled and brought her left arm up, her own black blade cutting swiftly through the air towards the male. His pale blue eyes flashed and he spun with his sword and blocked her blow. Kyter ducked around her and lunged with his sword, thrusting it straight towards the male's head.

The dark-haired male grunted and dove to one side, narrowly avoiding the blade. He rolled onto his feet but Kyter was there, spinning on his heel as he launched a high sweeping kick at the male. It caught him hard in the temple and sent him crashing onto the black stone floor.

Bleu snarled, catching her attention, and she wished she hadn't looked as he flew backwards through the air towards her, a white blast of energy exploding from his chest. She kicked off, launching into the air, slammed into him and wrapped her arms around him as she teleported.

The darkness evaporated as she landed and she set Bleu down on his feet. He huffed, tossed her a black look that left her in no doubt that he wasn't impressed that he had just been saved by his little sister, and then teleported, throwing himself back into the fray.

Kyter ducked beneath the silver arc of the dark-haired male's sword, dropping to one knee and launching his other leg out. He slammed his foot hard into the male's ankles, knocking him off balance. The male fumbled an attack, lashing out with his katana. Kyter rolled onto his back, pressed his hands into the stones above his shoulders, and flipped onto his feet, evading the blow as it harmlessly swept beneath him.

He landed in a crouch, pinned his sights on Fernandez, and roared again as he rushed the fallen angel.

Iolanthe joined him, unable to allow him to fight alone. He had demon blood in his veins but she wasn't sure he was strong enough to take Fernandez down.

Her heart stopped as Bleu shot past her and hit the largest stone of the altar so hard that it exploded, raining black fragments down on the area around the temple.

He hissed, flashing his fangs, and pulled himself onto his feet. His legs gave out beneath him and she screamed as the sorcerer blasted him again, pinning him to a column, and the dark-haired male attacked.

Kyter landed a blow on Fernandez, splitting the fallen angel's lip and sending him staggering backwards.

She had to help her brother.

Iolanthe teleported and landed on the dark-haired male's back. She wrapped her legs around his head, fell backwards and twisted as she planted her hands onto the floor, using her bodyweight and all of her strength to flip the male over her and slam him into the ground. He grunted on impact and she sat on his back, grabbed him by his hair and smashed his face against the black stone.

A hot blast struck her in her back and sent her flying into Bleu just as he found his feet. He grabbed her and fell backwards with her, toppling over the column. She landed on top of him and he wheezed, his face screwing up in pain.

"Have you put on weight?" he rasped in the elf tongue and she had half a mind to hit him.

She teleported off him instead and went after the sorcerer who had struck her with the spell.

The second she appeared, pain lanced her side. She cried out and clutched her left hip, expecting to find it wet with blood.

It wasn't.

Because it wasn't her pain.

"Kyter," she hollered and lifted her eyes to find him.

He stood with his back to her, both hands clutching Fernandez's black broadsword where it skewered his side. Her stomach somersaulted and she threw her hands forwards, using all of her strength to create a blast of telekinesis powerful enough to send the fallen angel flying. The blade pulled free of Kyter's side and he staggered forwards a few steps, growling and snarling, fur rippling across his shoulders.

Fernandez spread his black wings, halting his ascent, and swept his blade through the air.

He pointed it at Bleu.

Bleu bellowed in agony that chilled her blood in her veins and fell silent.

She turned slowly, afraid of what she would see, and her heart didn't slow even when she saw her brother lying on the black floor of the temple, his eyes closed and his stomach shifting with each slow breath. He was out cold but he was alive.

She wasn't sure how long he would remain that way if she didn't do something though.

The dark-haired male stood over Bleu, his katana raised above his head and poised to strike.

His icy blue eyes slid to her, a sadistic glimmer of pleasure in them.

184

Kyter was gravely injured and Bleu was unconscious. She had to do something now to turn the tide in their favour or they were all going to die. They weren't strong enough to defeat Fernandez and his men.

Her heart steadied.

They weren't, but someone was.

Barafnir.

If she could summon him, she could command him to fight Fernandez and kill him and his men.

The dark-haired male looked to his master. Fernandez started to nod.

"Wait!" Iolanthe dropped her blade.

The metallic ring of it hitting the ground seemed to freeze everyone in place. She swallowed hard and drew in a fortifying breath.

Fernandez's crimson eyes slid to her and he landed a short distance from Kyter where he kneeled just beyond the edge of the circle engraved on the black stone floor, clutching his bleeding side.

Iolanthe called the dagger to her and held it out to Fernandez.

"This is what you wanted. I believe it is the item you seek, but I have not been able to verify it. That is why we came here. I needed to ensure it was the item and not another clue."

Fernandez furled his black feathered wings against his back and eyed it with interest. "Will it summon the demon?"

"It will summon *a* demon. I cannot be certain it will be Barafnir as you desire." She held the dagger out towards him, refusing to let her hand shake and betray her nerves.

The fallen angel lowered his sword and held it out beside him. The fair-haired sorcerer hurried forwards and took it from him, carefully cradling it and bowing his head. Fernandez motioned with his hand. Behind her, the dark-haired male huffed and sheathed his weapon.

She went to approach Fernandez but he halted her with a cold glare.

"Summon this demon. If it is the one I hired you to locate, I will allow you all to live." He looked from her to behind her and then down at Kyter. "If it is not, we shall start by taking one of the males with us back to the guild, where he shall be our honoured guest, and you will decide which it will be."

Iolanthe had the feeling that honoured guest was a sick way of saying that either her brother or Kyter was destined to be tortured violently and ceaselessly until she found the right artefact, and she would have to live with the knowledge she had put them there.

Her stomach rebelled at the thought and her hand shook against the dagger.

"Come, Iolanthe. Summon this demon… or perhaps you need an incentive already?" Fernandez took a step towards Kyter.

Her heart jerked and she rushed out, "No. I will do it. Just… leave him be."

Kyter growled and clutched his side, blood spilling from between his fingers, his pain echoing on her body. He looked back at her, his golden eyes imploring her to be careful. She nodded, turned her back to him, and stared at the dagger.

This had to work.

This was the temple.

She frowned.

The dagger was the key?

When she had been looking for it, speaking to the demons, they had referred to it as the key of Barafnir. But if it was the key, where was the lock it fitted and the gate it opened?

She looked around her, her gaze straying to Bleu where he lay sprawled at the dark-haired male's feet, breathing shallowly, a black and purple bruise discolouring his right temple and cheek. Anger curled through her veins, heat that burned and set her blood on fire. The male would pay for harming her brother. Fernandez would pay for harming Kyter.

She edged closer to the altar to check it and check Bleu at the same time. The blow to the head was the only injury he had sustained. The dark-haired male's eyes tracked her, intense and focused, sending a cold shiver through her. She curled her lip at him and he smiled, as if the sliver of attention she had given him had been tender or affectionate and not laced with hatred.

Iolanthe moved away from him, loath to leave her brother near the male while he was vulnerable, but unable to stay near him. There was something wrong with the dark-haired assassin, something that deeply disturbed her. It was more than the fact he had made her the focus of his demented obsession since they had first met. It had to do with his power. It was darkness, the sort that an elf could fall into if they weren't careful, becoming a twisted creature and losing all of their purity and goodness. Turned towards evil, never to come back.

She looked at the circle engraved on the black stone floor, searching it again. No cracks where a dagger could fit. No clear instruction on how to use it. She felt Fernandez's eyes on her, his focus intensifying. He was losing patience.

A muffled grunt coming from behind her made her look back at her brother. He frowned and slowly raised a hand to his head, a groan escaping him. Relief swept through her but fear drove it down again. Kyter's pain was growing worse. If she could get near him, she could teleport a medicine for him to take.

"Let me heal him," she said with a glance at Kyter and Fernandez shook his head. She wouldn't give up. She took a step towards him, her fists clenched at her sides, and stared hard at Fernandez, feeling as if she was facing the Devil himself as his countenance darkened dangerously. "Please. I cannot focus… not while he is in pain."

"You care about this one," Fernandez murmured and looked down at Kyter and then back at her. "He means something to you."

The master assassin held his hand out towards her and the dagger shot from her palm and into his. He closed his fingers around it and grabbed Kyter, yanking him around to face her and tearing a pained cry from him. He fisted Kyter's sandy hair from behind him and pressed one edge of the dagger against the front of her mate's throat.

Her stomach lurched and she held her hands out, desperate to stop Fernandez but afraid that any move she made would see him carrying out his threat.

"I believe you might focus better now, not worse. Prove me right, Iolanthe, or this male you care so much about will be nothing but a sack of bones and blood." Fernandez stooped behind Kyter and tipped the blade up, forcing his head up with it.

Kyter tensed and growled through his fangs.

Rage burned through her, her blood becoming wildfire in her veins, an inferno that awakened a fierce need to recall her blade to her hand and cut Fernandez down with it.

She drew in a deep breath and Kyter's golden eyes widened. He had read her intention.

"No." Kyter grabbed Fernandez's hand and the dagger and tried to break past it as her black sword reappeared in her grip.

The dagger nicked his throat, painting a thin red line across the right side, a bare inch above where she had bitten him.

A bead of his blood rolled down the blade to the tip.

Black light burst from it and a shockwave exploded across the temple, knocking her backwards and hurling Kyter forwards, onto the engraved circle. He pressed his bloodied palm into the black stones to keep himself from hitting it face-first, ending up on all fours in the centre of the triangle.

Ribbons of shadows swirled like tendrils from his hand and curled around him, and he shoved up onto his knees and arched backwards, his face to the black sky of Hell as he roared.

Iolanthe clutched her side, screaming as fire blazed through it, tears streaming down her face.

Fernandez stared dazedly at the dagger in his hand and then at Kyter, and then behind her as the swirls of black smoke blasted past her. She looked over her shoulder at the altar and her eyes widened as the darkness gathered there, filling the space between the two columns at the back of the temple, beyond the broken dais.

Her heart lodged in her throat as the darkness rippled and the pain in her side faded before disappearing completely.

A leg emerged from the shadows, clad in black armour, each plate edged with crimson. Another followed it and then a bare arm broke through the darkness, the tendrils clinging to it before dissipating. She could only stare as the immense male finally stepped free of the black smoke, his seven-foot frame rivalling the fallen angel's but his shoulders far broader and his armour ending at his waist. His broad chest was bare, each powerful honed muscle on display. His arms were as thick as her thighs.

He turned fierce golden eyes on Kyter where he knelt in the centre of the engraved circle, breathing hard.

"I was told you were dead," the demon snarled, his deep voice vibrating through her. His huge smooth black horns curled through his jet hair from behind the tops of his pointed ears, twisting around to flare forwards besides his temples like deadly daggers. He took a hard step forwards, shaking the black platform and growled, revealing his sharp teeth and fangs. "I was told you did not survive birth."

Iolanthe had a feeling that he wasn't glad that Kyter had survived. A shiver ran down her spine as she recalled what the demon in the fae town had told her.

Barafnir had taken great pains to hide the way of summoning him.

That way was his blood.

She looked back at Kyter as he lumbered onto his feet, swaying a little before straightening, and lowered his hand from his side. The wound was gone but the blood remained, staining his skin.

Blood that had spilled on the dagger and on the circle.

Blood that had given her the ability to read the language written on the blade.

Blood that had come from his father.

Kyter was the key.

Not the dagger.

The dagger was the lock, the power within it unleashed by a single drop of Kyter's blood. Together they had activated the markings on the temple floor and opened the shadowy gate to his father.

Fernandez recovered first. "I order you to kill these people."

Barafnir turned flaming golden eyes on him. "I do not answer to you."

The fallen angel snarled and pointed the dagger at him. "I spilled the blood that summoned you. You will do my bidding."

The demon didn't move. He narrowed his gaze on Fernandez and then dropped it to Kyter again.

"Your hand spilled your own blood. You placed it upon the circle. You have summoned me. Speak your desire." Barafnir curled his lip, revealing his fangs again, and Fernandez looked ready to throw the dagger at him.

The demon was telling the truth though. Kyter's hand had been on the dagger when it had cut his throat, but the fallen angel's had been too. The demon had been given a choice of masters and he had chosen his son.

He had chosen death.

Kyter would use the one order he could issue to have the demon kill himself. He would use it to have his vengeance.

She looked back at Kyter, her heart pounding at a sickening tempo. Only a demon stood a chance at defeating a fallen angel. She couldn't let him have his vengeance. They wouldn't survive another fight with Fernandez and his men.

Kyter's golden eyes narrowed on his father.

Iolanthe shifted to intervene, opening her mouth to tell him to stop.

He snarled.

"Kill the angelic bastard who dared to threaten my mate."

Her heart stopped.

Barafnir smirked, pressed his left hand to his chest, and lowered his head. "As you wish."

CHAPTER 26

Kyter struggled to keep up with the fight between Fernandez and Barafnir. The demon had disappeared and reappeared behind Fernandez barely a second after accepting Kyter's order to kill the fallen angel.

Fernandez's two assassins had leapt into action and Bleu had gone after the fair-haired sorcerer with a vengeance, his violet eyes flashing with grim determination and his black spear a blur as he had launched his first attack. Iolanthe had gone after the dark-haired male, a vision of deadly grace as she alternated between attacking with her telekinesis and her black blade.

So far, Kyter had switched between them, moving as swiftly as he could, but his focus had always been split between his fight and his father's one.

Barafnir and Fernandez clashed high in the air above him, their huge wings battering each other as they exchanged blows. He wasn't sure who was winning and he didn't care. All he wanted was the chance to study his father in action, discover any weak spots the demon had, and then he would set his plan in motion.

Both Barafnir and Fernandez would die and that was all that mattered to him.

Iolanthe grunted, seizing his attention, and he raced towards her as she staggered backwards, her right arm still raised to protect herself from the silver katana the dark-haired male wielded. There was something about that weapon that linked it to the male, giving him the ability to inflict pain in any cut the blade made.

The elf armour his mate wore protected her body, including her hands, but not her head. The male had figured that out and was focusing every attack on her face now, attempting to land a blow that he could use to disable her, keeping her writhing in pain.

Kyter roared and shifted, his bones quickly snapping and transforming as fur swept over his skin and his tail formed. He leaped free of his clothing as he completed the change, landed in a crouch on the black ground and sprang at the male. The male turned towards him and hastily raised his right arm to shield himself, his pale icy eyes wide and his scent reeking of fear.

Kyter sank his fangs into the male's arm, crunching straight through the bone, and snarled as the assassin roared in agony. A deep sense of satisfaction raced through Kyter's blood. He slammed hard into the male and took him down, pinning him beneath his full weight. The male cried out again as Kyter tightened his grip, tasting blood, and violently shook his head, savaging the male's arm.

The male retaliated, bringing his sword around in a deadly arc.

Iolanthe kicked it from his grip and it clattered across the stone circular base of the temple and struck one of the broken columns.

It didn't stop the male from attacking. He rolled with Kyter, fighting to get Kyter beneath him, and Kyter kicked his back legs, slashing with his claws and tearing through the black long sleeve top the male wore. He would gut the bastard if that was what the male wanted.

The male ripped his arm free of Kyter's grip, launched to his feet and stumbled across the temple.

Heading for his sword.

Kyter rolled onto his paws and sprinted after him, pressed down hard on his last stride and launched through the air in a graceful arc. He landed heavily on the male's back and growled as he sank his teeth into the nape of his neck, seizing hold of him. The male grunted as he hit the stone flags and Kyter pinned him there. Every dirty look and disgusting thing this male had given and said to Iolanthe came rushing back and he couldn't stop himself as his instincts rose to the fore, primal and intense, demanding blood.

He slammed one paw down on the back of the male's head and clamped his jaws down harder on his neck. Flesh gave beneath his fangs and blood flooded his mouth as the male screamed and writhed, fighting to lift Kyter's weight off him.

Kyter tightened his grip and growled as bone crunched and the male stilled, the scent of death swiftly clinging to him.

He released the body, threw his head back and roared his victory at the dark sky of Hell.

Above him, Barafnir stopped and looked down, his black-edged-golden gaze brimming with curiosity. Blood rolled down the demon's broad chest, a mixture of his own and Fernandez's.

It would run in a torrent when Kyter was done with him.

Kyter narrowed his eyes on the demon and growled, baring his fangs. Tendrils of darkness flowed through his muscles and bones, sinking into his veins and his blood. He coaxed and nurtured them, until they spread deeper and wider, filling him, and he knew that his eyes were changing, altering towards the same darkness that had begun to consume his father's eyes.

The eyes of a demon.

Black as night.

Gold like fire.

"Kyter." Iolanthe's sweet voice brought him back from the edge and he closed his eyes before she could see what was happening to him.

She knew he was part demon, but he still wasn't sure how she would react if she saw how that part affected him. Not only the internal changes and the terrible need for violence it awakened in him. The physical changes too.

How would she react if she saw his irises were now black and his pupils were little more than gold vertical slits in their centres?

He snarled as he transformed back and she moved away from him, only to return a moment later. When he opened his eyes, she stood before him, holding his black combat trousers and his boots. He took them from her and pulled them on.

"Bleu?" he said and looked for the elf male.

Bleu battled a short distance away, nimbly evading the spells the fair-haired sorcerer cast at him. Kyter went to move in that direction but Iolanthe's hand on his arm stopped him. He looked back at her, meeting her violet gaze. She squeezed his arm and looked beyond him to her brother.

"I will aid him," she said and then her voice dropped to a whisper. "You do what you must do… but be careful."

He nodded, slid his arm around her waist and pulled her to him for a brief kiss before letting her go to her brother's aid. She was right and he was no match for the sorcerer. Physical attacks he could evade and deal with. Spells were a different matter. Iolanthe and Bleu could teleport out of their path or use telekinesis to knock them awry. If he tried to fight the sorcerer, he would only be in the way, and he felt sure that Bleu and Iolanthe could handle the man together.

His fight lay elsewhere, around one hundred feet above him.

Fernandez and Barafnir clashed again, huge swords cleaving at each other, their wings working overtime to keep them in the air.

Kyter needed to get them down onto his level.

He picked up the discarded katana and flexed his fingers around the grip, biding his time as he watched his father clashing with the fallen angel. He was weaker on his right side. Fernandez had dealt a hard blow to that arm and Barafnir naturally favoured his left hand.

Barafnir's sword punched through Fernandez's side, easily penetrating his black armour. The fallen angel grunted and cast his hand forwards, and used his powers to pull the demon closer to him. The sword slid deeper, coming out of his back, but the angel was grinning, flashing sharp fangs as he swung his own blade, aiming it at Barafnir's neck.

The demon disappeared in black smoke, his sword with him, and Fernandez's face screwed up in frustration, his red eyes glowing from beneath his black helm. The fallen angel's anger gave way to pain as he grimaced and clutched his side. His black feathered wings faltered and he dropped out of the air, landing hard on the ground a short distance from the temple, the impact shattering the rock.

Barafnir appeared beyond Fernandez and the fallen angel turned towards him, giving Kyter his back, and readied his broadsword.

Kyter grinned.

Kicked off.

Sprinted towards the fallen angel and leaped high in the air. Fernandez whirled to face him, his red eyes shooting wide, and began to bring his sword up. Too late. Kyter roared as he brought the katana down with all of his strength behind the blow and sliced clean through the fallen angel's shoulder and diagonally down his chest.

The blade stuck on a point on the male's ribs but it had done its deadly work.

Fernandez staggered backwards as Kyter landed and released the sword. The fallen angel eyed it, shock written across every line of his face as he started to lift his hands towards the hilt where it protruded from a spot in the centre of his chest.

From his heart.

The fallen angel raised his eyes to Kyter and for a moment Kyter feared his aim had been off and the male was about to make him pay dearly for trying to kill him.

Red light burst from around the katana and Fernandez threw his head back and bellowed as veins of it spread over his armour, growing in intensity until they blinded Kyter.

He looked away just as the ground rocked, a shockwave sent him flying, and something warm and wet rained down on the area.

It smelled like blood.

Kyter grimaced. He didn't want to look but he needed to see if Iolanthe was alright.

He opened his eyes, curling his lip at the grim sight in front of him. Pieces of flesh littered the black land and obsidian feathers drifted down on the warm air. Iolanthe stood off to his left, beside her brother, over the body of the sorcerer.

Her black armour covered in bits of Fernandez.

If Kyter had known that fallen angels exploded on death, he might have waited until Iolanthe and Bleu had been with him again, able to teleport him out of the blast zone, before killing Fernandez.

Barafnir picked himself up off the black ground and turned murderous black eyes on Kyter.

"It seems you failed to kill Fernandez," Kyter said as he found his feet and rose to his full height, facing his father across the wide strip of rocky ground.

The demon male bared his sharp teeth, the pointed tips of his black horns flaring forwards as he beat his enormous dark leathery wings. The jagged obsidian mountains behind him were a fitting backdrop for the demon as he stood with his head held aloft and his immense body covered in blood.

His father.

A strange sense of calm came over Kyter. He stood on the precipice of fulfilling a need for revenge that had been steadily building within him throughout his entire life. It felt strange to find himself here, facing a demon who had been nothing but a ghost before today, a nightmarish phantom that had ruined his mother's life and had shaped his own without ever making an appearance in it.

As he stood facing Barafnir, he couldn't help thinking that he looked nothing like him. If it weren't for the darkness that lived within Kyter, born of his demon genes, he might have been able to convince himself that Barafnir wasn't his father.

His mother had been right all those times when he had asked about Barafnir and she had told him that he was the spitting image of her father—a noble and powerful jaguar male.

He should have believed her rather than believing she was coddling him and lying to protect him, convinced that it hurt her to see him because he looked like his father and was a constant reminder of what she had been through at his hands. He should have been stronger and had faith in her love for him, taking strength from her words rather than allowing doubt and darkness to cloud his mind and his heart.

She had been the one pure source of affection and comfort in his life before he had met Iolanthe and he should have guarded her better.

He should have been there to protect her from the bastard standing across from him, just as she had protected him by raising him in secret. She had given him the chance to grow into a strong male and a capable warrior, one powerful enough to take down a demon.

He curled his fingers into fists at his side and stared across the black ground at Barafnir, hiding none of his anger and pain as he held the demon's black-and-gold gaze.

Killing the bastard who had held her captive, ruined her life, and had then murdered her wouldn't change what had happened, but it was going to make Kyter feel a whole damned lot better.

He couldn't bring his mother back, but he could avenge her.

"I guess that means I still get one order." Kyter tapped his chin, pretending to think, and then grinned. "I order you to kill yourself."

Barafnir didn't move. A slow smile spread across his lips.

Kyter didn't like it one bit. "I *order* you to kill yourself."

Barafnir's smile turned cold and evil. "No one steals my prey from me. You killed the one who summoned me. I shall avenge him."

"You son of a bitch." Those crude words leaving Iolanthe's lips caught Kyter off guard and he couldn't stop himself from staring across at her as she stormed forwards. "You cannot change who your master is as you please."

"I do not like this term… *master*. I have only one master. I mean to keep it that way." The huge demon male slid her a dark look that promised pain. "I mean to ensure no one can summon me again."

Barafnir's black gaze returned to Kyter.

"It is time you died."

Kyter flexed his hands, his claws breaking through the skin of his fingers, black and sharp as his demonic side rose to the fore once again.

"My thoughts exactly." He went to kick off and black smoke engulfed his father.

It dissipated just as quickly, revealing an empty spot where the demon had been.

"Kyter." Bleu's deep voice and the shiver that ran down Kyter's spine was all the warning he needed.

Kyter hurled himself forwards into a roll, narrowly avoiding the sword that slashed across at waist height to him from behind. He sprang onto his feet and turned in time to see Bleu snarling and thrusting with his spear. The black sharp tip of it struck the broadsword Barafnir wielded and shattered the blade in half.

Barafnir roared and swung the remains of his blade, a section still several feet in length, at Bleu. Bleu teleported and reappeared in the air above the demon, swept his spear above his head and arched back. His violet eyes narrowed on Barafnir's wings, he grasped the shaft of his spear in both hands and swung it over his head, aiming for them.

Bleu was a genius.

Disabling the demon's wings would give them an advantage they needed. Kyter kicked off, his claws at the ready as he charged towards the huge demon male. Bleu's spear nicked the demon's right wing and the male swung a meaty arm at the elf. It struck Bleu in his stomach and he shot across the black terrain, hit the ground and rolled a short distance before coming to a halt.

Kyter didn't pause to see whether Bleu was okay. It would take more than a hit to the gut to take down the dark elf. It had probably only served to piss him off.

Barafnir turned towards Kyter, swinging his blade. Kyter pressed down hard on his last stride, sprang into the air, and sailed over his father's head. He stretched down with his right hand, dug his claws into the bony part of the black leathery wing to anchor himself, and swung himself down onto his father's back. He grasped the demon's right wing and slashed across the membrane with his other hand, rending long gashes in the skin.

Barafnir roared, reached over his head, grabbed Kyter and threw him. Kyter hit the basalt ground hard and skidded across it, grimacing and grunting as a thousand sharp pebbles sliced into his skin and his side burned from the impact.

Iolanthe appeared beside him, crouched to check him and then lifted her head and hissed at Barafnir. She teleported before Kyter could stop her, reappearing behind the demon, already swinging her blade. It slashed up the demon's bare back and across his right wing, cutting into the muscle and bone.

Barafnir twisted at the waist, bringing his sword around with him, and Iolanthe nimbly flipped backwards, evading the blow, and sprang forwards the second she landed on her feet, her black blade zooming ahead of her, aimed at the demon's chest.

Kyter was on his feet and running for the demon's back, his gaze locked on the male's left wing.

Bleu staggered onto his feet, shook his head and teleported just as the immense demon smashed a thick arm into Iolanthe's chest, sending her flying. Bleu appeared in mid-air, caught her and landed hard, setting her down before sprinting towards Kyter and the demon.

Barafnir turned on his heel and swung his sword, cutting through the air towards Kyter.

Kyter hit the deck, sliding feet first across the black ground beneath the blow, and grabbed Barafnir's left leg as he shot past it. He clutched it, using it as an anchor to pivot himself around behind the demon. He pressed his free hand into the dirt, shoved hard as he used all of his agility to twist his body and swing his legs up, and grunted as he launched himself feet first at Barafnir's left wing.

The soles of his boots connected hard with the base of the wing, sending Barafnir staggering forwards. Bone crunched and snapped, and Barafnir roared, the vicious sound echoing off the jagged black mountains surrounding the valley. Black smoke swirled around the demon again and he disappeared. Kyter's feet fell forwards, he arched his back and flipped onto them, landing in a crouch.

His gaze immediately sought Iolanthe. She swayed on her feet, her left arm tucked against her chest, and he growled as he felt her pain radiating through his bones. The demon had broken it.

Bleu skidded to a halt halfway between him and Iolanthe and looked back at his sister.

Kyter's stomach dropped.

Black shadows shimmered behind her.

"Iolanthe!" He bolted for her, growling as his legs burned from the exertion.

Bleu teleported.

Neither reached her in time.

Barafnir appeared behind her, grabbed the blade she held in her right hand and had twisted it free of her grip before she could move an inch. Kyter bellowed as the demon grinned and slashed down her back and she screamed and arched forwards, her pain blazing through him.

Kyter sprinted harder, pushing himself to the limit and beyond it as he saw red, anger exploding through his veins and darkness consuming him. He closed in on Barafnir, his sights locked on him even as Iolanthe collapsed onto the black ground.

The fucking bastard would pay for hurting his mate.

He would pay for hurting his pride.

He would pay for killing his mother.

Bleu appeared as the demon was about to deal a second blow, his spear coming up fast to knock the black blade from the male's hand and send it tumbling through the air. He snarled something in the elf tongue, grabbed Iolanthe around her waist and teleported with her.

Kyter swept through the spot where they had been a split-second later and roared as he launched himself at his father, his claws at the ready. They grew longer, black talons that matched the ones tipping his father's fingers. A demon's claws.

A demon had killed his mother.

A demon had devastated his pride.

A demon had harmed his mate.

He was no demon.

He was a jaguar.

He transformed in the air, roaring as his body shifted much faster than it had ever done before, his gold and black fur covering him in the span of a heartbeat as he leaped free of his clothing.

Barafnir stared at him through shocked wide eyes.

Kyter opened his jaw as his paws slammed into the demon's chest, twisted his head and bit down hard on the male's thick throat. The force of the blow took the male down beneath him and Kyter clamped his jaws tight, crushing his windpipe and suffocating him as he landed on top of him. The demon battered him, clawing at his flank and trying to break free of his grip.

He held on, weathering the blows and the pain, not feeling them as everything faded away leaving only raw agony behind, the grief of losing his mother, and the fury of seeing his mate injured. Those violent emotions ruled him, keeping him in his jaguar form despite the pain of each slash and blow Barafnir dealt. His jaws ached, his limbs shook, and still he held on, sensing the life slowly draining from the demon beneath him.

He was no demon.

He was a jaguar.

He would never be a demon. He would never become his father.

He was born of a jaguar, to a long line of jaguars, each more powerful than the last. His lineage was pure and strong, and it beat within his heart with each breath he drew, instilling that strength in him. He was proud to be a jaguar. No one could take that away from him.

The demon's hands closed around his neck, throttling him, but Kyter didn't release him. He held on, using the last of his strength as it began to fade to keep his jaws clamped around the demon's throat. His head spun and his muscles turned to water as he ran out of air, but he wouldn't release the demon. He locked his jaws, refusing to surrender his prey. He would kill him and avenge his pride and his mother. He would set himself free from the tainted blood that ran in his veins. He would see his mate safe.

Even if he had to die with him to do that.

Barafnir's fingers loosened and fell from Kyter's neck.

The scent of death filled Kyter's nostrils.

He collapsed against the demon's body, his teeth still buried in his throat, his strength all but gone. His head swam, the sounds around him distorted and vague as fatigue crashed over him, threatening to drag him under the black waves.

"Kyter." The soft female voice curled around him, broken and fragmented but luring his hearing into focusing on the sweet melody because he liked it. It was familiar and comforting. Everything he needed as he sank slowly into the gloom. Her words came clearer. "Let him go now."

He couldn't. He didn't have the energy to move. It hurt too much.

Gentle hands bravely slipped into his mouth and prised his locked jaws open, and the demon's neck fell from them. A tender palm cupped his face and fingers brushed through his fur.

"Come on, Kyter… you dare do this to me." She stroked his forehead and his ears, her fear rushing through his blood together with the pain of every laceration that covered his body.

Every laceration that she experienced too.

His mate was in pain but she was focused on him, placing him before her own needs. His beautiful Iolanthe.

"Irritating cat." She shook him hard with one hand and he managed a growl, baring one fang at her as his top lip curled.

She laughed but there was no joy in it. There was only immeasurable hurt and fear. He was frightening her. His brave and confident mate. He didn't want to scare her. He didn't like it when she was afraid. She stroked his fur again, harder this time, before clutching it in her fingers and holding on to him.

Her hand shook against him. "Stop playing dead… because Bleu is threatening to bring medicine."

Kyter grunted and wearily rolled onto his front, sliding off the demon's chest and landing on his side on the ground. He tried to get onto his paws but his legs gave out as the haze in his head cleared and a thousand emotions roared back to life, ripping away what little strength he had gathered. The agony of his injuries and the fatigue from the battle combined with the pain of his grief and the knowledge that he had brought so much death to his kin and it was too much for him to bear.

He chuffed, the sound mournful, filled with the ache he felt inside.

Iolanthe continued to stroke him with her good arm, offering comfort that he soaked up, absorbing every drop of it to help him battle the violent waves of his feelings and regain some control over his body so he could shift back. If he could shift back, he would be able to handle them all and they would no longer own him. His jaguar side was too sensitive to emotions. He needed to shift in order to tamp them and his pain down.

He focused on Iolanthe as she murmured to him in the elf tongue, picking up the word for fated male. Ki'aro. That word warmed him, filling his heart with light. His mate. He could feel her pain and her need to see he was alright. He mustered his strength for her sake, wanting to allay her fears and give her comfort too. His female needed him.

He pulled himself away from the demon and Iolanthe to give himself space to shift.

Kyter slowly opened his eyes and growled as he transformed back, using every drop of the strength he had gathered to complete the shift. When the final bone had cracked back into place and his fur was gone, he rolled onto his back and breathed hard, fighting the pain burning him to ashes inside.

Iolanthe covered him with something, concealing his hips, and kneeled beside him as her brother approached them.

"You worried me." She stroked his brow and he issued an apologetic smile. He hadn't meant to scare her. She had scared him too. "I thought you were going to die."

"Never," he croaked and she smiled but there were tears lining her lashes.

They cut at him, making the lie taste foul in his mouth. He hadn't wanted to die, but he had been willing to, and he wasn't sure what that made him, but he didn't like it. He blamed the lack of air supply to his brain. It had made him forget what a wonderful and beautiful mate he had in this world.

He slowly raised his hand and cupped her cheek. "I've only just found you. I'm not going anywhere... not until I've had a thousand years with you and then a thousand more."

Her smile wobbled on her lips and she clutched his hand to her face, her violet eyes searching his. "I will hold you to that."

She lowered her gaze and he frowned at the sudden awkward edge her expression took on.

"What is it?" He swallowed hard as Bleu appeared above him, crouched and grabbed his shoulders, beginning to haul him up into a sitting position, no doubt so he could administer the foul and torturous medicine Iolanthe had mentioned.

Iolanthe looked down at her knees. "I am sorry that you did not get your vengeance."

Kyter frowned, his heart starting off at a pace. The demon wasn't dead? No. He was dead. Kyter had sensed it and scented it on him.

"What do you mean? I killed him." Kyter grimaced as he shoved off Bleu and his eyes shot towards Barafnir, expecting to see him getting onto his feet or teleporting away.

The demon lay where Kyter had left him.

With Iolanthe's black blade sticking out of his heart.

His gaze leaped back to her. She had killed his father.

"I could not stop myself. He was going to kill you. I had to choose whether to hold back and trust that you would survive or follow my heart and ensure you survived." She raised her eyes to meet his, an apology in them that she had no need to give to him. "I do not wish to live in a world without you in it."

Bleu might have gagged but Kyter wasn't paying attention to the elf. He grabbed Iolanthe's right arm and pulled her into his embrace, grimacing as every injury on his body burned white-hot. She grunted and hissed, her pain colliding with his as the deep wound on her back blazed and lightning shot up her left arm.

"Tell me this part of the bond disappears when we complete it," he whispered into her ear and she shook her head.

"I am sorry," she murmured against his bare chest, her voice laced with the pain he could feel flowing through her.

"Don't be." He stroked her braid and loosened his hold on her, not wanting to hurt her but unable to release her. He needed to feel her in his arms, safe now. Free from the assassins. "You saved me, Iolanthe... gods, you saved me. Not just from my father... but from a life filled with loneliness and pain, and a world where I had nothing left. You made me see that I had everything that I desired and needed if I only opened my eyes and looked beyond the dark shadows that clouded my mind to the light."

He had wanted to blame himself when he had realised that he could have stopped the devastating attack on the village if he had only been there, and he could have saved his mother.

He could have handed himself over to his father and the demon might have let the others live.

He couldn't take the blame though. He couldn't let it rest solely on his shoulders. His pride had driven him away. The blame rested on their shoulders too. Rather than accepting him as the jaguar he was, they had seen only the demon blood in him, and they had persecuted him for it. They had taken everything he had ever strived to give to them—his strength, his loyalty, his love—and had thrown it in his face.

He had taken the blame enough in his short life, feeling it piled onto his shoulders from a tender age. It had taken meeting Iolanthe to give him the strength to stand up, cast aside all of his fears about his mixed blood and how others would judge him for it, and cast aside the need he felt to beg for scraps of affection from a pride who had acted more like his enemy than his family.

Iolanthe had accepted all of him, no questions asked and no scorn cast at him. She had accepted him not as a jaguar or a demon. She had accepted him as Kyter and she loved him as he was. It was there in her eyes as she looked at him, even though he knew that his were as they had been from the moment he had attacked his father.

Black irises with gold elliptical pupils.

He shouldn't have feared she would judge him or turn away from him because of them. He should have known she would only hold him closer and love him more deeply, showing him that she didn't care about where he had come from. She loved all of him. Unconditionally. Eternally.

And he loved her.

Kyter dipped his head to kiss her.

Bleu coughed and shoved a vial between them. "I am still here and I am not going anywhere until you two drink this."

Kyter closed his eyes and sighed at the same time as Iolanthe laughed, the light sound teasing his ears. He had a feeling that Bleu was going to make his life hell for the next few years at least, but he would put up with it, because something told him that Iolanthe was going to put him through hell for eternity. It wouldn't be long before he and Bleu bonded over being dragged on expeditions, exchanging stories about her treasure hunts gone wrong, and generally racing in to save the day and her backside.

First though, he had a promise to keep, one that he knew would help Bleu begin to overcome his dislike of seeing him with his sister.

He opened his now-golden eyes and pinned her with a hungry look.

They had dealt with his father, and they had dealt with her client.

Now they were going to deal with their bond.

By the next full moon, Iolanthe would be his mate.

CHAPTER 27

Kyter prowled through the trees, moving from limb to limb, a silent shadow above his prey. The monkey chatter died as he approached and they fled their refuge, breaking out in all directions and scattering to avoid him. They were safe today. He had no interest in anything other than his prey.

She walked the floor of the rainforest far below him, her black backpack shifting with each sensual step she took towards her destination. He flattened onto his belly and crawled along a thinner branch, spreading his weight.

A bird of paradise called and she stopped, her green eyes lifting to the canopy above her, seeking it.

She was beautiful.

And she was his.

A soft smile played on her rosy lips and then she started walking again, skilfully avoiding each root and rock that lay in her path, finding her way across the bumpy terrain with ease. Her booted feet made no sound. Not a single twig snapped beneath her light step.

She brushed a rogue strand of her blue-black hair back, neatening the long thick plait that hung down her back beside her black pack. It bounced with each step, shifting against her tight dark violet camisole and luring his gaze down to the small pair of black shorts she wore. He struggled to keep his eyes off them, knowing if he looked that he wouldn't be able to tear his gaze away.

He had cursed her from the moment she had changed into them. They showed off far too much of her long toned legs and cupped her backside in a way that made him want to growl. The thought of her walking into his pride's village dressed like that, so much flesh on show, made him want to growl for a different reason. He would kill any male who dared to look at his mate with desire in his eyes.

She had been made for his eyes only.

Another bird flitted across her path and she twisted at the waist, lifting her hand towards it. The tiny colourful creature turned towards her, wings fluttering as it darted around in front of her. She smiled, stealing his breath with her beauty as her lips curved and her eyes sparkled. The bird edged closer to her outstretched hand and he marvelled all over again at the incredible power and beauty of his mate as it landed on her fingertips.

He had never in all his existence seen a wild bird do such a thing.

They all fled him whenever he tried to get close to them, but they flocked to her.

She petted it and it lingered a moment longer and then took flight, disappearing into the trees.

Incredible.

Iolanthe brushed her hand around the back of her neck, drawing his gaze to it, awakening a deep hunger to press his fangs into that sweet spot. She caught her braid, swept it over her shoulder, and released it. It swayed across the left side of her chest. Her fingers followed the braid and brushed across her breast, a sensual and slow caress that had his heart beating faster.

He reached a paw down to the next branch, his focus locked on her as he closed in.

A crack sounded.

Every inch of him went rigid as his senses blared a warning.

Branches lashed at him as the one he was on gave way and he dropped. One struck him hard underneath his jaw and flipped him onto his back in time for the next to strike him there and spin him around again. He hissed and twisted in the air as he cleared all the tree limbs and landed with a huff on his paws in the leaf litter.

Iolanthe appeared above him, her smile teasing. "Are you hurt?"

He growled at her and shifted back into his human form, and then sighed as he rose onto his bare feet. "Just a little dented pride."

She slipped the pack off her shoulders and offered it to him. He unzipped it, pulled out his black combats, and dropped the pack so he could tug them on, covering his nudity.

"What happened?" Her gaze drifted over him from head to toe and back again.

He shrugged and jammed his feet into his boots. "I was distracted."

Her smile only widened. "I did say I was not going to let you win your hunting game."

She had, and he had been determined to show her that he could stalk her all the way to the pride village and capture her before she could reach it. He hadn't anticipated she would use her deadliest weapon to her advantage though—her beauty.

He crouched and tied his boots, and then zipped his pack closed and slung it over his shoulder as he rose onto his feet.

"You win this one. I'll get you on the way back." He had been enjoying hunting her, and had been sure he could have got the jump on her if it hadn't been for the weak branch.

It had been a long time since he had taken to the trees. He had put on muscle and weight, both in his human and his jaguar form. He would be more cautious next time and would know which branches could support him.

"Maybe I will be a jaguar too on the way back." She said it casually but she knew what she was doing, stirring a fierce need to take her off the path and pin her to a secluded tree and have his way with her until she bit him and had enough of his blood to make that transformation.

He tightened his grip on the straps of the pack and grunted. "Maybe you will, maybe you won't."

She tossed a scowl over her shoulder at him and he smiled as she huffed and stomped along the path ahead of him.

He had figured out that she had a very limited window in which she could use his blood to shift. The ability seemed to be available to her for only a few hours, less than twelve. The last of his blood had left her system around a day ago. If she wanted to shift, she would need to bite him again.

And she would.

This time, he would bite her too.

He stalked after her and then moved ahead when they reached the steep slope that surrounded the village. He crushed his nerves, took her hand and helped her up it. She made it look easy, never once losing her footing on the mud and roots. He grabbed the tree at the top of the hill and hauled himself up, pulling her up with him.

She stopped, her gaze fixed down the other side of the slope.

"This is your home?" she said as her eyes took in the single storey thatched wooden buildings on their stilts.

"No." He didn't take his eyes off the village as her gaze drifted to him. "Maybe it was once… a very long time ago. It's just a bad memory now. My home is in London."

Her hand slipped into his and she linked their fingers, pressing her palm to his. "I like your home in London… although it is a little noisy."

He smiled and squeezed her hand, recalling how horrified she had been when they had visited it briefly to gather some fresh clothes for him and had arrived around midnight, during the club's busiest hour. The music had been pumping. The crowd had been heaving. Iolanthe had looked as if she might teleport back to Hell.

He had convinced her to follow him into the back of the building. Her wide eyes had taken everything in as she had passed through the busy club, including the bar staff.

She had scowled at Sherry.

Kyter hadn't been able to stop himself from smiling when he had felt the jealousy in his little elf. He had been about to tease her about it when Cavanaugh had caught his eye and he had silently thanked the male instead, and fielded a very curious but dark look. One that Kyter knew had been aimed at Iolanthe. The big snow leopard shifter had looked as jealous as Iolanthe had felt on seeing Sherry, leaving Kyter feeling that Cavanaugh had left a woman behind or lost her somehow, and that the female had been his mate.

Kyter intended to ask him about it when they returned to Underworld.

Right now, he had other business that needed his attention.

He led Iolanthe down the muddy slope to the village. Several of the pride males looked at her and he growled at all of them, flashing his fangs in a warning. The wise bastards instantly averted their gazes and he walked a little taller, his chin tipped up and a touch of swagger in his step as he took pleasure from seeing the males so subservient.

Females stopped to watch them as they passed, and one male raced ahead to the main building in the centre of the village and rushed up the steps, disappearing inside.

A second later, the grey-haired elder of the pride emerged from the building.

Kyter strode up to the middle of the open area in front of the building and stopped a short distance from it, refusing to move any closer. If he did, he would have to tip his head back to look at the elder, and he was damned if he was going to look up at the male.

He released Iolanthe's hand and held his out to her as the pride gathered in a circle around him, silently asking her to give him what she held in her safekeeping. She nodded, drawing the curious gazes of the females surrounding them. They wouldn't know what she was. Her ears were normal and her eyes were green. He had asked her to conceal herself because he hadn't wanted the pride to stare at her the way they stared at him, as if he was a monster.

When some of the males dared to look at her again, Kyter bared his fangs on a growl, the sound vibrating in his throat and warning them away. The elder raised an eyebrow, a flicker of disbelief in his eyes.

Kyter wanted to smirk and tell the bastard that he had a mate, but he was above it. He had come here for three reasons, and getting back at his pride or gaining their acceptance wasn't one of them.

He was about to fulfil the first reason.

Iolanthe teleported the demon's head into her hands and placed it into his. He held it aloft for everyone to see, clutching it by one black horn, and then tossed it across the dirt courtyard. It rolled and landed facing the elder.

"It won't change what happened... but it will stop it from happening again. No demon will bother you anymore." Kyter wiped his hand on his black combat trousers and didn't wait for anyone to acknowledge what he had done. They wouldn't thank him. He didn't need them to either.

He hadn't really done it for them.

He caught Iolanthe's hand and pulled her towards the fringes of the village, to an area that had gone to grass, lined with thick bare wooden poles around four feet tall. Each pole bore claw marks, scented by the kin of the jaguar buried beneath.

He had done it for his mother, and he had done it for him.

This was the second reason he had come back to this place.

He stopped in front of his mother's grave with Iolanthe, his golden gaze locked on the wooden pole that bore only his marks and his scent.

"I wish you could've met," he whispered as he stared at the grave, fresh pain beginning to well up in his heart as he thought about Iolanthe meeting his mother. "She would have been happy that I had a mate... and that I was happy at last."

Iolanthe lifted her other hand, caught his cheek and gently pressed, bringing his head around to face her. She tiptoed and kissed him, the softest one she had ever given him, one overflowing with love and tenderness.

She settled back beside him and smiled at the grave. "I am sure that she is with her ancestors and that she knows, and she is happy for you, Kyter."

He blinked to hold back the tears threatening to fill his eyes and clutched her slender hand, sending a silent prayer of thanks to those ancestors for giving him such a wonderful mate.

"She is happy for us," he said and Iolanthe nodded, slipped her hand free of his and shifted beneath his arm, nestling close to his side with her right hand pressed against his bare chest and her head resting above it.

He curled his arm around her shoulders and held her, giving himself a moment to be with his mother, etching this final memory of his village on his mind, because he would never return. There was nothing here for him now.

When the light began to fade and the heat of day gave way to the warmth of the evening, Kyter sighed and said a silent goodbye to this place, but not to his mother and his ancestors. They would be with him wherever he went. In his heart.

He turned with Iolanthe and slowly headed back through the village, ignoring the way everyone stopped to watch him as he passed.

When he reached the main building, the greying elder came out again.

"Stay," the male said and the village fell silent, the air growing thicker.

Kyter released Iolanthe and looked over his shoulder at the male.

"I have no reason to be here." Kyter looked the man in the eye as he said that, not hiding how he felt about the village or the people in it. They meant nothing to him, because they had made it clear a thousand times that he meant nothing to them.

"We need strong warriors and you have a female to protect now. You have a duty to do."

Iolanthe raised a single fine black eyebrow. "What does he mean?"

Kyter schooled his expression, hiding how amused he was by trying to guess how she would react when he explained.

"The old man thinks you should start popping babies out for the pride."

She laughed and shook her head. "Perhaps in another thousand years."

The smile that had been working its way onto his lips faded as it dawned on him that he had that span of time now, or at least he would have it soon, when their mating was complete. He looked down at Iolanthe, filled with an urge to rush to his third and final reason for being back in the rainforest.

"I only have one duty now," he said to the elder and took hold of Iolanthe's hand again, already backing towards the exit of the village with her. "My duty is to my woman and apparently there's a lost temple around four hundred kilometres north of here that she's itching to explore. Maybe in another thousand years I'll convince her to have kids, but when I do, I won't raise them in a place that will make them feel there's something wrong with them... sorry... I have a new pride now."

He turned and tugged Iolanthe towards the slope, his pace increasing as they closed in on it and left the village behind. She sidled closer to him and ran her free hand up and down his bare arm, her gaze burning into his body and the sweet fragrance of desire mingling with her exotic scent.

"I have a more pressing itch and I do not need to deliver the artefact to my client for another four months."

Kyter smiled over his shoulder at Iolanthe. "Plenty of time to scratch that itch then... and I have just the claws to do it... and the perfect place."

"*The* perfect place?" Her eyes lit up, violet chasing away the green in them, telling him that she remembered what he had said to her before they had fought Fernandez and Barafnir.

His smile widened and he nodded.

"I could teleport us," she said and her eagerness only increased his, making him want to take her up on that offer.

But he wanted to see her face when she saw the waterfall too, and he wanted the moon to have risen when they reached it.

He wanted it to be perfect.

For her.

Kyter led her through the rainforest, down secret paths that only he knew, deep into an area of steep ravines and lush nature. He looked back at her from time to time, drinking in the way her eyes sparkled as she took in all the rare flowers that only blossomed here, orchids that made the trees their homes, and the exotic birds as they swooped across her path or flitted around her.

He could feel her delight running through him, the pleasure she took from nature, and it left him feeling as if they truly had been made for each other. Both of them gained incredible pleasure from the natural world, and his pleasure only increased now that he could share it with her and share in how happy it made her.

He slowed as he heard the waterfall in the distance and wended his way down the steep path that looked like little more than a section of hill that had slipped in one of the storms. Ahead of him, through the trees, water glittered.

He brushed aside each shrub that hindered him and Iolanthe, holding them for her as she passed, and released her hand as he held back the final one. His gaze tracked her as she slowly walked forwards, her head coming up and the amazement she felt rushing through their link and into him.

She reached the edge of a large flat rock and looked back at him, a breathtaking vision against her backdrop of the four separate misty falls that leaped over the rocks and dropped into the dark pool below her. The water rippled, reflecting the moonlight and the stars that hung above them in the inky dark blue sky. Iolanthe turned on the spot, her violet eyes drinking everything in.

It felt like forever since he had been here and had basked in the beauty of the hidden pool nestled among the leafy green trees, but he didn't remember it looking as beautiful as it did now, with Iolanthe standing in the middle of it.

She said something in her elf tongue and beamed at him.

It might have been 'race you in' because suddenly she was naked and had leaped off the flat rock, diving into the pool around ten metres below.

He had intended to take the path down but he could display a little male prowess for his female.

Kyter dropped his pack and stripped off as he stood at the edge of the ledge, watching Iolanthe as she performed a perfect backstroke below him, her bare breasts breaching the water and making him hurry. He wanted to be down there already, sweeping her up into his arms and suckling those dusky peaks as she moaned his name.

She swam directly beneath him on her front, flipped onto her back and slowly paddled away, her eyes on him the whole time.

He tossed his combats on his boots and stood naked above her.

She crooked her finger.

Kyter obeyed. In style.

He planted his hands at the edge of the flat rock, kicked his legs up into a perfect handstand, dipped his weight down on his arms and pushed off. He spun in the air, twisting and turning, before performing a forwards roll and streamlining himself for a perfect finish to his dive. He plunged deep into the cooling water, kicked off the bottom and came up directly below Iolanthe.

Her legs kicked above him, treading water.

Kyter grinned and came up behind her, and grabbed her around her waist.

She shrieked and the birds in the trees took flight, startled from their roosts.

Kyter laughed until she elbowed him in the head, making it end in a grunt. She twisted in his arms, grabbed his shoulders and shoved down hard, sending him back under the water. Her laughter rang through it as she kicked off, swimming away from him towards the falls.

Kyter broke the surface and swam after her, driven to give chase. He easily closed in on her and grabbed her ankle, yanked her backwards through the water and turned her at the same time, pulling her into his arms with her front against his. She spluttered and wiped the water from her face.

"Were you impressed?" he murmured as he swam with her, kicking his legs and gliding through the water with her towards the falls on the right of the four.

She wrapped her arms around his neck and toyed with his wet hair. "When you scared the life out of me or when you performed the twisty dive thing?"

"The latter."

She wriggled her nose and was about to answer when the spray from the waterfall rained down on them and she looked back over her shoulder towards it.

"Kyter... what are you doing?" She tried to break free but he tightened his grip on her, refusing to let her escape him.

His right arm hit the underwater ledge and he planted his right knee on it and scooped Iolanthe up into his arms as he rose onto his feet. She clung to him and gasped as he waded through the thigh-deep water with her. Her gasp became another shriek as they passed under the waterfall, the cold water pounding down on them, and then faded as they reached the other side.

"Taking you somewhere more private." He set her down on her feet, keeping hold of her bare hips, and slowly guided her towards the boulders that lined the back of the recess.

Her eyes darkened.

Kyter backed her into a large smooth boulder and bent her over it. He held on to her hips and kissed down her throat, tasting the water on her warm skin. She moaned as he reached her breasts and clutched his head, his name leaving her lips as a breathless whisper. He could feel her need. It pounded in him too, a deep beat that enslaved him, driving him to obey it.

He moaned and suckled her nipple, tugging it into a firm peak before kissing across her chest to her other breast and doing the same to that one. Water lapped at his thighs, the sound of the waterfall drowning out the world around them, leaving only their ragged breathing and their moans as he explored her body with his mouth.

He held her waist and pushed her higher on the rock, so he could kiss lower still, heading towards the apex of her thighs. He wanted to taste her again and feel how hot and wet she was, primed for him as he was primed for her. His cock throbbed, jerking against his stomach, hot and heavy and hungry to be inside her. His fangs itched, the need to sink them into the nape of her neck overwhelming him.

She spread her thighs for him, an invitation he would never turn down, and clung to the rock above her as he dropped his head and speared her with his tongue. She was warm and slick, her taste making his length pulse again.

"Kyter," she murmured, the sweetest thing he had ever heard as he felt the emotion behind it, the need and the hunger.

"I want you to be mine, Iolanthe," he whispered against her flesh and stroked her with his tongue, eliciting another cry from her lips. "Will you be mine?"

She nodded. "Forever, Ki'aro... forever."

He swirled his tongue around her, his gut tightening as his need spiralled, almost slipping beyond his control.

"Forever isn't enough for me," he murmured between each stroke and swirl, each moan she gave to him. "It isn't enough with you. I want more."

She chuckled and it ended on a moan. Her fingers ploughed through his wet hair, danced down his cheek, and slipped under his jaw. She lured him up to her with nothing more than a gentle touch and smiled at him as he braced himself above her, breathing hard, straining as he resisted the urge to ease himself into her.

"It is not enough for me either." She slipped her hand around the nape of his neck and drew him down for a soft kiss, one that flooded him with warmth and light, and he felt all of her love for him as she whispered against his lips, "Forever and a day. We will have forever and a day."

He nodded and pressed his forehead against hers. "Forever and a day."

It was a promise.

He dipped his head and kissed her, and she wrapped her legs around him, pressing her heat against his rigid length. He groaned and slid his hand between them, grasped himself and lowered the crown to her entrance. He swallowed her moan as he eased into her and then grasped her hands in his and pinned them to the rock above her head as he began to thrust, driving deep into her, long strokes that had her panting against his lips as they kissed.

Kyter poured his love for her into that kiss, wanting her to feel it as he could feel hers and know that this moment meant everything to him.

She meant everything to him.

He slowly quickened his pace, his softer thoughts giving way to ones that filled him with a need he had been denying for what felt like too long now. A need to claim her. His fangs lengthened and she moaned as she stroked them with her tongue, sending hot shivers blasting down his spine and up his cock.

"Iolanthe," he husked, clutching her hands and fighting to control himself as his deepest instincts awakened, demanding he take the female beneath him and bind them as mates.

"Kyter." Her soft tone, the gentleness and understanding in it, and the unspoken permission, tore a moan from him.

His beautiful mate. He would cherish her forever.

From this night forwards, they would belong to each other. They would stand by each other. They would fight for each other. They would be one.

He growled as he surrendered to his need and pulled out of her, flipped her onto her front and entered her again. He grasped her hip, raising it away from the rock, and plunged deep into her. Her moan echoed around him, the hunger and arousal behind it driving him on as it coursed through him.

He bared his fangs and clutched both of her hips as he thrust into her, as deep as he could, and she grasped the rock in front of her, bracing herself. She moaned with each meeting of their bodies as he pumped her, his guttural grunts mingling with the softer sounds of her pleasure.

She raised her backside higher and he groaned, his fangs lengthening as he slid into her, feeling every inch of her wet hot core as it clenched him.

"Kyter." Her breathless moan teased him, goaded him into taking her harder.

He pushed her against the rock, so her breasts pressed against it, and planted his left hand against it near her shoulder. His left knee raised her leg and he braced it on the boulder, spreading her thighs as he rose over her, his right hand holding her hip in place. She arched forwards, her head raised and mouth open as she moaned, taking each deep thrust of his cock.

Her braid fell away from her nape as she looked over her shoulder at him, her fangs long between her lips. He growled and couldn't hold back any longer. The need was too strong. It crushed the last of his control. He grabbed her right arm and pulled her up so her back was against his front as he thrust into her from below, her left leg still raised up by his.

He snarled, angled his head as his balls drew up, the tightness of her sheath bringing him right to the edge, and sank his fangs into the nape of her neck. She cried out and he grunted against her as he thrust harder, deeper, claiming every inch of her as her blood flowed down his throat.

She twisted her arm free of his grip, latched her hand around his wrist, yanked it up to her mouth and sank her fangs into it.

Kyter growled and grunted against her nape as heat blasted through him and she cried out, her body arching away from his as her sheath quivered with her climax, milking his cock. He managed another thrust before the pleasure that had detonated within her rocked him, multiplied one hundredfold by their bond as it completed itself, twining them together.

He breathed hard as he spilled himself inside her, his knees weakening beneath him, trembling as he struggled to bring himself down from his high, from the bliss of mating with her.

She took another slow pull on his blood that had him jerking inside her in response, quivering in time with her, and then released his wrist and licked it.

Kyter had more difficulty convincing himself to release her.

He wanted to stay like this forever.

His body made the decision for him when his knees gave out, sending him crashing into the water. Iolanthe gasped and spun to face him, her lips painted red with his blood. He had never seen a more glorious sight.

She stifled a smile, caught his arm and pulled him up to her, so his backside rested on the boulder. He waited for her to tease him as she settled against him, between his legs, her hip nestled against his thigh and her breasts against his chest.

She kissed him instead, another tender one that touched him right down to his soul.

"I love you, Kyter," she murmured against his lips.

He sighed, gathered her against him, and held her. "I love you too."

He stroked her back, running his fingers up and down her spine, before turning her so her back pressed to his front. He licked the nape of her neck, sealing the marks he had placed on her. Marks of their mating.

She was his now. He was hers.

He wrapped his arms around her and held her, absorbing her warmth and the love he could feel in her, and how it felt to be mated and loved.

He had meant every word he had said to the elder. He wouldn't regret leaving this place behind because he had a new pride now. The sort he had always wanted.

Iolanthe wasn't the only other member. He could see now that his eyes were open that he had made himself a new pride a long time ago, welcoming people like himself into it, under the banner of Underworld. Cavanaugh and the others were his pride. Iolanthe was his pride. All the people who had accepted him, cared about him, and had stuck with him.

He pressed a kiss to Iolanthe's shoulder and closed his eyes, all of his focus on her and how much he loved her. His mate.

She meant everything to him and he would keep his promise.

They would always be together, side by side, partners in the deepest sense of the word.

Their love would last forever.

And a day.

ABOUT THE AUTHOR

Felicity Heaton is a New York Times and USA Today best-selling author who writes passionate paranormal romance books. In her books she creates detailed worlds, twisting plots, mind-blowing action, intense emotion and heart-stopping romances with leading men that vary from dark deadly vampires to sexy shape-shifters and wicked werewolves, to sinful angels and hot demons!

If you're a fan of paranormal romance authors Lara Adrian, J R Ward, Sherrilyn Kenyon, Gena Showalter, Larissa Ione and Christine Feehan then you will enjoy her books too.

If you love your angels a little dark and wicked, the best-selling Her Angel series is for you. If you like strong, powerful, and dark vampires then try the Vampires Realm series or any of her stand-alone vampire romance books. If you're looking for vampire romances that are sinful, passionate and erotic then try the best-selling Vampire Erotic Theatre series. Or if you prefer huge detailed worlds filled with hot-blooded alpha males in every species, from elves to demons to dragons to shifters and angels, then take a look at the new Eternal Mates series.

If you have enjoyed this story, please take a moment to contact the author at **author@felicityheaton.co.uk** or to post a review of the book online

Connect with Felicity:
Website – http://www.felicityheaton.co.uk
Blog – http://www.felicityheaton.co.uk/blog/
Twitter – http://twitter.com/felicityheaton
Facebook – http://www.facebook.com/felicityheaton
Goodreads – http://www.goodreads.com/felicityheaton
Mailing List – http://www.felicityheaton.co.uk/newsletter.php

FIND OUT MORE ABOUT HER BOOKS AT:
http://www.felicityheaton.co.uk